**John Harris** was born in 1916. He
*Sea Shall Not Have Them* and w
Mark Hebden and Max Hennessy. He was a sailor, airman,
journalist, travel courier, cartoonist and history teacher. During
the Second World War he served with two air forces and two
navies. After turning to full-time writing, Harris wrote
adventure stories and created a sequence of crime novels
around the quirky fictional character Chief Inspector Pel. A
master of war and crime fiction, his enduring fictions are
versatile and entertaining.

# JOHN HARRIS

# THE
# SLEEPING MOUNTAIN

HOUSE OF
STRATUS

This edition published in 2001 by House of Stratus, an imprint of Stratus Holdings plc, 24c Old Burlington Street, London, W1X 1RL, UK.

www.houseofstratus.com

Typeset, printed and bound by House of Stratus.

A catalogue record for this book is available from the British Library.

ISBN 0-7551-0222-3

'For the past three weeks the mountain had been vomiting clouds of smoke, but the smoke seemed to be produced so normally that it was permissible even for those inclined to look upon the dark side not to dread a catastrophe.'

Report from *The Times*

Although no mountain by the name of Mont' Amarea exists, nor a town by the name of Anapoli Porto, there is just such a mountain on another island, and there was just such a town.

My thanks are due to the staffs of the Volcanological Department of the University of Naples, and the Geological Department of the University of Florence, who together with others helped me to transpose an actual event from this other island to Italy.

## *one*

Probably because he was engaged in nothing more than scratching with a conte crayon on the back of an old menu card, Tom Patch became aware of the sound and the movement from the earth long before anyone else.

It started as a whisper and at first he thought it was just the wind getting up again for another freak storm like the one which had flung the tiles off the old houses round the Porto that morning, and sent a muddy swirl bubbling through the mountain-stream beds to the beach and out in a yellow-brown cloud across the water of the Tyrrhenian.

He had come creeping out with the rest of the islanders as the rain had died away, pushing through the crowds in the dark alleys behind the harbour where the puddles picked up splinters of light, past the strings of washing, seeking the sunny corners where every open window was now draped with airing blankets and mattresses.

He lifted his head, waiting for the gust that would rattle the menu card in his hands and whip up the scraps of paper into little spirals in the air. But it didn't come and, relaxing again, he took out a cigarette. As he lit the match, though, and held it up, he saw the flame begin to dance and, remembering how many drinks he'd had, he wondered for a moment if his hand had finally become unsteady. Then he saw the waiter in the bar behind him cock his head and he realised that the sound was audible to others too, and he became more vividly aware of the scene in front of him – as

1

though it were a film which had suddenly slowed down into separate pictures.

The murmur came from way down – out of reach of the day's glare. It emerged from hundreds of feet below the leaning buildings whose roof-levels of red and grey pantiles made a jagged backdrop to the harbour. It was blown out over the Tyrrhenian by the spring breeze that shrivelled the bare vineyards rising in terraces behind the town, in clear view to Patch as he sat in a trembling air he could sense rather than see. The bells of goats mingled with it as they came down the steep road between the last little villa on the outskirts of the town and the great white house dominating its eastern flank, more like a palace than a dwelling-house, with its turrets, its castellated walls, and its cypressed gardens.

It pierced the high piping of the gulls along the sea wall and the sound of a mandolin on one of the fishing boats drawn up on the beach – even, in spite of its faintness, the raucous croak of an election car down by the harbour that had shattered the peace like an assassin's bomb with its loudspeaker and for the fiftieth time that day made Patch feel like a displaced person, reminding him that, in spite of his rooms in the Porto, the fishermen's district of crevasse-like streets and narrow-gutted buildings where politics were as natural as breathing, he was really no more a part of the island than the other foreigners who lived in the aloof little villas outside the town, residing on Anapoli for a variety of reasons that ranged from arthritis to straitened finance.

Perhaps because of the noise about the town, none of them – apart from Patch – noticed the sound at first, for it came gently, hardly as a breath, in fact. For a time it went completely unheeded among the multiplicity of teeming streets and squares that made up Anapoli Porto, as they clung to the cliff above the beach of grey volcanic sand in an incredible kaleidoscope of light and shade.

Even the people at the other side of the Piazza dei Martiri didn't catch it in the long second when it was obscured by the loudspeaker and the voice of the man in the Via Garibaldi who was haranguing a few disinterested loafers from a soapbox dais decorated with an Italian flag. Beyond the ugly statue of Garibaldi which occupied the centre of the square, a bill-poster who was plastering the walls with Communist sheets went on filling in the spaces the party in office had left, so that the political protagonists seemed to be carrying out a wordy warfare in slogans, debating with each other, coming out with new posters to answer the accusations in the opposition's reply to their own last one.

He had plodded along the edge of the piazza, daubing the pillars of the ancient Museo with 'Vote for Bosco' and 'Vote for the People's Party', placing his sheets carefully so as not to obscure the efforts of the wall-daubing fraternity who had been at work among the gaudy new posters and the fluttering ribbons of the old ones with whitewash and tar filched from the harbour. Finally, just as the murmur started, he'd found a space at ground level where the cycling enthusiasts of the island, untouched by the fevered finger of politics, had apparently lain flat on their faces to placard their adoration of their own particular hero with an '*Evviva Coppi*' or two; and stepping back to discuss its position and its value with the group of ragged small boys who were accompanying him, had spread another poster, 'Vote for the People's Friends', as though it were an argument he had overlooked, the slap of his wet brush obscuring the first hint of the sound as it stole into the square.

As it increased in strength, the man two tables away from Patch lifted his head and looked at the sky.

3

He had arrived ten minutes before in a taxi, his uniform jacket and felt hat indicating immediately to Patch that he was from the ship which had arrived a day or two earlier to take away a cargo of the island sulphur. She was moored to the Molo del Porto, small, elderly and not very smart, leaning against the black basalt blocks as though she were holding the hillside up, her appearance belying the impressive name painted across her counter. *Great Watling Street,* it said in square white letters. *Great Watling Street, London.*

He had stood on the shadow-striped cobbles under Garibaldi's upraised arm, arguing over the fare with the driver, obviously grimly enjoying himself in a private and execrable brand of Italian, and it was as he seated himself, clearly satisfied with his linguistic acrobatics, that the sound began to swell into a growl.

As it increased to a rolling echo, Patch pushed back the straw hat he wore, frayed round the brim like an ill-tended hedge, listening, his eyes on the spot where the transparent ultramarine of the sea touched the cobalt of the sky. His breath seemed to halt for a moment in his chest and he found himself noticing how the sunshine picked out the ochre, black and sienna tints of the ruined Aragonese castle which jutted out behind the houses, sharp in the glass-clear air, and caught the sides of the coastguard station among the palms.

Then as more people moving across the square lifted their heads, he realised the sound was making itself heard to everybody, spreading, it seemed, across the purple sheet of the sea and through the emptiness of the heavens which were crossed by fanning streaks of cloud from behind Mont' Amarea as it towered behind him up to the crater where a wisp of vapour, like a grey-white feather, streamed over its slaty sides.

He saw the taxi-driver motionless alongside his taxi, the bill-poster with one frozen hand outstretched across another gaudy sheet, and a group of loafers in the shadow of the

Museo, their eyes switched sideways as they tried to see two ways at once.

Around them, above them and beneath them, they could all hear it now – a rumbling sound like a cart passing over the cobbles of the Porto. It seemed to hang in the air like thunder, quivering in the silence, then a tile crashed and the windows all round the square started to rattle violently as though someone were behind them beating them with a heavy fist, and a flock of pigeons exploded noisily into the air beyond the Museo.

Without any assistance from the driver, the door of the taxi shut with a bang. A girl in a tight skirt, crossing the piazza on a bicycle with a long packet of spaghetti under her arm, had dismounted and was staring at the bell as it tinkled on the handlebars without any effort on her part. A priest, heading round the back of the Church of Sant' Agata, halted in the doorway as a shower of dusty plaster fell nearby, glanced quickly at Mont' Amarea, and folded his hands and waited, muttering Hail Marys. The loudspeaker car and the soapbox politician shouting in the Via Garibaldi had suddenly become quiet so that they could all hear across the evening silence that lay over the whole of the Porto.

Patch's glass was drumming heavily now against the metal of the table and the spoon was tinkling with lunatic frenzy in the saucer of his coffee cup. The two early carnations, wilting wretchedly in the centre of the table, were shaking frantically and he noticed without alarm that the dust was dancing in little puffs between the cobblestones at his feet.

Then the quivering died away as suddenly as it had come, and everything became still again.

5

# t w o

---

For a moment, as the murmur and the movement died away, the piazza was still, as though the film had stopped and everyone had become petrified.

They were waiting for the next murmur and the next movement, then, as none arrived, they all came to life again, as if someone had started the film moving once more. The man from the ship cocked his head upwards, looking like a dog which has heard a noise in the night. Then he turned quickly towards the Via Garibaldi where you could see the topmasts of his ship between the houses that split the glare in a wedge of shadow, like an axe-stroke across the sunshine. He was obviously concerned for her safety, but she was still there, still resting her fat bottom gently on the grey sand of the low tide, gathering weeds and garlanded by her own refuse.

Emiliano, who owned the bar where Patch sat, came to the door and stared upwards at its bizarre façade and tower with bulging mild brown eyes. He had built it with his own broad back before the war and in his enthusiasm to make it impressive had painted pillars on it, a bellicose fresco and an artificial window complete with shutters and even curtains, and finally, lower down on the blue-washed walls, a picture of the Virgin Mary with the words, *O Maria, Tutta Bella Lei, O, Gloria, O, Onoria, O, Amore,* to make up for his repeated absences from Mass.

'*O, Mary, all that is beautiful, O, Glory, O, Honour, O, Love,*' ought to be enough, he had fervently hoped, to offer some measure of protection to his property in times of trouble.

He studied the plaster for cracks, as he always did after a rumble from Mont' Amarea, his flabby cheeks blue with a two-day old beard, his great paunch covered by a voluminous white apron that was spotted with wine and coffee and marked in a brown smear where the arc of his stomach rubbed constantly against the polished counter, then he disappeared again behind the great engine of the Espresso machine, talking with his hands to his customers.

'*Uno scoppio*,' Patch heard him say. 'An explosion.'

The taxi-driver had opened the door of his taxi and, as Patch watched, he slammed it shut again, staring at it with a bewildered expression on his face. The bill-poster completed the hanging of the sheet of paper, shouting over his shoulder to the girl with the bicycle and to the two or three men who had run to the point where the Via Garibaldi joined the piazza so they could stare at the mountain. Then he left it, 'Vote for the People's Friends', hanging a little lop-sidedly, as he slammed his brush back into his bucket and hurried away, still shouting and gesturing with his free hand, to pick up the posters of the opposition and hang them too. The girl with the bicycle smiled nervously as he called to her, then she remounted and rode off into the Via Garibaldi, blushing as the men on the corner stopped chattering to themselves and stared approvingly at her legs as she passed. The small boys who had been watching the bill-poster were screaming in a group that had been joined by several women and became attached eventually to the men on the corner of the Via Garibaldi.

The priest was disappearing inside the church. The loud speaker car by the harbour and the politician in the Via Garibaldi, taking advantage of the arrival of more people from their houses and shops, had opened up again and were trying to shout each other down once more. Then Emiliano and a couple of his customers returned to the door of the bar to stare at the mountain and the feather of vapour that drifted away from the summit, then they too joined the group on the corner, arguing noisily. A few windows had been flung open and people had begun to appear on balconies, pushing out the crooked shutters which were still closed on the higher floors where the sun had penetrated a few minutes before.

The man from the ship was staring upwards again, as though he half expected the sky to drop in on him at any moment, his mouth open, his eyes blank and questioning. Patch grinned and called out to him.

'Take it easy,' he said. 'It's as normal here as a baby's breathing.'

The other stared curiously back at Patch's lean face and black hair and the thin prominent nose that gave him the look of a handsome eagle.

He was still busy drawing, a lean colourful figure in a paint-daubed shirt and faded cotton trousers that hung off his hips, his face half hidden under the frayed fringe of the battered straw hat.

'You English, Mister?' the sailor asked. Patch looked up and grinned again.

'Sure. Name's Patch. Tom Patch. You off the ship?'

'That's right.' There was a vague relief in the little man's voice – as though it were a comfort just then to find a fellow countryman – and he moved across and sat by Patch. 'Fred Hannay's the name,' he said. 'I'm master. Just come on this run. Toulon, Balearics and Naples and here. Back'ards and forrards like an overwrought squirrel.' He spoke with a thick North Country burr, clipped, broad and ugly. 'Listen –' he paused, his eyes still troubled ' – what was that just then? It felt as though something damn' big just broke wind.'

'It did. It was the mountain.' Patch indicated the massive bulk behind him with his crayon, then bent over the menu card again, glancing up occasionally at Hannay with shrewd black eyes that made the little man feel uncomfortable. He took the cigarette Patch pushed across between pencil strokes, a startled look on his face.

'You mean it's going to erupt or something?' he asked.

'I very much doubt it,' Patch reassured him with a smile. 'A touch of flatulence, I should say.'

'Jesus!' Hannay glanced again at the mountain, then he gestured at the piazza.

The bill-poster was just disappearing into the Via Garibaldi. The girl on the bicycle and the priest had already vanished. The loudspeaker and the politicians were giving it all they'd got again, appealing to the people who now lined the fringes of the piazza – the loafers, the shopkeepers, Emiliano, the man who kept the hairdresser's, one of his customers, still swathed in linen, the bent little creature who sold coral rings in the cavernous shop next to the Museo, the fruit-sellers from the steps of the church, a man who had appeared with a plate of spaghetti in his hand, the beggar who had been asleep in the sun, still and silent as a bundle of old rags until a moment ago, his barrel organ stuffed into a corner, out of the traffic. The taxi-driver was standing by his taxi with Emiliano's waiter, demonstrating the extraordinary behaviour of the car door. He had it open again and Hannay saw him close it with his foot, his hands held high in the air. 'Look,' he was saying. 'Just like that!' The piazza, dormant a moment before, was suddenly alive and noisy, with more people coming out of doors every minute.

'Doesn't it worry them?' Hannay asked, indicating the noisy vitality in the square.

'It doesn't appear to,' Patch said, and Hannay realised for the first time that he hadn't even bothered to change his position, hadn't even stopped scratching on the menu card.

'It didn't appear to worry 'em last time either,' he went on cheerfully. 'All they did was have a few bets on the date of the next one. I suppose that's what they're talking about now – whether they've won or not.'

He looked up at Hannay's bewildered face and went on to explain. 'The mountain's not erupted since 1762,' he said. 'And in its time the place's been ravaged by the Greeks, the Trojans, the Romans, the Venetians, the Portuguese, the Spanish, the English and, not so very long ago, the Germans and the Americans. What's a rumble or two? It's rather like telling a monkey it's got another flea.'

Hannay was staring up at Amarea, still unconvinced, and Patch grinned and tried to soothe the doubt out of his eyes. 'It's been doing it for years,' he said. 'Nobody worries unless it puts the lights out or damages the telephone lines. Then they complain to one of the observatories and a commission arrives weighed down with importance and instruments and bursting with the desire to reassure everybody. But since you can't very well use a plumber on a volcano, that's about all they can do. They potter around the place with gravimeters looking grave and knowledgeable and when they go away all they appear to have done is issue a report saying there's nothing to worry about. The Mayor sticks it up on the town notice boards and everybody's happy.'

Hannay listened with interest and, as Patch finished, he lit the cigarette Patch had pushed across. Drawing in a lung-full of smoke, he spluttered violently and took the cigarette out of his mouth again quickly. 'Christ,' he muttered in awed tones, staring at it with suspicion.

He looked up. 'You smoke these Eyetie things?' he asked incredulously.

Patch nodded. 'I have to. I ran out of English ones years ago.'

A thought crossed Hannay's mind that hadn't occurred to him before. He glanced at Patch, lounging at the other side of the table under the withered orange trees that lined the pavement, still drawing happily.

'You live here or something?' he asked.

'Yes.'

'Why?'

Patch looked up. There was nothing offensive in the question and he attributed it to Hannay's North Country curiosity. He considered for a moment before replying, and came to the conclusion that there didn't seem to be any reasonable answer. There were plenty of places in Italy far more accessible that he could have lived in, and he could only put it down to a natural contrariness that he should have preferred Anapoli to the more traditional places with their wealth of free models and easy colour.

His constant efforts to avoid conventionality in his work had led him on a long road from one chilly studio to another, in London, New York, Paris and Rome, with models who failed to turn up for fear of not being paid, with never enough to eat and never anything at all to drink, until at last the irrepressible exuberance for life that still managed to show through in his paintings had caught the interests of the critics and had started a fashion in the popular galleries with nothing much to offer but weary modernism. He had suddenly found himself not having to seek commissions but dodge them and had made his way to Italy and finally to Anapoli, he decided, largely as a means of avoiding the infectious limpness of twentieth-century art.

He looked across at Hannay, with his square red face and blue unemotional eyes and decided that perhaps he wouldn't understand even if he tried to enlighten him, so he plumped in the end for the simplest explanation.

'I live here because I don't like Capri,' he said, gesturing with the menu card at a fly. 'Besides, it's cheaper.'

Hannay didn't seem to appreciate his efforts to save him trouble and looked aggressively back at him.

'What's wrong with England?' he demanded.

'What's right with it?'

'It suits me.'

'That's fine then.'

Patch gave the sailor a beaming untroubled smile that somehow managed to annoy him and went on with his scribbling.

Hannay stared for a moment, puzzled by his indifference to what was the be-all and end-all of his own life.

'How d'you manage to live here?' he asked.

'It's very easy. I wash. I shave, I eat and sleep. The usual.'

Hannay frowned. 'I mean, what do you do?'

'I paint.'

'Oh!' Hannay seemed startled, as though he were immediately out of his depth, and faintly disappointed, for he had half expected Patch to be nothing more than a remittance man he would have had the pleasure of disliking. To Hannay no one who worked for his living had a right to be so indolent about it.

'What do you paint?' he asked doubtfully.

Patch looked up and smiled again, conscious of Hannay's disapproval. 'Faces,' he said. 'I rent a couple of rooms from an old dear called Meucci round the corner. Come and have a drink some time. You can't miss it. You can hear Mamma Meucci arguing a mile off.'

He casually threw across the menu card as though he had lost interest in it and Hannay stared at a fanciful likeness of himself, executed entirely in scribble, and surrounded by vignettes of the people he had seen about the piazza – the taxi-driver standing under the Garibaldi statue deep in argument with Hannay, the bill-poster and the group of small boys, Emiliano and his waiter, discussing the mountain.

'That's good,' he said, pleased and beginning to regard Patch with a greater degree of warmth. 'Annay'll have that framed.'

12

He paused. 'My wife had an uncle was an artist,' he went on. 'Oils. We've got two of his pictures at home. 'Ighland cattle. All hair and horns.' He stared at his fingers for a moment. 'They look as if they'd been painted with brown paint on brown paper. He once did me. You'd have thought I'd been struck by lightning.' He gave a nervous laugh. 'I made a fire-screen of it,' he explained.

Without thinking, he took another puff at the cigarette and began to cough, then he fished in his pocket and pushed a green tin across to Patch. 'Have these,' he said. 'Ship's Woodbines. Better than them bombs you smoke.'

He tossed away the Italian cigarette Patch had given him and, begging a Woodbine back, made himself comfortable, blowing smoke rings in silence for a moment, his eyes vaguely troubled again.

'Isn't it a bit like sitting on a land mine, Mister? – living 'ere, I mean.'

Patch thought the question over as he fished a couple of old envelopes from his back pocket. It had never occurred to him before to consider what went on inside the mountain underneath his feet. After two years of living in the Porto, with the islanders' indifference to Amarea becoming as much a part of his everyday life as the old walls and the daubed signs, 'Hail, the Queen of Heaven' and 'Up the Soviets', that adorned them, he had long since taken it for granted that there was nothing to worry about. The mountain's previous episodes of activity were all as lovingly remembered in the bars as its symptoms and had been related to him so often that he had come to regard them with much the same indifference as he regarded Mamma Meucci's complaints about the neighbours.

'It is a bit, I suppose,' he said, starting to draw again on one of the envelopes. 'But they've been sitting on it for hundreds of years. You get to like it in the end, in fact. It keeps your behind warm in winter. And, so far as I know, not more than half a dozen or so have ever been hurt by it. Even the big bang of 1892 only brought down a lot of soot.'

Looking like an anxious pug, Hannay was casting another glance over his shoulder at the mountain behind them, massive, sombre and silent, its sides brassy-gold in the glare that hit them at a tangent and slid into the clefts lower down as the island dropped abruptly into the Tyrrhenian.

'Could it erupt?' he asked.

'I doubt it. Not now. In any case, it had better not.'

'Why not?'

Patch gestured at the fly again, finished his drink and ordered two more, then he leaned across the table, indicating to Hannay to listen. Through the narrow streets that wound up to it from the harbour, the sound of the loudspeaker car filtered into the piazza again, rebounding off the crumbling walls of the old buildings where the grass grew in the angles and along the gutterings.

'That's why not,' he said. 'If the mountain erupted, they'd have to postpone the election.'

Hannay snorted and Patch grinned.

'They'll be arguing over the result of the voting six months after it's finished,' he pointed out. 'But I'll lay you a pound to a penny that they won't be discussing the mountain tomorrow.'

Hannay looked around him. The piazza was quietening down. Patch's prophecies seemed as though they might be correct. The taxi-driver was starting up his car. The bill-poster was busy plastering the walls with posters once more. The politician from the Via Garibaldi was trudging across the square to the Via Venti Settembre on the other side, to tackle the loungers there who had come out to join the crowd and were now leaning against the wall, passing a cigarette from one to another. As he moved beneath the women on the balconies, they catcalled after him but he took no notice of the laughter and continued, an earnest, humourless, shabby figure in black, with his banner and his tricolour under one arm and the two boxes that made his dais slung by a piece of frayed string over the other. Emiliano and his friends had gone inside now to continue their discussion over the bar with the barber and his customer who still unconcernedly wore his linen swathe. The little boys had grown tired of the mountain and were playing a game. Only the crowd on the corner of the Via Garibaldi were still chattering excitedly to newcomers. Life seemed to be settling down again to normality.

'Eruptions aren't allowed to interfere with elections here,' Patch explained cheerfully. He reached out and finally swatted the fly with a newspaper. 'Got the bastard,' he said triumphantly. 'Besides,' he went on, 'Forla would lose a lot of money.'

'Who's Forla?'

'Forla's olives. Forla's lemons. Forla's wine. Forla's the sulphur you've come for. Forla's Anapoli and Anapoli's Forla.' Patch waved a hand towards the turrets of the vast house on the hill. 'That's Forla. He keeps his antiques there and the best part of his art collection. It's one of the finest in Italy – all Botticellis and da Vincis, with a few fat Rubens thrown in to show he's catholic in his tastes. He even bought one of mine for his house in Rome. He owns everything here, damn' near. Even the mountain – so I suppose he's got it as well under control as the rest of them.'

'Does he live 'ere?'

'Not he? Would you, if you could afford to live in Rome? He hasn't been near the place for eighteen months. His nephew, Orlesi, runs it for him.'

'Why would he lose a lot if the mountain erupted?'

'It would drive away the inhabitants, and they're leaving the islands fast enough as it is. They don't like being so far from the big cities and the football and the television. And then who'd get your sulphur, who'd tend the vines and the olives? Who'd look after the tourists when they come? They don't get many here but they give 'em the full treatment.' Patch sat back. 'The mountain *can't* erupt,' he concluded firmly. 'Perhaps a little coloured smoke, or a pretty red glow at night like Stromboli. But that's all.'

Hannay stared at Patch, beginning to wonder just what sort of man he was. He was clearly a man of confidence and skill. Even in the scrappy drawing he had thrown across the table the technique managed to show through. But his apparent indolence, his untidiness and faded clothes, puzzled Hannay as much as his indifference to everyone else's opinion and the deep lines of humour on his face that contrasted so strongly with his cynical comments.

'You lived here long?' he asked.

'Two years.'

'Why here?'

Patch looked up, and decided to dodge the determined questioning once more. 'I've nowhere else,' he said.

He seemed as undisturbed by the mountain as the rest of the Porto and Hannay began to feel a little happier about sitting on an island beneath which the unknown shifts of rock appeared to be as normal as the morning sun.

'Don't you ever go home?' he asked.

'This is home.'

'What about your friends?'

'I've got none. I never did have many but I reduced the number radically when I made the mistake of quarrelling with the people back home who can make or break you. Gnomes, mental pygmies and push-Baptist schoolmarms, most of 'em – though they seem to do damn' well out of it,' he added ruefully. 'My friends decided I was a distinct risk and dropped me like a hot brick.'

'Fine friends you've got.'

'Most of 'em have wives and families.' Patch shrugged philosophically. 'I'd never rate a couple of lines from some rat-faced reviewer in a trade weekly back home now.'

Hannay sat back, enjoying this introduction to what was to him an entirely new world. Then he became aware of a youngster about twelve standing alongside him, a handsome boy with a grave brown face and dark eyes, who wore an ill-fitting jacket and trousers that looked as though they'd been cut down from someone else's suit. One of his cheeks was discoloured by a bruise that stretched from his eyebrow to his jaw.

Alongside him was an ageing mongrel dog which wore a muzzle that hung uselessly on its chest; and the boy smiled as Hannay stared at him, and heaved the muzzle over the dog's jaws.

'For the rabies, signore,' he explained gravely. 'All dogs must wear muzzles for the hot weather.' As he straightened up, the dog promptly squatted down and freed its head once more, then sat up, grinning.

Patch was studying the boy, frowning. 'You've been fighting again,' he said severely. 'You've got a black eye.'

'No, Signor Tom.' The boy turned to him, unsmiling. 'It's my uncle.'

'Beating you again?'

'Yes, signore.'

'What for?'

'I was late home last night, Signor Tom.'

'Why?'

'I don't like going home.' The boy swung away from Patch and began gesturing at Hannay. Patch grinned.

'He wants a cigarette,' he pointed out. 'Here, Cristoforo.' He tossed a Woodbine across and the boy caught it and lit it from Patch's, inhaling the smoke with deep grateful gasps.

'Cristoforo's my best model.' Patch swung the boy round and pushed his chin up carelessly with the back of his hand.

17

Cristoforo stood motionless, his fingers still clutching the cigarette so that the smoke curled up in blue tongues along his arm. 'Look at those bones. Sharp as T-squares and clean as right angles. A draughtsman's dream. That's what Cristoforo is. Pure Greco. All set squares and French curves. An architect could draw Cristoforo.'

The boy was still standing with his head turned, his shoulders held back, motionless as the statue of Garibaldi in the middle of the piazza.

'They have faces here,' Patch went on. 'Not pieces of pudding. Look at those nostrils and that upper lip. Better than those pre-Raphaelite virgins with buck teeth you hire back home. Look at his eyes. Colour. Colour all the time. Beautiful, expensive, exotic colour. And all for free. It used to cost me a fortune back home to get some wall-eyed witch who couldn't sit still and whined all the time about the cold. All right, Cristoforo, relax.' The boy dutifully lowered his head and took a drag at the cigarette.

'I've painted Cristoforo as often as I've painted anyone,' Patch concluded. 'It works out well, too. Cristoforo's an orphan. I used to pay him once but the uncle he lives with – a big brute called Angelo Devoto – took all the money. So now I buy him a good meal whenever he wants one and give him cigarettes.'

'I don't 'old with kids smoking,' Hannay growled.

'They all do it.' Patch turned to Cristoforo. 'Good, Cristoforo?'

'*Si*, Signor Tom. *Grazie*.'

'In English, you little blighter. It's useful to know English. Make lots of money if you speak English. Say it again.'

'Yes, Sir Tom. Thank you.'

The boy spoke the words precisely but Patch was suddenly not paying attention. Both Cristoforo and Hannay were aware that his interest had been caught by a girl crossing the piazza, and he was drawing her quickly, his eyes half-closed, patently admiring her figure and the way she swung her hips as she walked.

'Where've you been today?' he asked over his shoulder, the tone of his voice indicating that only part of his mind was on Cristoforo, the other busy with the drawing he was making of the girl.

Cristoforo's expression had changed subtly at the question, and even Hannay noticed the difference.

'On the mountain, Signor Tom,' the boy said. 'We hunted snakes and lizards. Myself and Antonio Gori and Matteo Lipparini.'

The girl disappeared round the corner into the Via Garibaldi and Patch threw down the envelope in disgust and turned to Cristoforo again.

'Find any?' he asked.

Cristoforo's brows came down so that the hair that fell over his forehead almost covered his eyes. His expression was anxious as well as puzzled and even Patch was aware of the doubt behind his pause.

'Signor Tom, that is funny,' he said eventually. 'There are *no* lizards. Usually there are many. Today there are none. And no cicadas. There were no snakes either, signore. Not one snake, and under the folds of the lava and in the cactus bushes there are usually many. I've found them often.'

Patch reached for the glass of vermouth in front of him.

'Where are they then?' he asked cheerfully.

'Signor Tom, I don't know. We look for many hours but we find no snakes at all. And no lizards. Nothing. The mountainside is empty, signore. Empty. There's no living thing up there.'

# *three*

---

Cristoforo's words seemed to hang on the still air like the rumble from beneath the ground and the vibrations that had come up through the layers of the earth's crust.

Patch swung round in his chair, the boy's anxiety insinuating itself into his mind. Cristoforo was standing alongside him patiently, one hand behind his back, the other holding the dwindling cigarette pinched between forefinger and thumb.

Patch stared at him. 'No snakes, eh?' he said lightly.

'No, Signor Tom. No snakes. Not a bloody one.'

'Not a *what*?' Hannay sat up abruptly, looking as though he couldn't believe his ears.

'Not a bloody one,' Patch said placidly. 'My influence, I'm afraid. I try to teach him English but it's surprising what he picks up in addition.' He drew on his cigarette for a second then addressed the boy again, still inclined to regard the matter as a joke. 'Snakes' day off today,' he suggested cheerfully. 'Snakes have got to have a day off like everyone else.'

Cristoforo paused before replying. He knew from Patch's mood that he'd been drinking.

'Signor Tom,' he said earnestly. 'I think it is the mountain. I didn't want to stay. I came down at once.'

'The mountain?' Hannay leaned forward, his square, peeled red face curious.

'Did something happen on the mountain?'

Cristoforo thought for a moment, trying to remember exactly what *had* happened. He had been sitting on a rock among the folds of dead lava, high up where the sea seemed no more than a rippling blue sheet and the clouds that hung about the crater seemed almost within reach. He had been gnawing at a piece of bread and sausage, and farther down he could hear the shouting of his friends.

It was only the sighing of a non-existent wind and a sudden vibrating of the earth that sent a little stream of dusty gravel dropping gently from where he sat on to the leaves of a myrtle bush just below him that gave him any indication that anything unusual had occurred. He had watched the leaves bend slowly under the weight of the gravel then, as it slid to the earth and the leaves jumped up again, he had turned and stared at the mountain top. Then he had noticed that Masaniello, his dog, was standing up, its face to the crater, its manner suspicious and, without knowing why, Cristoforo had been oppressed by a feeling of fearful inscrutability about him, a strange dread as everything stood still in a queer drawing back of time.

He had remembered then that in addition to the inexplicable absence of lizards and little grey vipers, the noisy thrumming of insects was missing also on the scrubby slopes. The silence around him seemed monstrous and curiously violent.

He had glanced upwards, conscious for the first time of the stuffiness of the atmosphere and the smell of sulphur that drowned the scent of wild thyme and mimosa and cypress, aware for the first time of the brooding bulk of the mountain above him, and he had crammed the rest of the bread and sausage into his mouth, obsessed by a sudden fear that he would be left behind when darkness fell. Jumping from the rock, he had shouted after his friends, his cries muffled by the fullness of his mouth, and gone leaping after them like a young goat, jumping from fold to fold of the ringing grey lava.

He drew a deep breath to try to explain.

'Signor Tom,' he said. 'There was a big noise like the one a few moments ago, and a wind without anything stirring.'

Hannay gave the mountain an uneasy glance and drew quickly on his cigarette. Patch was sitting up now.

'That's nothing,' he said. 'There've been rumbles before. You're used to rumbles. We all are.'

'Yes, Signor Tom.' Cristoforo was looking as uneasy as Hannay by this time. 'There've been many before, but none like this one.'

'What was special about this one?'

'It had a feeling, Signor Tom. It was only small – smaller than the last one a few minutes ago – but I felt it all around me. It was there with me. It was alive. I was afraid, signore. I'm still afraid. It's even down here in the Porto.'

'What do you mean?' Patch was staring at him now. 'Down here in the Porto?'

'Signor Tom' – there was a hint of bewilderment in Cristoforo's voice – 'there are no snakes on the mountain, because they have all come into the town.' He paused while Patch absorbed the information, then he went on excitedly: 'They killed three this week behind the garage. My uncle killed one near the mole. They've been killing them all week in the vineyards. Matteo Lipparini lives in San Giorgio. His father's a foreman. He brought one home which he killed himself. He said it was the fifth in three days. He threw it on a fire in the garden. You could see the skeleton.'

The humour had gone out of Patch's face now.

'Antonio Gori's uncle was bitten when he was working on the sulphur,' Cristoforo went on. 'He was very ill. And the gardens on the slopes have been full of quail. It's as I said, signore, there's nothing left on the mountain. No lizards, no snakes, no quail, no pigeon. Nothing. They've deserted it.'

Patch lit a cigarette and studied Cristoforo through half-closed eyes. He wasn't a nervous child or one given to wild imagination. He spent a great deal of his life among the slaggy streams of cold lava and he knew the mountain as well as he knew his own hand. He was an expert on the sea-shells found in the harbour at low tide and could identify a bird while it was still only a speck in the sky. And Patch was already aware of his uncanny reading of weather signs. He had predicted that morning's violent storm the previous day and long before there had been any sign of it, as though his skin were sensitive to pressures in the air that didn't affect other people. He knew when rain was coming and when it was going to be warm, and when the winds were building up in the islands to the south.

Patch studied the troubled young face a little longer, his eyes on the narrow features and the alert intelligent black eyes, then he shrugged off his serious mood.

'You imagine things, Cristoforo,' he said.

Cristoforo shook his head, his face still grave. 'Signor Tom, there was also a great deal of smoke.'

'There always is.'

'No, signore. Steam. But today there was smoke.'

Patch drew on his cigarette and breathed out slowly, glancing at the mountain and the little plume that drifted to the east on the wind.

'It looks the same to me,' he said.

'When you get closer, signore, you can see it is different. It is thick and dark. As when they burn oil and tyres behind the garage in the winter when the visitors have left. But the smell wasn't that smell. It was like Forla's sulphur.'

Patch and Hannay were silent, and after a while Cristoforo took his leave, trailing an olive twig along the cobbles. At the other side of the piazza, he was met by some of his friends, who had been washing a couple of withered apples at the pump, and they began a game that consisted of throwing rubber shoe-heels into chalk-numbered flagstones against the peeling colour-wash of the houses. Hannay was disturbed to see coins change hands among them.

He watched them for a while, his eyes on Cristoforo.

'Nice kid that,' he said over his shoulder. 'Wish we'd got one like 'im, me and Mabel. We always wanted a family and never managed it. Thought we might adopt one but we kept putting it off because you never know what you might get.'

Patch had started to draw on the table cloth, an absorbed expression on his face. 'You could have Cristoforo for a few thousand lire,' he said, looking up. 'Uncle Angelo would agree – '

Hannay turned quickly, and there was an eagerness in his heavy face that surprised Patch. 'Honest?' he asked.

' – providing,' Patch concluded, 'that you adopted Uncle Angelo and probably all the other relations as well. About a million, I should say, at a rough estimate. They'd like the chance of going to England, too.'

Hannay scowled. 'Come off it, Mister. I'm not joking.'

Patch looked up and smiled. 'Neither am I. A quarter of the population of Italy wanted to emigrate after the war. On Anapoli, where they were forgotten by the relief organisations it was as high as a half. Angelo Devoto was among them. He thinks you can live without working in England.'

Hannay was silent for a while, obviously still thinking of Cristoforo. 'He was a bit put out then,' he said. 'About the mountain, I mean.'

Patch considered. 'Yes. Cristoforo's no fool. But he thinks too much.'

'All the same he'd been scared.'

'He's only a kid, and a rumble *would* scare him. The mountain's dead.'

'It didn't feel dead to Fred 'Annay. It felt very much alive-o. 'Aven't they got an observatory or something here to keep a check on it?'

'They were going to have. They even put the foundations down. Then they ran out of money and decided the mountain was dead anyway. Forla keeps his cars in it now.'

Hannay thought for a moment. 'Suppose it isn't dead? What would you do?'

Patch drew in a sweeping line that broke his crayon and looked up. 'Take a boat to the mainland,' he said.

'Wouldn't you stay?'

'I couldn't care less about the bloody island.'

'Fine attitude for a man who's made his home here,' Hannay reproached.

Patch looked up again and met the cold glance from the bright blue eyes across the table. He grinned, putting Hannay down as a psalm-singing, Bible-thumping, praise-the-Lord-and-pass-the-ammunition sort of sea lawyer who probably made life miserable for his crew with Sunday prayers and lectures on morality whenever they made port.

'That's the worst of being one of these decadent artist types,' he said, enjoying the irritation in Hannay's expression. 'Maybe I'm just contrary. Let's have another drink. Emiliano's waiting for me to drink myself to death so he can put up a marble plaque outside, "*Here sat Thomas Patch, the English painter*," just as they've done with Gorki in Capri and Sorrento. He's a great one for celebrities, is Emiliano. It helps with the tourists. Looks so important on a postcard home. And I think he feels it would be so much better with "*Died of drink*" at the end of it to add a touch of poignancy.'

He slumped in his chair, still drawing, an unashamed grin on his face.

'God knows,' he said, 'I'm game enough to help him so long as he calls half-time occasionally and stops for spaghetti and a smoke.'

Hannay stared at him, unsmiling and clearly disapproving. 'That's a smashing future you've got mapped out for yourself,' he commented severely.

*f o u r*

When Patch eventually left Emiliano's, Hannay stared after his lean figure with its paint-daubed shirt, the faded pale-blue trousers, and the jaunty straw hat.

Then he turned slowly in his chair and looked thoughtfully up at Amarea, stretching away behind the town, bare and ugly, the grey, scorched-looking summit changing to purple as it sloped down to the villages of San Giorgio and Colonna del Greco that stood out on the skyline like a couple of broken teeth; then to green, and finally into sunbursts of colour where the early azaleas and the oleanders burst into flame along the side of the road that led round the island to Corti Marina and Fumarola in the north.

In spite of what Patch had said about the mountain, he wasn't entirely satisfied. The mountain had rumbled. Therefore, it was anything but dead. The animals were leaving the slopes. That clearly indicated that with their surer instinct they were afraid. Fat lot of good it was, saying it had done it before, he thought. Hannay was quite unconvinced. It was his duty as master to protect the interests of his ship and he felt that here he had a case that required further investigation.

He turned round as he became aware of Cristoforo standing alongside him again, his face grave, his dog sitting behind him.

'Are you a sailor, Sir Captain?' the boy asked.

'Yes, lad, I am,' Hannay said, his voice warm with friendliness.

Cristoforo smiled, dazzling Hannay. 'I would like to be a sailor, too,' he said.

'Would you? Why?'

'My father was a sailor. He was lost at sea. I don't suppose you need a man on your ship, do you, Sir Captain?'

'Why? Do you want to leave Anapoli?'

'*Sì*, signore.'

'Wouldn't you miss it?'

'Not bloody likely, Sir Captain.'

Hannay frowned. 'Sailors don't use words like that,' he pointed out, hoping God and all seafaring men would forgive him for the monstrousness of the lie.

Cristoforo accepted the rebuke humbly. 'Very well, Sir Captain. I'll not use such words any more. Signor Tom taught me them. He laughs at them.' He paused, thinking. 'Sir Captain, I would work hard on your ship.'

'I'm sure you would. But you're just not old enough, son.'

'I'm thirteen,' Cristoforo said proudly.

'You'd have to be fifteen to work on my ship.'

'I could tell them I was fifteen. No one would know.'

'I would. I'd have to put your age down on the ship's papers.'

Cristoforo seemed to regard this as a minor difficulty. 'You could tell lies, Sir Captain.'

'No, I couldn't.'

'Why not?'

'Because it's wrong to tell lies,' Hannay said firmly. 'And if the captain told lies, the crew would tell lies.'

Cristoforo thought this over for a moment, seeing the sense in it. 'I think we shall have to think carefully about this,' he said gravely.

Hannay stood up, placing a hand on the boy's shoulder with an instinctive gesture of friendship. 'I think we shall,' he said. 'This uncle of yours – have you ever talked to him about being a sailor?'

'Yes, Sir Captain.'

'Would he let you go? If you were old enough, of course.'

Cristoforo was downcast immediately. 'No, signore. I don't think he would. He says I beg cigarettes better than he does. He says I can get money for odd jobs that he can't get.'

Hannay patted his shoulder. 'Well, perhaps we'll have to try to change his mind for you. A boy needs a future.' He gave the boy a smile, so that his face was transformed from the stiff, self-righteous mask that Patch had seen into something friendly and human. 'Now perhaps you can tell me where I can find out something about that mountain? Where's the library, for instance? Or the museum? I've got some business to attend to.'

Cristoforo looked up eagerly, anxious to help. 'By the Town Hall, signore. I'll show you. Is it important business?'

'I think so.'

'Then why not see the Mayor himself? He's there now. I saw him go with Tornielli, his assistant. There's been some trouble. The Communists hung a red flag outside the door and there was a fight. Why not see *him?*'

Hannay considered. 'Aye,' he said finally. 'Why not?'

The Town Hall, originally the palace of the Duke of Anapoli, was a shabby brick building faced with stone to give it dignity. Across its pretentious front, let into the façade in new stone, was the carved legend, '*L'antica qualità della città emerge dalle devastazioni e disastri dei secoli,*' the twentieth-century sentiment of some ambitious official who had tried for party promotion with an attempt to encourage the belief that a fascist revolution was no more than the ancient spirit of Italy reasserting itself.

Ignoring the crowds who were filling the square and the policemen who were trying to persuade them to leave peaceably, Hannay translated the legend in the same solemn way that he waded through all notices and signs in every port he visited in an effort to improve his command of languages, then he tramped up the steps and through the gloomy corridors where the duke had once held court, casting a disapproving shipmaster's eye along the shabby walls and the chipped plaster.

He was fortunate in finding the Mayor in his office – he always believed in going to the fountainhead instead of worrying over minor officials – and he thrust aside all the protesting clerks who claimed he should have had an appointment.

'How can I have an appointment,' he said in that wonderful Italian of his that sounded as though it had been born in Bradford, 'when I only arrived on the island the other day?'

There seemed no answer to the question and he was shown into the waiting-room by a tall slim young man with the sculptured head of a Medici portrait.

'My name's Tornielli,' he said. 'Can I help you?'

'Maybe,' Hannay replied. 'It depends who you are.'

The young man seemed startled by his bluntness. 'I'm the Mayor's assistant,' he explained. 'In his law office in the Via Venti Settembre, of course. Not here. What can I do?'

'Nothing,' Hannay said. 'I haven't come to consult him about law. I've come to consult him about my ship in the harbour.'

The young man smiled nervously and tried to argue but, in spite of his accent, Hannay could speak Italian well enough to give him as good as he got and the dispute was growing noisy when Vicente Pelli, the Mayor, came to the door himself.

He was a short fat man with pendulous cheeks, dark spaniel eyes flanking a long nose and plump white hands that were constantly on the move. He signed to Tornielli and, showing Hannay into his room, personally held out the chair by the desk for him to sit down. The young man placed glasses of pale vermouth before them.

'You're fortunate to find me here,' Pelli said in English. 'But the Communists have been causing trouble. You can see the crowds. It's over now.' His heavy eyebrows rose as he stared at Hannay. 'You're from the ship in the harbour, of course, Captain. There's something you want?'

Hannay nodded. 'I'm interested in that mountain behind the town. I want to know if it's going to erupt?'

Pelli laughed outright. 'Erupt? Amarea's extinct. We've long ago ceased to fear it, Captain. The peasants regard it with affection. It keeps the wind off them.'

He leaned forward, his elbows on the desk, his fingers making a spire. 'Surely there's nothing to cause anxiety?' he said.

Hannay flushed but gave no ground. He was sitting bolt upright in his chair, his red face stern. 'What about all that noise just now?' he asked. He had no more intention of being put off by Pelli than he had by Patch.

'I heard no noise.' Pelli cocked his head gaily.

Hannay scowled. 'You could hear it in the square lower down – the Piazza Martiri.'

Pelli stared at him, then he turned to the young man who was bending over a table near the window reading a paper. 'Piero,' he said, 'did you hear any noise?'

Tornielli turned round and there was a pause before he spoke. 'No, Signor Pelli,' he said. 'I heard nothing.'

Pelli turned to the indignant Hannay and spread his hands.

'I heard it with my own ears,' Hannay said. 'So did lots of other people.'

'The Piazza Martiri's notorious for its excitability.'

As he gazed at the Mayor, Hannay's features were marked with a clear disbelief. He had already decided he didn't like

31

Pelli, for all the vermouth and the welcome and the apparent willingness to be helpful. Hannay was a cautious slow-moving man with a natural distrust of smoothness and too many smiles. In spite of what Pelli was trying to tell him, he knew the rumble as he had heard it must have been noticeable to everyone in the Porto, and Pelli's attempt to convince him it was nothing more than his own imagination antagonised him.

He looked hard at the Mayor and then at Tornielli but they were both ingratiatingly friendly.

'I *heard* it,' he insisted, a suspicious expression on his face, 'and I want to know if my ship's safe down there. I'm a ship's captain and I've got to think of things like this.'

'Of course. Of course. But you can be quite certain, Captain, that your ship *is* quite safe. Amarea's extinct.'

'It didn't sound extinct. In fact, they tell me it's made these noises before.'

Pelli nodded his head. 'There *have* been occasions,' he said. 'Very rare, though. A shifting of the rock below the surface. No more.' He smiled. 'You can rest assured, Captain, that Amarea, extinct though it is, is carefully watched. Experts from the universities on the mainland still visit it every six months and make tests. They're well aware of the noises it makes from time to time and they'd warn us if anything were likely to happen, I can promise you. We can't start worrying now when we've never worried before. If people worried over mountains, there'd be no Naples, no Castellamare, and no Catania in Sicily.'

Hannay was still not entirely satisfied. 'It sounded a pretty *loud* noise to me,' he said doggedly. 'Even if *you* didn't hear it. Don't you think it might be a good idea to have 'em check up on it? I look like being here some time and I don't want to take any risks with my ship.'

'Signor Captain' – Pelli rose – 'believe me, if I thought there were any danger, an expert could be summoned very quickly. But Italian volcanoes are all of the same type and they give plenty of warning. Remember, we have two of the most active in the world not far away and we know a little about them, I think.'

Hannay pushed back his chair with a deliberate movement that indicated his dissatisfaction. He was aware already that he was going to get nowhere with Pelli, but the Mayor's reassurances were just a little too glib to put him off. While he knew nothing about volcanoes, when he got his teeth into a principle nothing in the world could shake him off, and Pelli's easy friendship in no way budged him an inch.

'I always thought,' he said slowly and with meaning, 'that with a volcano, *anything* could happen – even with an Italian volcano.'

Pelli laughed. 'You've read too much about Pompeii, Captain,' he said. 'A lot has been learned since then.'

Hannay finished his drink and stood up. 'Well,' he said, 'I can't say I like it even now. And I'll like it even less if it does it again. On the other hand, thank you for helping.'

As the door closed behind him, Pelli sat back, his smile gone, his black eyes curiously bright. Then he lit a cigarette, puffing at it slowly. The young man behind him had turned round and straightened up.

'I did hear it,' he said abruptly.

Pelli nodded. 'So did I, Piero.'

'The staccatos have been coming more frequently,' Tornielli pointed out. 'There was one last week.'

'I know, I know.' Pelli waved his hand. 'But they're nothing.'

'We don't know much about it. 'Tornielli seemed nervous. 'People are talking. Shouldn't we get someone here from the mainland – ?'

Pelli sat up abruptly. He was a man dedicated to freedom and the belief that the only hope for his politically sundered country was a democratic government. To that end he was desperately anxious to retain his tenuous hold on Anapoli and was prepared to take risks because of it. 'Certainly not,' he said brusquely. 'We can't have some irresponsible geologist from the mainland going about uttering warnings just now. He could do untold harm. Volcanologists are delightfully vague when it comes to making prophecies – I've heard them – and what he said could be misconstrued. The election's only three weeks away, Piero. People could easily be panicked. The Communists might even use what he said to drive our voters away and a vote from everybody's our only hope of victory. They might even start a scare as they did at Vicinamontana in Calabria. They blamed the flooding there on the Christian Democrats. They said they'd neglected the Ruffio dam, and they'd do the same sort of thing here if they got half a chance.'

'I suppose they would.' Tornielli stood in the middle of the room, fiddling doubtfully with a pencil. 'All the same, people are beginning to notice.'

'That's why we mustn't have any geologists here,' Pelli said sharply. 'People are talking too much already. It's the most natural thing in the world to talk, of course, but that doesn't mean that what they say is right.' Piero continued to fiddle with his pencil, still unconvinced.

'I'm not happy about the mountain either,' Pelli said, brushing aside his doubts. 'But I don't think it's dangerous. Obviously rumbles are bound to cause anxiety. But we mustn't forget that with every one of them the Communists are just that little bit more happy about the result of the voting. They're the only ones who're likely to gain anything from the sort of panic that our friend the English captain's suffering from.'

'I heard that the Communists were complaining about the mountain in the Piazza Martiri last night,' Piero said.

'Of course they were.' Pelli sat back and gestured with wide-open arms. 'Of course they were. It suits their purpose perfectly to encourage the belief that the mountain's dangerous. We all know just how many years these odd rumblings have been going on.' He pointed with a pencil, jabbing with it as though it were a stiletto. 'But have the Communists ever worried about them before? Of course not. Then why are they worrying now? Because there's an election on. Many of our voters could afford to leave Anapoli for a few weeks if they wish. The Communists' supporters, for the most part, can't. Therefore any false alarm such as our friend the captain subscribes to can only decrease the number of our friends and leave the Communists exactly as they were. It's up to us to deride all this talk of danger before it does us any harm. The balance in the voting's too delicate to upset it for a mountain that's been rumbling uselessly on and off throughout most of its existence. After three hundred years of it, we can safely forget it for another three weeks.'

# *five*

---

It was dark and the crowds had dispersed by the time Patch reached the Via dei Pescatori where he lived. The dim night-streets were still a little noisy with groups of young men shouting and gesturing in doorways and across the pavements, and he felt bored and left out of all the arguments that were going on.

Just above the harbour, he turned into a narrow street like a chasm where the scents of cheese and olives and ravioli and uncorked wine came out at him in gusts with the whiffs of charcoal and the smell of ancient stone, and pushing through the great half-opened door of a peeling block of apartments whose shutters hung awry and unpainted at the windows, he mounted the stairs to the rooms he rented from Mamma Meucci.

Through an open door above him he could hear Mamma Meucci herself, already hoarse from shouting, carrying on one of her everlasting arguments across the narrow street with the old woman who lived opposite and spent all her time in the window watching what went on in Mamma Meucci's rooms and passing on the information to the neighbours. Then, as he trudged up the stone steps where the children had chalked their names on wet days and gouged faces in the cracked plaster, the stomachic boom-boom-boom of a trombone played by old Tornielli, the caretaker, came up the well of the winding staircase in the 'Jewel Song' from Faust.

Somewhere among the rafters a baby was crying – there was always a baby crying – and the wasp hum of a sewing machine; and the sound of two older children arguing while their mother threatened to knock some sense into both of them; some wife tearfully begging her husband to stay home; and through it all a wireless blaring out a popular song – '*Il bosco è ingiallito, da quando sei partita tu*' – in a shuddering dispossessed way as though it didn't belong to anybody.

It was a great barracks of a place, noisy, none too clean and anything but private, but in his self-dependent, self-absorbed way that ignored the need for anything in the nature of comfort Patch loved it. It was too chipped and scarred to be called beautiful but it had life and colour and light and people – and it was the people and the life and the colour he crammed into his pictures that sold them to the galleries.

He listened for a moment, pausing on the stairs to enjoy the variety of sounds, the straw hat on the back of his head. 'All at home,' he thought. 'The whole barmy lot. All wrapped up in their own little worlds of words and music.'

As he halted by the next flight of steps, he saw Piero Tornielli, old Tornielli's son, at the top with Cecilia Leonardi, who lived in a third-floor apartment. He was gesturing importantly and with a touch of arrogance, the immaculate clothes that went with his job with Mayor Pelli oddly out of place on the dark stairs.

As he saw Patch, his gestures drooped and he frowned quickly, his eyes flickering sullenly downwards, so that he looked exactly like Patch's portrait of him, the *Young Man in Love*, that graced Forla's Rome house – dreamy with jealousy and torn by internal strife.

'Signor Patch,' he said uncertainly. He had been on the point of descending and he now stepped back to let Patch pass.

'No, no! Signor Tornielli!' Patch smiled and, with a caricature of a gesture, stepped back too.

Tornielli hesitated, trying to will Patch to move first, but holding the battered straw hat across his chest, Patch leaned nonchalantly on the banister and waited, and finally Tornielli's bluster collapsed. He gave a quick unhappy glance at the girl then ran down the stairs, not looking up at Patch as he passed him.

Patch watched him go before mounting the steps. The girl's blue eyes were on him all the way up, resentful and challenging. 'Why do you do that?' she asked in English. 'You know he hates it.'

'It pleases me to see the collapse of the legal mind.' Patch grinned. 'Every time we meet here, Cecilia, we have that little passage of arms. He always gives in. I'm waiting for the time when he'll try to punch me on the nose. I'll buy him a dinner if he does.'

'Piero's only young,' Cecilia pointed out defensively, as though she were as old as Patch instead of only nineteen.

Patch grinned again, feeling vaguely sorry for young Tornielli. He knew his tormenting was senseless and cruel and perhaps included a degree of gasconading for Cecilia's benefit. He was constantly promising himself he wouldn't do it again, but there was a quality of petulant vanity about the boy, a querulous self-assertion that drove Patch to debunk him. Somehow, Piero didn't belong in that haggard building with its disfigured paint work and the washing that plastered its façade – a stranger in spite of being born and brought up there among the noisy inhabitants whom Patch set down with such gusto in his paintings, just as he found them, hard-working, lazy, proud, profane or religious. Piero had been clawing his way for ages out of that class of society, forgetting as he went where he came from, and aiming for the arrogant and self-important, the better-than-the-rest class that to Patch was always like a red rag to a bull.

'Has he asked you to marry him lately?' he asked.

Cecilia frowned. 'Piero's been asking me to marry him since he was twenty. Since before you came here. Ever since my grandfather and his father decided it would be a good match. I'm still saying no. But I don't laugh at him.'

Her eyes were sullen as she looked up at him, a small figure in a yellow dress that lit the shadows.

'You make too many enemies,' she said.

'They're more exhilarating than friends.'

'You don't care, do you?' She looked puzzled and uncomprehending, and vaguely worried about him. 'I don't understand you not caring. I don't understand *anybody* not caring when they make enemies.'

'Piero's not an enemy. Perhaps he'd like to push me down the stairs, but no more.'

'Piero takes himself – and me – very seriously.' She was vaguely hostile towards him, even defensive towards Piero because he was young like her and unsure of himself. 'Sometimes he makes me afraid. He sets such store by this arrangement of his father's.'

'He'll get over it.'

She looked up at him, smiling a little, a suggestion of contempt and pity in her expression. 'How little you understand us,' she said.

He stared at her for a second, sobered by her seriousness. God, he wondered, why can't I get at the thoughts behind those eyes? – all the fears and doubts of youth, all the gaiety and the pride. There was nothing could make a picture so much as the character beyond the flesh and bone. That was where all the great portraits came from, the Mona Lisa and those magnificent Titians and Barbaris.

He wondered even if he knew her features too well, for he'd painted them so often he could almost do it blindfold. She'd modelled uncomplainingly for him through the whole of the stormy two years he'd lived there and in between had helped Mamma Meucci to feed him when he was too absorbed to feed himself, had sewed on his buttons, washed his clothes, tidied his room whenever he permitted her, typed his letters at the office where she worked, quarrelled with him, even told lies to free him from the irresponsible love affairs he embarked upon.

Theirs was an odd relationship. For the most part, he hardly noticed her when he was absorbed in his work, bullying her to hold her head still when he was painting her, thoughtlessly making her stand for hours while he caught the details of a drape he'd wrapped round her, then as she finally rebelled against his domination in a flood of impassioned Italian, suddenly becoming alive to the fact that under the sulky surface she was a pretty girl with fire and laughter in her veins and taking her off on some riotous picnic at the other side of Anapoli in a hired car or in a boat to one of the neighbouring islands.

He woke up as he realised she was watching him, too.

'Any coffee, Cecilia?' he asked. 'I feel a bit fuzzy round the edges.'

'Has there ever not been any coffee?' she demanded.

He laughed at her hostility. 'That's what I like – the warm glow of welcome. I'll come in.'

Without returning his smile, she held the door open for him, and he crossed the little studio that old Leonardi, her grandfather, had once used for photography, but which was now rapidly falling into disuse from lack of clients. By the door was the glass frame that had originally hung in the street until the wind had blown it down. It was still full of brown portraits ten years out of date with a background of rustic seats and waterfalls, their edges growing green-grey with damp and age. On the bench there were boxes of long-developed plates, but no sign anywhere of new work. The whole place smelled of cleaning but the pungent odours of acids and developers had long since vanished.

Cecilia moved ahead of him into the apartment and watched him drinking his coffee for a while, his lean predatory nose in the cup, then she moved to the window. The Tyrrhenian was picking up the stars and a few white birds like puffins were mewing over the headland. The lights from the ship in the harbour were doubled in the water alongside, like sequins against the oily surface, and at the other side the windows of the flat-fronted houses glowed yellow in the mirror-still waters of the bay. In preparation for an open-air meeting, the loudspeaker car was still tearing the quietness to shreds down by the harbour with a gramophone record of a brass band, and a dog was howling in retaliation in one of the narrow courtyards.

'It's hot tonight,' she said.

'Election fever,' he pointed out.

'Elections!' Her eyes flashed as she turned on him, and he thought how young she looked with that small face of hers, how incredibly young in the yellow dress that made her seem slighter than ever. 'There's nothing in anybody's mind but elections. But it isn't elections. I don't like it. It makes me afraid.' She moved closer to him. 'There was another staccato today.'

Patch looked up quickly. 'Cristoforo says there were two,' he said. 'But what about it? The mountain's been rumbling for fifty years on and off.'

'The mountain's been there for forty million years,' she said, her blue eyes bright under the smoky lashes. 'And everyone still says nothing will happen because nothing's happened for fifty years. What's fifty years in forty million?'

He found her vehemence amusing. She was very pretty with her slim figure and her small hands and ankles, her rebellious mouth and the hot blue eyes, and he began to wonder why he had never done anything about it.

41

'Fifty years,' she was saying. 'It's no longer than an afternoon in a lifetime, no longer than it takes you to put your hat on.'

'I know it isn't, Cecilia.' He tried to calm down the anger in her, the sort of indignant anger he hadn't managed to rouse in himself for years. 'But nobody's losing any sleep over it. Believe me, nobody's worrying.'

'Nobody worried *last* time,' she said. 'They won't be worrying *next* time. They'll be singing and making love and producing children and holding elections, then – poof – ' she snapped her fingers ' – suddenly there'll be no elections and no songs and no love and no children.'

Patch looked up as her anger curled round him. He had been able to thrust aside Hannay's fears as those of someone unfamiliar with the ways of the island and Mont' Amarea. Cristoforo's he had thought were merely those of an excited child. But now, here it was again, the doubt behind all those eyes that turned upwards towards the mountain every time it rumbled. Here again was that silence that came after the vibrations, when they all waited for the next move that didn't arrive, a silence full of crowding thoughts of what went on under their feet where the white-hot rock shifted uneasily miles down where no one could measure it, a silence that brought home to them their own lack of knowledge, their uncertainty, and that bare ugly mountain behind the town, dark now, probably treacherous, and certainly unknowable.

Cecilia was still watching him, her eyes hot, and he shifted restlessly under her gaze. 'Cecilia,' he said, waving his cup, 'apart from rumbles and a little ash and smoke, the damned mountain's been silent for two hundred years.'

'So – ' she swung fiercely round on him again, her face close to his, ' – it follows it will be silent for *another* two hundred?' She shrugged, suddenly deflated, and tried to smile. 'Perhaps it's nothing,' she said, turning towards the window again. 'Perhaps it's just the heat.'

A blare of cacophonic noise from the loudspeaker van by the harbour exploded into argument up the narrow street and burst like an intruder into the room. As she frowned and glanced towards the window, Patch stared approvingly at the curve of her thighs and hips in the yellow dress and the lines of her breast and neck and shoulders. Then she swung round and looked at him frankly, suddenly very young again as her eyes lost their heat and became large and defenceless, her expression unguarded.

'The staccatos are coming more frequently,' she said. 'And the mountain seems so close.'

He moved nearer to her. 'Cecilia, I'll be going to Naples soon,' he pointed out with a gentleness that seemed oddly out of character. 'If it worries you, come with me and get away from this place. I could use a model. You hate Anapoli. You know you do. You're a bit like the mountain yourself, in fact. You're always simmering on the point of an explosion.'

She smiled up at him, her eyes bright, and shook her head. 'There are plenty of models in Naples. There are models for the asking there.'

'None I'd rather paint than you.'

'I don't want to come. Naples is a big city to be alone in with you.'

'You'll stay here looking after your grandfather for ever.'

'That's why I came here when my mother died.' Her voice held the islanders' fatalistic acceptance of life that never failed to antagonise the cheerful realist in Patch.

'Oh, to the Devil with why you came!' he said. 'You're too damn' pretty to be an old maid or married to some fool like Piero, with a house full of children and only the church for consolation. Come to Naples. I'd be around to look after you.'

'Like you did with Mrs Hayward when she went to Rome?' Cecilia's eyebrows lifted.

Patch's smile changed abruptly to a scowl. His entanglement with Mrs Hayward, the acknowledged leader of the middle-class foreign colony on the island, the set that totally ignored the poor of the Porto and aped the aristocracy and the business magnates who found their way to Forla's palace, had been the general property of the Via Pescatori for some time. 'Why bring her up?' he said. 'I didn't mean that.'

'Giovanetta Pariani then? Or Margharita Silona? Or – ?'

Patch had been watching her affectionately but now his quick temper rose.

'Where the hell do you get all these god-damned names?'

Cecilia was laughing openly at him now, enjoying his discomfort. 'I've only to keep my ears open. You weren't very careful when you first came to Anapoli. If I looked further, I suppose I could find more names from Naples, and Sorrento and Capri and Florence.'

'I was painting Margharita,' he explained noisily, and for Cecilia without a great deal of conviction. 'Not that she was any good. She's got no neck and feet like a pair of waders. I was never in love with the damned woman.'

'You never are.'

He studied her for a moment, at a loss for something to say, baffled by her skilful handling of him, the sure knowledge of his secrets that she used like a weapon against him, then he turned away, still oddly concerned that she should know more of life than Anapoli could offer her.

'Naples will be coming to its best just now,' he said over his shoulder. 'We could go to Capri. Or Ischia.'

She shook her head. 'No,' she said. 'I'm not coming. I know you too well. I know of all the other girls who've been with you.'

'You could still come to see the lights.'

She turned away from him. 'I'd be running away if I did.'

He looked up, irritated by her stubbornness, and baffled by her concern with what seemed to him nothing more than merely a mountain with a stomach disorder.

'Running away? From what?'

'Something's – going to happen,' she persisted. 'I know it is. I can feel it.'

He grinned, admitting defeat. 'OK, then, you can feel it. You can certainly feel something. That's obvious. But perhaps it's nothing more than indigestion. Or the election. Or another storm like this morning. Anything on God's good earth. You should enjoy yourself before it happens. I do. For the first time in my life I'm doing what I like and for the first time in my life I can afford to. I don't have to flog my pants to buy brushes, or my shirts for money to haggle with an old Shylock in a junk shop over some dreary painting I want to use the back of for a spanking new idea that warrants decent canvas. It's hard when you're happy to get upset about a mountain that doesn't know whether it wants a belch or a haircut.'

## *six*

---

The following evening, Patch was painting as he changed his clothes, standing by the window, holding his trousers up with one hand as he angrily jabbed lemon yellow paint at a large canvas with the other. Around him were the odds and ends from his studio which he had collected for Mamma Meucci to remove, in his weekly effort to make the place more presentable; the boom he had borrowed, an assortment of dirty pots and pans, the empty bottles, the paint-spotted newspapers. In the middle of the task, the painting had caught his interest again and he was now completely absorbed, the clearing up forgotten, the dressing he had started in the middle of the clearing up forgotten too.

Mamma Meucci came panting into his room with bread and cheese and wine, the whole of her amiable fourteen stone wobbling with eagerness, the odour of garlic from the kitchen that clung to her clothes sweeping before her like a miasma. The two children who came with her immediately crossed to the spare easel and stared at the painting of Cecilia Leonardi which Patch had started the previous night.

'Her nose is too long,' one of them commented severely. 'She's not as pretty as that either.'

Patch threw down his brush angrily.

'How many times have I told you not to come into the bloody room without knocking?' he shouted, swinging round on Mamma Meucci. 'I'm not dressed. And get those blasted *bambini* out before they knock something over.'

Mamma Meucci brushed aside the two children who fled towards her. 'Signor Tom,' she shrieked, laughing breathlessly. 'What does it matter if I see you undressed? I'm an old woman and God made you all the same. Many times I've seen my husband without his trousers. Whenever it happens there is a new *bambino*.'

Shaking with laughter, she edged backwards towards the corridor, knocking over the pile of household implements he had stacked up for her to remove, and sending them crashing to the floor.

'Signor Tom,' she panted, picking them up one after the other and stuffing them under her arms. 'Almost you make me forget. There is a letter for you. The Signora Hayward left it with old Tornielli.'

Patch put down the brush he had picked up again and stared at her for a moment, puzzled and suspicious. It was unlike Mrs Hayward to visit the narrow alleys of the Porto. She belonged to the hotel with its bright colours and potted palms and the little newspaper stand which in the season sold the *New York Herald Tribune* and the *Paris Soir* and the fat magazines from across the Atlantic, all out of date but food and drink to the enthusiastic elderly ladies who came eagerly to Anapoli to see the Greek remains in Colonna del Greco and to examine the Church of Sant' Agata and then found none of the comfort beyond the gaudy foyer of the hotel that they were used to in Venice and the Vittorio Veneto in Rome.

He opened the letter slowly, his mind still on the writer. It stood out a mile to everyone – and everyone in Anapoli Porto was always interested in everyone else – that Mrs Hayward, an immigrant to Anapoli from the displaced British official classes in India, had made the frantic marriage of a young woman on some God-forsaken station where her husband was perhaps the only eligible man. She had pounced on Patch the minute he had arrived on the island and was still, after two years, loath to take her claws out of him.

It. was an affair which had fluctuated for her between ecstatic heights of excitement and the depths of misery and vindictiveness when Patch fought to hold her at arm's length during the periods when she grew reckless. For the most part its impetus had been given to it by Mrs Hayward's desperate craving for vitality after her husband's cheerful dullness, and it had moved in fits and starts throughout his occasional visits to the mainland.

Still holding his trousers with one hand, Patch dropped the envelope on the floor where Mamma Meucci stared at it indignantly, and read the note.

'*Dear Tom –* ' the passionate hurried scrawl went well with Mrs Hayward's garish blondeness, ' *– Must see you. Important. Let me know when.*'

It contained a hint of the old desperation, the old craving for excitement, and Patch was growing tired of Mrs Hayward's hysterical desperation. He had no wish to become embroiled again in any affair with her, with all the embarrassment it meant for him and the misery it meant for her. He stared at the letter for a moment, then he grinned at Mamma Meucci and screwed it up into a ball.

'Anything important, Signor Tom?' Mamma Meucci was quivering with curiosity, bursting to know the latest on the affair.

Patch picked up his brush again and shook his head. 'She wants me to referee a boxing match,' he said. 'That's all.'

Mamma Meucci gaped at him disbelievingly, then she stepped into the corridor, dropping the broom and the buckets with a clatter as though she had crashed into something.

'Signor Tom – ' her voice came to Patch excitedly as she backed into the room, ' – there is someone to see you!'

'Oh, my God, no!' Patch exploded again. 'It's like a bloody railway station in here with people running in and out all the time. Tell 'em to go away. Tell 'em I'm sick. Tell 'em I'm dead!'

Mamma Meucci cackled hoarsely and seemed to grope into the dimness of the corridor as though rummaging into a dark cupboard. It was Hannay she produced, and she pushed him into the room with both hands flat on his back. He looked a little sheepish and stood uncertainly by the door, at a loss for a moment as Patch completely ignored him.

He was in front of the easel again by this time, absorbed in painting once more, placidly holding his trouser tops while he dabbed lemon yellow on the canvas.

Hannay watched for a while, listening to Mamma Meucci's noise in the corridor as she drove her children away, and the arguments from above and the oompa-oompa of old Tornielli's trombone that floated up the staircase to join the yells of the baby and the shouting of the squalling children; then he stared round the shambles of Patch's living-room, with its discarded clothes and bits of statuary, the enormous brass bedstead littered hopelessly with drawings and old shoes in magnificent confusion, and the picture of the Virgin Mary that Mamma Meucci had hung on the wall when she had first discovered Patch was a painter and now spent most of its time backside-outwards because Patch couldn't bear to look at the appalling workmanship, all the odds and ends of an artist's studio hopelessly intermingled with the paraphernalia of what fragmentary domesticity Patch possessed.

Hannay coughed but Patch seemed to have been stricken with deafness. He cleared his throat noisily and tried again, but with the same results.

'Hell,' he said at last, to draw Patch's attention to himself. 'I thought I was never going to find you. Proper rabbit warren, this place, innit?'

Patch finally condescended to notice him. 'It's all right,' he said. 'Except when it rains. Tornielli won't repair the roof.

He says he's no head for heights and it's easier to let it fall in.'
He hitched up his trousers a little and crossed towards
Hannay. 'Here, stand like this for a bit.'

He jerked Hannay's arm up and while he was still startled
into motionlessness hurried back to his canvas.

'Ere, what's the idea?'

'Don't move, you bloody fool! You'll come out as
Mercury picking fruit. You look as though you could be the
champion fruit-picker in the whole of the world. That's the
best of Italy. Models are so cheap. Pity you've got a face like
an old sea-boot. You'd do well at it.'

'Am I in a picture?' Hannay seemed pleased as he spoke
over his shoulder.

'Your jacket is. It's much more interesting than you are. I
want the fold of the sleeve. It's always a sod from this angle.
Come and look. You can move now.'

Hannay moved to the easel, then his expression changed
as he stared. 'What's that?' he asked.

'*Primavera*,' Patch explained enthusiastically. 'Spring. It's
a copy of Botticelli in modern dress with a touch of Bastier
Millais. Ever seen Millais?'

'No.'

'You've not missed anything. This is much better. It's the
period of awakening after a war. There'll be four. Summer's
the high noon of prosperity, Autumn's the gathering clouds,
and Winter's war again. War's seasonal these days, after all,
isn't it? Like it?'

'They look like a lot of pansies to me,' Hannay said
bluntly. 'Look how that bloke's standing. He looks as if he's
caught himself on something.'

Patch stared at him, stung by the criticism.

'What's biting you?' he demanded. 'In need of a drink or
something?'

'Sort of,' Hannay admitted. 'But I get dead sick of boozing
with Anderson, that Number One of mine. All he talks about

is the women he's slep' with. 'E makes me ship sound like a knocking-shop.'

Patch grinned. 'I'll join you,' he said. 'I've got plenty of time.'

He put down the paint brush and adjusted his trousers. 'I was just trying to tidy the place up,' he said. 'I was supposed to be doing it when you arrived. Mamma Meucci's done it once today but it seems to fall apart again the minute I come in.'

He stacked a pile of magazines into Hannay's arms and gave him a push. 'Shove 'em in the corridor,' he said. 'Mamma'll shift 'em.'

Hannay disappeared and when he returned he hesitated in the doorway, clearly troubled by something. 'I saw that nipper again today,' he said. 'Cristoforo.'

The overtones of anxiety in his voice made Patch straighten up from where he was folding his clothes over a chair.

'He'd been up the mountain again,' Hannay said. 'He was scared. He said the smoke was worse. He said you could even smell it.'

Patch had stopped fiddling with the clothes. 'I should tell Cristoforo to leave it to the boys in the observatories,' he said gently. 'They know the score.'

Hannay said nothing, standing by the door as though only a charge of dynamite would shift him. He seemed annoyed. 'Suppose it erupts?' he said eventually. 'I saw Vesuvius in 1944.'

'Well, I didn't. It should be interesting.'

Hannay stared at him, infuriated by his indifference. 'Did you know I went to see the Mayor about it last night?' he asked.

Patch grinned. 'Sure. Tornielli lives here. We get to know everything that opens and shuts at the Town Hall. Goes through the building like a dose of salts. Tornielli's the Adonis who helps Pelli.'

'He doesn't seem very bothered,' Hannay said. 'The Mayor, I mean.'

'Neither does anybody else. Except you, that is.'

'Don't they? That just shows how much you know about the place.'

The words struck a chord as Patch was reminded of Cecilia's comment the previous night: 'How little you understand us,' she'd said.

'Well, then, who is worrying?' he asked. 'You're the only one I've seen who's doing any bitching.' He lost interest in the clothing he was trying to tidy and threw it behind a curtain.

'Cristoforo's worrying,' Hannay said.

'He's only a kid.'

'And there was an old geezer I heard talking in a café down there. An old bloke with long white hair looked like Old Nick down on his luck.'

'That's old Leonardi.' Patch straightened up from jerking the curtain into place. 'He was here when the bang occurred in 1892, so he considers himself the mountain's personal custodian and friend. He even calls himself "Doctor" Leonardi but he's no more a doctor than you are or I am. He's got no instruments, no charts, nothing. But he's been prophesying disaster ever since the turn of the century. Nobody ever takes any notice of him now. He lives here, too. On the floor below. We have everyone worth knowing in the Via Pescatori. I'll have to introduce you to him. He'll scare your tripes out with his talk of volcanoes. You'll love it.'

Hannay looked disappointed but he showed no signs of moving, and Patch lost his temper, 'Oh, hell, man,' he said. 'You've got a fixation about the bloody mountain!'

'No, I 'aven't.' Hannay seemed indignant to the point of anger. 'I mentioned it to that Orlesi bloke when I saw him today – the chap who runs the sulphur for Forla. If anybody's got a fixation it's you and him and all the others who think there's nothing happening up there on that flipping mountain. I talked myself black in the face to him. I might just as well have saved me breath. What noise? says he, as if I was something the cat had brought in. What smoke? What rumble? Like he'd gone deaf and blind and bloody daft. I could have sloshed him one across the jaw. What smoke? My God, it's there plain as the nose on your face. All he did was wag his mitts at me and dodge the subject. Understand my meaning?'

He drew a deep breath while Patch waited for him to continue. 'I suppose you know,' he said, 'that he's having trouble with the sulphur workers? They can't work for talking. Did you know that? I bet you didn't. Well, *they* wouldn't stop unless they'd got reason. That's why they haven't started loading me yet. I was ahead of me schedule when I arrived here. But now – ' he left the sentence hanging in the air, heavy with contempt for Italian organisation.

'Look,' he said eventually, 'it's my opinion Orlesi and Pelli and their pals don't *want* to hear that mountain. They're frightened of it upsetting business, like you said. Don't you think you ought to give 'em a bit of a push?'

There was silence for a moment because Patch couldn't think of anything to say. Hannay was one of those worrying, nagging little people who are always canvassing for a lost cause. If he hadn't been a ship's captain, he'd have been president of a league to reduce taxes or to stop them putting up the rates, or standing for Parliament on a platform of anti-vivisection.

'For Christ's sake, why me?' he asked at last.

Hannay stared back unblinkingly. 'Influence,' he said simply. 'It wants somebody with influence. I thought you was pulling my leg with all that talk about Thomas Patch, the painter. Now I know you weren't. Everybody knows you.

Even Anderson, my Number One. Suppose you went to the Mayor and told him you'd got the wind up – '

'But I haven't.'

'You can say you have.' Hannay was getting irritated.

'You could say you was worried about the mountain.'

'It's not *my* affair.'

'It's everybody's affair.'

'Then why the hell don't *you* go? Your ship's in danger if anything happens. That makes it *your* affair.'

'I've been once,' Hannay said angrily. 'And a fat lot of good I got out of it too. If I go again, they'll just tell me to take me ship away if I don't like it.'

'Well, why don't you?'

Hannay's face set in an expression of tortured patience.

'Well, for one thing, I'm supposed to stay 'ere till I get what I came for,' he said. 'And for another, I'm not just thinking of me ship. I'm thinking of a few other perishers, too.'

'A few others? Who, for God's sake, who can't look after themselves?'

'All these Eyeties. All these damn' people on the island.'

Patch was frankly baffled. Hannay clearly considered it his duty to concern himself with Mont' Amarea and everybody's right to expect his concern.

'You seem to be bloody fond of the Eyeties,' he said.

'Oh, but I'm not.' Hannay shook his head and there was in his face that smug expression that made Patch want to throw something at him, a secure self-righteousness, but at the same time a consciousness of being right that was curiously disarming. 'Anything *but*, Mister. I think they're a treacherous lot of bastards. They nobbled me in Venice in 1940 before the war had even started and I spent the whole blasted shooting match as a prisoner. That's why I'm the driver of that little sardine tin I've got instead of one of the company's bigger ships. I missed all the best chances. They went to the blokes who'd stayed out of the bag and collected all the medals.'

There was no bitterness in Hannay's voice. He was merely stating facts, without any bias against the people who had passed him over or against the men who had been chosen in his place. 'I was Third Mate on the *Orloway* then. The bastards held up the ship's manifest. They wouldn't give us a clean bill of health. They did all they could to stop us leaving. The old game of diplomacy. Understand my meaning? 'Annay was all for pushing off and chancing it but the captain was an old grannie. He tied himself in knots like an old woman's entrails trying to sort things out. But it didn't work. Mussolini declared war and a naval party just walked aboard and 'Annay went into an internment camp. Where do you think I learned to speak Italian like I do?'

'I often wondered.'

In spite of his grin, Patch was disturbed by Hannay's stubbornness and the clear feeling of anxiety that prompted his interest in the islanders' safety.

'If somebody else went, they might begin to take some notice,' Hannay continued. 'There must be something in it, they'd say, or people wouldn't be scared. You could say you'd been asked by the rest of the English people on the island to enquire.'

'I'll wait until they do.'

Hannay snorted disgustedly. 'Don't you ever feel no sense of responsibility?' he demanded.

Patch shrugged. 'Who ever heard of a responsible artist?' He looked at Hannay for a moment, puzzled. 'It's no good going on at me,' he said. 'I like this place. I picked it out of the whole damn' world to live in. Now you come, skittish as an old streetwalker looking for a fight, and start pulling it to pieces.'

'I'm not pulling it to pieces. I want to know what's going on. I want something certain. Not some half-baked political reply.'

'Well, ask somebody else. If I tried, I'd probably make a mess of it anyway. I hate being practical. I'm a thinker, not a doer.'

'You could try.'

Patch turned slowly. 'Do you go round the world in your little boat stirring up trouble everywhere you come to?'

'No, I don't. You know damn well I don't.'

Patch swung away again and spoke over his shoulder. 'Then, for God's sake,' he said, 'leave me alone. I came here to get away from people who liked to mind my business. There are too many of 'em in this world. Some of 'em are politicians and some of 'em are newspapermen but they all suffer from the same mistaken impression, like you do, that they've a right to tell people what to do. Besides, I'm not the type to follow a cause. My name's Tom Patch, not Joan of Arc.'

Four days later, as Mont' Amarea cast violet shadows along the sea, Alfredo Meucci, Mamma Meucci's husband, puffed at the scrap of cigarette end he had rescued from his pocket.

His fishing boat was drifting gently near to Capo Amarea and behind him, as the boat swung, the ruins of the Aragonese castle shone in blocks of purple and pink as the early morning sun slanted across it. The mountain stood over the town like a crouching lion.

He sat back, watching the bobbing corks of his lobster pots close inshore and enjoyed the last puffs at the crumbling cigarette end. He had three more pots to drop before he could return home to Mamma Meucci's breakfast.

As he threw the cigarette away, the throbbing engine in front of him set the headboard of its casing rattling as the propeller lifted out of the water on a sudden steep swell that slid obliquely across the headland, and Meucci turned his lined mahogany face in the direction it had come from, watching for a repetition, his hand on the tiller to counter it.

'That was a big one, Tomaso,' he said to his companion, who was sitting in the bows cutting up the heads of Tyrrhenian mullet for bait.

Tomaso, his tangled black curls over his eyes like a mop, gazed towards Capo Amarea, his brows drawn down in a puzzled frown.

'That's the third,' he pointed out. 'Where are they coming from?'

The two of them stared across the smooth water that lifted in translucent meadows of blue and watched the big swell roll away towards the open sea.

'There's no wind,' Tomaso pointed out. 'There's been no wind since the storm the other day.'

Meucci didn't answer. He was staring out beyond the headland, his eyes fixed on a stretch of ruffled water. He squinted at it for a moment longer, his eyes unwavering as he concentrated, then he bent over the engine.

'Let's move on,' he said abruptly. 'We'll work towards that patch under the headland. There's something there. The water's moving. It might be fish.'

Putting the engine into gear, they moved inshore again and emptied the rest of the lobster pots, Tomaso scooping the dripping baskets out of the water expertly, removing the lobsters, jamming the head of a mullet in place with a sharpened stick and dropping them quickly into the sea again. Then Meucci swung the boat's head towards Capo Amarea and the disturbed water he had seen. His face was expressionless.

He shut down the engine as the boat slipped into the cold shadow of the headland, a gloomy place of wild dark cliffs where black water slopped at the rocks and the crying gulls flew alone. Tomaso busied himself with lines and bait, whistling. 'The Blessed Madonna's probably brought us a shoal,' he said cheerfully. He looked up as his companion didn't reply and he realised that Meucci had become strangely grave. He stopped what he was doing and swung round. 'What's wrong, Alfredo?'

Meucci was staring round him, his face puzzled.

'There are no fish here,' he said with certainty, sniffing the air like a dog. 'Perhaps it's nothing to do with the Madonna at all. Perhaps even it bears the thumb-print of the Devil.'

Tomaso looked at him wonderingly and turned back towards his work, subdued by the older man's gravity, chilled by the shadow of the headland and the sudden depth of the sea. He baited hooks for a while longer, then he leaned over to wash the slime of dead fish from his fingers, but as he brought his hand out of the water the look on his face changed to surprise. 'Alfredo,' he shouted. 'The water's *warm* here!'

Meucci let go the tiller and leaned over the side. As he straightened up, he was also staring with puzzled eyes at the sparkling drops that fell from his wrist. Silently he put his hand into the water again, withdrew it, then leaned over and shoved the engine into gear once more, fiddling inside the engine house, as though he were looking for something to do.

The bewilderment that had given way to gravity had changed again to something akin to superstitious fear. There, in the shadow of the headland where the sun very rarely penetrated, the water was never anything but cold as the grave. The whole area of sea under the cliffs had a soggy dampness that went with the shadows and the mournful cries of the gulls and the black craggy rocks where the seaweed washed backwards and forwards like the hair of drowned sailors. In a lifetime of fishing in every inlet and bay of the island, Meucci had never known the water anything but icy.

'Why is it so warm, Alfredo?' Tomaso repeated, thinking suddenly quiet.

Meucci was staring again at the drops of water among the thick black hairs on his hand.

'Why is it so warm, Alfredo?' Tomaso repeated, thinking the old man hadn't heard him.

Meucci lowered his hand and started to life again.

'I don't know,' he said slowly, not looking at Tomaso. 'I don't know, Tomaso. Perhaps even it was *hot* not so long ago.'

Even as he replied, the engine started to run raggedly and he switched it off with the precise movements of a man not familiar with mechanical things. Around them the silence under the headland seemed immense after the thump-thump-thump of the engine. Then another of the tremendous unexplained swells hit them and the boat swung alarmingly as the huge dark ripple slid beyond them across the bay.

Meucci regained his balance and, bending over, examined the engine.

'We'll use the sail,' he said, half to himself. 'It's no good trying to cool engines with water as hot as this is.'

'Alfredo – ' Tomaso's anxious voice broke sharply in on his musing and he swung in the direction of the pointing finger, ' – look, the sea's alive!'

A vast slow bubble was rising to the surface near them, white and empty and glassy, and as it burst in a thin film of spray that caught the sun edging round the headland, they saw wisps of steam break from it and lift away into the air. Then they noticed other wisps of steam all round them and realised the sea was stirred by other bubbles. Meucci and Tomaso stared at them, frozen by surprise, Tomaso's knees bending slowly until his head was low behind the gunwale of the boat, only his nose and eyes above its edge.

'Alfredo, what's happening?' His voice was only a whisper as though he were afraid of being overheard.

'The swells! This is where the swells come from!' Meucci was crouching too, now, both hands resting on the gunwale of the boat, listening.

'*Ascolti*, Tomaso,' he breathed. 'Listen! Do you hear that noise?'

Tomaso, his eyes wide, cocked his head and together they could hear a rumbling, low and muffled, as though it came from under the sea.

'What is it?' Tomaso twisted on his knees in the slimy bottom of the boat, his eyes fixed again on the brown face of Meucci. 'It's like a coffee-pot when it starts to boil.'

He glanced at the sea then at Meucci again, both of them aware now of the eeriness of the sound below them, and the sensation of being surrounded by something malevolent.

'Do you notice the smell, Tomaso,' Meucci whispered. 'It's the smell of brimstone, the smell of the Devil.' He crossed himself quickly.

Tomaso sniffed. 'It smells like Forla's sulphur lorries,' he said in more matter-of-fact tones.

With eyes opaque with bewilderment, Meucci stared at the boiling sea for a second longer, then he scrambled to his feet and grabbed for the sails with the clumsy movements of a frightened old man.

'Quickly –' he seemed impatient and anxious to be away from the spot, ' – get the lines inboard, Tomaso. We'd better head home. I'm hungry.'

## *eight*

When Patch went down to the mole, blinking in the sun rebounding from the walls in a dazzling glare that hurt the eyes, the crowd round Meucci's boat was like a flock of sea-gulls round a patch of garbage. There were men and women and children, most of them from the harbour area, many of them barefooted and all of them talking at the tops of their voices. Behind them, the narrow houses, washed in pinks and yellows and blues which had peeled off to a scaly tawdriness or had run in the recent heavy rains into great tear-stains beneath the windows, stood like a stage set for a play. Somewhere beyond them, in a blare of sound that seemed to rattle the windows and shudder the lopsided shutters, a loud-speaker car was playing patriotic songs, but it went unheeded for once like the strings of garlic and the bunches of pimentoes and the twine and the buckets in the empty little shops whose owners argued round Meucci's boat.

Meucci himself was pottering with the engine, his head inside the casing. His face was grave and he was saying nothing. It was Tomaso who was doing all the talking.

Behind them lay the bulk of Hannay's ship, nearer to the end of the mole, sharp and clear in the sun which picked out the rust marks where the water had run out of the scuppers. Across the foredeck, a string of underwear was stretched motionless in the still, hot air; and half a dozen Lascar firemen hung over the rail, watching the raggle-taggle of people arguing round the fishermen.

Cristoforo was sitting on an old lobster pot on the fringe of the crowd, his dog beside him, its muzzle under its chin. Patch lit a cigarette and held one out to Cristoforo. To his surprise, the boy shook his head, though he looked at the cigarette a little wistfully.

'Signor Tom, I have stopped smoking.'

Patch raised his eyebrows. 'Since when?'

'Since yesterday, signore. The Captain Hannay says it stunts the growth.'

'Who wants to be big?'

'I do, Signor Tom. The Sir Captain says I will never make a sailor if I'm small.'

Patch grinned. The sun, coming over the mountain, was warming to his back and he felt pleasantly lazy. He had been working since daylight with the frenzied energy that sometimes caught him, and he felt now like sitting and absorbing the colour, the reds and blues of the crowd round the boat, the sharp block of black from the ship and the grubby pastel shades of the houses in the background.

Then he noticed Cristoforo studying the sky. It was already the vivid trembling azure of the travel posters and against it the mountain stood out in sharp greys and purples.

He watched the expression on the boy's face for a while. He was a handsome intelligent youngster and it seemed a pity that he would end up like most of the other children of the harbour; without a church-going, God-fearing mother to hold him straight; slapped by the nuns, cheeking the priests, chased by the police, fighting with the older boys, each day growing more raucous-voiced and sharper with his wits. Then he remembered what Hannay had said about adopting him and it occurred to him that, in stopping Cristoforo smoking, he had already made the first move towards it. Suddenly Patch felt better about Cristoforo and found himself prepared to bet on Hannay's success.

Instead of teasing Cristoforo again, he spoke gently and with real interest.

'What can you see up there, Cristoforo?' he asked, staring up into the sky with him.

'It's not what I *can* see,' the boy said. 'It's what I *can't* see.'

'Well, then, what *can't* you see?'

'Birds, Signor Tom. No birds.'

Patch indicated the seagulls squalling on the water round the scraps of fish Tomaso was throwing out of the bottom of the boat. 'What are they?' he asked.

'Migrating birds, I mean, Signor Tom. Where are the swallows?'

Patch stared up into the clear sky too and then it occurred to him with a shock that he had also missed the sleek forms of the swallows, their smooth aerobatics round the houses and their chattering on the red pantiles of the roofs opposite Mamma Meucci's in the early morning before the traffic drowned their cries.

'That's right,' he said wonderingly. 'There are no swallows. They're late, this year.'

'They're not late, Signor Tom,' Cristoforo said firmly, 'They won't be coming now. They should have arrived long since from Africa and even gone north. They've just not come. Neither have the martins and the orioles and the warblers. The sky's empty.'

Patch frowned, his mellow mood gone in an instant. He knew immediately that this was another of those odd inexplicable things that were troubling Hannay, another strange augury of evil.

'Perhaps it's the heat,' he said. 'It's hot today, Cristoforo.'

Cristoforo shook his head. 'No, Signor Tom. Not the heat. That would *bring* them, not send them away.'

Patch drew on his cigarette for a while and squatted down alongside the boy. 'Cristoforo,' he said seriously. 'Have there been any other curious things? – any other things like no lizards and no snakes, and no swallows?'

'Alfredo Meucci's seen things today, signore,' Cristoforo said solemnly. 'That's why there's a crowd round his boat. Tomaso's telling everybody now.'

Patch stared at the noisy group, squinting against the sun. 'What sort of things?'

'The sea, Signor Tom. Bubbling as though it were boiling. Off Capo Amarea. The Sir Captain's trying to find out what caused it.'

'Is Captain Hannay there?'

'Yes, signore. He's at the front of the crowd.'

Patch puffed at his cigarette and looked at the group of people for a moment. Somewhere, stirring at the back of his mind, was a distinct uneasiness that he didn't care to admit to, and he straightened himself abruptly.

'Let's go and join them, Cristoforo,' he said.

Hannay looked up as Patch pushed through the crowd. He was dressed in grey flannels, held up by red braces. His jacket and cap were missing.

'You heard what's been happening?' he asked Patch, his Yorkshire accent as blunt as himself.

Patch nodded and turned to Meucci who immediately smiled nervously. 'Cristoforo says you've been seeing some pretty strange things, Alfredo,' he said.

Meucci sat silently for a moment, one brown knotted hand resting on the engine which he wiped slowly with a piece of old rag, almost as though he were leaning on it.

'There was warm water, Signor Tom,' he said cautiously. 'In some places, in fact, it was hot. Hot enough to bubble. And great swells that rose from the bed of the sea and moved without wind.'

Patch looked at Hannay and found the Yorkshireman's eyes fixed on his face unwinkingly. Across the silence they heard the high-pitched sound of a motor scooter going up the hill out of the town, and the blare of the loudspeaker car.

'Has anything like this happened before, Alfredo?' Patch asked.

Meucci leaned on his rag again and considered, while the crowd waited for his reply. He was remembering a rushing of wind about him when there was no wind, and oppressive air in spite of clear sunshine. Then he remembered rumbles coming out to him across the bay, transmitted, it had seemed, by the lifting water – and the freak storm of a few days before which had come smashing down on the startled island out of a clear sky and a dazzling visibility, bringing short steep waves crashing on to the beach and lashing the palms by the harbour into a frenzy of tumbled fronds. It had built up in monstrous leaden clouds to the south-west in a few minutes, spreading sluggish purple fingers across the still air, until from the sea had come a desolate whine that had sent the bewildered fishermen heading nervously for the lee of Capo Amarea.

Meucci looked up at Patch cautiously. 'There have been things,' he said slowly, and went on to explain what he had seen. 'Only last week something frightened the gulls out there by the Cape.'

'What gulls?' Patch found this thing about him – this intangible thing that was beginning to surround them all – was beginning to be creepy.

'They were feeding,' Meucci was saying. 'And suddenly they all flew up into the air.'

'A fish?' Hannay asked. 'Was it a big fish?'

'It was no fish, signore. There were no fish today. I've been a fisherman all my life and I know when there are fish. I can smell fish.'

Patch watched Meucci puffing gratefully at the cigarette he had offered to him. The things that were worrying Hannay were beginning to take root in his own mind.

The crowd was silent now, gaping.

'Have these things happened before, Alfredo?' Patch asked.

'Occasionally, Signor Tom. Once now and then. But now they all happen together.'

Patch stared at the cigarette smoke hanging on the still air in blue whorls that changed shape as they drifted. The atmosphere seemed lifeless and suffocating. Hannay appeared to be gathering himself together for more questioning.

'Do you remember 1892?'

The question seemed to drop like a bomb into the silence.

They all knew what the date meant. There was no one on the island who didn't know what had happened in 1892 and they all guessed what Hannay was thinking. Several of them had been thinking the same things.

Meucci's eyes switched to Hannay and he started to wipe the engine again quickly.

'I am only a boy, signore,' he said cautiously. 'I am still at my mother's knee. Only Dr Leonardi remembers that far back.'

'Maybe.' Patch took up the question. 'But you've lived all your life here, Alfredo. You've talked to people who would remember. What about Mamma Meucci's father, for instance? He was a fisherman. He'd remember. Didn't he ever talk about it? Did *he* feel winds then and see bubbles? And warm water?'

'Warm water, signore. He felt warm water. He said so. I remember. Very warm water.'

'What about winds?'

'He said the weather was bad – but only over the island. While everywhere else had sunshine, here there were thunder-storms – like the one the other day, I suppose – and a great deal of lightning. And the air was heavy. So heavy, he said, it was as though he was carrying a great load.'

'Like now?'

Meucci thought for a moment. 'It is certainly oppressive, Signor Tom.'

'Suppose the mountain *did* erupt, Alfredo? Would everyone get into the boats? – as they did then.'

Meucci smiled and shrugged. 'Signor Tom, you can't get the whole of Anapoli into a few fishing boats and a few private yachts. Perhaps the ferry would help if it were in, but even so it couldn't take everyone.'

'No one was left behind in 1892. Were there *more* boats then?'

'Of course. The authorities had ordered an evacuation. There were warnings.'

'Alfredo – ' Patch spoke as seriously as he could, ' – are we having warnings *now*?'

There was silence again as everyone waited for Meucci's answer but he turned back to the engine and slowly began to wipe the casing again with his rag. There was a stubborn closed-down expression on his broad face, as though he had no wish to speak.

'Meucci,' Patch persisted. 'Are we having warnings now?'

Meucci looked up, his black eyes troubled. 'Signor Tom,' he said soberly, 'the Lord in His Mercy wouldn't destroy us without first sending word.'

# nine

Patch said nothing as he turned away. The crowd began to chatter again and he could hear Tomaso's voice, scared and noisy. The gulls were edging closer, shrieking and moaning as they wheeled above their heads in the empty sky.

'I'm just going to 'ave me breakfast,' Hannay said, appearing at Patch's side. 'Come and have a cup of tea.'

They crossed the poop deck of the *Great Watling Street*, between the canvas-covered lifeboats and the refrigerating plant and the engine-room ventilators where Hannay was in the habit of taking his daily walk at sea, and climbed the ladder towards the bridge. Hannay opened a door to a tiny saloon almost filled by an oblong table and four swivel chairs all screwed to the deck. At one side was a dresser bearing a tea urn, above which hung a picture of the Queen, and at the other a cracked leather settee where a ginger cat sprawled, obviously in the family way.

Hannay pushed the cat to the floor and made room for Patch.

'That bloody cat,' he apologised. 'Soft as a brush. Let's all the toms 'ave their way with 'er.'

He slumped heavily into one of the swivel chairs, his peeled red face serious. Patch sat on the settee and it was only when the indignant cat streaked for the door that he realised Cristoforo and his dog were still with them.

'Got a new deckhand,' Hannay said with a grin. 'Shapes well. Chris boy, go and tell the cook to give you a plate of bread and dip or something. You look hungry.'

As the door shut behind the boy, Hannay looked up at Patch. 'Taken a real fancy to that kid,' he said. 'I think Mabel would like him.'

He waited until the steward arrived with a dish of greasy bacon and eggs, then he looked up again at Patch. 'I'm thinking of seeing this chap Devoto who looks after him,' he said. 'Thought I might get the kid a job aboard of a ship.'

'I hope you're successful.'

Hannay frowned at the sarcastic note in Patch's voice. 'Don't you think I could do it?' he asked. 'I know lots of people in Naples who'd pull a few strings for me.'

'If I were you, I'd just whip him away and say nothing. It'd be easier and Devoto wouldn't be surprised to find he'd disappeared. Why can't you just smuggle him aboard and up-anchor? It'd be simpler.'

Hannay seemed startled and shocked by the suggestion. 'I couldn't do anything like that,' he said.

'Why couldn't you?'

Hannay was staring at his plate. 'When you've spent all your life living by rules,' he said, 'you don't go and break 'em some time just because it suits you.'

'My God, you've been well brought up.'

Hannay sat back in his chair. 'I was brought up Non-Conformist,' he said. 'Church three times on Sundays. Kids should be seen and not heard. Hell fire and damnation if you went off the straight and narrow. Sometimes, I think it's a pity there isn't more of it. What are you?' He seemed with an effort to thrust Cristoforo out of his mind and his manner became brisk again.

'Me?' Patch was startled by the question. 'Me? A bit of hell fire might have done me good?'

'You've been here a long time, haven't you?' Hannay said unexpectedly.

Patch studied the ugly red face opposite him for a moment. 'Why do you ask?' he said.

'Just interested. You come to save money?'

'I couldn't save money on a desert island,' Patch said ruefully. 'I was in America with an exhibition and some fool discovered I once helped at a Communist meeting when I was at art school. They started twittering like a lot of maiden ladies at a baby show. Un-American activities and so on. It didn't help the exhibition much. Especially when one of those pernicious columnists they have got hold of it. I was called before the committee who were running the show and questioned about my politics, my morals, my girl friends, the size of my grandfather's hats, everything you could possibly conceive might cross a man's mind.'

'I bet that pleased you.'

Patch grinned. 'I stood it for a bit, then I told them that while they were hell on wheels as organisers, otherwise they were a lot of old grannies. There was a slight argument.' Patch smiled faintly in reminiscence and Hannay suspected that, in spite of the disaster, he had managed to enjoy himself. 'I told them their mental stature was that of a set of dwarfs and that they'd have been better running a whelk stall than an art exhibition. I thought I might as well have a good time. I knew I was done for. I was suspect. I was tainted. I was anti-Christ. I was anti-bloody-everything smug and proper they stood for, in fact – and damn' glad to be,' he added with feeling. 'I was shown the door.'

'And you had to go home?'

'No.' Patch managed to look faintly embarrassed. 'I told you. I'd already got on the wrong side of the people who matter there. So I came here. They like painters in Italy – even stylised Beardsleys like me – and painters like them.'

'Are you a Communist now?' Hannay asked.

'My God, no! It was one of those things kids of nineteen and twenty do at university and art college. Like eyeing girls in tight sweaters. All I did was help at a meeting when I was too young to know any better. A week later I had a passage of arms with the candidate over the way he kept calling me "brother" and fetched him one with a pint pot.' He paused and glanced quickly at Hannay. 'Where's all this questionnaire leading?'

Hannay looked up, surprised at Patch's perception, for he *had* been leading up to something which had been worrying him a little. He studied Patch for a while over his plate, then he made one of those bewildering switches in conversation Patch had come to expect from time to time. He seemed to have forgotten Cristoforo completely.

'I 'ad an English bloke and his wife come to see me last night,' he said. 'Big chap. Talked like he had a plum in his mouth. His wife was a blonde. Snappy bit but going off. Name of Hayward. Said they knew you.'

Patch thought immediately of the note he had ignored and wondered if it had had any connection with this visit to Hannay.

'What did they want?' he asked.

Hannay shovelled a forkful of bacon into his mouth. 'They were a bit upset. They were doing a bit of poking about, if you understand my meaning. Sort of trying to get to know if I'd take them and a lot more like 'em to the mainland if the occasion arose. They was tearing it up a treat for a bit. Nearly had me crying.'

Patch's head came slowly up from the mug of tea he held. First Cristoforo, then Hannay, then Cecilia – now, it seemed, the whole of the British colony. What had been a small cloud on the horizon a few days before was growing now into a storm, dark and disturbing. He began to understand the meaning of Mrs Hayward's desperation.

'What occasion precisely were they thinking about?' he asked.

Hannay helped himself to more bacon and indicated the mountain with his fork.

'What did you tell 'em?'

'What *could* I tell 'em? That I wasn't going yet but that they was welcome as deck passengers when I did go. Only it made me think, see? First them. Now this here fisherman. Maybe he'd like to go too, if he had the chance. Only he hasn't – any more than Cristoforo has, or your pal with the bar has, or any of 'em, for that matter.'

Patch stared at the earnest little man in front of him, baffled by his unswerving interest in everybody else's business.

'You seem bloody keen to poke your nose in,' he said.

Hannay stared back at him, his bulging blue eyes as placid and undisturbed as a pair of glass marbles. 'You ever read anything by John Donne?' he asked unexpectedly, and Patch was as startled by the question as he was by the knowledge that Hannay had ever heard of John Donne.

'Yes,' he said. 'He was a bit like you. He liked to elect himself keeper of the public conscience.'

Hannay ignored the comment. 'I've got a book of 'is. Some queenie who once signed on as a deckhand left it behind when he jumped ship in Sydney. They brought it to me with his stuff. It's dead clever. Lots of things to make you think.'

'That was the idea.'

'There was one bit I've never stopped thinking about. I've read it. Lotsa times.' Hannay put his head back and began to quote as though he were reciting the *Rules of the Road for Mariners* – or running through a paragraph from a signalling manual or a *North Sea Pilot* – sonorously and in a completely unembarrassed manner which made Patch squirm. ' "*No man is an ilande,*" ' he said, ' "*intire of itself.*" It's old-fashioned, see. "*Every man is a piece of the Continent, a part of the maine; if a clod be washed away by the Sea, Europe is the lesser...*" then there's a bit more, and it finishes "*...any man's death diminishes me, because I am involved in mankind*".'

Patch found himself oddly moved, not by Hannay's quotation or by the fervour with which he recited it, so much as by the obvious way he believed in what he was saying. He found himself staring with a certain amount of awe at a humanitarian whose humanity was cloaked by a rough exterior and a set of tasteless catch phrases that dropped off his tongue every time he opened his mouth.

Hannay was opening his eyes now, his rocky face transformed by the light that seemed to glow behind it. 'That's the bit I like best,' he said. '*Involved in mankind*. If a bloke's nice to you, it becomes part of you, see? If he's dead rude, the same applies. In other words, if anyone's in trouble, you can't bloody well walk off and ignore 'em just because they're Eyetalians or whatever else they are.'

'You ought to be a lay preacher,' Patch said.

'I am,' Hannay replied blandly. 'When I'm home.'

Patch sat back and studied Hannay. He had obviously been listening to a lecture in which Hannay's intention to convince him that he ought to concern himself with the mountain's activity was only thinly disguised.

'What would you do then,' he asked, 'if the mountain went off pop? You're obviously a do-gooder and you obviously think I ought to do a bit of good myself. So we might as well know what *your* ideas are at least, before I start telling you there's nothing doing. What would you do?'

Hannay answered firmly and without a pause to consider, so that Patch felt faintly ashamed of his cynicism: 'I'd fill me ship,' he said, 'with anybody what wanted to come – Eyetalians, English or bloody old Chinese – till she was sinking under the load. And then, if there was one we'd left behind that we could take, I'd turn round and come back for him. That's what I'd do, Mister.'

*t e n*

---

Cecilia was waiting on the landing outside her door when Patch returned, curiously depressed by his meeting with Hannay down by the mole. It seemed that Anapoli had suddenly presented him with a problem that had to be faced, and with his easy-come-easy-go nature that enabled him to live in uproarious untidiness, so absorbed in painting that he forgot even to eat, he hated facing up to problems.

He smiled at her, glad to shove his troublesome thoughts to the back of his mind, then her voice took the smile off his face.

'Mrs Hayward's in your room,' she said.

'Oh, my God! I forgot all about her. What's worrying her? Is it the mountain?'

Cecilia smiled at his uneasiness. 'It can't be you. Her husband's with her,' she said, and Patch was visibly relieved. 'My grandfather's entertaining them.'

Patch laughed unashamedly. 'Come up and fetch your grandfather, Cecilia,' he said. 'Come and have a drink. For God's sake, come and stop her cornering me.'

'Mrs Hayward doesn't approve of me.'

'I don't give a good God-damn of her opinion. I don't think I ever did really.'

He grabbed her hand before she could protest any further and pulled her up the stairs after him.

The Haywards were sitting among the fantastic untidiness of Patch's rooms, trying not to notice the dirty glasses and the clothes he left lying around, and the damp stain under the window. By the wall, a couple of dachshunds they had brought with them sat licking themselves.

Old Leonardi was offering drinks and jabbering away in his own peculiar brand of English in an attempt to be friendly. With his loose false teeth, his white hair and sharp pointed face, he looked like a seedy Toscanini. His stiff white collar and clip-on bow tie and the black alpaca coat and spats he wore made him look as though he'd been too long on a shelf and taken off without being dusted.

Mrs Hayward's full lips were tight with irritation but she smiled as Patch entered. Then the gesture died immediately as she saw Cecilia behind him. She was obviously dressed to impress and Patch knew it wasn't for the florid, hearty man in the club tie who was trying to excuse himself from old Leonardi.

She nodded towards Cecilia who was producing clean glasses from a cupboard. 'You might have dispensed with some of the company, Tom,' she said softly. 'You know the Porto's not quite my cup of tea. I was expecting a quiet tête-à-tête!'

Patch smiled maliciously, rejecting her hints. He helped himself to a drink to give himself time to think, knowing he would have to answer cautiously or she'd have him back at that damn' club they ran, all pink gins and bridge and whirring fans and silent bartenders – as though Hayward and his cronies were trying their best to reproduce the India they'd all been glad to get away from – a place where they all grew nostalgic for 'home' and spent their time complaining about the decadent Socialists who had lost the Empire.

'You're asking too much,' he said. 'You ought to know the Porto's not the place for tête-à-têtes or even quiet.'

Mrs Hayward was sitting quietly, with poise and a self-assurance that hid the unhappiness and the desperation that lay under the surface. She was dressed in a pale blue frock that was clearly chosen to go with her eyes but which, with her blonde hair, only managed to look too youthful and wrong. She was staring across the room at Cecilia and Patch knew immediately she was jealous.

Her next words confirmed it.

'She's pretty,' she said. 'Do you sleep with her?'

'Oddly enough, no. It's something they taught me in the Boy Scouts, I think.'

She accepted the glass he offered her. 'When are you coming to see us again?' she asked. 'Don't you feel it would do you good to get away from this occasionally?'

'I'll get by. God will provide.'

She smiled, trying not to show her annoyance. 'Don't be difficult,' she said. 'You know what I mean.'

He grinned. 'Too right I do. That's why I haven't been.'

'Why didn't you acknowledge my note?' Mrs Hayward's face became sulky and full of annoyance at the realisation that he was neglecting her, annoyance mixed with disbelief. 'I left it with the caretaker.'

Patch began to move away hurriedly. 'Tornielli's a bastard with letters,' he said over his shoulder. 'He can't be bothered to climb the stairs. He flushes 'em down the lavatory.'

Mrs Hayward clearly realised he was lying but she said nothing and, as he crossed the room, Hayward joined him. His manner was a little nervous. He was a big shuffling man who was easily intimidated and Patch had always seemed to him more noisily Italian than English with his black hair and hawk's nose. Hayward had had a strong suspicion for a long time that something had been going on between Patch and his wife whenever he left the island, and he approached him now with an expression of diffidence on his podgy features. He hadn't wanted to come at all and had only been encouraged to do so by his wife's desire to see Patch again and the worry that was crowding in on him. The other worries that nagged him because he never had enough money and because his wife embarrassed him in front of his friends were small by comparison with this new one. Those were weekly worries, daily worries, hourly worries that he got used to, such as whether the rate of exchange would grow more favourable and the small pension he received from the British Government would buy him more than it did last year. His present worry was connected with Mont' Amarea, for Hayward was afraid of it suddenly.

Someone had been burning rubbish in a garden below his own when he had left and the acrid smell of smoke, killing the scents of the oaks and the pines and the firs that came off the slopes, had made him curiously nervous.

'Look, old boy,' he said abruptly in the flat, uncertain voice which had thickened with the effects of too many brandies in India when the monsoons had been too trying. 'Several of us have been a bit anxious for some time about the mountain – '

Leonardi tagged on to him quickly. 'It's dying,' he said at once. 'The experts say so.'

'You've got some information?' Hayward asked and Patch could see he was eager for reassurance. 'From an expert?'

'No.' Leonardi shook his head vigorously so that his ill-fitting false teeth seemed to rattle in his mouth. 'I have no dealing with *experts*.' He made the word sound like an insult. 'They are old-fashioned and mean-minded because I am now old and all I can do is arrange tours up the mountain for foreign schoolboys whose only wish is to throw stones into the crater to try to make it explode.'

He gave a gigantic shrug that seemed to rest his shoulders on his ears for a moment, then he twirled on his toes, pirouetting like a creaking ballet dancer, and pointed dramatically at Hayward.

'But when they say it is dying, they are, of course, right.' He jabbed his finger at Hayward who took a step backwards. 'We all get nearer to death as we grow older. But' – another jab – 'there can be quivers even from a dead body.'

'That last tremor made five in four weeks,' Mrs Hayward said – indignantly, as though she blamed it on inefficiency.

Leonardi turned, champing his teeth, and jabbed at her. 'There were *fifteen* in 1917. Fifteen in one year, increasing in speed and violence. I forecast disaster. The island is in a state of panic and rescue boats are evacuating. People beat their breast and pray to the Madonna. What happens?' He shrugged. 'Nothing. Nothing, Signor 'Ayward. It simply stops.'

'What do you think about it now then?' Hayward said. 'The mountain, I mean. All these queer happenings.'

'I have issue my warnings.' Leonardi stood on tiptoe and raised a thin finger to point at the ceiling, his jaws working, looking like some elderly oracle. 'I have issue my prophecies. I have tell them the island is in danger once more. Only' – the figure crumbled into a frail, foolish old man – 'only they tell me that I issue my warnings also in 1917 and 1931. In 1924 and 1943. And 1918 and 1919 and 1920 and 1921 and every year until this year when I issue them again. They tell me I am mad. I am only an old lunatic who has made a mistress out of a mountain.'

He cackled suddenly, a dry laugh, like the rustle of old leaves in a gutter. 'But, ask them yourselves,' he said gaily. 'Ask *them* to be certain. And even the experts will say the same as I do. No volcano is dead unless it does not erupt for ten thousand years. And even then it might surprise us.'

There was silence as he finished speaking. Hayward stared at his fingers for a moment, then he seemed to start back to reality. He waved his glass and addressed Patch.

'There's a considerable amount of uneasiness in the town all of a sudden,' he said.

'Where?' Patch asked. 'I've not seen any. Only a few crackpots like us. Everyone else's behaving normally – going to work, sleeping, eating, fornicating.'

'Well, perhaps not here, old boy. These people are Italianos. They've lived all their lives under the mountain. I meant among the English people. Lots of 'em are worrying. A lot of our crowd have been talking about it. We've been thinking someone ought to try to get some real advice. It's always possible that the mountain is entering an active phase again.'

He sipped his drink as he finished speaking and began to wish that his interests had been wide enough to include the Porto where all the frightening rumours he had heard had started. At least, there he might have got at the truth. Besides, looking at Patch, he suspected that he might have had a much more noisily enjoyable time in the Porto than he did at his wife's cocktail parties with the same old set and the occasional startling stranger like Patch she produced.

Mrs Hayward took up the conversation from where she sat on the arm of a settee, looking over her glass at Patch with a cat-like smoothness that infuriated Cecilia.

'I think someone ought to ask the authorities to make tests,' she said. 'It's silly for us to be sitting around wondering what the score is when they could find out so quickly.'

Patch jiggled his drink around in the bottom of his glass. 'Surely to God in this day and age there'd be plenty of warning,' he said. 'They've got gravimeters and God knows what on the mainland and in Sicily.'

'And none here,' Leonardi ended significantly. 'We are over a hundred miles from the mainland.'

Patch began to get angry. 'Oh, hell, what if it *does* erupt? People lived right under Vesuvius in 1944. They came to no harm. They just got out of the way of the lava.'

He was beginning to find this obsession with the mountain irritating. He was content enough to let it rumble and smoke if it wished so long as it didn't interrupt what he was doing. He had managed to paint through a series of riots over Algeria in Paris and he felt that no mountain could be more terrifying than a mob of angry Parisians. He was inclined to fling the lot of them through the door.

'If those people under Vesuvius could get out of the way of an eruption,' he said, 'so can we.'

'Perhaps we could. Perhaps we couldn't.'

Patch swung round as he heard old Leonardi cackling quietly behind him.

'Well, didn't they?' he demanded.

Leonardi chuckled and jigged from one foot to the other as he brought out a trump to kill Patch's ace. 'In Martinique in 1902,' he said, 'when Mont Pelée erupts, it wipes away thirty thousand people and a town in three or four seconds. It isn't lava which kills them. It is burning gases. It sweeps them into the sea in one second. Two seconds later they are all dead, boil-alive. If they had been evacuate they would have lived.'

Mrs Hayward's mouth went hard and Patch scowled. 'But listen – '

Leonardi held up his hand again and gave one or two ruminative clicks.

'Krakatoa, in the East Indies, shatters an island to pieces, also the people on it. Even our Lord Vesuvius destroys Pompeii in a few hours.' `

The room became silent again except for the clicking noise as the old man's jaws worked. In the background, Cecilia was standing quietly by the bottles and it suddenly occurred to Patch that he was the only person in the room who wasn't afraid of the mountain.

'Look,' he said. 'It seems damn' silly to come to me with your worries. I'm no expert. Why don't you just pack up and go and live on the mainland where it's safer?'

'I don't think you realise,' Hayward said stiffly – as though it hurt his pride to admit it. 'We're not wealthy. We can't afford to give up everything and leave. We came to live here in the first place because it was cheap and we could live as we'd been used to living.'

Mrs Hayward was turning to Patch again, and he knew from her manner she was trying to indicate to Cecilia the subtle intimacy that comes from shared thoughts, shared secrets, shared passions, an intimacy that Patch no longer returned.

'You know, Tom, of course,' she said, 'that nobody's doing a damn thing. They're only concerned with the election. They're not worrying about us – any of us.'

'Why *should* they worry about us?' Patch asked. 'Just at the moment they're busy trying to stop the Communists getting hold of the islands. And when you consider how many unemployed there are and what a rotten deal they get from the big shots like Forla, who supported Fascism once upon a time until the British and the Americans took him up after the war, they've got a bit of a job on. That's what makes elections so interesting here. One side wasn't acceptable yesterday. The other side isn't acceptable today. Let them sort that lot out and then they'll worry about the mountain.'

'If they don't get the damned election over soon, everyone will leave Italy and serve 'em right. People like our crowd, I mean.'

'I don't suppose the Italians give a damn about that.'

'Yes, but I mean – even the post has gone haywire. Haven't you noticed?'

'Nobody ever writes to me.'

Cecilia saw the look in Patch's eyes and took away his glass but he recaptured it a moment later.

'Look at that awful road up the hill,' Mrs Hayward went on. 'They started mending it and now they've just left it. We have an awful job getting the car out.'

'Use the bus.'

'It never runs on time.'

'Come and live in the Porto.'

Mrs Hayward looked at him quickly, knowing she was beginning to annoy him but unable to stop. 'I'm tired of their beastly slogans,' she said shrilly, the anxiety and the desperation beginning to show through her coolness. 'They think of nothing but their silly election.'

As she finished speaking, a motor-cycle roared down the narrow street outside, the echoes of its exhaust rattling up the crooked walls and slamming backwards and forwards from side to side. Everyone in the room was silent. Behind it, they heard a car moving along, its horn going to summon attention. Then, above the noise, the loudspeaker blared out. It was Pelli's car, on the way from the Piazza del Mare to address an open-air meeting in the upper town.

'We fight,' it announced, 'for the very soul of Italy. Remember Poland. Remember Hungary – '

'There they go,' Mrs Hayward said furiously and by now the façade had cracked and she was only a tired, angry, frustrated woman who was using this problem of the mountain and the election as a whipping boy for all her personal troubles. 'Worrying about Communists and Socialists and Democrats and Catholics and Fascists and not giving two hoots about us. We could all be blown into the sea for all they care.'

'That'll be fine,' Patch said with a grin. 'All going to Heaven at once. I always thought how dreary it must be on your own. Like a new boy.'

'Look' – Hayward seemed embarrassed and a little humble, too – 'you know a great many people here, old boy.' He was obviously choosing his words with care. 'Everybody knows you. You've got a lot of influence. More than you realise. We thought you might care to approach someone in authority here for us and get 'em to do something. I've tried but they say they're too busy with the election.'

'I shall be busy, too,' Patch said cheerfully, 'directing the American tourists to the best spot to take their photographs.'

'It's no time for joking, Tom,' Mrs Hayward snapped.

'I'm not joking,' Patch said. 'Personally, I couldn't care less what happens to the mountain. I'm sick of people complaining about it. It's a lovely mountain. If anything *does* happen, which I still doubt in spite of everything, I'll be there on the mole with the best of 'em, kicking and biting and scratching to get to the front. But for the moment, I'm going to go on enjoying myself. If you're worried, go and arrange with the captain of the *Great Watling Street*. He's got transport. I haven't. You ought to have a lot in common. He'll scare you silly with his talk of the mountain and you can scare him.'

Hayward glanced at Patch, defeated, then he touched his wife's arm. 'Maybe you're right, old boy,' he muttered unhappily. 'Perhaps we'd better go and see this chap again. We'll let you know what he says in case you want to take advantage of it yourself.'

He moved towards the door, collecting the dachshunds as he went.

Mrs Hayward halted in front of Patch, her face hard and angry. 'You've not been very helpful,' she said. 'You're getting soft. You should get out of the Porto once in a while. Visit people.'

He laughed. 'Come and see you, for instance?'

Hayward was waiting outside the door now, staring backwards from the dark corridor, holding the dachshunds, tubby, patient and ineffectual.

Mrs Hayward's eyes rested on Patch's face for a fraction of a second before the door closed.

'You could,' she said.

# eleven

During the night Patch woke up unexpectedly, bathed in perspiration and aware of a sound filling the room like the noisy escape of gas. Then he became conscious of people in the street below and the chatter of voices.

He got out of bed and dressed quickly. The courtyard was full of human beings and from the street by the front door Mamma Meucci's breathy shriek was very noticeable among the chattering, distinct even above the hissing sound that penetrated the confusion of alleys and courtyards and balconies where the tomato and basil plants occupied every inch of space among the washing.

Both the Meuccis were there, arguing with Tornielli and each other and shouting up to the old lady across the street who was a cripple and unable to descend the stairs.

Mamma Meucci broke off as she saw Patch and rushed across to him.

'Signor Tom,' she shrieked. 'The end has come. The Holy Souls in Purgatory protect us! The mountain's about to erupt!'

Then he realised that it was from the darkness high up behind the town that he could hear the hissing. It came from the direction of the crater and was back-grounded by a dry clacking sound.

Its very unusualness was frightening, its very unexpectedness enough to set the hair at the back of his neck standing on end. But even through the apprehension that started in him as he remembered the grisly pictures Dr Leonardi had drawn, he realised that in spite of the noise there was no other apparent sign of danger.

He gave Mamma Meucci a cigarette as she clung to his arm, and lit it for her. She drew on it greedily, her eyes wild. 'Holy Mother of Mercy, we've not heard it like this since 1931,' she said, blowing out smoke and waving her hands at him. 'Signor Tom, we are all awakened by the noise. Little Stefano starts to cry. Then he wakes up Giuliano and soon we are all awake. Signor Tom, what should we do?'

Patch stared up into the darkness beyond the houses, surprised that Hannay and Cecilia and Cristoforo and all the others had been right. There seemed no longer any question about the mountain being dead. It obviously wasn't. But he could still see nothing to indicate danger and the noise was already growing less.

He patted Mamma Meucci's arm. 'If I were you,' he said, 'I'd go back to bed.'

'There you are, Mamma.' Meucci appeared from the crowd as Patch finished speaking, and smacked his wife's fat behind. 'You hear what he says. We are still here. It's only a lot of noise. Nothing more.' He gave her a shove. 'Get back to bed. Signor Tom says go back to bed. I say go back to bed. *Now* are you satisfied?'

His wife turned swiftly on him. 'Are *you* satisfied, Meucci?'

Meucci's gaiety dispersed abruptly and as he glanced at Patch there was that same look in his eyes that expressed the doubt and bewilderment that Patch had seen by the harbour the previous day. Then he smiled quickly and pushed his wife again.

'Quite satisfied, Mamma. Now let's go back to bed or the children will be shouting.'

Now that they were all awake, though, nobody seemed to want to go to bed. Through the excitement engendered by the violent hissing – as though a gigantic jet of steam were being released – it was obvious that they preferred to cling to each other's company. Even argument was reassuring in the unexpected racket the mountain was setting up. Bottles of wine appeared, and coffee, and even plates of pasta, and what had been a startled rush for the communal comfort of the street ended up as a slightly hysterical party.

Patch stayed for a while, then he grew tired of the crowd and set off back to his room. On the way, he caught up with old Leonardi labouring up the stairs. The old man seemed delighted by the turn of events.

'In the full moon it'll come,' he said excitedly. 'You see. With the full moon. For thirty years I've been wrong but one day the laughter will turn to tears when I'm proved right.'

He trudged on up the stone steps, heaving his creaking legs up one after the other, conscious of the drag of his old body. There had been a time when he had skipped up the stairs to his apartment as he had skipped up Amarea to make the investigations for the charges that had always proved wrong, so wrong, in fact, so regularly wrong that it had become an obsession with him that he must be right.

'Come and have a coffee,' he said to Patch, 'and I'll show you the photographs I take when I climb Stromboli in 1935.'

In the shabby apartment, Patch brooded over the self-portraits of old Leonardi in mountaineering clothes posturing on folds of cold lava, then as Cecilia brought in the coffee, they noticed the hissing from the mountain had ceased and only the high-pitched clacking sound remained.

'Amarea's quiet again,' Cecilia said.

'It's not quiet inside,' old Leonardi said gaily, clicking his teeth and waving both hands to indicate effervescence. 'That's why we hear banging still. That's why we have the staccatos. They tell me you could see the glasses jiggling on the tables in the Galleria Umberto in Naples before Vesuvius erupts in 1944. Even Pompeii is shaken to its foundations just before it is destroyed. This place is part of the Campi

Flegri – the Flaming Fields of the Romans. There have been rumblings here since before Christ.'

Patch yawned suddenly with tiredness and old Leonardi, seeing him, felt tired himself. But for a different reason. Thirty years, he thought. Thirty years of interest in the mountain behind the town that had lost him all his money, involved him in lawsuits and dwindled his business to nothing, thirty years when he had ceased to be a prophet and become only an old crackpot of whom nobody took any notice any longer. He clicked his teeth ruminatively. No wonder Patch was yawning. They'd heard it all before. He'd been nearly right so many times, he thought the mountain played its tricks deliberately.

He put away the photographs and pottered off, clicking away, and as the door slammed, Patch and Cecilia sat over the coffee, saying nothing. The clacking noise had almost subsided now and it was quiet again outside except for the sound of people in the street. They could hear the chattering and even singing and the high shriek of Mamma Meucci, now turning to laughter. Then they heard the harsh voice of Bruno Bosco, the Communist candidate, who lived just down the hill. 'Even the mountain's protesting against Pelli,' he said, and there was a burst of laughter.

Patch looked at Cecilia, remembering how when he had first arrived on Anapoli, the crater of Amarea had been a favourite picnic spot, and tourists had been in the habit of visiting it to see the thin jet of steam which escaped through a fissure in the rock. He had been taken there himself by Cecilia in the first weeks he had known her and had been entranced by the view and the loneliness and the colour – and Cecilia. She had been happy then, young and untouched by anger. This morose hostility towards him was something that had grown inexplicably in her over the last year.

Then he remembered he had taken Mrs Hayward too trying to capture some of the first magic, and had failed, and the trip had seemed only a dreary adventure, with Mrs Hayward complaining all the way back about the distance and the heat of the sun.

'There'll be no more Easter-Day picnics in the crater for a while, Cecilia,' he said. 'Especially if there's any dirt.'

'There'll be dirt,' she said. 'And eventually probably a lot more than dirt.'

He stared at his coffee-cup. 'Cecilia,' he said after a while. 'Why do you believe there's danger? Why now? Why this time? It's happened before. Even this noise has happened before. Why didn't you expect danger last time?'

'Why? Why?' Her eyes flashed angrily. 'Why? Always why? You're constantly falling over that word. It's like a weight round your neck. Why should I do anything? Why must I worry? Why can't someone else? And now, "Why are you afraid, Cecilia, when you weren't a week ago?" I don't know why I'm afraid now. I only know. I only know there should be an observatory on Amarea but there's never been enough money to build one. I only know that in Italy there is never enough land to spare so that people have to huddle round volcanoes.' She stood up, hugging her elbows. 'If only there were someone with enough initiative to do something about it!' She turned on him tempestuously 'It only needs someone to ask to set everything in motion. It only requires one person to go and put the idea into the Mayor's head. Just one. I've already asked Piero. He won't do anything.'

'Poor Piero,' Patch said. It must have been baffling to the stiff, humourless boy, brought up as he was to expect respect from a future wife, to find himself saddled with a mutinous girl trying to break out from centuries of convention, a rebellious personality who was not prepared to accept courtship as he understood it, with admiration for male virtues, to be followed by marriage with dutiful obedience.

'Poor Piero,' he repeated, with a certain amount of sympathy.

She turned on him. 'Poor Piero!' she said. 'Sometimes he makes me afraid. I can see the whole of my life being walled up in Piero. He said that politics were not a woman's concern. How long has Amarea been politics?'

'I don't know,' Patch said. 'But it could be that it is now.'

She began to pace up and down the room. 'If only I were a man,' she said. 'If I were, I'd ask Pelli myself. Or Bosco. I wouldn't care.'

Patch sighed, feeling old. In her youthful indignation, in her indifference to derision and her desperate seriousness, there was a rare vitality that seemed lacking in everyone else, and he was a little saddened by the thought that the same rebellion had died away in himself.

'Cecilia' – he leaned over and put down his cup – 'does it occur to you that perhaps Pelli doesn't want to know about the mountain? Perhaps Bosco doesn't. It could make a difference to the voting if anything were said by them, if anything were done. In view of the nearness of the election, they probably feel they might be wiser to wait.'

'Nobody would be that dishonest.'

Patch shrugged. 'Let's not call it dishonesty,' he said tolerantly. 'They're business men. Their business is politics. They've got to take a risk sometimes and they probably think they can afford to take one now.'

'Not with other people involved.'

Patch sighed, thinking how when he had been Cecilia's age issues had seemed for him too a little too clear cut. Black must have been too black for him also, and white too shining bright. As he had grown older, he had begun to see there were greys.

'Pelli's not dishonest,' he said. 'He's just being cautious.'

Cecilia gestured irritatedly, impatiently. 'I still feel someone should demand some action,' she insisted.

'Cecilia,' he said, chiding her affectionately. 'Give 'em a chance. There's only a week or two to voting day. I suppose they feel they've a right to get that over first. Surely, if the mountain's done nothing of note since 1762, they needn't worry for another two weeks.'

Cecilia turned fiercely towards him, a small angry figure, resentment flaring up inside her, sick with disappointment that she could persuade no one to do anything in this matter that so concerned her. The disgust for everyone's indifference was an indigestible lump in her throat.

For a second as she stared at him, the room was in silence and Patch realised that practically all sound had already ceased from the mountain. The night outside was still and only the people now talking in the street disturbed it.

'Have you read my grandfather's books?' Cecilia said, gesturing angrily towards the old man's study. 'All those books he has in there, about volcanoes and earthquakes?'

'No.'

Cecilia's eyes were bright under the heavy brush-strokes of her brows, 'I have,' she said. 'They're full of dead people who gambled on another two weeks.'

## *twelve*

Although the noise from the mountain had stopped when Patch woke the following morning, the commotion in the street seemed to have been going on all night. Nobody had wanted to go to bed and Patch had clung to sleep as though he were balancing on the edge of a precipice.

As he reluctantly let it slide away from him, he realised he could still hear Mamma Meucci's shriek, though the singing had stopped and there seemed to be a louder note of alarm now in the babble below. Then he heard Alfredo Meucci's voice and he wondered why he wasn't off Capo Amarea attending to his lobster pots.

He was still in a half doze when Mamma Meucci pushed her way in with his coffee. Her face was ashen and slack and her cheeks shook as though she had malaria.

'Signor Tom,' she said as she put down the tray. 'The Holy Souls in Purgatory have pity on us. It is the beginning of the end. There's been a fall of ash on the slopes. If there'd been a wind, it would have been all over the town.'

Patch was sitting up in bed now. The atmosphere in the room seemed stuffy and made breathing difficult, and he was still half-asleep. He peered round him, trying to fight off the drowsiness, and gradually he became aware that the place was full of the dusky twilight that comes before sun-up, and he woke up abruptly.

'God, Mamma,' he said indignantly. 'It's still dark! What time is it?'

Mamma Meucci stood in the centre of the room, her hands to her face, her fingers outspread and pressing the flesh of her cheeks into rolls. 'The Lord have mercy on us, Signor Tom,' she said. 'It isn't darkness. It's the mountain. It's smoke over the sun. It's dirt.'

Patch stared at her, then he jumped quickly out of bed and crossed to the window. Over the crater of Amarea there was a flat layer of grey cloud, clinging in the still air to the mountain top. Through its fringe, the sun gleamed in a dull yellow ball that was too weak to throw a shadow. The whole town seemed to be oppressed to an unnatural greyness.

'That's what the mountain threw out,' Mamma Meucci mourned. 'Meucci says an old man in San Giorgio was suffocated last night. He'd got ash dust in his mouth when they found him.'

When Mamma Meucci had gone, Patch dressed slowly and walked thoughtfully down the stairs to the street.

At the point where the Via Garibaldi debouched from between the crooked houses into the Piazza Martiri, a crowd had gathered, strung out in chattering groups towards the statue of Garibaldi. There was another large group of people outside Emiliano's, standing among the orange trees and flowing under the arches of the Museo and into the barber's shop where a man with a wet towel round his head was holding forth noisily to the other customers. Old Leonardi was prominent among the arguing, clicking and pointing with that odd pirouette of his like an aged ballet dancer as he gleefully prophesied disaster.

Around them the children who normally played in the piazza stood in a silent bunch, scared by the serious faces of the men, their angry voices and fierce gestures. Patch could see Cristoforo there, waiting a little to one side with his dog as he always did, big-eyed, tousle-haired and motionless, as he had often seen him on the mountain, as though he were listening for hidden sounds that were beyond the power of anyone else to catch. Over the group that was posed in a half-circle – as though set for a Rubens portrait, Patch thought – were the flat-fronted houses and beyond them the grey-blue cone of Amarea, silent now but brooding, a menacing, heavy-shouldered shape backgrounding the town.

Emiliano called from the crowd as he appeared, and pushed forward a young man with a taut, scared face, in a shabby black suit and a shirt without a collar, the dull brass of his stud showing at his throat. The big, dark eyes in his swarthy features showed the flat despair of a peasant faced with disaster. There was no resentment, merely acceptance, for disaster had been part of his heritage for generations, but there was something in his hopelessness that stirred Patch into wanting to help.

'This is Marco Givanno,' Emiliano explained importantly with a two-fingered gesture at the young man. 'His father died last night in San Giorgio. You will have heard, I expect.'

Patch nodded, with a feeling of being caught up in some strange sort of nightmare. It seemed odd to be face to face with someone who had been suffering from the sly violence of the mountain at the very time when down in the Porto they had all been inclined to regard the noise more in the nature of a joke than anything else. It had a sobering effect on him, far more than the sight of that grey cloud of dust over the crater where the sun glowed through, peering like a short-sighted orange eye.

'I think my father was dead when we found him,' the young man was saying to Patch. 'He'd been sleeping outside because of the heat. My brother Giuseppe and I brought him straight down here.' He gestured at a ramshackle little green vehicle with sacking curtains by the kerb, and a bunch of gaunt men in overalls, and went on with a desperate appeal in his voice.

'If you've any influence at all, signore,' he said, 'I beg you, in the name of the Lord Jesus who suffered on the Cross, to get to know what we are to do. In San Giorgio we have this dust falling all the time these days.'

The cloud of dust over the sun had cleared when Patch returned to the square later in the morning.

The crowd was still there but the Givannos had gone to arrange about the inquest on their father, and the core of the crowd was round Hannay who was haranguing an agitated Emiliano in an angry, frustrated way. He wore his uniform jacket with the four tarnished rings of his rank, grey flannel trousers and a grey felt hat. His face was scarlet with arguing and his eyes were blazing with excitement. He seemed to be trying to form some sort of committee to see the authorities.

'Aren't *you* afraid of that damned mountain?' he was asking Emiliano as Patch approached.

Emiliano was staring back at him, his eyes large and troubled. 'Signor Capitano, I've *always* been afraid of the mountain.' He gestured with a fistful of whirling fingers under Hannay's nose. 'I've lived here all my life and I've not yet got used to seeing the steam that comes from it.'

'They say it's smoke now,' Hannay snapped.

'Smoke then, signore. It's all the same.' Emiliano shrugged and let his hands drop heavily to his sides. 'I'm as worried as you are. I think all the time of my bar. I build it with my own hands. I rebuild it after a landslide knocked down the rear wall and I rebuild it again after the war when a bomb blows in the front. Last night I listen to Amarea and I pray' – his ready hands assumed the attitude of prayer – 'I pray that I am not going to have to rebuild it again. If I could, I'd leave the island now.'

'Well, why don't you?'

'I can't afford to. Fortunately, I'm reassured by the knowledge that if anything *does* happen I am near enough to the mole to be among the first to get on a ship.'

Hannay leaned forward. 'Look, I want to go and see Pelli. I want someone to come with me. Why won't you?'

'Signor Capitano, it might make trouble.'

'Trouble?' Hannay snorted. 'What sort of trouble?'

Emiliano flapped his hands and tried to explain. 'Suppose it gets to the sulphur workers that people are complaining down here. You know what they're like. They'd start complaining, too. And then work would stop. I don't want to be the cause of that. Trouble in the Porto always starts trouble among Forla's people. And Forla owns this land. Forla owns this property. Forla owns my bar. On Anapoli there aren't enough of us and there's too much of Forla.'

'What about all the other shopkeepers?' Hannay demanded loudly. 'Surely there's a traders' association?'

Again there was that nervous fluttering of Emiliano's hands. 'Of course there is, Signor Capitano. And who do you think is the biggest trader on Anapoli?' The whirling hands grew nearer. 'Forla belongs to the small traders' associations because he owns small businesses. He belongs to the big business associations because he owns big businesses. Forla's reached out and touched everything.'

'But surely – '

Emiliano's hands came up again and Hannay grabbed them angrily in his own and held them down.

Emiliano sighed and submitted with a heavy despair.

'Do you think, Signor Capitano,' he said slowly, releasing himself, 'that the shopkeepers want everyone to *expect* danger on Anapoli? The mountain hasn't erupted yet and if we tell everyone it's going to, what would happen to all the money that comes here in the shape of tourists? The season's not far away and we need the season. This is not Capri. This is a *poor* island. Pelli says it's safe. He told you it was. I've got to believe *somebody*.'

He tapped his forehead significantly and gestured again with his bunched fingers. 'We don't believe in danger,' he concluded, 'because we don't *want* to believe. We're masters at putting off until tomorrow the worries that trouble us today. Let's leave it at that.'

It was as he turned away in disgust from Emiliano that Hannay became aware of Patch standing alongside them.

'Hah!' He pounced immediately. 'There you are. Where've you been? I've been looking all over for you. What about it now, eh?'

Patch lit a cigarette, unmoved by his excitement. 'What about what?' he said. 'I can see your soul's stirred to cataclysmic proportions and you're about to blow a gasket.'

'I suppose you were sleeping like an 'og in your bed,' Hannay snorted. 'The bloody mountain blew off a fine old fart in the night.'

'I know. I heard it.'

Hannay seemed surprised that Patch had been so alert. 'It was dead grim,' he said. 'It was fizzing wicked. 'Annay was listening.'

'As it happens, so was Patch.'

'Well' – Hannay was stirred to the point of hoarseness – 'are you still going to be 'og-tied by your bloody brains and intellect and still not do anything? You said you'd try if the English people asked you. Well, they asked you. Last night. I know, because they came to see me afterwards. And I'm asking you now. I want to know what's on and so does everybody else. But nobody'll do anything. They're all scared. "Tomorrow. Tomorrow." That's all they say. Well, tomorrow's no good for me. I'm going to see Pelli now.'

'I don't think it would do much good,' Patch said quietly.

'Why not?' Hannay was bursting at the seams with eagerness, his whole body quivering with the desire to get on with something. 'Go on, tell me. Why not?'

Patch shrugged. 'Because,' he said, 'I've just been to see him myself.'

*thirteen*

---

As Patch spoke, the crowd turned to face him. The word of what had happened seemed to fly round immediately. Mamma Meucci, who had been engaged in an argument with a fruit vendor, immediately broke it off and drew nearer. The group of men in the barber's shop came out with the barber and the little man who sold coral rings in the dark room next door.

Then old Leonardi, who had remained behind to clear up some point which had held his attention, came flying out in a sort of hop-skip-and-jump movement, all flying arms and bony legs, and sailed straight into Patch without any preamble.

'What did he say?' he asked eagerly. 'They've appointed me to watch the mountain? They realise it's dangerous? They agree to provide a gravimeter?'

Patch took a deep breath, conscious of all their eyes on him.

'He says there's no danger,' he said heavily, and at once a sigh seemed to rustle round the circle of people about him.

'No danger!' Old Leonardi rose on his tiptoes and pointed dramatically at the sky, clicking indignantly. 'No danger. But I've seen danger for weeks. For years. And now it's come.'

Emiliano moved back to his bar, but he was shaking his head, and old Leonardi chased after him, an agitated scarecrow figure, to persuade him to protest. The crowd began to split up into arguing groups and it occurred immediately to Patch that no one was very satisfied.

Hannay let them go before he spoke. He had been standing silently in front of Patch, his eyes narrowed, the redness of his face fading.

'You've been to see him?' he said eventually. 'Already?'

Patch nodded.

'Why didn't you tell me? I'd have come too.'

Patch shrugged. 'Would it have helped much?'

Hannay scowled and ignored the question. 'What did he say? I mean, why did he say there was no danger?'

Patch thought about it for a moment. He had entered Pelli's office unwillingly, feeling he had been caught up in something he had no wish for. The anger generated in him by the despair of the Givannos had already been dying and he had begun to feel foolish, wondering how to say what he had to say without appearing neurotic and nervous. Pelli had been so engrossed with the election the anxiety of the Givannos had seemed mere hysteria brought on by grief.

'He was amused and very tolerant,' he said.

'Tolerant!' Hannay exploded.

'He was very sorry about the dust-fall,' Patch went on. 'Chiefly, I think, because it makes people leave the island and reduces the number of his voters. Then he went on to blame the old man's death on the shortage of houses.'

'Shortage of houses!' Hannay seemed unable to do anything but repeat the more outrageous points from Patch's description of the interview after him. 'What's he think this is? An election stunt?'

Patch smiled. 'He might at that,' he said. 'He's pretty cute. He didn't give much away. He read me a lot of statistics on disease and ill-health. I think he was trying to blind me with science. That rabbit Tornielli was there, disliking me even through the back of his neck while he sorted out facts for his lord and master.'

'Go on.' Hannay hurried him over the personal details.

'He told me I represented only a handful of people – which is right enough – and that thousands on the island were still going to work in the normal way, which again is right enough. He also told me some story I didn't quite catch about the Communists starting a similar scare in Calabria by blaming the flooding at Vicinamontana on the authorities, and ended up by pointing out that everything I had in my mind was merely supposition.' Patch shrugged. 'And again, he was right. Dead right. It is.'

'Didn't you tell him everybody thought it was important?'

'Certainly. But he didn't think it was as important as winning the election. He even explained how they hoped to do it, and scaring voters to the mainland wasn't one of the ways.'

Hannay followed Patch across the square in silence and sat down with him as he lowered himself into one of the bright little chairs outside Emiliano's. He seemed staggered by Patch's news.

He had never really expected Pelli to do much, but to discover that he intended to do nothing at all seemed to have cut the ground from under his feet.

Then his crusading spirit revived abruptly and he sat up, prepared to dispute until nightfall if necessary Pelli's decision.

'How's he know the mountain's not dangerous?' he demanded. 'Has he got God-given information? Does he have the ear of the Almighty or something? He's no special pal of God's.'

'Come to that, neither are we,' Patch said urbanely. 'He said he got his information from Forla's observatory.'

'You told me it was a garridge.'

'Of course it is. It was an excuse. He wanted to get rid of me. God's truth, man, if anyone should know the mountain, the islanders should.'

'They do.' Hannay indicated the chattering groups in the square. 'Ask Meucci. Ask Cristoforo. Ask this lot. Look at 'em. You'd hardly say they was curling up of laughing, would you?'

He had lit his pipe and was puffing smoke rings furiously. 'How about the Communists?' he asked suddenly. 'Will they help? I'll go to anybody who does things instead of sitting on his fat little embongpong.'

Patch grinned, beginning to enjoy his discomfiture. 'You're too late again,' he said. 'I've been there, too.'

Hannay seemed to bounce upright in his chair. 'You've what?'

'I went there while I was still mad at Pelli. Bolshies don't go in for love and kisses. They prefer a boot up the backside to a bouquet of violets and I was in just the right frame of mind.'

Hannay had taken the pipe from between his teeth and was sitting with his mouth open now. Once more he seemed staggered by Patch's initiative – and vaguely cheated, as though he had missed all the excitement.

'What did they say?' he asked at length.

Patch grinned. 'The same. Bosco's no fool. A fool wouldn't have organised the resistance group here that he did during the war. The Germans had a torpedo-boat base on the island, but Bosco had 'em licked even before the Americans landed. Bosco knows how many beans make five. That's why he dresses like a street-corner boy and shares his cigarettes. He knows it's good for business.'

'What was *his* excuse?'

'He didn't offer any. Commissars don't. I think he'd like to blame it all on Pelli or the priests.'

'Did he offer to do anything?'

Patch shook his head. 'He's not getting mixed up in anything he can't wriggle out of. He prefers to watch Pelli fall by his own inertia, instead of pushing. He gave me a lecture on the appeal they're making to the middle classes – together with a short jeremiad on Forla. You'd be surprised how much I've learned about politics this morning.'

'Is that all he did?'

'Not quite. He said he'd produce a poster. A nice Pelli-baiting poster – enlarging on the danger and on Pelli's refusing to do anything about it in case it lost him votes. He knows damn' well Pelli intends to do nothing – from the very fact that I'd gone to see *him*.'

Hannay seemed to resent Patch being able to see a funny side to his own frustration. 'Fat lot of good a poster'll do anybody,' he growled. 'It'll only scare people away.'

Patch held up one finger. 'Not Bosco's voters,' he said 'For the most part, they *can't* leave the island even if they want to. They can't afford to. He doesn't give a damn about his own supporters reading it. It's Pelli's voters he's hoping to attract. They *can* afford to go. If it scares anybody away, it'll be Pelli's supporters. Bosco can't lose.'

Hannay snorted. 'It's a dirtier game than Pelli's playing.'

Patch nodded. 'Pelli will be after my guts for this.'

Hannay seemed stunned with disappointment. 'Is that the best you could do?' he asked.

Patch sat up angrily. 'The best I could do?' he said. 'It might interest you further to know that I telephoned the newspaper on the mainland. But they're not interested, either.'

'Why not?'

'Because they're busy with the election, too. They've got their own axe to grind like everybody else. Besides, old Leonardi's already rung them up. Three times. They're sick of Anapoli and its bloody volcano. They even told their correspondent here to drop it. It's old news. It's as dead to them as Queen Anne until it goes off pop.'

Hannay seemed repentant but not abashed. 'I thought we might have done more,' he said.

Patch slouched down in his chair and made himself comfortable. 'I once swore I wouldn't play with political parties again as long as I lived,' he said. 'Now I've done it. And you can bet Bosco will make fine political capital out of it, too,'

Hannay was staring at the bulk of Amarea, his expression thwarted.

'OK,' he said heavily. 'I'm sorry. Only – well, an old man's been suffocated.'

'Maybe he's the last.'

'Aye' – Hannay was still unsatisfied – 'and maybe he's only the first.'

## fourteen

With Patch's visit to Pelli and Bosco, all attempts to do anything about Amarea seemed to come to a stop. Even the mountain itself ceased to encourage any untoward anxiety. The small plume of vapour continued towards the east but there were no other manifestations of its activity in the area of the Porto and there was no further word from the Haywards, so that it seemed they had let the matter drop too.

Only Hannay seemed prepared to go on worrying but, as obviously nothing was going to be done, he contented himself with making life as difficult over the delayed load of sulphur as he could for Orlesi who, with his connections with Forla and therefore with the power that held the islanders in thrall, was a natural enemy to Hannay.

It seemed, from his protestations at the delayed loading, that he was anxious to be off, but Patch still suspected that had he been presented with his sulphur and told to take his ship away immediately he would have been disappointed to the point of despair. Every time he dragged Patch round to Emiliano's for a drink or a coffee, he seemed to be dwelling on a bed of thorns, edgy and waiting for the next event that might prove him right.

When it came, it came not from the Porto but from Fumarola on the north side of the island, and on land belonging to a farmer by the name of Amadeo Baldicera.

Fumarola was an untidy little village built on the slopes where the mountain fell abruptly into the sea, a collection of crowded houses with a piazza projecting like a pier into the water. It was strung along the black ribbon of the main road that circled the island, in the North the thoroughfare for donkeys more often than cars; and Amadeo Baldicera's farm lay just above the village, a prosperous little holding that managed to provide employment for two men besides Baldicera and his family. The afternoon was oppressively hot. There seemed to be no air anywhere and the place never seemed to have awakened from its noontide doze. The courtyards were oases of quiet as everyone lingered longer than normally over their mid-day meals, so that it was a matter of pride to Baldicera that he was about, trudging through the shimmering heat in the direction of the little dam he had built on the sides of Amarea.

His mind was busy with the problems of his farm and it was not until he was on top of them that he became aware of the pathetic feathered shapes lying in the stunted grass of his field, some of them still feebly moving, beating their wings weakly against the ground in an effort to rise.

He stopped dead and stared down at the starlings, his eyes scared. There had been other occasions recently when he had found a dead bird in his fields. He had even seen one drop out of the sky, struggling to control wings that no longer seemed to function, so that it had hit the ground in a steep glide and a flat bounce that broke bones. At first he had not worried but as other small corpses had appeared he had begun to be anxious, and to find two – more, three–dozen of them lying on the ground, their wing feathers splayed, filled him with alarm.

For a while longer, he stared at the birds, glancing around him uneasily, then he turned on his heel and walked quickly back towards his home. There, he explained what had happened to his wife and, putting on a jacket, he set off on his bicycle into the village for the home of Don Dominico, the village priest.

Don Dominico was a withered old man with a face like a wrinkled walnut and the calm dark eyes of the plaster saints in his own shabby church. He listened silently to what Baldicera had to tell him, then he reached for the black shovel hat he wore. Closing the door on his untidy home and taking out his own rusty bicycle, he slogged back with Baldicera to the farm, the skirts of his soutane tucked up around him.

Parking the bicycle, he walked across the fields with Baldicera and his wife and son and they stood together, all four of them, in a row, and stared down at the lifeless bodies of the birds.

'This is the second time,' Baldicera said heavily. 'And often I've found an odd one.'

Don Dominico wasn't listening. He was staring up at the ash-grey slopes of Amarea and the plume of smoke that hung on the crater, his eyes narrowed against the sun and his own unhappy thoughts.

'What do you make of it, Father?' Baldicera said, and his next words indicated what *he* was thinking. 'You know, of course, that the hot springs in the village have become hotter, don't you?'

'I do,' Don Dominico said quietly, thinking of the sweating messenger. who had arrived on his doorstep to put an end to his afternoon doze the previous day.

'The last time was in 1762,' Baldicera's son said. 'And you know what happened then.'

'I know all that, my son.'

'That's not all, Father – '

Don Dominico lifted a thin hand on which the veins had begun to stand out, knotted and ugly, as the flesh had dropped away with age. 'I know it's not all, Amadeo,' he said. 'I've ears and eyes myself.'

Baldicera scratched his head unhappily. 'Father, my cattle have been restless at night. The horses in the stables – '

Don Dominico's hand went up again – as though he were giving a blessing.

'Amadeo, my own dogs have not slept easily.'

Baldicera stared at him, and the priest was aware of the eyes of the woman and the boy also fixed on him, and he felt his responsibility lay heavily on his thin shoulders.

'What is it, Father? What's happening?'

'I don't know, Amadeo.'

'There must be some explanation. What should we do?'

Don Dominico felt very tired and conscious of the size and number of his flock. There were times – and this was one of them – when he would gladly have exchanged the service of the Lord for a pension and the chance to rest his old bones.

'What should we do?' Don Dominico, glanced at Amarea as he repeated the question. 'First of all, I think it's time other people knew of these events. We must let someone know.'

It was Emiliano who introduced Don Dominico to Patch and Hannay. He had listened at his bar in his lugubrious way to the old man's shy and rather hesitant account of what had happened in Fumarola, nodding vigorously and wringing his hands at the appropriate moments. There was a public meeting going on in the next square and it was hard to hear over the racket, but Emiliano paid careful attention, then, as the old man finished, beckoned to him to follow.

The piazza was full of strangers and neither Patch nor Hannay, sitting outside in the shadow of the Garibaldi statue, looked up as Don Dominico appeared beside them. Then they realised Emiliano was there, too, and even Patch was stirred by the faint scent of trouble. As he swung round Emiliano cleared his throat to catch their attention.

'There is somebody here, Signor Tom, whom you might like to meet,' he said, flapping a hand at Don Dominico and pushing a chair forward. 'I told him about you seeing the Mayor.'

Don Dominico sat down, sweeping his dusty skirts away from the big black boots he wore. Hannay pushed a glass towards him and Don Dominico accepted the drink gratefully. For years his feet had never strayed far from the path between his home and the village church and outside Fumarola he felt lost. He was tired, too, now, and thirsty, and a little depressed. He watched the faces around him for a change of expression, then he went on to explain what he had seen on Amadeo Baldicera's farm, and the other things that had caused so much uneasy speculation at the other side of the island. Hannay sat on the edge of his chair, looking rather like a terrier waiting for a biscuit as he listened. Patch leaned back, fanning himself with a newspaper. Emiliano's busy hands were occupied with lighting a cigarette, but his eyes were fixed on the priest's.

'It's been suggested,' Don Dominico went on, 'that somewhere on the slopes – perhaps near Amadeo Baldicera's field – there may be a new fumarole we don't know about which is leaking gas and that the birds which pass close to it are being affected. If there is such a fissure and the mountain *does* start to be active, it could be that it will open wider, for the lava rises to the cracks in the earth's surface. And if it did – ' He stopped and smiled apologetically.

Emiliano flapped the match he'd been using until the flame was extinguished – vigorously – as though he needed something to do. Hannay leaned forward. Patch sat up at last, and Don Dominico stared at the ruby glow in his glass, a wash of defeat in his faded eyes. Then he looked up.

'They said at the Town Hall there was nothing to be afraid of,' he continued. 'But I am not so sure. I wondered if you would perhaps like to see Don Alessandro, at the Church of Sant' Agata. He's a man of great ambition. His brother's a bishop and he'd like to be a bishop, too.'

Hannay's interest was caught immediately. 'Go on, Father,' he said.

'He's young and enthusiastic,' Don Dominico went on. 'He has energy and influence. He has the ear of Monsignor and even beyond. For such a small place as Anapoli, Don Alessandro's an important man.'

Patch leaned forward. 'Father,' he said. 'Why don't you see Don Alessandro?'

Don Dominico smiled again. 'I'm an old man,' he explained. 'And perhaps not a very efficient one. Don Alessandro and I have had a great many differences of opinion. He's a great driving force and I am getting tired and stubborn. It's like having a greyhound harnessed to a goat. He has a great deal of influence but not much patience. We are all a little afraid of him, and if I saw him I might be at a disadvantage from the start. We've had too many disagreements in the past. On the other hand' – he looked up with a child-like smile – 'you, if you were to approach him as you did the Mayor on behalf of the foreign residents of the island, might succeed where I would fail. At the very least, you might learn a great deal. Then what you knew, *we* should know, too.'

# fifteen

Don Alessandro was not in the church when they arrived, but there were several women sweeping the entrance where the dust had sifted in through the great door during the past two days, unnoticeable in its fineness, obscuring the colours of the mosaics and the gilt on every angle and curve. The women were talking quietly as they worked, heedless of the girl kneeling before a group of candles and the young man with a shabby briefcase crossing himself with holy water from the font.

They stood for a moment looking for the priest, and Patch noticed that Hannay, in spite of his Non-Conformist upbringing, genuflected solemnly towards the altar before they turned away, heading for the gardens behind the church and Don Alessandro's room in the crypt.

Don Alessandro looked up briefly from his desk as they were shown into his study, a stone-walled room lined with books and heavy oak. His thin ivory-pale face was taut with concentration and his bloodless lips were pursed with effort.

He had been writing a speech for a Catholic Women's Meeting and had been trying hard to construct one which came down heavily on Pelli's side and yet sounded like a speech in support of the Church of Rome rather than of a political party.

'Forgive me a moment,' he said, 'while I finish this sentence. We mustn't put weapons in the hands of the Church's enemies by using the wrong word.'

He wrote a little more, then looked up. 'The doctrine of Christ,' he said precisely as he put down his pen, 'is irreconcilable with those materialistic principles which, if we accept them, can only mean desertion of the Church and ceasing to be a Catholic.' He smiled. 'The Holy Father in Rome stated that as long ago as 1947.'

Listening to him, Patch found himself comparing him with the friendly, shabby old man from Fumarola and was startled to realise he was as chilled by the frightening efficiency as Don Dominico.

'I'm afraid I must limit our interview,' the priest was explaining. 'I have a meeting shortly. I'm going to tell them how they ought to vote in the coming election. The conscience of a sincere Catholic obliges him or her to give the vote to the party which accepts Divine Law and the Christian moral doctrine, and ever since Cardinal Schuster said that followers of Communism or other movements opposed to the Church of Rome cannot obtain absolution, we've held a whip hand. This is a Catholic country.'

To Patch the gloomy stone walls seemed to grow in oppressiveness as Don Alessandro pushed aside his papers and prepared to listen.

While he explained the reason for their presence, the priest sat motionless, one pale hand resting lightly on the desk. He had been disturbed in the Church of Sant' Agata by the rumble from the mountain the week before. He had become aware of the movement of the earth under his feet as the chandelier tinkled behind and above his head in the gilt and purple entrance. He had looked up, troubled, at the crash of plaster outside, but he had seen no movement except for a faint shivering among the crystals.

He hesitated before he replied. He disliked getting himself involved in lay matters – he considered the election anything but a lay matter because it affected the Catholic conscience of the community and therefore demanded all his attention –

and he knew that already the Mayor and his own arch-enemy, Bosco, had been interviewed on this matter of the mountain and had refused to do anything about it.

'The mountain seems quiet enough,' he began cautiously. 'But if there is danger, it is the will of the Lord.' He indicated the life-size plaster Christ on a rough-hewn cross on the wall. 'I can do no more than offer prayers.'

'Father – suppose there were an investigation? Suppose some expert were prepared to say there *was* cause for concern.'

Don Alessandro summed up for himself in his precise way the possibilities that might arise from such an event. It was a nicely poised question. Such problems made him feel more a diplomat than a priest. Immediately, his mind flew to the voting he was so concerned with and the disastrous results that could arise from any wild statements of danger.

'Knowing the mountain's history,' he said slowly. 'I would naturally deeply suspect any such statement and I should welcome any delay in its publication that would give time for it to be checked and re-checked. Any such irresponsible suggestion of danger could lead to a mass evacuation, and the people are leaving the islands too fast as it is.' He permitted this to sink in before continuing: 'They never return when they go and we shall eventually end up like Stromboli, with empty houses and no people. We should never hasten such an event. We need the people here. We have a live and living church and must keep it so. The Bishop has spoken to me most clearly on this subject.'

The priest's pale face showed two pink spots of anger and watching his eyes, glittering like brown burning glass, Patch began to feel he was in the presence of a fanatic. He could almost imagine Don Alessandro presiding at an Inquisition, or permitting the destruction of a community as a scourge to the public conscience. To Don Alessandro suffering and spiritual cleanliness were probably one and the same thing.

113

Although he managed to cloak his opinions in ecclesiastical trappings, there was little doubt but that he had much the same feelings as Pelli and Bosco about calling for help.

Patch drew a deep breath and tried again.

'Father,' he pointed out. 'Nobody wants to leave yet. It's reassurance they want. That's all.' He was speaking from his heart, not because he was being goaded into it by Hayward or Hannay. 'People are becoming afraid, Father. They only ask for an investigation. No more. The Mayor and his opponents are too busy to seek one. Forla, who is powerful enough to make them, is not on the island. Won't *you* undertake to force their hand?'

Don Alessandro spread his pale fingers in his lap and appeared to be counting them.

'Any such investigation,' he said, 'would inevitably lead people to suppose there was danger, and such a supposition could only lead people to stop work – particularly those who work high on the slopes of the mountain, Forla's people.' Patch sat up quickly, and Don Alessandro raised his eyes. 'Signor Patch, this church stands only by the charity of Forla and by the aid of his family. If I started taking sides with the forces which are opposed to the things the Forlas represent, those gifts might stop.'

Patch frowned. He noticed that Hannay was fidgeting heavily in his chair.

Don Alessandro had sat back now, his hands folded, his black-garbed figure tranquil. 'Signor Patch,' he concluded firmly, 'I shall pray, of course. But I cannot become involved in any dispute. This church couldn't exist without the Forla family. Since the growth of the present materialism, the men of the island have left us but the Forlas, though they no longer live here, have continued to support us in a way no one else can any longer afford, and I will not have the Church of Sant' Agata reduced to the penury of some of the churches of Italy. It is something I feel most strongly about.

Everything in it was contributed by the Forlas. The tomb of the Duke of Anapoli was rebuilt by them when it was in danger of falling down. The duke's remains were originally disinterred from an inaccessible grave on the mountainside and placed in the church by the Forlas. They built the façade and the steps which are our pride. It is *all* Forla.'

---

Patch found himself stumbling to his feet, followed by Hannay, while the sharp, intelligent eyes of the priest accompanied them to the door. He had expected to be laughed at and had been untouched by Pelli's gentle mockery, but the deliberate refusal of Don Alessandro had shaken him to the point where he could no longer think rationally about it.

He had accepted Hannay's challenge to see Pelli and Bosco and now Don Alessandro because he had thought the issue had seemed clear-cut and simple. The mountain either was or was not entering an active phase. And if it were, then obviously it should be investigated with all possible speed. It had seemed so straightforward at first, but now politics and patronage had become involved and the issues were obscured by all sorts of side-issues that touched upon it.

'I've had enough of this affair,' he said, exploding into the sunshine. 'You're getting me involved with the bloody politics of the place – you and Leonardi and the others. From now on, sort it out yourself. I've finished.'

Hannay stood for a long time in silence by the entrance to Don Alessandro's garden, a short, square figure, his hat on the back of his head, staring after Patch's lean nervous shape striding across the square. Behind him the sun streamed through the scimitar leaves of the palms that framed the entrance to the courtyard and striped the flagstones with jetty shadows. The oleanders were bursting into blossom round a noseless statue of Tiberius which had stood by the mole until some antiquary had carried it into the town and erected it by the church.

He knew Patch's accusations were genuine enough but he felt with all the force of his upbringing that even if there were no danger from the mountain – and he sincerely believed there must be – it was still the duty of someone to make certain. In spite of his lonely life at sea, Hannay was still securely part of humanity. He belonged to people and people belonged to him. In his ingenuous way that reduced everything to its ultimate simplicity, he had a firm belief that human beings were a family and there was no part in the shape of things that permitted him or anyone else to turn his back on unhappiness – or, for that matter, happiness. He extracted his share from both and he couldn't see, being as he was, that anyone else could feel differently.

He fished unhappily in his pocket and dragged out the stubby pipe he smoked. Sticking it between his teeth, he smoothed his rumpled jacket into some semblance of neatness then thoughtfully removed the pipe from his mouth again and began to pack it with tobacco. He was lighting it when he became aware of Cristoforo standing alongside him.

'Sir Captain' – Cristoforo smiled nervously, unsure of Hannay's mood – 'I am here.'

Hannay threw away the match and ruffled Cristoforo's hair as he stood poking at the dust with his toes, waiting for Hannay to speak.

It seemed right and proper to Cristoforo to remain silent while Hannay thought. Hannay was a man with responsibility and he needed to think.

It would probably have startled Hannay's humble soul to realise that Cristoforo admired him so tremendously, but to the boy he represented integrity and honesty. Even his rebukes over Cristoforo's smoking had the ring of truth about them, for he was taut and clean himself and always shaved – organised in a country where organisation was at a premium. Even Patch, with his utter indifference to everything – people, meals, clothes, even cleanliness – when he was engrossed in painting, seemed disorganised to Cristoforo and all his life he had wanted to be organised.

He waited a little longer for Hannay to speak, then he smiled nervously and looked up.

'They tell me, Sir Captain,' he said, 'that the men from the sulphur refinery have gone back to work. They've heard that the Mayor says there's no danger. There'll eventually be enough sulphur to load the Sir Captain's ship.'

'That's fine, Cris boy.' Hannay was still far away.

'Will the Sir Captain then depart?'

'Eh?' Hannay was still busy with his thoughts. 'Why, yes. I'll have to go then.'

'The Sir Captain could not, perhaps, somehow take me? I've arranged that Matteo Lipparini in San Giorgio should take my dog. He loves him well and he wouldn't be unhappy. If there is likely to be any difficulty, perhaps I could hide myself on the ship. Then no one will know and when the ship has left I will appear and you'll not be responsible. No one will then be angry with you.'

Hannay stared in front of him. Struggling with the complicated machinery of a small boy's mind, he was finding the interview was getting a little out of hand.

'People who do that,' he explained 'aren't allowed ashore. You'd have to stay aboard and come all the way back.'

'Perhaps the Sir Captain's wife might have me. I can't remember my mother, signore.'

There was loneliness in the boy's appeal and Hannay found himself considering what Mabel's reactions would be to the sudden and unexpected appearance of Cristoforo in their modest semi-detached. He could almost hear her: 'The boy looks half-starved. He needs feeding up.' He could see her running round the kitchen in a frenzy of haste to provide a meal before Cristoforo fell apart at the seams. He could imagine her rushing upstairs and fishing out some clean sheets and clothes. Could imagine –

'Cristoforo!' He pulled himself up sharply before his thoughts ran away with him. 'That'd be impossible.'

'Wouldn't the Sir Captain's wife like me?'

'I'm sure she would.'

'Then what can be wrong?'

'Look, Chris boy,' Hannay said heavily. 'For us to do that, your uncle would have to give his consent. Without it, I can't do a thing. And the time's not right to ask him just yet.'

Cristoforo stared at the ground again. 'But if he says no' – his face was blank with bewilderment – 'what are we to do? You want me to come. I wish to come. He will say no. I know he will. Something ought to be done.'

'Yes.'

Cristoforo glanced up at Hannay, conscious of his troubled manner, and he thrust his own cares aside loyally. 'The Sir Captain is worried?' he asked.

'Yes.'

'What about, Sir Captain?'

Hannay gestured wearily. 'You. Me. Lots of things. The mountain, for instance.'

'Can't something be done about the mountain, Sir Captain?'

'Yes, but nobody'll do it. It wants someone to have a look at it. There are plenty of people who could, but nobody'll ask 'em.'

He fished in his pocket and slipped a thousand-lire note to Cristoforo. 'Here,' he said gruffly. 'Go and buy yourself something.' He glanced up at Amarea and seemed to be sniffing the air. 'And if anything should 'appen, just you set off for that ship of mine, uncle or no uncle. Double quick.'

'Double quick?'

'Fast. *Rapido. Mollo rapido. Capisce?* Understand?'

'*Si*, signore.' Cristoforo gave Hannay a beaming smile of comprehension. 'Signor Patch has taught me. Fast as bloody hell.'

*seventeen*

---

Cristoforo thought for a long time about Hannay's words. He had no feeling of indebtedness to him, for he had no knowledge of what Hannay wished to do for him. All he knew was that Hannay had expressed the need for an investigation of the mountain and his disgust that no one would undertake it. The issue seemed simple enough. Cristoforo begged a lift to San Giorgio and went to the home of Matteo Lipparini, whose father, in addition to working for Forla, kept a tiny peasant farm holding above the village. From Matteo's mother he begged a hunk of bread and a piece of sausage and, stuffing them into the pockets of his ragged coat, set off towards the mountain top.

If Hannay could show courage and intelligence and because of them become master of a fine ship – in Cristoforo's eyes the *Great Watling Street* had grown in bulk and majesty – then so could he. By doing so he might even convince Hannay that he was capable enough to be a sailor without the consent of his uncle, and so start earlier on the ladder that led upwards to a ship of his own.

Matteo had not responded to the suggestion that he should accompany Cristoforo, so the boy advanced alone up the winding path that led to the summit, finally pausing a long way below the crater, tired, thirsty, and oppressed by the silence of the mountain and the increasing conviction that the last craggy slopes might be beyond his strength and skill.

He stood among the fold of dead lava and stared upwards with a sense of loneliness. Above him the column of black smoke drifted slowly upwards into the rain clouds that were beginning to gather, sullen onlookers of his minuteness.

The mountain had a brooding stillness about it that worried him. In the last week or two it had ceased to be his friend and had become a surly, sulking thing, indifferent to his affection for it, vaguely threatening in a way that Cristoforo couldn't describe, even before the steam that waved gently from the summit had changed to the present thin but steady column of smoke.

Cristoforo had never seen the mountain smoke before, though he knew from what he had heard that smoke in itself was no reason for alarm. Plenty of people older than himself had seen the smoke at various times, had seen it grow to a thick column on which the lights reflected from the sea played in various colours, only to die away eventually and be replaced once more by the wisp of steam.

Below him he could see the sea, like the mountain grey and threatening and with none of its normal friendly colours, and to his right Anapoli Porto, spreading in a cluster of pink and yellow and blue buildings along the coast round the little harbour where the *Great Watling Street* lay, with Captain Hannay on board.

Momentarily he wished he were down there in the flowered streets among the oleanders and the pots of geraniums where people could reassure him with their movement and sound, where there were voices instead of this incredible silence. Never before had Cristoforo been so conscious of the mountain's stillness.

To others, perhaps, the mountain had always been silent but to Cristoforo, who was acutely aware of these things, there had been movement and life about him. Now there was nothing. The folds of rocks were empty, the bushes gave only before his own blundering. Even the threatening sky above his head was empty. There was nothing, not even insects, it seemed.

He pressed on a little further, vaguely uneasy but anxious to reach the summit. He had never been so high on the mountain before, had never quite left behind him the scented vetch and juniper bushes and finally the wiry brown grass so that he was among the scorched rocks and cinders and the pockmarks of ancient agonies where the stony lava flows were thick and black and tortured. San Giorgio lay below him, among the silvery groves of olive trees and the sparkle of oranges, a huddle of muddy-looking yellow houses clustered round a shabby campanile. He could see goats and a few dots of chickens and then he saw a black-coated figure move round a house at the upper end of the village where the Lipparinis had their home just below the threadbare little farm of the Givannos. He suddenly wanted to turn round and head down again to the companionship of human beings.

He put his hand out to touch the head of his dog. Masaniello had shown a marked reluctance to snuffle at the holes and indentations that pitted the slopes of cold lava – perhaps because of the absence of wild things, for it was long enough now since they had deserted the mountain for the tracks to be cold – but more likely, he realised, because the dog was also oppressed by the silence and unfriendliness of the mountain top.

As his questing hand failed to find the smooth brown head, it startled Cristoforo to realise that the dog was not alongside him, and he stopped in his tracks and turned. Masaniello was grinning anxiously at him, its tongue hanging out, the muzzle under its chin.

' 'Niello,' he called. ' 'Niello.'

He whistled softly and the dog's stern wriggled as it tried anxiously to make up for its disobedience by wagging its tail.

' 'Niello,' he said again, more sternly, but the dog, although it stood up, still refused to move.

Cristoforo, anxious himself and wanting to expend his anxiety in anger, strode back to the dog and cuffed it. Then he took a piece of string from his pocket and, tying it to the dog's collar, set off again.

The dog followed him – but reluctantly, and then Cristoforo noticed that, as it hung back, the hair along its spine stood on end, and it eyed its surroundings with marked hostility and suspicion. Cristoforo began to be conscious of a prickling along his own neck, and when the dog finally sat down again and refused to go any farther he was frankly scared.

He glanced up at the mountain, just in time to see a burst of smoke issue from the summit, rather like the puffs that came from Hannay's lips when he blew smoke rings, then the steady thin stream of black continued as before.

Cristoforo looked round at his dog, unconsciously seeking some excuse to return. Then he became aware of the mountain's sounds – a steady rumbling, very low-pitched and almost inaudible, that was mixed with a faint hissing sound like a train letting off steam in the distance. He stopped dead, more anxious to turn his back on it than he liked to admit, but he could still see no sign of danger. Only the dog, squatting behind him, its hair bristling, its eyes rolling, indicated that all was far from normal.

Then the mountain gave another puff of smoke and the dog slithered round on its haunches and bolted down the path, burning Cristoforo's hand as it dragged the string through his fingers. Thirty yards away, it took up its position again and sat waiting for him, its mouth in a grin, its eyes and forehead anxious.

'Coward,' Cristoforo said angrily, speaking out aloud to give himself courage. 'You ought to be ashamed of yourself, ' 'Niello. There's nothing to be afraid of.'

The dog's grin widened but it didn't lift its seat from the ground.

'Very well,' Cristoforo said. 'I'll go on my own.'

As he set off again, he noticed that there was moisture in the air and as he stared up at the grey-blue clouds that trailed their bellies along Amarea's crater he laughed.

'Rain,' he said to the dog. 'You're afraid of rain.'

The rain seemed to fall a little more heavily and Cristoforo debated whether he was wise to risk getting wet, but he decided to chance it and pressed on a little farther up the mountain. Then he realised that the spots that fell on his face were warm and stinging.

He put his hand to his cheek to wipe them away and was surprised to find a smear of grey on his finger tips. Then he saw that the backs of his hands and his clothes were spotted by the same grey-brown stain. He stopped dead and slowly passed the fingers of his right hand over the back of his left. To his surprise, the spots ran into a smudge. He stared at it, sniffed at it, even tasted it.

He noticed then that the road and the folds of ground about him were also spotted with the grey, moist substance and that the fine dust that had fallen on the slopes during the previous days was turning to the same colour.

His lips began to move as he started to pray quietly.

'*Gesu mio, misericordia!*'

For a moment, he stood, muttering out loud to give himself confidence, then he heard a faint sigh high up in the sky above him among the clouds that pressed the air down into a suffocating closeness. Suddenly the stillness became more intense. It had been silent before but now it seemed that in spite of the high-pitched sigh, the silence had been magnified a thousand times in a way that prickled along his skin.

Ahead of him the mountainside was blurred. The cloud bottoms seemed to have been dragged down in wispy tails that touched the slopes and there was a strong tang of sulphur in the air, the sickly smell that always clung to the clothes of the workers in Forla's refinery. He felt something brush across his face again and, looking up, saw the sky was full of a dark moisture.

'*Mamma mia!*' The exclamation burst out of him, loud in the silence. 'Mud! It rains mud!'

Stupefied by the phenomenon, he stared at his hands a little longer, then fear took hold of him and he turned and fled, catching his foot against a rock so that he went sprawling at the feet of his dog. Picking himself up, he set off again, the dog alongside him, running silently and desperately down the slopes towards San Giorgio.

## *eighteen*

That night a storm of unusual intensity broke out over the island.

The clouds which had been hanging around the tip of Amarea all day seemed to gather companions from nowhere, ugly black galleons anchored to the mountain where the column of smoke, thicker than during the day, mingled with the vapours of the cloud formations. During the evening, the thick black cumulus changed its shape and spread until the sky was covered with flat, oppressive-looking formations that held down the heat and sent the people hurrying through the streets from their work, casting nervous glances up over their shoulders.

The heavy air seemed to beat down until Patch, struggling in the poor light over his *Primavera*, found himself sweating. Then a door slammed somewhere in a sudden gusty wind and the room was lit by a flash of lightning which was followed by a clap of thunder that rattled the windows. Immediately, the rain began to fall from the angry-looking sky, at first in long slow drops that splashed leisurely against the panes one after the other, and then in a growing downpour of straight glassy splinters that streamed across the window in a steady sheet of water, and bubbled under the ill-fitting frame and down the wall to form a pool on the red tiles of the floor.

The rain seemed to have quietened the normal gaiety of the building and there was no sound about the place beyond the drip of the rain; and the steady tapping of the water seemed somehow linked to the general mood of frustration.

Listening to it, Patch was curiously reminded of the defeat in the eyes of Don Dominico as they had informed him of Don Alessandro's reaction to their visit. He had not shared Patch's anger, but had accepted the news with a calm fortitude that didn't match the hopelessness in his eyes. 'Don't be too angry, my son,' he had said gently. 'Our church is as plagued with ambitious men as any other organisation.'

At any other time, Patch might have shrugged off Don Alessandro's indifference, but just now it all seemed bound up with the growing feeling that nobody cared. Once Patch himself had not cared, but the studied indifference of everyone with influence was making him angry and suspicious and he was beginning to care very much.

Gradually, as the evening advanced, the downpour eased off, but there remained a lurid glow under the clouds, and the trickle and gurgle of running water round the dilapidated old building made music with the plop-plop-plop of a leak in the corridor.

The sound of feet outside caught Patch's attention, then there was a bang at the door and he whirled round as Hannay entered. He was dressed from head to foot in a long glaringly yellow oilskin that was topped by the grey felt hat soaked to blackness by the downpour.

He nodded at Patch without speaking and, removing his hat, shook the water out of it all over the floor.

'Rain,' he said.

'I've noticed it.'

Hannay looked angry and Patch thought he was going to start all over again about the mountain, but instead he fished out his pipe and lit it, blowing smoke into the room in angry puffs like some furious dragon as he walked up and down for a while in a sailor's short promenade before he spoke.

'I want you to come with me and show me where Cristoforo lives,' he said at last. 'I'm going to beat the living daylights out of that bastard who looks after him.'

He was obviously deeply moved and his anger had not the cold, impersonal quality it had had about the mountain, but something stronger that seemed to sear his soul.

'I'm going to give him one across the jaw,' he said ferociously, obviously enjoying the prospect. 'And see how *he* likes it.'

Patch pushed a drink across to him without speaking and Hannay tossed it back quickly.

'What's happened, man?' Patch said. 'For God's sake, calm down.'

'He's been beating the kid again,' Hannay snapped. 'He's got weals all round his legs. Just because he went up the mountain. He did it for me, I think. He came on my ship, scared stiff because he'd seen mud dropping out of the sky. God, as if he hadn't enough on his slate without that. Then when he went home that bastard lit into him, because he went without asking permission. A strap he'd used. You can see the marks of it. He's so scared he'll get another he won't show me where the bastard lives.'

'I take it you're talking about Uncle Angelo Devoto?'

' 'Course I am,' Hannay snapped. 'Who else?'

'You might have told me.'

'Well, you know now, anyway.' Hannay seemed impatient to get on with the job. 'Coming?'

Patch poured himself another drink. 'Yes,' he said, slowly and deliberately to give Hannay a chance to calm down. 'I'll come. I'll show you where he lives. But only on condition you sort yourself out a bit first. He lives three floors up and in your present mood you'd probably try to throw him out of the window.'

'No more than he deserves,' Hannay said, but perceptibly he began to quieten down.

'And if I might make a suggestion,' Patch continued, 'I should forget about beating him up for the present if you're keen about adopting Cristoforo.'

'What do you mean?' Hannay seemed disappointed.

'Do you want to adopt Cristoforo? '

'Yes.' Hannay paused before he spoke but, having made his decision, he seemed in no doubt about it.

'You've asked Mabel?'

'Mabel won't quarrel with me. Not over this.'

'Then a smash in the jaw's not very likely to produce results, is it? Why not keep calm and make an offer for the kid? Knowing Devoto, I wouldn't guarantee he'll respond, but you can try.'

Hannay stared at the empty glass in his hand for a while before replying. When he looked up again, he seemed in control of himself. 'Okay,' he said. 'Maybe you're right. Let's go.'

Devoto lived at the bottom of the Via Medina down by the mole. Outside, at the bottom of the steeply sloping street, the grimy children played in the thin rain, instinctively avoiding the puddles as they ran. Across the windows the dripping washing that no one had bothered to take in shut out the light above the slimy pavements and slapped against the crooked walls with their cracked plaster and broken brick-work and the strings of indentations where bullets had bitten into them in the street fighting of 1943.

They picked their way through a puddled courtyard full of rubbish and climbed a set of rickety iron steps. Pushing through a doorway, glassed with multi-coloured panes, they groped across a dark landing, and headed up more stairs, stone stairs with barely enough light to see by.

Hannay thundered on the door of Devoto's apartment, and waited impatiently, his aggressive humanity bristling like the hairs on a dog's back, determined to affect some business deal that would result in Cristoforo's removal from the ugly building. He had been itching for days to meet Devoto, anxious to point out the boy's thinness, his threadbare clothes, his poor shoes, and the fact that only Patch, with his sporadic generosity, had ever seemed to show any interest in his meals.

They were let in by Devoto's wife, a tired-looking little woman who had once been pretty, with a child in her arms, and Hannay was startled to discover that Cristoforo's uncle was only ten years older than Cristoforo himself, the youngest of a set of brothers of whom Cristoforo's father had been the oldest. He was big and handsome, dwarfing Hannay, and in no way abashed by his poverty.

Patch introduced them, then stood back and let Hannay do the talking. He started off with his usual bull-in-a-china-shop rush.

'You Cristoforo's uncle?' he barked in his dreadful Italian.

'I am, signore.' The big man with the sly eyes bowed mockingly. 'Devoto, Angelo, at your service.'

'I'm wanting to speak to you.'

Devoto grinned. 'I've been expecting you, signore. I understand you would like my Cristoforo to go to England.'

For once, Hannay was startled. He had not expected his mission to be known.

'It's not a bad idea,' he said gruffly. 'He might be better looked after.'

Devoto put his hands behind his back and stared at the ground, rocking on the balls of his feet.

'It is a bad thing,' he said weightily, 'to put such ideas in a boy's mind when they're totally impossible.'

'They're not impossible,' Hannay rapped. 'He's on my ship now. Covered with bruises. I thought I might even adopt him. I've come to see you about it.'

Devoto didn't answer for a moment and Patch studied the bleak, shabby room with the inevitable picture of the Virgin, the great brass bedstead alongside a table littered with the remains of a meal, and the *prie-dieu* that was obviously never used. Devoto's wife stood silently in a corner by a paraffin stove, the baby held awkwardly on her hip, not speaking, washed-out, beaten, and hopeless. Devoto's bold greedy eyes had lit up but he made no move to indicate his thoughts.

'There are many official documents to complete,' he said cautiously.

'They could be arranged.' Hannay found he disliked Devoto even more than he thought he could.

'He means a great deal to me.' Devoto was speaking in a fine ringing voice he seemed to enjoy using. 'He's a comfort to my wife and a joy to my children.'

He glanced round towards his wife and Patch saw her eyes signal a message to him, an appeal to accept whatever was to be offered without delay.

Hannay in his anger, had not noticed the glance. 'If he means so much,' he said, 'why don't you look after him? Treat him better?'

Devoto shrugged in self-justification. 'Sometimes he is very self-willed. All boys are. A man must discipline them. I promised my brother before he died. And how can a poor man do better for him than I do? I've many troubles.' He smiled. 'Two boys and a girl. One a baby. And another on the way. I've no work.'

There was a pause and Patch watched Devoto, trying to read the thoughts behind the handsome face. Beyond him, there was a pale patch of damp on the wall that looked curiously like a seedy halo behind his head.

'I'll take Cristoforo off your hands,' Hannay was saying. 'That'd make it easier for you, wouldn't it?'

For a second, Patch thought he saw hope again in the hopelessness in the woman's face, then she looked at her husband's blank expression and the hopelessness returned.

Devoto had spread his hands. 'Signore, Cristoforo means more than that to me. I wouldn't like to be parted from him.'

The woman started to take a step forward, her mouth open as though to protest, then she stopped, and moved back to her corner, silent.

'How much do you want for him?' Hannay asked bluntly. He fished in his pocket and threw his wallet on the table.

Devoto glanced at it and smiled faintly. 'Money becomes wine, signore. It's soon gone. A job does not. That's what I want.'

Hannay frowned, puzzled, and glanced at Patch for a lead. 'I can't give you a job,' he said.

'Then take me to England with you,' Devoto said. 'And help me to get a job. There are jobs in England. Unlike Italy, there are more jobs than people.'

'What about your family, Devoto?' Patch put in quietly from his position by the door.

Devoto turned and gave him a flashing smile. 'They would be all right. I would send them money.'

'We should never hear from you again!' The words burst out of the woman's lips almost as though she had no control over them. '*Gesu mio*, we get little enough when you work *here!*'

Devoto's heavy face didn't alter in its expression. 'Many Italian men work abroad,' he said, turning to Hannay again.

His wife became silent and slipped back into the corner, and Patch had the feeling that she would suffer the consequences of her interruption later.

Hannay had said nothing during the outburst. He seemed to be trying to weigh Devoto up, trying to get to the bottom of his refusal of the money and the demand for a job.

'I can't take you to England,' he said slowly.

'You've a ship, signore. Who's to know I'm aboard, apart from you? If I'm not to accompany Cristoforo, who after all still needs the care of someone who understands him – his own flesh and blood – then, signore, Cristoforo can't go. I couldn't permit him such unhappiness.'

Hannay glowered at Devoto, dwarfed but undaunted. 'Cristoforo's happiness has got nothing to do with it,' he snapped. 'I'll make it worth your while. Even if I took you to England, they'd never let you stay.'

'Then that seems to end all the argument, signore.'

'Angelo –' The woman stepped forward again, her face desperate, but Devoto signed her to silence with a gesture.

'Signore,' he said. 'In Naples, – the women borrow each other's babies to beg with. Everything that holds out the smallest gleam of hope is clung to by the hopeless. Cristoforo appeals to people. Visitors give him money. People who won't employ me get him to do jobs for them. I can't let him go except in return for what I ask.'

Hannay stared straight ahead. 'They'd never let you ashore,' he said.

'It's easy to arrange these things.'

'Not on my ship.'

'Then I'd advise you to forget all the hopes you had of taking away Cristoforo.'

Devoto picked up the wallet and handed it back. Hannay swallowed, holding in his anger. 'If I could smuggle you aboard,' he said, 'what's to stop me doing the same with the boy?'

'Me, signore.' Devoto indicated the window through which they could see the flat sheet of the grey sea beyond the runnels of rain on the dirty glass. 'My rooms overlook the mole. I can watch Cristoforo whenever he leaves the house. I've no work so I'm not otherwise engaged.'

'It gets dark.'

'I don't think he'd defy me. And if I'm in any doubt, there are always the police to search your ship.'

He smiled and moved towards the door. 'It grows dark now,' he pointed out as he opened it for them. 'I hope Cristoforo will not be late home.'

Standing in the crumbling archway that led to the courtyard, Patch and Hannay watched the rain for a while. It seemed to have a quality of blackness, a dreariness as dark as Hannay's mood.

Through the open window above them, they could hear the sound of an angry argument.

Hannay seemed shocked. He had confidently expected success and seemed unable to accept the fact that Devoto could not be bought.

'It would 'ave been better if I'd clocked him one after all,' he said heavily. 'I never fancied adopting a kid till I knew how he was going to turn out, but I thought Cristoforo seemed to just about fit the bill.'

He stared at the rain for a little longer then he seemed to cheer up. 'I'll come again,' he said briskly. 'I think he's holding out in the hope I'll offer him more. He'll give way when he sees I don't intend to.'

'I shouldn't be too certain,' Patch warned him.

'Hell, I was half-way there.' Hannay seemed suddenly to recover his optimism. 'It only wants time. Why would he hang on to Cristoforo when they don't want him? His wife would be only too glad to let him go now.' He indicated the window above them and cocked his head to the sound of the two angry voices. 'You can hear them now.'

Even as they listened, there was the sound of a blow and a cry of pain. Then they heard the crash of breaking glass and the wail of the baby, and the soft whimpering of a woman.

Hannay looked upwards, his expression again one of unhappiness and uncertainty.

'I don't think his wife has much say in the matter,' Patch said soberly. 'I think you'll have to take him with you if you want Cristoforo.'

'But why? He don't want work. You can see that a mile off. And I'd pay him well.'

Patch shrugged. 'His money wouldn't last long here. He's got relatives and they'd be on to him like a pack of ravening wolves. He wants to go to England because he's sick of his wife. Ask Emiliano. He's a bit of a Casanova and he wants fun and games again. But the only way he can get fun and games is to live where he's not known. In England, for instance. Even the mainland's too near and they'd find him too quickly.' He paused and stepped out of the shelter of the archway into the rain. 'So you see,' he concluded, turning to wait for Hannay, 'he sets rather a lot of store by the *Great Watling Street* and you.'

## nineteen

The rain had increased as Hannay left Patch by the mole and headed for the *Great Watling Street.* Patch watched him stride away, then he hung about for a while, undecided what to do with himself. In the end he called in at Emiliano's but the place seemed surprisingly different without Emiliano's great paunch and waving hands behind the bar.

'He's gone to a meeting,' the waiter said from his unaccustomed place behind the Espresso machine. 'I don't know where. Something about the mountain, I think.'

He brought Patch's drink round the counter to him and set it on the end of a group of trunks stacked in a corner of the bar.

'From one of the houses up on the slopes,' he said, indicating the luggage. 'The old American woman. There are some more behind the bar. They're to be collected in the morning when the ferry comes in. She's leaving. And she's not the only one.'

Patch sipped his drink thoughtfully. The exodus from Anapoli was starting, in spite of Pelli and Bosco and Don Alessandro.

'They say several of the yachts left this afternoon, too,' the waiter went on. 'Looking for better weather. And they say the Givannos are going to leave San Giorgio for good. They brought the children and the old lady down in the van this afternoon. They've moved in with relatives in the Via

Garibaldi until after the funeral. All but one of them who's staying to look after the farm. They won't go back.'

When Patch reached home, Mamma Meucci was waiting for him, and as he put his umbrella aside, she brought him a meal of bread and cheese and wine.

Putting down the tray, she tried to assimilate his mood, and looked dolefully at him, her round face dropping.

'*Che tempo miserabile*,' she mourned, shaking her head until her cheeks wobbled. 'What awful weather! We've had no spring this year and my sister in Naples writes what wonderful sunshine they're having there. They've missed all our storms. They just sit on top of Amarea and never go. They say whole families are leaving San Giorgio.'

'One family,' Patch corrected her. 'The Givannos. They moved into the Porto for the inquest on their father.'

'It's over.' Mamma Meucci cheered up at the realisation that she knew something he didn't know. 'Today. Didn't you hear? The doctor from the Piazza del Popolo said it wasn't the dust that killed him. He'd had a chest complaint for years. They decided it was a natural death.'

She went out of the room, still muttering to herself, and Patch stood at the window, gazing at the puddles gathering in the roadway and the water bubbling in the gutters. The clouds were blotting out the peak of Amarea now, but as he stared a flash of lightning forked across the sky, coming, it seemed, from the very heart of the mountain. The clap of thunder that followed set the knife tinkling against the plate on the table.

The unease that had started with Cristoforo was spreading The grapevine was carrying it round the island and Patch found it had reached him now, and he turned away from the window, suddenly conscious of a desire to know more about volcanoes.

Placing a piece of cheese on a slice of bread, he went out of the room eating it and down the stairs to the Leonardis' apartment.

He was startled by the number of people he found there and when he saw Emiliano he realised that this was the meeting the waiter had referred to. Old Tornielli was there, too, and the barber from the Piazza Martiri, and the rest of the Emiliano's customers. As he closed the door, Cecilia came out of the kitchen carrying a bottle of wine. Her expression was mutinous but as she saw him the suffused anger immediately changed to pleasure.

'Come in! Come in! Old Leonardi bounded forward in a succession of awkward leaps that set his knee joints cracking. 'Come in!' He clicked his teeth and flung a finger violently upwards to the ceiling. 'We petrify ourselves with talk of Pompeii. We discuss which will be the better – to be trapped in a river of fire or to choke to death under a cloud of lapilli. There is another rumble today. That makes about four in a week, and when "swarms" of earthquakes appear an eruption is imminent. At Ilopango there are eight hundred in one month.'

'I came to borrow some books.' Patch swallowed the last of the bread and cheese, and Leonardi whirled energetically and swept the room with wide-open arms.

'I have no books,' he said. 'I never read books. I've some albums of photographs, but they're a little dusty and I doubt whether they'll make you sleep. The only books I possess are my authorities on volcanoes.'

'Those are the books I came for.'

Leonardi laughed a little hysterically and embraced him, pressing him against the food-spotted alpaca jacket so that he could smell the garlic on the old man's breath and hear the champing of his teeth.

'Welcome to the gathering. Come and join us at discussing dusty death. Now we have an Englishman, we might get somewhere. One Italian, twenty ideas. One Englishman, one idea – one good idea.'

The others looked up as Patch was pushed into the lounge – and to Patch, his senses alerted by the oddness of the atmosphere about him, the feeling of living at twice the normal speed, the gathering had an air of excitement about it, even of Leonardi's hysteria verging on panic. He was reminded again of the defeated look in Don Dominico's eyes and found he was desperately anxious to know the truth.

'The rain comes down as mud on San Giorgio this afternoon,' Dr Leonardi led off with a grisly cheerfulness. 'The boy Cristoforo told Emiliano. I'm surprised the captain Hannay hasn't come. We invited him. The dust the mountain throws up touches the clouds and the rain there turns it into mud. It's a very curious phenomenon.'

'San Giorgio's dying,' old Tornielli announced in a sepulchral voice. He had heard the chink of glasses and had entered pretending he had arrived to inspect the plumbing, and was now determined to enter the spirit of the thing and make a good job of his gloom. 'Before long there'll be no San Giorgio.'

Patch looked round, faintly irritated by the atmosphere in the room – as though they were all sitting round mourning a corpse – and he could see it had affected all the others too. Only Leonardi was cheerful, but it was the cheerfulness of nerves. He was the expert who had been waiting fifty years to predict just such an event as now seemed on top of them and yet hadn't the skill and the reputation to make anyone listen to him.

Cecilia appeared beside Patch and offered him a glass.

'They're a lot of old grandmothers,' she said angrily. 'They've been sitting there an hour now – just talking.'

Patch stared after her as she turned away, startled by the vehemence in her voice.

'We've been deciding that someone ought to go on the ferry tomorrow,' Leonardi said, offering him a cigarette with a gesture. 'It's due in at daylight. If we can't get the authorities to do anything here, then we must try the authorities on the mainland.'

'You're a glutton for punishment, aren't you?' Patch said. 'There's an election on there, too.'

'They'll behave differently on the mainland,' Leonardi pointed out confidently. 'It's their job to listen to complaints. And they haven't a personal interest in Anapoli like Pelli has.'

He grinned at Patch with a sudden surprising malice. 'Piero called in,' he went on. 'He told us Pelli wants to see you. It seems Bosco has produced some posters that Pelli objects to. For some reason, he blames you.'

'Thanks for letting me know,' Patch said dryly. 'I'll make a point of not being around. Maybe I'll go with the committee to the mainland to see the experts. Who's going? You?'

Leonardi's eyes widened. 'Ah! 'He raised one finger like an exclamation mark. 'That is where our problem starts,' he said. 'I can't go. I've my business to look after. People come every day for photographs. There is suddenly a rush. Maria Gori's expecting her seventh and Innocenzo dArpa's getting married.'

You old liar, Patch thought. You've no business left to attend to. They wouldn't come to you for photographs if you were the last photographer on God's good earth.

Old Leonardi could expertise in cafés and bars but he knew his hit-or-miss prophecies would never stand up under the precision instruments of the experts, and he was afraid of being laughed at.

He glanced at Emiliano.

'I'd go, Signor Tom' – Emiliano thumped himself on the chest with a gesture – 'only' – his demeanour altered and he seemed to shrink – 'only I have my bar to think of.'

Patch began to grin, beginning to feel better, beginning to feel that their behaviour brought reality to the fantasies they were imagining. He sipped the wine Cecilia had handed him. 'And Tornielli's got to mend the roof,' he said. 'And Meucci's afraid of missing the fish. The trouble with the lot of you is that none of you wants to make a fool of himself. Well, neither do I. So, if you won't go, and I won't go, and nobody else will go, what do we do now?'

Cecilia put down the wine bottles on the table, but her hand was trembling and she knocked one of them over so that the red wine splashed on the floor like blood.

'I shall go,' she said.

# *t w e n t y*

It was still raining the next morning when the passengers began to go on board the *Città di Salerno*, the white-painted ferry for the mainland that was lying alongside the mole.

The leaden sea was ruffled by the wind that seemed to be blowing in circles round Amarea and by the rain that pounded down on the taut awnings covering the fore and after decks, indications that when the ship had left its base the sun had been shining.

Patch wandered among the few people standing on the mole huddled against the rain; the youth with an armful of umbrellas he was trying to sell; Cristoforo, waiting in the hope of tips for running last-minute messages; an old man with a barrow who trundled luggage about the town; the Haywards, seeing off an old American woman from one of the villas on the slopes.

As he passed, Mrs Hayward grabbed his arm and pulled him towards her. 'Anybody would think you didn't know us, Tom,' she said.

She laughed in a brittle way that was entirely mirthless, putting on an act for her husband's sake, and Patch thought there was nothing quite so jarring as an affair gone sour, nothing so miserable as the performance that had to go on for everyone else's benefit. Without taking her eyes off him, she spoke to her husband. 'Edward, do me a favour. I'm right out of cigarettes.'

Hayward fished in his pockets cheerfully, and she frowned. 'No, I don't want one now,' she said shortly, and Hayward stopped fumbling. 'I've none for later.'

'Oh, right-o, old thing.' Hayward sighed, knowing she wanted to speak to Patch alone, and shuffled off with the two dogs, patient, woolly and forgiving. She moved closer to Patch immediately.

'Why haven't you been to see me?' she demanded as her husband disappeared. 'You've had plenty of opportunity. Is it that little Italian piece?'

'No,' he said. 'I've been busy.'

'You're always busy these days.'

'I know.' Patch tried hard to remain pleasant with her. 'It's amazing how tied up you get.'

Her voice dropped. 'Edward's playing bridge tonight,' she suggested.

Patch glanced over his shoulder, looking for Hayward, and she mistook his discomfort for caution.

'He'll be ages yet,' she said. 'Shall I expect you?'

Patch tried to meet her eyes. 'I don't think I'll make it.' he said. 'You see' – he grinned suddenly – 'I'm catching the boat.'

She looked surprised and disbelieving. He had no hat and wore no coat in spite of the rain. 'Like that?' she asked.

He began to wish again that Hayward would come back from the little bar with the cigarettes and stop her questions. But he knew Hayward, with his patient, forgiving affection, would probably be taking as long as he could over the purchase, and he controlled the irritation rising in him again. Mrs Hayward, in her search for excitement, had always been trivial but now she seemed pitifully so. 'It was urgent,' he said.

'I don't believe you.'

He shrugged, giving up the struggle.

'Why didn't you tell me you were going?' she went on angrily. 'I could have found an excuse to come, too. Anything to get away from all this damn' nonsense about the mountain. We could have gone to Rome.'

Patch looked round again, desperate for a means to escape.

'I didn't have time.' He was beginning to hate himself for this sordid little melodrama in which he had become involved. 'It was urgent.'

There was something in her face that told him immediately that she didn't believe him, in spite of the smile she kept there for everyone else to see. Her eyes had the desperate look he'd seen so often before.

'I've never known you go like this.' In her desperation, she was becoming shrill although she knew it was the one thing that irritated him most of all. 'I've never known you move fast in your life.'

'There's always a first time.'

He was still struggling to convince her when Hayward returned, clearing his throat noisily to warn them, calling to the dogs more forcefully than he need have done, and Patch managed to dodge away, thankful for his reprieve, her eyes following him all the way.

As he reached the shore end of the mole, a group of people appeared out of a muddy alley alongside the harbour, heading in a line towards the Via Maddalena, a group of boys chanting Ave Marias, some of them in shabby rain-spotted cassocks, a huddle of nuns, and Don Gustavo, a pimply-faced young man who was Don Alessandro's curate. Behind them, two men carried a colossal wreath of palm leaves and mountain flowers, obviously picked on the slopes of Amarea and home-made for cheapness; and after them two more men trundled a small hand-cart, gaily painted like an ice-cream barrow and bearing a rough coffin which was followed by a group of relatives telling their beads, the women moaning to themselves as they shuffled through the puddles. Among them were Giuseppe and Marco Givanno, and Patch suddenly realised he was witnessing the funeral of Amarea's first victim.

The little procession passed him as he stood in the rain, all of them, from the youngest to the oldest, indifferent to the weather, all of them in their Italian fashion preoccupied with death. Depressed by their poverty, he turned into the bar where all the ferry passengers crowded out of the weather, and found old Leonardi at the counter trying to choose a cheap bun for himself.

The old man didn't look at Patch. He knew he should have gone to the mainland himself instead of letting Cecilia go, but he hadn't the courage any longer to argue with people who knew as much as he did and more. He was too old. He couldn't face the effort. He couldn't face the looks and the sidelong glances that indicated he was crazy. The frustration at not being proved right had changed with the years to a cosiness that came from not being proved wrong.

As it happened, though, Patch ignored him and made his way towards Cecilia who was sitting at a table, her face pale and expressionless, a small suitcase by her feet. Piero Tornielli was with her, his coat draped across his shoulders like a cloak, holding one of her hands in both of his and talking in an undertone.

His expression changing as Patch appeared, he stood up abruptly, scraping the chair as he moved. A great heat of fury was already mounting inside him. His father had told him the night before that Cecilia was going to the mainland and immediately he had assumed it to be a move on Patch's part to take her away from him. He had not been able to sleep for the intensity of his hatred.

He took a deep breath, going again through the hours when he had lain in bed, nursing his dislike of Patch, recalling all the times when he had listened to him talking on the landing above with Cecilia, while blood-red curtains of jealousy swirled in his mind. He had suffered through the night, dreaming up moments of triumph, glorying in pictures to which there was no substance but which nevertheless provided balm for the wounds that his hatred wrought on him.

'What do you want?' he demanded, his voice harsh.

'Just a chair,' Patch smiled, sitting down.

Piero remained standing, staring down at him, the muscles of his face moving as he gritted his teeth.

'Why can't you leave us alone?' he demanded.

Patch looked up, surprised, then responded with sarcasm as he always did to Piero's aggressive jealousy. He waved his cigarette and turned his back on the boy. 'Believe me,' he said. 'I won't look.'

'I was saying good-bye to Cecilia before she leaves.'

'Odd.' Patch spoke over his shoulder. 'I'm most concerned with her departure, too.'

Piero's handsome face flushed and he shuddered with his hatred. 'She shouldn't be going on this wild-goose chase at all,' he said wildly. 'It's undignified for an engaged woman.'

'Piero,' Cecilia said quickly, incensed by his melodramatic concern, his improbable anger. 'Piero, we've already discussed all this, again and again and again.'

The boy bent over her and spoke in an angry whisper: 'If you must go, go with me. Wait until after the election.'

'It might be no good then.'

Piero seemed on the verge of tears with frustration. 'Cecilia, *tesoro*, I wish I could persuade you not to board that ship.'

'I'm going, Piero,' Cecilia said calmly, indifferent to his anger.

'Why? Why must you – ?'

Cecilia looked at him without smiling and laid a hand on his arm. 'You'd better go, Piero,' she said. 'You'll be late and you mustn't offend Pelli.'

Piero glared at Patch, thwarted and savage, as though the whole of his frustration and distrust were *his* fault and his alone. Then he kissed Cecilia's hand and swept out of the little bar like a cyclone.

'Dear me,' Patch said mildly. 'He's not very sound on departures, Cecilia.'

Cecilia sipped her coffee as though she hadn't heard, and Patch knocked the ash from his cigarette and glanced towards her. She was sitting very straight, very small, the dark hair curling round her ears.

'Cecilia!' – he paused before he spoke, and all the banter had gone out of him – 'they'll never listen to you.'

'I'll make them.'

Patch swung round in his chair to face her.

'Cecilia, they'll wonder why a man wasn't sent, why Pelli himself didn't come, or even your grandfather.'

'They'd never listen to *him*,' she said contemptuously. 'His warnings have come too frequently. Besides, he's afraid of being laughed at, like Emiliano and Meucci – and you.'

He stared angrily at her. 'Cecilia, I tried. What more must I do? Go down into the crater and come up with my ears full of boiling lava? There must be ways of doing this but obviously we haven't used the right ones. We must wait for more definite signs of danger.'

Cecilia's blue eyes flashed. 'There have been enough signs of danger already,' she said.

'Oh, God, how stubborn can you get?' Patch lit a fresh cigarette from the stub of the old one and paused before he spoke again. 'Cecilia – I'm coming with you.'

She looked up quickly, an expression of clear delight chasing the anger from her face for a fleeting second, then it had gone again and the happiness died out of her eyes in a glance of suspicion.

'Why?' she demanded.

He laughed outright. 'You know, Cecilia,' he said. 'For a moment, I thought you were pleased.'

'For a moment I was,' she said. 'I believed you were coming for the good of Anapoli. Then I thought again and I knew you weren't.'

Patch grinned. 'All right, then,' he said. 'I'm coming to look after you. I think you need a man around.'

'Some women do – like Mrs Hayward.'

'Cecilia, I'll just sit in the background and call you taxis and beat off anyone who tries to fetch a policeman.'

She gave him a little smile, melted by his teasing. 'You've no luggage,' she pointed out.

Patch fished in his pocket and gravely produced a toothbrush. 'There. I've travelled much further with much less.' It was her turn to laugh now, her eyes bright as she let him win her round. Patch's ability to make her laugh was always a relief after Piero's histrionic seriousness.

As she smiled at him, the sullenness gone from her face, a car that had come down the hill into the piazza began to circle the wide stretch of wet porter-coloured cobbles close to the mole.

'We must work for the socialism of the soil' – the raucous cry made Cecilia jump – 'we must destroy that capitalism that blinds a worker to slavery. We stand for a new dignity for the poor, for the destruction of the church dictatorship and the end of the leadership of the White House...'

'I love elections,' Patch said. 'Pity it doesn't mean that the people of Anapoli can take a vote on whether to cork up the mountain or not. Freedom congeals a bit when Pelli decides that even if they're right to demand action, he's righter to refuse it.'

The siren of the *Città di Salerno* boomed. The little ferry boat looked clean alongside the black bulk of the *Great Watling Street* which was blurred and indistinct through the rain further down the mole.

'Time to go,' Patch said. He picked up Cecilia's case and moved to the door. She followed him, her expression puzzled.

'Why are you really coming?' she asked, as he paused by the door.

He frowned, finding it hard to tell her of the night he had spent poring over her grandfather's books, to tell her even that he had discovered the truth in Hannay's claim that no man could be an island. For years he had gone his way, cloaked in his own ego – but now he had found that her distress and Mamma Meucci's worry and Don Dominico's doubt in Fumarola, even Hannay's anxiety over Cristoforo, had become personal, had linked him to the rest of them as surely as if he were bound by threads of flesh and tendon.

And besides, he was oddly scared at the thought that he'd be lonely without her in the flat below, without the sound of her singing in the kitchen, without the rare moments of gentleness and affection over the coffee. It was an awareness that had come suddenly to him, for in his absorption with painting he'd never considered Cecilia much except as a free model.

At first he'd thought the feeling sprang perhaps from the fact that she was pretty and there weren't a great many pretty girls among the sturdy stock of Anapoli, then he realised he had always listened for her voice and watched her covertly as she came and went on the stairs, with a wistfulness he had never noticed until now.

'I'm coming because I'm sick of myself,' he said, dropping into his old mood, and immediately concern came into her expression. 'Because it's time I had a change. Because there may be something in what you say about Amarea. Because, if something is done, I want to collect a little of the glory and say "I told you so". Because I'm sick of painting and I'm sick of drinking and I'm sick of the island. I'm sick of everything and I don't know why.' He chuckled suddenly, as a spark of devilry prompted his final remark. 'And finally because Pelli's after me.'

Cecilia's expression had become tender as she listened to him but at the mention of Pelli the anger mounted at once to her cheeks. Trying to keep her eyes away from his, she watched the mothers at the bar counter buying sticky sweets to occupy their children on the journey, the old women laden with bundles going to see married daughters on the mainland, the men with enormous suitcases of shoddy raffia goods they hoped to sell. But her glance found its way back to his face in the end, and she was unable to keep the anxiety out of her voice.

'What does Pelli want with you?' she asked.

'My skin, I suspect. A question of some posters. He came round to see me. Personally. Mamma Meucci sent one of the kids to Emiliano's to warn me. I bought this toothbrush ten minutes ago.'

Cecilia was standing stiffly upright now. 'Why not tell Pelli that what you said you believed?'

Patch shrugged. 'Because, little Cecilia, I'm not sure that I do. And I'm not the stuff that martyrs are made of. Pelli's boys might get excited if they bumped into me one night in the Via Maddalena. Some of Bosco's supporters tried to set their dogs on Don Alessandro last night, I heard. I'd rather wait until it's all over and I can walk down the Via Maddalena in peace.'

He looked out at the rain, then down at Cecilia and stepped outside.

'It happens also,' he said with a grin, 'that I know an American who might help. Man called Raphael. He's a geologist in his spare time and he's crazy about volcanoes.'

## twenty-one

The sun was shining when they reached the mainland the next morning. Piles of cumulus, in great continents, dappled the blue sea with yellow as they towered over the houses standing out in blocks of white paint and black shadow all the way down the hillside to the harbour. The palace of the old kings emerged from the mass of buildings in a yellow block of stone with the dome of the Cathedral gleaming alongside it.

A loudspeaker van was standing just inside the parking area of the basin as they climbed ashore.

'The beauties of this city are incompatible with the Marxian system,' it was announcing. 'The materialism of this creed does not – cannot fit into the culture of Italy –

'Oh, God,' Patch said. 'Here, too!'

As they headed for the jangling little trams that ran past the gate, a woman handed them a leaflet each, decorated with the hammer and sickle sign, and, across the road, three young men carried a banner on which was written: 'Bread and Liberty. Vote Communist.'

The hotel Cecilia took him to was a bleak little place near the station which went by the august name of the Albergo del Bello Sole. It was situated on the top floor of an ancient block of buildings and its rooms were as cheerless as the district that housed it.

They were too late to attempt anything that day so Patch took Cecilia to the opera, delighting her with one of the best seats near to the royal box, buying her flowers and enjoying her blushes as he handed them to her. She seemed quite different from the Cecilia he had got used to on Anapoli, alive suddenly and radiant, as though her moodiness had dropped away from her as they had crossed the Tyrrhenian, and he sat back, enjoying the vitality and the youth in her face as she applauded. Afterwards, he took her to a night club, bribing the attendant to let them in, and they danced until Patch became involved in a noisy argument with an American sailor and they found it wiser to leave.

Still laughing, they hired a carriage to take them home, a ramshackle affair smelling of old leather and brass polish, and he sat with his arm round her while the ancient horse plodded through the steep streets, the driver dozing on his box.

The night was milky warm and they could smell the sea, and they both had a feeling of freedom from the uneasy obsession with Amarea that existed in the Via Pescatori and Emiliano's Bar. Cecilia's happiness had not left her. Indeed it had grown, but the gaiety had subsided now and she was calm, as though all her old hostility towards Patch had never existed and they were back in the days when he'd first arrived on Anapoli and found her eager to help, to speak English with him, to show him around, to do all the little things that would make him feel at home.

Patch paid off the carriage by the Albergo del Bello Sole and they ascended in the creaking lift. As they stopped outside Cecilia's door, she slipped inside but half-closed it in front of him when he made to follow her.

'I'm not Mrs Hayward,' she said.

He stared down at her for a moment, then he grinned, admitting defeat.

'Thank God. She talked too much. Even in bed.'

'Poor Mrs Hayward,' Cecilia murmured. 'Did you treat her very badly?'

Patch laughed ruefully. 'If I did a bit of soul-searching,' he said, 'I suppose I'd admit I did. It was what she asked for, but that's no excuse.'

The following morning, Patch tried to insist on another carriage to the university but Cecilia wanted to walk and he found himself enjoying the warmth of the sunshine after the angry weather of Anapoli. He took her hand and they pushed through the crowded streets happily, both of them curiously light of heart.

There was a Communist demonstration near the docks, with youngsters carrying placards and banners and jeering at the American tourists who were coming off the ships and trying to find taxis out of the glare of the sun. Then a group of students from the university burst on to the procession and tried to break it up and a fight ensued. The struggle swayed across the street, more pushing and shouting than fisticuffs, and finally the police swept down and the crowds fled into the fly-blown little alleys behind the harbour like dust before a wind, upsetting the crude stalls of the street vendors and sending the shining fish and the eggs and the shabby trinkets flying.

'God-damn all politics,' Patch said, lashing out furiously, his good humour gone, as he dragged Cecilia out of the way of the running youths and steered her to the university.

A lecturer in the Department of Volcanology, situated in the top floor of a building that on one side looked over what had been a palace garden and on the other the city slums, led them along a wide, marbled corridor dim with shadows to a room marked with the name, *'Professor Camaldoli'*, where a small man with dark glasses and a long Neapolitan nose was reading a newspaper under the green shadow of an old-fashioned desk light. Spread in front of him were several other newspapers and all round him on the oppressive crimson wallpaper were lurid paintings of eruptions.

The little man behind the desk looked up over his glasses and smiled gaily, showing several gold teeth. He indicated a couple of Medici chairs in front of him.

'They tell me there was a fight near the harbour a little while ago,' he said cheerfully. 'How do you think the elections will go?'

'I don't know,' Patch replied. 'I'm not very interested.'

Camaldoli's friendly face fell and he hurriedly pulled forward a pad and a newly sharpened pencil.

'My apologies,' he said briskly. 'I get so carried away. So much is at stake. How can we help you?'

While Cecilia told him why they had come, Camaldoli listened in silence, his elbows on the desk, his chin on his clenched fists, the picture of interest. The minute she had finished, he sat back, picked up his pencil, toyed thoughtfully with it for a second, threw it down with a gesture, and spread his hands palms down on the desk.

'You say your name is Leonardi, signorina,' he said thoughtfully. 'Are you – would you be related at all to a Dr Leonardi, also of Anapoli Porto?'

'He's my grandfather.'

Camaldoli's cheerfulness had vanished as he opened the drawer of a steel file behind him and took out a folder. 'These,' he explained glumly, 'are Dr Leonardi's letters. The last one's dated six months ago – last autumn. It desires that we send an expert with gravimeters to make tests on Mont Amarea. It suggests also that, failing this, we should permit him the use of our instruments. If he only knew their value!' He raised his eyebrows at the aside. 'It suggests he might be taken on our staff as an observer. It suggests that the island's in danger of disintegration, following an eruption of Mont Amarea. It suggests, in fact, all manner of disasters.'

He placed the file in front of them, and turned the sheets of paper over with smooth pale fingers. 'This is another, dated the year before that. According to this one, Anapoli's about to be swallowed up in a vast subterranean explosion. This one, the previous spring, states that the lava is on the point of overflowing.

'Those are the warnings,' he explained. 'One a year without fail. These – he turned the file over and opened it at the back – 'these are what you might call urgent letters, not offering information but merely calling for help.' He paused and peered at the pile of papers. 'Nineteen twenty-two. That's the date on the first one, though there may have been earlier ones which weren't filed. They've come almost six-monthly ever since. We've a matter of over fifty. And we've not yet had a request from the authorities to go there over and above our normal routine visit. And Anapoli's still there.'

He paused, obviously trying hard not to be too depressing in spite of the unspoken hint of what he thought of their mission. 'Signorina,' he said. 'It's unfortunate that Anapoli's such a long way off. Perhaps because of that it's been a little neglected. But there's no money for small islands and dying volcanoes. We're not a government department. There is no government department concerned with volcanoes.'

He saw Patch's surprise.

'Is it so fantastic as it seems,' he asked, 'when you consider how dangerous it is to cross the road and how few people are killed by eruptions? However, we're hoping one day to erect observatories on the sides of every existing volcano. Small ones, of course, but the type of volcano we have here in Italy can largely be predicted without observatories. They have cycles and we can predict when the cycles are arriving with our instruments.'

'Is one arriving now?' Patch interrupted.

Camaldoli spread his hands and looked vaguely sheepish. 'It's not possible to predict exactly what a volcano will do,' he admitted. 'The science of volcanology is still in its infancy. But we check regularly. It's only three months since we had someone at Anapoli making gravimetric measurements. They travelled right round Amarea.'

'Can't they come again?'

Carnaldoli shrugged. 'We can't be in two places at once. Perhaps in a few weeks...'

He saw the look on Cecilia's face and hurried to explain. 'No volcano in Italy becomes dangerously active so quickly you can't afford to wait,' he said. 'And Amarea, in spite of the rumbles, has long since been pronounced dead.'

# twenty-two

In the days that followed, they tried everyone they could think of but the reactions were sickeningly disappointing. The officials of the Ministry of the Interior whom they contacted referred them back immediately to the university.

'It's no concern of ours,' they said. 'Not until *after* an eruption. Then we organise relief and help. Until then, only the universities are interested. Have you tried the Ministry of Education?'

Patch felt curiously like laughing. Somehow, the brooding viciousness of Amarea didn't seem to fit among the statistics showing the incidence of success among twelve-year-old scholars and the tendency of university students to leave when they were married.

At the newspaper offices, everyone was too busy with the election to investigate suggestions of neglect on Anapoli among the bigger issues at stake, especially after Dr Leonardi's repeated warnings that had never come to anything.

'We'll mention it, of course,' they said. 'But everything but the election and the international news is cut to a minimum at the moment.'

In the end, Patch even tried the British Consulate. But, 'This is an Italian affair,' they said. 'It's no concern of ours. Naturally if anything happened, we should do all in our power to help.'

Patch had to admit failure, but to Cecilia he tried to appear still confident. 'There's always Major Raphael,' he said cheerfully. 'He's a go-ahead type. Let's try him.'

When the clerk ushered them into his office, Raphael was admiring the view from the window. It was a pleasant view across the roofs with a strip of blue sea and the grey slopes of the mountains in the distance where the bay curved out to the headland. Just below him a large palm gave it an exotic African touch. The whole picture seemed to be splashed with gold and striped with shadow, and through the open window he could hear the gay trumpeting of motor horns and the high-pitched chatter of children's voices in the street below.

Raphael turned away from the view reluctantly as the door opened.

'Thanks, Hauser,' he said to the clerk, and came forward to meet Patch. He pushed chairs forward for them and sat down again behind his desk, brisk and efficient.

'Shoot,' he said vigorously. 'If it's in my power to do anything, I'll do it. You know that.'

Patch explained their mission and Raphael's lean handsome face looked owlish from behind his spectacles.

'Sounds rugged,' he said when they'd finished.

He thoughtfully pushed a photograph straight on his desk and Patch saw it was a pretty girl in an officer's uniform.

Raphael sat for a moment in silence, thinking, then he looked up again at Patch, his eyes mildly interested.

'Why have you come to me particularly?' he asked.

Patch hesitated before he spoke. It seemed fantastic that most of their fears were based only on the feelings of a young boy and a frightened girl and a stubborn sea-captain, none of whom had been born at the time of Amarea's last real evidences of activity, but it seemed even more fantastic that they couldn't persuade anyone to listen to them. He began to wish Hannay were alongside him, square and solid and immovable, to add his weight to the argument, In his self-righteous way, he was so convinced of danger, he could almost feel the stirring under Amarea through the soles of his shoes.

'We wanted your help,' he said. 'The authorities on the island won't do anything.'

Raphael's expression became immediately guarded. 'Why not?' he asked.

'Because they're too busy with the election.'

Raphael grinned at Cecilia. 'It's tough, isn't it? You can't get served anywhere.' He paused, swinging back to Patch. 'But, hell, if the thing's flinging out rocks and scoriae, they've *got* to do something.'

'It isn't flinging out rocks – not yet.'

Raphael's expression altered again, and this time there was a hint of doubt in his eyes.

'Then what is it doing?'

'Smoking.'

'Yeah, but what else?'

'Rumbling.'

'That's nothing.'

'All the animals and birds have left the place.'

'It happens regularly on Etna and Vesuvius and Stromboli. Etna's having a go now, in fact.'

'So is Amarea. It's smoking.'

'Steaming,' Raphael corrected.

'Smoking,' Patch insisted.

'Have it your own way. But it's not active enough to erupt. It's not erupted for two hundred years. I've got the data somewhere. There's been an occasional dusting of ash round the crater. Nothing more. Popocatapetl steams and that's extinct.'

'To me that's a reminder that it's active.' Patch felt that he was almost quoting Dr Leondardi. 'It's active until it grows grass in the crater. And then it could *still* be active.'

Raphael rubbed his nose. 'Maybe,' he agreed. 'But it doesn't *sound* very active. What else?'

Again Patch felt that sense of hopelessness. 'Nothing else,' he said finally. He glanced at Cecilia but she was sitting silently, allowing him to deal with Raphael on his own.

'Nothing?' the American was saying.

'No.'

'Well, what are you worrying about?'

'Oh, God' – Patch lit a cigarette quickly – 'it's something you can't explain. It's something you couldn't put down in an official report. You can just *feel* something's going to happen. I'm beginning to feel it now.'

Raphael was thoughtfully rubbing his nose again. 'Doesn't sound much to go on,' he said. He was silent for a while, then the buzzer on his desk went. He pressed a switch and Hauser's voice came on the loudspeaker.

'Lieutenant Andreas on the 'phone, sir.'

'OK. Put her through.'

He picked up the telephone. 'Hi, Freddy! How do you feel this morning?'

He listened, smiling, and Patch and Cecilia could hear the high-pitched voice of a woman in the earphone.

Raphael laughed into the instrument. 'Fine. That's fine,' he said. 'Only I'm tied up just now. But it sounds a good idea.' He glanced at Patch and Cecilia. 'Give me a minute or two, will you? I'll ring you back.'

He put down the instrument.

'Just got myself engaged,' he said, smiling. 'She's out here from home, too. Now, then, where is this place?'

He rose enthusiastically and crossed to a map of the Mediterranean on the wall.

'My, Tom,' he said 'It's a hell of a way out. I didn't realise it was so far. What can I do from here?'

'Nothing. How about coming and looking at it?'

Raphael's smile had disappeared. 'It would take a week to get there and back, and, man, that's a long time. I'd have to take some leave for that. 'And' – he began to look dogged – 'I've just got engaged, Tom.'

He suddenly seemed to realise he was not being very helpful. 'Just a moment,' he said. 'I've got an idea. You ought to be able to see if there's anything going on there from the air. The flying boys are always on missions over the Tyrrhenian. They could maybe lay one on over the island and take a look-see for you.'

He jiggled the telephone switch. 'Hauser,' he said. 'You know Major Holly? Get hold of him, will you?'

He dropped the telephone and came round the desk again, talking, pretending enthusiasm, but Patch knew his heart wasn't in it. He glanced at Cecilia but she was sitting silently in her chair, her face pale.

Raphael was telling them about a party he'd been to the night before when the telephone rang again. He reached out a long arm.

'That you, Nick? Listen, I want you to do something for me – '

He explained what he wanted, then stopped as the man on the other end of the line replied.

'What's that? Yesterday? Yeah, do that.'

He looked up at Patch. 'A ship reported smoke from your island,' he said. 'Thought it might be another ship on fire. One of the fighter boys was directed to have a look at it. Holly's getting the report now.'

He looked down at the telephone as the distant Holly spoke again.

'That all?' he asked. 'Nothing more than that? OK. Thanks. That helps a lot.'

He replaced the telephone with the expression of a man with a job well done behind him.

'You can go back and tell them there's nothing to worry about,' he said. 'That pilot said there was nothing to see.'

'What was he looking for?' Patch asked.

'Oh, nothing, particularly. He just had a look and then came home and reported it wasn't a ship.'

'Did he examine the crater?'

'Sure he did. The report says he could see right into it.'

'Seeing something's different from examining it.'

'Well' – Raphael began to look a little indignant – 'he went to look at a ship not a mountain. Why should he be interested in volcanoes? He's seen 'em all round here. He knows it's there. He knows it has a plume of steam – or smoke, if you want it that way. It's on his charts. Why should he lose any hair over it? He's probably flown over it dozens of times, like he has over Stromboli and Vesuvius and Etna. It's nothing new to him.'

'Look, Curt,' Patch said seriously. 'It's not just for me. There are other people involved. Even one or two Americans. We want some real advice.'

'What's wrong with that?'

'It's not advice. We want to start the authorities moving.'

Raphael frowned. 'Listen, Tom,' he said quietly, and there was stubbornness in his expression now. 'Get this straight: I don't want to tangle with the authorities. I'm here because I'm doing a surveying job for the fleet in Naples, that's all. And the United States Navy's not here to run the country. It's just what the Commies want – for us to poke our nose in where it shouldn't be, so they could claim interference and toss us out our base.'

'OK, thanks.' Patch rose. His smile was tired. 'Thanks, Curt. Let's go, Cecilia.'

'I just got engaged,' Raphael said despairingly. 'Things are different now.'

'It doesn't matter.'

'Hold it, Tom.' Raphael was scribbling frantically on a piece of paper, desperately trying to show how helpful he could be. 'How about seeing this old boy? Guy called Marotta. He's a bit of an expert. He's retired now, but I guess he'll help you. Especially if there's money in it. You can find him in Tazzi's Bar in the Galleria Savoia any time before noon. Marotta, that's his name. Marotta.'

## twenty-three

But Marotta was too old – too old and too infirm. In spite of the heat, he sat outside Tazzi's in a heavy overcoat, his sharp birdlike face and yellow skin indicating that he had been half-starved over a long period.

He listened politely to Patch, his attention still partly on the sound of the political arguments that came from the bars and shops and hairdressers' saloons in the high vaulted arcade where the tattered children begged for coins and the wings of the pigeons made echoes in the high glass roof, but his face never showed much interest except when they offered him another coffee and a drink.

'Volcanoes are born pranksters,' was all he could say. He repeated it – again and again interspersing his mumbled explanations of the workings of Vesuvius and Etna with it.

'Volcanoes are born pranksters.'

Clearly he had no intention of moving from his comfortable seat and, looking at his withered fingers and tired eyes, Patch felt he could hardly blame him. They contented themselves in the end with getting from him the name of a professor of geology who was acting as adviser on several building operations in the district and went to see him instead. But the professor was a smart professional with what was clearly a thriving practice and he seemed hostile from the first, going to enormous lengths to describe how busy he was and how big his fees would be. He seemed to regard Cecilia and Patch as a couple of nervous neurotics.

'How long has the mountain been there?' he asked, hardly troubling to hide the contempt in his voice. 'Millions of years. How many times has it erupted? Within human knowledge about three or four. Why should it choose this particular moment? If you're so afraid of Amarea,' he concluded, 'why not try Capri? It's very beautiful there and I can assure you there are no volcanoes.'

Patch bought a newspaper as they left, reading it in the trolley bus as they jolted down the hill.

In the streets beyond the tram tracks there were still a lot of students shouting out of doorways at their opponents and waving banners from windows, while crowds of children like flies enjoyed the noise and the excitement.

They found a little restaurant by the harbour overlooking the sea, where an elderly troubadour was trying to sing 'Canto nella Valle' to an American woman tourist, accompanying himself with refined gestures and sneaked glances at the verses on the card concealed in his left hand. Behind him, a stout business man swathed in a napkin studied the half-page-deep headlines announcing some new world crisis and linking it obscurely with the election. A loudspeaker at an outdoor meeting round the corner drowned with election slogans the café noises and the thin voice of the singer, but oddly, in spite of their failures and the racket about them, Cecilia seemed content. The city had a calming quality with its flowers and its trees and the glimpses of the bay that kept appearing through the houses as they moved about, which somehow each night had managed without fail to drive away the frustrations of the day.

'It's beautiful here,' she said, her hand across the table in Patch's.

'Pity he's flat.' Patch commented, glancing at the singer.

Cecilia drew her hand away quickly. Patch's remark had broken into her happiness and she suddenly saw that the

166

singer was old and his voice none too good, and that the café they were in was shabbier than she had thought under the gilt and the mirrors.

'Why do you say that?' she asked bitterly. 'I don't mind him being flat. I don't mind if he hasn't learned the words. Or that he's fifty and bald. I'm happy. I'm happy because it's warm and pleasant and because I like the lights on the water, and I like the singing. Why must you spoil it all?'

Patch smiled indulgently and secured her hand again. 'Don't take any notice of me, Cecilia,' he said. 'It's a habit I'll try to break.'

But the mood was lost and even when he tried to tease her, she smiled at him a little abstractedly so that he knew her thoughts weren't on what he was saying.

'Tom,' she asked at last. 'Do you think there's any hope? Of getting help, I mean.'

He paused before replying, then he dragged from his pocket the newspaper he had bought earlier and laid it in front of her significantly. She looked up at him, her eyes questioning, and he pointed to a paragraph at the bottom of the page.

In spite of their protests of disinterest, the newspaper had pursued their story about Amarea, and Cecilia found herself staring at what was a brief defence of Pelli. Apparently, he had reacted to Bosco's goading by sending a couple of policemen up Mont' Amarea to investigate. There had been nothing to see beyond a little dust and a little smoke. Even the lake at the side of the crater had looked quite normal, but the paragraph ended with a condemnation of Bosco and a claim that he had been trying to discredit the authorities who had merely taken this wise step to deprive him of his arguments. The breaking of the Ruffio dam and the flooding of Vicinamontana were mentioned – obviously as a parallel – and the whole story was a complete vindication of Pelli.

'I didn't mention this before, Cecilia,' Patch said gently. 'I didn't want to spoil the evening. But Pelli's swept the ground from under our feet. Nothing we can say to anyone will do much good now. They'll all quote this back at us.'

Cecilia looked downcast and he touched her hand across the table again. 'You asked me, Cecilia,' he said earnestly, wishing he could say something to take the disappointment out of her face. 'I'm as anxious as you are. Once I didn't care a damn, but you and Hannay seem to have an odd effect on me. You bring out the latent crusader in me.' He shrugged. 'Unfortunately, though, we're crusaders without a crusade now. Pelli's taken it away from us. We can't move anyone with this in front of them screaming out loud that we're a couple of crackpots with nothing to prove what we're saying.'

As they walked along the sea front, the lights of the city behind them sprinkled the hillside in blocks, and the neon signs on the dark bulk of the ancient castle by the harbour stood out sharply in a splash of colour against the night. Up against the sea wall the naphtha flare of a chestnut vendor spluttered noisily as the breeze caught it, and from a café a juke box blared out an Italian version of 'Somebody Stole My Gal'.

The Albergo del Bello Sole looked bleaker at night than during the day, with its solitary unshaded bulbs dragging the shadows out of the corners of the corridors. As the lift laboured upwards, Patch gently put an arm round Cecilia's shoulders and pulled her to him, and she leaned against him, saying nothing.

A wave of affection for him swept over her and she made no attempt to shut the door in his face as she had on previous nights. After a pause, he followed her inside the room.

For a moment, he fiddled with the light switch, twisting it round in its socket until it made its faulty contact and the bulb, inevitably too small, filled the room with a grey dusty light that seemed only to make it shabbier.

She watched him as he moved across from the door, a lean figure with curves of humour on his features. It was a face that had known joy and disappointment and triumph, a face that was capable, as she well knew, of tenderness as well as sarcasm. He was infuriating, unpredictable, at times intolerable, but extravagantly generous, and all the gentleness, all the warm comfort of shared troubles that she had in a world which sometimes in her youth seemed too big to be borne came in sporadic bursts from Patch in a way they never did from Piero. Piero demanded a one-way love that was armed with jealousy. Patch's affection was mature and sometimes barbed, but when he wasn't engrossed in painting, entirely unselfish.

'I'm glad we're going home,' she said at last.

It was hot and Patch took off his jacket and lowered himself to the edge of the hard bed. Cecilia sat down on the other side, her back to him, her earlier happiness dispersed completely.

'Why can we get so little done?' she said with a choked, furious anger. 'Why do so many people talk and do nothing else? I thought it was only on Anapoli we could achieve so little.'

'Cecilia, why *should* people do anything?' Patch turned towards her, trying to calm her, trying to protect her a little from her own impatience. 'The authorities aren't complaining.'

'But why not? Tom – ' she was pleading with him, trying to understand the evasions, the inertia, ' – they *ought* to complain.'

Patch felt a twinge of conscience. as though he had no right to shatter her illusions. 'Cecilia, this world's full of people who talk in half-truths. It's full of ambitious people, and even people who're so obsessed with doing good that

169

they manage to do harm to achieve it. It's a hard fact to face but it's easier when you do face it. The ones at the top sometimes forget the ones at the bottom. They're so engrossed with the big things they overlook the fact that there might be small things, too.'

He reached across the bed and laid his fingers softly against her cheek. Her unlined face looked young in its baffled anger and Patch was touched with a feeling of tenderness towards her.

'Cecilia,' he said. 'Remember what Marotta's friend said? Why not go to Capri? There's no danger there. There's no one shouting bloody murder because he can't run the world the way *he* wants it. I could get somewhere to paint. There are always rooms free at this time of the year in Anacapri.'

'Are *you* going?' She looked sharply at him. With the older civilisation that stood behind her and the blood of an older race that ran in her veins, she had always felt vaguely wiser than Patch and strangely condescending towards him, in spite of her youth; but suddenly there was no condescension, no anger, only a small frightened feeling that he might be leaving.

He was studying her features now as she turned and faced him. They were lost and afraid, and he desperately wanted to bring the smiles back to them.

'I'll have to go some time,' he explained. 'I am painted-out on Anapoli. Besides,' he added, 'Spring's here. The flowers'll be out. All the way up from Marina Grande. The sea'll be bluer than we've seen it at Anapoli for a long time. You belong there. Not in that ugly great building in the Porto. We could sit on the wall on the way up to Anacapri and splash paint on canvas until we're sickened with colour.'

She smiled weakly back at him, then she put her hand over his where it rested on her cheek.

'No, Tom,' she said. 'I can't. You're offering me nothing but a good holiday. Eventually I'd have to give it up. Piero's offering me marriage.'

Patch stood up and walked to the window. 'That's true,' he said slowly. 'And in spite of what I've said about Piero, I hope you're happy, Cecilia.'

He turned and looked at her, his lean face smiling, and in that moment she found the answer to all the questions that had been troubling her; the cause of all her guilt when she had found herself regarding Piero as a spoiled sullen boy who belonged to the past years of her life; the cause of all her pleasure when she met Patch every morning in the little café outside the hotel where they breakfasted; the cause of her anxiety at the thought that he might be late. All her rebellion against Piero's possessiveness and the ready acceptance of the match by her grandfather and old Tornielli, all the times when she had found it hard to be civil to Patch, all the reason for her anger that lay hidden deep in jealousy for the other women he knew, were explained as it dawned on her she was in love with him and had been for some time.

Patch was looking at his watch and she was surprised in her sudden nightmare of hope and misery and great joy that he could be unaware of how she had changed.

'I must go,' he said gently. 'It's getting late and I must leave you a reputation for Piero.'

'I am not making you go, Tom,' she said, surprised to realise she hadn't thought of reputations – either her own or Patch's. There had been a time once when Patch's had shocked her, and later when she had regarded it with tolerance. Now, suddenly, she realised how unimportant it was, how unimportant her own was, for that matter, as she tried to tell him of her new love, of the heart sickness and the sudden pain she was feeling, the fear, the sense of emptiness and fruitlessness that was growing on her.

Patch had glanced quickly over his shoulder at her from the door as she spoke. He could see her trembling and he knew it wasn't because of any chilliness in the room. Then he remembered the look that Piero always gave him, and what they all thought of him among the proper little villas above Anapoli Porto. There was no reason why Cecilia, looking as young as she did now, should be saddled with his past and all his weary old love affairs.

'Now you're being grateful – or something,' he said quietly, hardly daring to look at her.

'I'm not, Tom! I'm not!' She took his hand and hung on to it, pleading with her eyes, wondering why he didn't see the love that she felt must be glowing and obvious in her face.

He studied her for a while, all his instincts telling him not to turn his back on her.

'Then I am,' he said finally. 'And I'm not going to take advantage of it.'

He saw the unhappiness in her eyes and took her arms and, lifting her to her feet, kissed her hard on the mouth. Then, before she had time to respond, he released her and turned away.

Closing the door behind him, he stood in the corridor with his hands in his pockets, staring at his feet.

'God,' he said aloud. 'I must be getting old.'

*twenty-four*

---

When the *Città di Salerno* reached the island again, the weather was gloomy, growing steadily worse as they recrossed the Tyrrhenian.

Hannay was standing on the mole as the ship turned into the harbour. Behind him the houses, darkened with the rain of the last few days, rose in tiers like the icing of a battered cake, the windows with their sun-bleached shutters staring blankly across the water. Beyond them, the mountain emptied of habitation as it rose, except for a few small villas and the bulk of Forla's magnificent palace, built in a fold of the slope to catch the sun all day, then the purple, grey and green sides rose steeply to the ash-coloured peak half-hidden in the clouds, arbitrary and murderous.

Hannay watched the ship approach. He was frowning heavily for, in the last three days, Amarea had begun to manifest its activity with a new form of evil, a high-pitched whistle that had a curiously penetrating quality. It had started softly at first and he hadn't realised where it came from, then it grew gradually louder until now it had a faint fine piercing note but oddly enough still no direction, so that it seemed to come from everywhere at once.

It was audible in Hannay's cabin and in the saloon of the *Great Watling Street* when he worked with his books and his loading charts spread across the table; in Emiliano's when he walked there for his coffee or his evening drink; in the taxi when he went up to Orlesi's office outside the Villa Forla to complain about the delayed loading of the sulphur. It was louder up there on the mountainside – but still no more than the thin pipe of a simmering pot. Orlesi had pretended not to hear it, even when Hannay had drawn his attention to it, but Hannay had known all along that he did hear it, because when its pitch had changed faintly – so faintly the difference in the note was almost indistinguishable – Orlesi had stopped in the middle of a long-winded excuse about the loading and his eyes had flickered towards the mountain. His pause had lasted only a fraction of a second then he had continued as though nothing had happened, but it was long enough for Hannay to notice it.

Nothing more had occurred, however. The smoke had not increased and there had been no more ash dust on San Giorgio. And this high-pitched whistling had become so much a part of the everyday life of the town that even Hannay, as he worked over his books and telephoned his bitter complaints to Orlesi, had begun to accept it as normal.

He watched the *Città di Salerno*, for a while, admiring her captain's handling of her, then he turned and looked further down the mole.

A big yacht which had arrived in the night was moored there, all gleaming brass and chrome, from the stall of the yacht-club flag on her bow to the plated name, *Canzone del Mare,* screwed to her stern. A big car was waiting alongside, and luggage was being handed ashore and pushed out of sight.

A group of young men who had been standing watching, turned, stared at the approaching *Città di Salerno,* then almost like a company of soldiers, swung round and headed towards Hannay. In their lead, he realised, was Bruno Bosco, the Communist candidate.

Hannay recognised him at once from the pictures that placarded the town, a sharp-featured man with sly eyes and strong lines of humour round his mouth. Behind him, the squad of young men all seemed to be dressed remarkably alike and were all notable for their stern, expressionless faces.

Bosco appeared to recognise Hannay, too, for he stopped and addressed him gaily.

' *'n giorno, Signor Capitano*,' he said. 'I see Forla's with us at long last.' He indicated the yacht alongside the mole and Hannay nodded, wondering why Bosco should trouble to be so friendly with him, an English sea-captain with no vote.

'Still, we're bringing up our big guns too,' Bosco went on cheerfully. 'We've a meeting tonight and we have Deputy Sporletti on the *Città di Salerno*.'

Hannay still said nothing and Bosco grinned. 'Not that Sporletti's ever been a minister like Forla,' he explained. 'But a deputy's a deputy anywhere – and we don't see them often on Anapoli.' He paused and Hannay could almost see the thoughts turning over in his mind. Then, with his next words, he knew why Bosco had singled him out to be the object of his good cheer.

'I hear Signor Patch went to the mainland to find a volcanologist,' he said. 'Was he successful?'

'I hope so.'

Bosco's smile had vanished as he turned away. 'It doesn't suit our policy to have volcanologists on the island,' he said. 'I told Signor Patch so. Not now. Perhaps next week it'll be different.'

The gangway of the *Città di Salerno* was touching the black basalt blocks of the mole by this time and Bosco and his henchmen formed up in a line at the end of it. The first of the passengers were brushed aside as a small man with a mean mouth and thick glasses stepped on to the gangplank. Accompanied by a flourishing of clenched fists from Besco and his followers, he received a bunch of flowers and was borne away in the centre of Bosco's group up the Via Maddalena.

Hannay watched them go. It was drizzling again and the wind was whipping at his trousers. Behind the town, the blue hazy outline of Amarea rose to the clouds which flattened the thin column of smoke in a plate-like shadow.

The whistle was there still, lost somewhere in the clouds but quite distinct when the bustle along the mole quietened for a moment. Hannay listened to it for a while, picking it out from the cries of the people greeting relatives, his head cocked, almost wishing the mountain would manifest its internal activity with a few more histrionics. The whistle, in spite of its threat, after a time seemed no more dangerous than the singing of a kettle.

A noisy little Lambretta drew up alongside him and Piero Tornielli dismounted.

'Nearly missed her,' Hannay commented.

'I was delayed,' Piero panted. 'Has she disembarked yet?'

'Not yet.' Hannay stared up the gangplank. 'You just made it.'

'He went too, didn't he?'

'Who did?'

'Tom Patch.' Piero's intense gaze was on the ship. 'He thinks I don't know. But I do. Everybody in the town knows he went with her.'

Hannay glanced at the flushed furious face beside him, then he saw Patch and Cecilia at the top of the gangplank and began to move forward.

Patch seemed tired as he stepped ashore. Cecilia, who looked a little subdued, was immediately swept from the gangway by Piero.

'I hope you're satisfied,' he said loudly to Patch over his shoulder. 'I suspected some intrigue of this kind when I saw you waiting for the boat last week.'

Patch shrugged, with an indifference that humiliated Piero. 'I hope you're highly satisfied at having your theories proved right,' he said.

Piero's face went dark with anger and his whole body shook as he fought to find the biting reply that persisted in eluding him. He took Cecilia's arm to stop himself leaping at Patch and tried to lead her away, but she hung back to listen as Hannay stepped forward.

'Well?' he asked.

'Well, nothing.' Patch didn't seem to notice Piero's furious face.

'Nothing?' Hannay stared. 'You mean you've brought nobody back with you?' His eyes swung from Patch's face to Cecilia's.

'It's as Tom says,' Cecilia said quietly. 'No one would do anything. They all seemed afraid.'

She appeared to be depressed and glad to accept Piero's attentions, and Piero was startled enough to swallow his fury. He touched her arm again and they disappeared without saying good-bye.

An odd expression on his face, Patch watched the little Lambretta chugging along the mole with Cecilia sitting side-saddle on the rear seat, apparently indifferent to the voice of Piero who was shouting something at her over his shoulder. He seemed about to make some comment, then he thought better of it and turned to Hannay.

'What's happened here?' he asked. 'I know something has. You've got a face like an early Christian martyr.'

'Listen!' Hannay bristled immediately like a terrier after a rat. His head cocked on one side, he indicated that Patch should listen also.

'What's that whistling?'

'His royal highness. Fizzing like a bottle of ginger beer.'

'How long's it been doing that?'

'Last three days.'

'God, if only we could have taken it with us!'

'Well, you couldn't.' Hannay changed the conversation. 'The 'Aywards came to see me last night,' he said. 'Wind-up

177

again. It's this whistling, and they've heard I'll be off at the end of the week, see? Orlesi's finally got me sulphur. They've started loading at last.

He looked suddenly unhappy. 'I had another go at Devoto,' he said.

'And – ?'

'And nothing. You were right. It ain't the money he wants.' Hannay jammed his pipe into his mouth and sucked furiously on it for a moment. 'I wouldn't mind if I could only arrange something for the kid,' he said. 'I talked too much as usual. I probably made him think I could pull it off, and now I've had to tell him there's nothing doing.'

Patch made an effort to draw his mind away from Cristoforo by changing the subject.

'Will the Haywards go with you when you leave?' he asked.

Hannay looked up at him and seemed with an effort to thrust Cristoforo out of his mind. 'They said they would, but I don't suppose they will. They want their cake and eat it at the same time. Mind you, some of 'em, them what could afford it, have gone already. Hired a sailing boat when the whistle started and left for Sicily. Some more of the yachts have pulled out too – full up with all their pals. It's been a proper pantomime.'

He paused and glanced towards the fishing boats grouped off Cape Amarea. 'We haven't half had some rain while you was away,' he said. 'Rain and wind and thunder and lightning. The lot. They're scared now the lake in the crater's going to overflow. More people have left San Giorgio. I reckon they've got the wind up too. If they haven't, they oughta have. I have.'

## twenty-five

Mrs Hayward was waiting for Patch in his room when he returned. She was standing in the centre of the floor as he opened the door, her face flushed, her eyes hot, and he knew she had leapt to her feet as she had heard him in the corridor. He resisted the temptation to turn round and walk straight out again.

'So you're back,' she said.

'Yes.' Patch went to the cupboard and poured himself a drink. 'It begins to feel like it. All the old familiar faces.'

'No wonder you went. She went too! What happened?'

Patch's back was to her and he looked up over his shoulder. 'Nothing,' he said, with a smile. 'Curiously enough, nothing.'

Mrs Hayward pressed close to him, so that he could see the lines on her face that she tried so hard to hide. 'I suppose you've had a wonderful time,' she said bitterly. 'It's been murder here, with that damned mountain acting the fool again. I thought I'd go mad. And now you come back and glibly tell me nothing happened.' She laughed sarcastically. 'You don't expect me to believe that, do you? I can't imagine you losing your grip to that extent.'

Patch looked at her with an urbanity that infuriated her. 'No,' he said. 'I'm not losing my grip.'

'You're hardly the type to pass up on a chance.'

'It's one of those things the great sporting public will understand.'

She stormed to the window, baffled by his calmness, his good humour, her inability to ruffle him, then she swung

179

round on him again. 'I never thought I'd see Tom Patch – the great Tom Patch – losing his head over some sexy little slip of an Italian girl.'

Patch turned round to face her. He was still calm but his eyes were angry. 'I'm not the *great* Tom Patch,' he said. 'I'm just plain Tom Patch, and I've been travelling and I'm tired. My God, I'm tired! I'm tired of people chivvying me to do things and other people chivvying me not to do things. For your information, though I don't suppose it'll do any good because you won't believe it, Cecilia didn't go off for a dirty week-end with me. She went because she's got more guts and courage than all those bloody fools who're crying "wolf" about the mountain and aren't prepared to do anything else. Leave her alone, for God's sake! And leave me alone, too!'

He swallowed the drink and slammed the glass down so hard on the table he broke the stem. Then the door banged behind him and Mrs Hayward, her face sagging and suddenly old, heard his feet clattering down the corridor outside.

Patch clumped down the stairs, surprised to find he wasn't angry or tired any more, surprised at the ease with which he had concluded the affair. He suddenly felt better, as though he'd shifted a weight from his shoulders, and he walked towards the Piazza Martiri, too busy with his elation to notice the crowds.

The square was jammed with people and a shabby band in green frock coats decorated with peeling gold braid stood near the Garibaldi statue trying to gather numbers for Bosco's meeting. Flags had appeared at the windows while he'd been away, the national tricolour interspersed with streaming slogans and the red banners of the Communists. The bell over the church of Sant' Agata, echoed from the hillside by its companion bell of Sant' Antonio, was beating through the blare.

There was a crowd in Emiliano's. Hannay was there, completely entrenched among the group who formed the custom of the bar, clothed in authority and listened to with respect; and so was Giuseppe Givanno from San Giorgio. They were talking about the mountain and it was obvious that if Pelli and Bosco and Don Alessandro were content to let things slide, *they* weren't.

The feeling of doubt in the Porto seemed to have given place to one of distrust, the sort of distrust that had torn Italy for generations, the distrust of the North for the South, the distrust of the peasant for the landowners and for the authorities who appeared to ignore them. There were still more peasants on Anapoli than there were tradespeople and even people like Emiliano were only one generation removed from them.

Patch ignored them for a while, staring into his empty glass, his mind busy, not even hearing the flat voice of Hannay as he made his comments from time to time. Then the bitterness in the things they were saying reached through to him with the suspicion of centuries against leaders like Forla and Pelli and Bosco and even, for that matter, for the politically minded priests like Don Alessandro. They had learned years before to trust no one but themselves and being back among them began to stir Patch's blood.

'All anybody does is talk,' young Givanno was saying angrily, banging the counter to stress every word. 'There are other lawyers here on Anapoli besides Pelli. Why won't *they* do something?'

Emiliano leaned over the counter, his dark eyes wide, one hand waving gently. 'Do you think *they* want the Communists to win the election any more than Pelli does?' he asked. 'One more Communist in power, they say, means one more muscle in the Party's arm.'

'They forget the mountain killed my father.'

Emiliano's shrug symbolised the uncertainty, the lack of conviction that lay over their fears even now. 'We don't know,' he observed. 'The doctor said not at the inquest.'

'We know better.'

181

'All right then,' Emiliano said. 'There's been a bit of dust. I can stir up as much with my broom. A few belly-noises. I make worse myself after a meal.'

'It's more than that,' Givanno said angrily. 'The people of San Giorgio know it's more than that.'

'Pelli doesn't live in San Giorgio,' Emiliano shouted, beginning to get excited. 'And neither do the doctors and the lawyers!'

He reached for his drink, then stopped, staring out of the window. 'Now what is it?' he said.

He jabbed a long finger at the glass and Hannay and Patch and Leonardi crossed towards him. The bar became silent immediately as the others turned away from the counter.

Old Tornielli was hobbling across the square, shouting, and they could see from the movement on his lips rather than from the sound of his voice what he was saying.

'Signor Tom! Signor Tom!'

Patch swung the door open and the old man almost fell into his arms.

'What is it, Tornielli? What the hell's wrong?'

'Signor Tom! Alfredo Meucci and the fishermen – !'

Patch looked quickly at Hannay as Tornielli struggled for breath. 'What about Meucci?' he asked.

'Signor Tom,' the old man panted. 'Fish! Thousands of them! Millions of them! Thousands of millions! All dead and floating! Half-cooked! Boiled alive! The whole fishing fleet's come back loaded. They've enough to last a month. Mamma Meucci says come quickly. Papa Meucci's very angry and she's afraid he'll do something crazy. There's a lot of shouting and the police are there.'

There was dead silence for a moment then Emiliano dropped a glass behind the counter. It didn't break but it bounced against an enamel tin and on to a wooden floorboard. The crash startled everybody into movement.

'Come on,' Hannay said.

# twenty-six

The crowd on the mole had spread into the Piazza del Mare by the time they arrived. The fishermen had left their boats and were gathered in a group, watched by a bunch of suspicious policemen. Every one of them seemed to have a fish in his hand, showing it to someone else, pointing with it, gesturing with it. There were fish everywhere – in mounds, in baskets, in boxes, and even as the group from Emiliano's appeared they saw a fight break out as someone tried to help himself while the fishermen argued, and a couple of policemen joined in immediately. The smell of fish and salt water seemed to fill the whole square.

Among the fishermen were the farmers from the hillsides who were in town as usual to meet the *Cità di Salerno* and for the market which was always held on the day the ferry boat arrived. There were also a few people from San Giorgio, Fumarola, Colonna del Greco, and the little peasant holdings round Corti Marina, shabby gaunt men and women, trading from their carts and their bicycles and their mules. Many of them had walked across the side of the mountain and were expecting to walk back.

They were standing among the fishermen, edging out of the tides of people in the market where the smells of cheese and wine and fish hung about under the canvas-covered booths, their baskets and their rickety little stalls, even the shopping they had come for, forgotten. They were listening to the arguments and gradually joining in as they became

183

more excited, for clearly the fishermen didn't consider the finding of the fish that loaded their boats an element of good fortune.

'It's wrong to pick up fish that are dead and dying,' Meucci was shouting, waving a young cod, while his wife stood alongside him wringing her hands and looking piteously around her for someone to stop the uproar. 'A man ought to find his fish alive – even if it's harder work.'

'It's the mountain!' Dr Leonardi burst into the group like a banshee. His white locks flying, his teeth clicking madly, he pushed them all aside to make room for his gyrations, and spun round in the middle of the circle of people, his pointing fingers jabbing away, his black eyes glittering with excitement. 'It's the mountain. It'll come at the next full moon. I've been prophesying it for years.'

For once there was no laughter.

'Maybe he's right this time,' Meucci said heavily.

As Patch pushed through the crowd, Mamma Meucci grabbed his arm. 'Signor Tom,' she begged. 'Tell him to be careful what he says! Tell him to be careful!'

'For the love of God, woman,' Meucci said angrily. 'I'm not going to kill anybody!'

'Where did you find the fish, Alfredo? Patch asked above the din.

'Off Capo Amarea, Signor Tom.' Meucci pointed with the cod. 'Where we found the bubbles. Thousands of them. Acres of them. All belly-up and floating. Every one of them. In a long line that pointed to the heart of the mountain. As though a current of hot water had passed through a big shoal of them. They'd been boiled as they swam. Look.'

He swung up the codling and broke the skin.

'Look! Look at it, Signor Tom. Look at the flesh. No live fish ever had flesh like that.'

He jabbed with a horny finger at the opaque whiteness, all the sheen of freshness gone from it.

'As though it had come straight from the pan,' he said.

'There's a vent under the sea there,' Leonardi screeched, swinging round to fling a finger in the direction of Capo Amarea. 'It's worked for years. Now it's blown its stopper out. That's what killed the fish.'

He almost crooned the words and a noisy babble of talk broke out as they were passed from mouth to mouth. The place was full of gesturing people and several of the peasant women sitting on the edge of the pavement, surrounded by their families and bundles, got up and joined the crowd, and the alleys between the stalls began to empty as more people were attracted by the shouting.

Hannay was questioning young Givanno and he indicated the mountain as he turned to rejoin Patch, pushing through the throng of people, dodging the gesturing arms and avoiding the excited children.

'Pretty, ain't it?' he said.

The smoke pall seemed no thicker than on the previous day but it reached noticeably higher than it had a week before and suddenly, even with the noise of the gesticulating peasants, Patch realised that the whistle had ceased.

'It's stopped,' he said to Hannay. 'The whistling's stopped. Listen.'

'Of course it's stopped!' Dr Leonardi whirled on him. 'When you lift the lid of a simmering kettle, it stops singing. But it starts when you put it back again.'

He launched into a long description of the interior workings of a volcano, then someone started shouting and they all turned to see who it was. Bosco was standing on a cart by the Customs House. Alongside him were Deputy Sporletti and his group of followers.

'People of Anapoli,' Bosco was shouting. 'Why don't you insist on your rights? Mayor Pelli's your servant, not your master. Go and *demand* help from the mainland.'

There was a burst of cheering and Bosco began to work himself up, confident of the crowd's support.

'People of San Giorgio,' he said, addressing the shabby group which stood separate from the others. 'You've already suffered. People of Corti Marina. Centuries ago your village was wiped out. Don't leave this town today until you've been assured of safety.'

'That's it!' The voice was that of young Givanno who pushed forward, barging people aside in his excitement. 'Don't go away until they do something.'

A stall was pushed over as the crowd surged forward, the owner adding to the din as he argued and threatened, picking up his belongings in between the gestures. A barrel of fish was knocked over and the silver stream got among the feet of the crowd.

'Squat on the Town Hall steps until something's done,' Givanno yelled. 'Sell the chickens in the Mayor's office. That'll make him think.'

There was some nervous laughter and the old women on the fringes of the crowd sat down near the mole while their menfolk began to argue among their carts again, among the mules and the stalls of old clothes and the startling colours of the foodstuffs, pushing and shoving at the crowd to make room as more people became involved. Even while the uproar was going on, families were dumping their belongings on the pavement, clearly intending to stay, quarrelling with passersby who fell over the bundles.

'Storm the Town Hall,' Bosco was yelling. 'Go and see the Mayor now. He's there all right. He's drinking with Forla. I've seen him.'

'Lead us, Bruno,' Giuseppe Givanno shouted. 'Lead the way. We've plenty to talk about.' He grabbed at Bosco's sleeve, almost dragging the jacket off his back as he appealed for leadership.

Bosco jumped from the cart and set off towards the Piazza del Popolo and immediately the crowd began to follow,

Mamma Meucci dragged along with them as she clutched Meucci's arm to hold him back. Another stall went over with a splintering of woodwork and the crash of glass, and someone started singing the '*Bandiera Rossa.*' There was a little laughter, but on the faces of most of the crowd there was an expression that suggested they were after justice.

There was a noticeable sense of readiness in the Piazza del Popolo. A few policemen in their black and red uniforms were standing by the Town Hall and, as the crowd appeared, they split up and seemed to flex their muscles. The shopkeepers had already begun to put up their shutters and a few fruit-sellers who had been sitting hopefully under the arcade of the Archivio, chattering in agitated bursts about the mountain, picked up their baskets and moved out of the way hurriedly. The balconies overlooking the square were crowded already and a few clerks had appeared at the windows of the Town Hall, attracted by the noise.

The policemen hitched up their belts and spread out as the crowd surged into the piazza and gathered in front of the Town Hall, oozing to right and left of the steps like a heavy liquid. Noticeably, Bosco, had disappeared from the front and had picked a spot on the pillars at the entrance to the Archivio where the families of the farmers camped out when it rained, surrounded by all the gaudy arguments on the posters. As he climbed up, the women and the children rose from among the baskets and bundles and crowded to listen.

He was chattering gaily with his followers while the crowd swarmed round the steps of the Town Hall, shouting.

'The Lord Himself's on our side today,' he was saying to Deputy Sporletti. 'In spite of what the priests say, in spite of Don Alessandro's Masses and his Hail Marys for a win for Pelli. This is too good an opportunity to miss.'

'Come on, Mother,' he shouted to a group of women standing among the baskets of vegetables and the crates of chickens. 'Unpack your goods, again! You won't be going

home yet! Your men are staying till the Mayor does
something.'

There was more laughter and several of the farmers began
to spread their belongings more wholesale on the pavement,
much to the annoyance of the shopkeepers alongside the
Archivio, who began to shout and push people away from
their doorways.

The crowd was chanting now. 'Where's Pelli? We want
Mayor Pelli. We want action.'

Someone threw a fish towards the Town Hall and a
policeman ducked hurriedly. It landed at the top of the steps
and slithered out of sight. Then Pelli appeared, a cigarette in
one hand, a sheet of paper in the other, and waved for
silence. He looked pale but confident. Two or three of his
followers were with him, and Patch noticed Piero Tornielli
standing in the shadows just inside the doorway.

'Quiet! Quiet, everybody!' Pelli shouted. 'Please don't
panic. The situation's completely under control.'

'Under control? What about the mountain?'

Pelli swung dramatically and pointed over the roof tops
towards Amarea. The drifting column of smoke was
mingling with the low clouds still.

'What about the mountain?' he asked. 'It's doing no harm.
It's holding your houses up as it's been doing for centuries.'

'It's killing the fish,' Meucci yelled, waving his codling. 'If
it goes on there'll be no fish left in the Tyrrhenian.'

'Nonsense! There are more fish than that. And besides, if
the fish are floating, you don't have to search for them. That
makes your job easier, doesn't it?'

There was a laugh from somewhere among the farmers
and Pelli smiled, the politician getting the mood of the
crowd.

'It's giving us signs,' Leonardi shrieked suddenly. 'It's
warning us.'

'Hello, old Leonardi,' Pelli said. 'You there again? You still
issuing your warnings? When was the last one? Six months

ago? And what happened then? Nothing? Is nothing going to happen again?'

The angry faces were thawing out and a few of the men were grinning at old Leonardi, whose reputation was well known.

'Listen to me,' Pelli called. 'What damage has the mountain done?'

'It killed Givanno,' Leonardi screeched.

'Did it? The inquest said he died naturally.' There was a confused babble of conversation as the crowd began to discuss the old man's death, and Patch could hear young Givanno's voice yelling indignantly.

'Look at the mountain now,' Pelli shouted, interrupting them. 'Look at it. Does it look dangerous? It always looks like that.'

'It's smoking,' someone shouted.

'So am I!' Pelli held up his cigarette and there was a flurry of laughter. 'It's often smoked. It was smoking yesterday and the day before. You're worrying for nothing. Didn't I arrange for someone to climb to the crater and inspect it? What did they find? Nothing. You're being stirred up by troublemakers. But contrary to what your clever friends tell you, Mayor Pelli doesn't sit all day doing nothing. A scientific commission's already on its way up the mountain. Did you know that? What they discover will be available to you as soon as I receive their report.'

Leonardi began to dance on tiptoe and shout.

'Who are these experts? Name them!'

'You're certainly not one, old Leonardi,' Pelli shouted back. 'According to you, we've had a disaster here every six months since 1922. But there are a remarkable number of people in this piazza for a town that's been wiped out every six months for thirty-five years. We all look remarkably well and our buildings look excessively strong!'

The crowd laughed again and old Leonardi grew more furious.

'Name them! Name these experts!'

'I don't even know them myself. They were met at the boat and taken straight away to work. Your Moscow friends were so busy meeting their political masters from Rome they failed to notice the rest of the passengers. They were driven up the mountainside with their instruments. They're there now.'

'The bastard's lying,' Hannay exploded indignantly. 'Nobody came off that flipping ship looking like a geologist!'

'I have one other thing for you!' Pelli's shout interrupted him. 'One other thing to reassure you. You've all heard of Signor Forla.'

There was a chorus of boos and Bruno Bosco began to yell abuse from his pillar.

'Traitor! Fascist! White House toady!'

Pelli grinned. 'Signor Forla's here on the island. He's here in the Town Hall, in fact. He's here on your behalf. He's just handed me a report from his own observatory. It was brought to his yacht this morning when he arrived.'

He held up the sheet of typewritten paper he had in his hand. 'The instruments he has there have reported nothing unusual.' He grinned again, sure of the crowd now. 'Listen,' he said, his tones warm and bantering. 'One thing more – how often does Signor Forla come to this island?'

'Never,' Bosco yelled. He was puzzled now and watching Pelli's moves, his mind working quickly to counter them.

'Thank you, my friend,' Pelli said smoothly. 'Then why would he come now if there were any danger? Surely with all his money and all the houses he has to choose from he'd stay away from this one?'

The crowd had grown quieter. Even under the arcade of the Archivio the shopkeepers had stopped quarrelling with the farmers and were listening. Pelli had obviously made them think.

Then Forla appeared at one of the windows by the balcony and waved. There was a chorus of boos but they died quickly and dissolved into muttering.

'By God, he's got it across,' Patch said, admiring in spite of himself.

'One last thing!' Pelli's voice rang out across the square, strong and confident. He knew he had them on his side now. Bosco and his small coterie of followers were shouting on their own and politics were forgotten.

'One last thing!' Pelli raised his arms for attention once more. 'We are taking steps at this very moment to inform the authorities on the mainland by telephone.'

For a second, there was silence, then a storm of cheering, and Pelli grinned.

'You've no need to fear,' he said. 'I always maintained there was no need to fear. I promised long ago that at the first sign of danger, I should act. Well, although I don't believe in this danger we hear so much about, I have acted. Because you were anxious and many odd things have occurred, and my enemies were trying to make political capital out of them.'

There was a burst of ragged cheering and a definite appearance of relief among the crowd as they began to turn away. The policemen seemed to relax visibly and started chattering among themselves. Then Pelli, obviously determined not to lose a perfect opportunity, started to harangue the crowd.

'You have been stirred up, friends,' he shouted, 'by that rabble-rousing faction who call themselves politicians. Believe me, people of Anapoli, their only idea is to stir the people against authority – '

There was a thin burst of cheering and Hannay pulled at Patch's arm in disgust.

'Come on, for Christ's sake,' he said, and they pushed their way out of the crowd.

## twenty-seven

Before dark, someone saw a taxi draw up at a side door of the Town Hall and Forla appeared with Pelli. There were quick handshakes then the taxi drew away and roared out of the piazza. There were a few boos but somehow the sight of Forla heading up the hill to his vast, expensive palace reassured everyone more than anything else and the farmers started to pack the few belongings they had brought with them once more and the first family set off out of town, in an ancient van that groaned from the square in a cloud of blue smoke. Behind them followed a mule cart and another straggling family carrying parcels on their heads like Arabs.

Mayor Pelli, standing on the balcony of the Town Hall, watched them leave.

'They're going, Piero,' he pointed out to Tornielli. 'Forla did the trick. I wonder why he came.'

'Orlesi,' Piero said shortly. 'He's having trouble with the sulphur workers. They say he sent a radio message to the yacht in Naples and asked him to put in an appearance. It'll quieten them down. He'll be gone in a couple of days.'

Pelli turned round. 'Piero,' he said. 'I saw the man Patch in the crowd again. He was with the fisherman, Meucci.'

'He lives with Meucci,' Piero said.

'Do you know him well, Piero?'

'I live in the same apartment building.'

'You must know something then. I've heard it said that he was once a Communist.'

Piero took a deep breath. In his heart was an intense hatred for all the condescension with which Patch treated him, for all the humiliating incidents on the staircase that made him feel like a small boy, for the studied indifference with which he had been received on the mole that morning.

'He's a born trouble-maker,' he said.

Pelli puffed at his cigarette thoughtfully. 'Bosco was quick over the fish,' he said. 'It was a good job Forla was here. I didn't like telling that story about the scientific commission.' He was a little ashamed at the untruth, but he consoled himself that even if it weren't correct, it was nearly so. It was his intention to ask for a commission. He had found himself driven on to the defensive by Bosco and had seized on the idea to get back the initiative. He told himself for the hundredth time he had done right. There could be no immediate danger – if there were danger at all. It didn't seem possible. He couldn't somehow associate disaster with himself and his home and his island.

'We'll get in touch with the universities on the mainland, all the same,' he said uneasily. 'I'll write at once. We can put everybody off until they send someone. I'll put out a proclamation of some sort this evening, in fact. Even if they come straight away, they'll not arrive before the eve of the election and anything they do the following day can't affect the voting. It's all so ridiculous, having to indulge in these antics. Everyone's getting worked up over nothing. It's happened before. Look, it's quiet now!'

'The calm before the storm,' Piero said.

Pelli looked at the young man quickly. 'Don't you believe it's quiet, Piero? He asked.

Piero frowned. There were many things on his mind just then, and the mountain seemed just one more barb in his flesh.

'It *sounds* quiet,' he said sullenly.

'Don't you think it *is* quiet?'

A dreadful feeling of doubt began to rise in Pelli's mind, and for a moment he felt the decisions that were cropping up were too big for him to face alone.

He lit a cigarette and drew on it nervously. 'Anyway, thank the Lord there's no sign of danger now,' he said.

He glanced up the road out of the town, satisfied with his plans, content that he had done all he could according to his political conscience. There was nothing to indicate the unquiet earth that had killed old Givanno and the thousands of fishes off the cape. Nothing but the thin column of smoke rising steadily into the darkening sky.

---

# twenty-eight

That evening Pelli's proclamations appeared – after dusk so that few people would be around to ask awkward questions, and the streets were emptying by the time Piero Tornielli began to make his tour of the town notice boards in the three squares.

The Piazza del Mare was deserted when he stopped outside the Customs House, but five minutes after he had gone, Hannay halted on exactly the same flagstones Piero had occupied. as he paused to read the public notices and documents, a habit he had always followed in foreign ports to improve his linguistic abilities. His eye caught the slip of paper Piero had pinned up a few moments before and his lips moved as he read it through carefully. Then he jerked his jacket straight on his taut square body and set off up the hill towards Mamma Meucci's.

Patch was painting when he arrived and he looked up as Hannay opened the door.

'Oh, Christ,' he said wearily. 'Not you again, for God's sake! What's happened now?'

Hannay ignored him and crossed the room towards the easel, staring at the painting critically enough to put Patch off his work.

'I should say you still got that bloke's leg wrong,' he said, jabbing a horny thumb at the canvas.

'And I should say,' Patch retorted, 'that you don't know the first god-damn thing about it.'

195

Hannay seemed quite unmoved and Patch began to work again. He knew Hannay hadn't come to discuss art and he was suddenly sick of his agitating and old Leonardi's parrot cries about the mountain, and the whole political set-up, all the evasions and equivocations, all the semi-truths that were fed to them and the super-truths that led to nowhere. Mrs Hayward had been to see him again and his head ached from the ugly scene that had ensued, the pleading, the misery and the vindictiveness. He felt he wanted to run downstairs and find Cecilia and take her off to the mainland again, away from the fantastic comic opera atmosphere that had begun to exist on Anapoli.

Hannay said nothing for a while, watching him paint, then he dragged out his pipe, lit it and started blowing rings of acrid smoke into Patch's eyes as he worked.

'Bosco's meeting didn't go so well,' he said conversationally. 'His deputy pal didn't fancy being chased into the sea by a red hot volcano and he discovered he'd got to get back. He caught the boat again. Bosco's playing hell in Emiliano's about it. Dead smart, the way Pelli got one up on him.'

'Fair's fair,' Patch said indifferently. 'He was one up on Pelli before.'

'Pelli's got some proclamations out,' Hannay went on. 'About the mountain and them experts he said he'd got. I've just been reading one. It's a lot of tripe.'

'Like the paper he flourished on the Town Hall steps,' Patch said cheerfully. 'That was tripe too. It was a letter of instructions to the polling officer in Corti Marina.'

Hannay's heavy face was shocked at the suggestion. 'How do you know?' he demanded. 'You couldn't see.'

'The old dear opposite!' Patch indicated the old woman sitting in the window across the street observing the inhabitants of Mamma Meucci's with interest. 'She's got a granddaughter Donatella working in the Town Hall. She was carrying a pile of letters across the corridor when Pelli went on to the steps. He snatched the top one as he passed. She's only fifteen and she was scared at losing it. Nobody saw it happen but her. She told Grandma and Grandma told Mamma Meucci. Mamma Meucci told me. Poor little Pelli. Bosco's pushing him into things I'm sure he wouldn't do if he weren't so scared of losing.'

Hannay scowled. 'He never sent no message to the mainland either,' he said. 'Did you know that?'

Patch started to paint again, still cheerful, still unmoved by Hannay's excitement. 'No, I didn't. But it doesn't surprise me. He only said "steps were being taken" and that's a political phrase to mean they're still only thinking about it. How'd you find out?'

'My Number One, Anderson.'

'Has he got a grand-daughter Donatella working in the Town Hall too?'

Hannay grunted. 'He's been knocking off the girl on the switchboard – you know what he is. The whole business is beginning to whiff like a ten-day-old kipper. You know what I've been doing all day? I've been loading crates on my ship for Forla.'

He brought out the item of news quite casually, but he had waited deliberately to produce it and it made Patch drop his mask of indifference at once.

'For Forla?' He put down his brushes at last.

'That's it. On 'Annay's ship.' Hannay puffed on his pipe as though he were working up a head of steam. 'You shoulda seen the panic. Orlesi came to see me personal. I had to radio the agents for approval. It means a special trip, see. But Forla's paying through the nose and it's only a small deck cargo. They gave me the OK. He had the stuff on the mole by the time I gave him the go-ahead. He said it was machinery.'

Patch was looking puzzled.

'Only it isn't machinery,' Hannay said.

'Well, what is it, then?'

'Furniture. Paintings. Some damn' fool let go the brake on the winch and one of the crates landed on the deck with a bang. It was full of pictures. He's getting rid of his collection. In fact, that's what he came for, I'll bet.'

Patch found it hard to believe what Hannay was trying to suggest. 'Perhaps he's loaning them to a gallery,' he said. 'They've left the island before.'

'Would he loan silver and furniture as well?' Hannay asked. 'Some of them there cases have got marble in 'em. There's a bloke in one with a helmet and no drawers. I've had a look on the quiet. And they've been loading silver on the *Canone del Mare* all evening.

'How do you know?'

' 'Ad a look. Me and Anderson. They brought a van down the mole when it started to get dark. They kept it well covered up but they forgot us. We could see from the bridge.'

'All that way?'

'Telescopes, Mister,' Hannay explained blandly. 'They put it in the main cabin. They was in a proper 'urry. It ain't even packed properly.'

'Have you told anyone?'

'Only you.'

Patch stared at his cigarette end. 'Poor bloody little Pelli,' he said compassionately.

'*Poor* Pelli!' Hannay snorted contemptuously. 'He's right in there dodging like the rest, Mister. As for that Forla he ought to be strung up by his thumbs. Standing there trying to make everyone think they're safe when all he's come for is to empty his flipping house of everything that's valuable.'

## twenty-nine

Hannay stayed late with Patch before setting off for his ship, and it was with some surprise that Patch, drinking a last coffee in Emiliano's before going to bed, saw him burst through the door just as he was about to leave.

'Now what the hell?' he asked. 'Forla taken his crates back? Or has Orlesi thrown a fit?'

'Cut it out,' Hannay said brusquely, his expression a mixture of anger and anxiety. 'It's none of that. It's Cristoforo.'

Emiliano leaned over the bar, his large eyes dark with sympathy, his hands clasping the handles of the coffee machine.

'He's disappeared,' Hannay went on. 'I've got him outside. Devoto, I mean. He come to me, wanted to know where I'd hidden him. It took me an hour to convince him I hadn't got him. And when I found *he* was serious I started to get the wind-up too. The last time he was seen, he was going up the hill out of town. He's got an aunt up there or something, but she hasn't seen him. I think he's gone up to San Giorgio and I want you to help me find him.'

Patch finished his coffee and hitched up his sagging trousers. 'What the hell has he gone to San Giorgio for?'

'I don't know. Maybe because it's about as far as he can get from *him*. I think it's because the bastard won't let him come away with me. I told him I was ready to leave, you know, and he's not been home since. He's got a pal up there

199

in San Giorgio, hasn't he? I've heard him talk about him. Matteo Lipparini or something. I'll bet he's there and I want to be around when that bastard finds him.' Hannay kept bringing out the word with repetitive explosiveness, as though he drew some pleasure from it. 'Besides which, in case you 'aven't noticed, the kettle's started singing again.'

'Oh, Christ, no!'

They went to the door and stared up into the dark sky. The sound that came from behind the town was almost imperceptible but it was clearly the beginning of the whistle again.

Devoto was standing in the square near the statue of Garibaldi, his big body lounging against the plinth, his handsome face dark with suspicion, and Hannay glared at him with undisguised hatred.

'I don't trust the bastard,' he said. 'He might have a go at the kid when he sees him and I might not be big enough to stop him. He's a heavyweight. I'm only a bantam.'

'OK,' Patch said. 'I'll come. Let's get a taxi. There'll be no buses at this time of night.'

'Signor Tom,' Emiliano said gently from the doorway. 'Let me take you. My van's in the square and I have finished now.'

The atmosphere in the little vehicle was tense as Emiliano drove them out of the town. Hannay crouched on a box in the back with Patch, sitting opposite Devoto, a sort of armed truce existing between them. Emiliano sensed the tension too, and talked all the time from the front, gesturing with his hands and laughing nervously, so that the van seemed to drive itself more than be driven.

San Giorgio was almost in darkness when they arrived, only a few lights showing in the village street. As they stopped to ask at a house for directions to the Lipparini small-holding, Patch was aware of a deep sighing noise about him as though a wind had sprung up and was stirring the trees, but the air was still and the leaves were undisturbed against the night sky.

For some reason he began to wish he were down in the Porto. The crowded houses and the narrow streets there suddenly seemed to have a warmth and affection that glowed against the loneliness of the bare mountain.

When they arrived in the farmyard, lights were glowing in the Lipparini house, a tiny low-roofed building lit with oil lamps, that seemed full of people from Lipparini himself and his wife, through two or three generations. From the doorway, beyond the barking dogs, they saw Cristoforo immediatedly, still wide awake and big-eyed at the far side of the room, hugging Masaniello. He said nothing, sitting silently with two or three older children as he listened to Hannay and Devoto arguing with Lipparini in a growling undertone.

Then Lipparini shook his head. 'He's not going,' he insisted. 'The boy is afraid. No boy should be afraid like that.'

'I'm his guardian.' Devoto brushed past Hannay. 'I say he must come home.'

'Mamma – ' Lipparini called over his shoulder, ' – we must get advice. Go and fetch the priest. He'll tell us what to do.'

His wife hesitated, not certain whether the instruction was meant to be a bluff or not, and it seemed to Patch that the whole affair had a tinge of melodrama about it – with the scared faces of Cristoforo and the women caught by the light of the oil lamps, and the angry figures of Hannay and Devoto in the doorway, both of them quite obviously ready to start another quarrel.

Then, while they were still waiting for Lipparini's wife to move, the sighing noise about them changed until it became a low grumbling sound, like an ominous hollow growl at the back of a dog's throat, and immediately, everyone's eyes left

Cristoforo's face and swung up into the darkness above them.

'Holy Mother of Jesus!' Lipparini's wife crossed herself quickly, and for the first time Patch caught a glimpse of the doubt that existed up there in San Giorgio, and the fear that the Givannos had spoken about after the death of their father.

The breathy grumbling grew louder and louder and Patch felt the ground tremble, almost as though it were one of the distant thunderstorms that sent the lightning flashing across the Tyrrhenian like the sweeping beam of a search-light, rattling and rumbling over the curve of the sea, as sullen as distant gunfire.

As it died, a violent crack shuddered the mountain and brought everyone inside the smoky little room to their feet. At once, they heard the restless noise of animals behind the house and the dogs which stood behind Lipparini began to bark again.

Cristoforo was completely forgotten as the whole lot of them tumbled out of the house and stood in the farmyard, staring at the sky. Through the clouds along the ridge of the slope, they could see the moon and the brilliant stars. Then one of the dogs stopped barking and started to howl, throwing its head back and letting out a series of melancholy cries that echoed round the house. Immediately all the others started to howl too.

'Quiet, Aldo! Quiet, Asa!' Lipparini snapped, and in the silence that followed Patch felt the hair at the back of his neck standing on end.

Over the thick silence, they heard shouts from farther down the slope, nearer to the village, and the howling of more dogs among the huddled houses.

'Listen,' Hannay said. Over the increased rumbling above them they heard the noise of rattling stones, and the first thing that occurred to Patch was that one of Lipparini's goats had knocked down a wall. The same thought appeared to occur to Lipparini and he stepped forward, but everything had become still again and silent, and he turned, at a loss, and stared at the others. Below them the village seemed to have awakened abruptly, and they could hear more shouts now over the fold of rocky soil where the farm stood.

'It's stopped again,' Emiliano said, pointing.

The whole group of them, the four of them who had arrived in the van, Lipparini, the womenfolk and the old people, and the scared-looking children, were staring up the slope. Above them the yard led out into the fork of two deep narrow lanes, almost like sunken roads that headed higher up the slopes to the Lipparinis' scrubby fields and threadbare vineyards. Farther up, they could see two spots of light where another farm stood.

Then the mountain started its racket again and the dogs began to back away, growling deep in their throats, the hair along their backs bristling

'Aldo! Asa!' Lipparini called them but the dogs refused to return to his side.

'Look! Look!' His wife shot out a hand and they saw the lights above them disappear abruptly.

'That's the Givannos' farm,' Lipparini said. 'Young Marco's up there alone. Something's happened. We ought to go and see.'

'You're not leaving here,' his wife said quickly. 'Not till daylight. The Lord have mercy on us, we don't know what's happening – '

Above the sounds of the mountain, they heard a series of shouts from the direction of the Givannos' farm and then silence, a thick silence that had a sinister quality.

'I'm off home,' Devoto said. Swinging round, he stepped forward to grab Cristoforo's arm but Emiliano moved into his path, his big stomach thrust out. Devoto bounded off it, and Hannay grabbed the boy and swung him aside.

'Give him to me,' Devoto shouted furiously, recovering himself.

'When you've calmed down!' Hannay shouted back.

'Give him to me!'

The argument developed into a struggle which to Patch looked like one of those sad newspaper pictures of estranged couples fighting for possession of a child, both men pulling at the pathetic figure of Cristoforo cowering between them, and they all forgot the mountain and stepped forward to separate them.

'Let him go,' Patch shouted in Hannay's ear above the babble. 'You've got no authority to do this, you damn' fool! You'll only make it worse for him.'

It was while they were still struggling that they heard the clattering of rocks again and a grinding noise as though huge boulders were moving against each other. The quarrelling stopped and Cristoforo was ignored abruptly as they swung round once more, their eyes trying to pierce the mountain blackness.

'It's an avalanche,' Hannay said.

'Signore,' Lipparini said. 'You've never heard an avalanche. There's not enough noise.'

In spite of themselves, they were all beginning to edge backwards towards the road that led to the village.

A donkey came clattering towards them, its dainty feet slithering and stumbling over the rocky path, and they heard the splintering of wood and a crash that sounded like a gate falling.

'That's the Givannos' donkey!' Lipparini made a grab for the animal and missed, and as the sense of something inexplicable and malevolent about them grew, the lips of the women began to move.

'Holy Mother of Mercy, have pity on us,' Lipparini's wife was muttering. 'Holy Mother of God, watch over this farm.'

They could now smell a warm humid heat that seemed to be drawing closer, heavy on the clear mountain air, like the smell of boiling vegetables.

'Get the children together,' Lipparini said abruptly, and the women began to gather the children into a group, Hannay and Devoto hanging about near Cristoforo.

Patch had begun to move slowly out of the farmyard up the hill, trying to see what was happening, and Lipparini caught up with him by the gate,

'Do you see anything, signore?' he asked.

As they stared, the clouds parted and the moon came through briefly and the two of them, their ears assailed by the stony cacophony from the mountain, saw a swiftly moving wall of what looked in the darkness like slimy soil coming towards them. It seemed about ten feet high and they could see it was steaming. Then they realised the roadway was full of water which was warm against their shoes. A big fig tree higher up the road bent over before the hideous moving mass and toppled, and they saw the heavy viscous flow swing round the trunk and sweep on towards them.

'Holy Mother of God!' The words broke out of Lipparini's mouth in a croak, and he turned back into the farmyard at a run, shouting a warning.

'Get the children out of here, Mamma,' he yelled.

Emiliano was already stuffing the smallest ones into his van. 'Run,' he was shouting to the older children. 'Run! Run down to the village! It's mud!'

He slammed the doors and dropped into the driving seat, and the van jerked out of the farmyard, bouncing down the stony road followed by the barking dogs, all the children shrieking and pawing at the windows. The women, the old people, Hannay and Devoto set off after them.

'Givanno,' Lipparini said to Patch as they disappeared. 'We've got to get to Givanno! He's on his own up there.'

He moved forward, seeking a way round the moving mass, but he found himself face to face with a farm cart being pushed sideways down the hill by another horrifying wave that wilted the vegetation in front of it. Then the cart caught its near wheel in a rut, toppled over, and was buried within seconds, and the two of them turned and set off after the tail lights of Emiliano's van and the shouting family as they streamed down the hill.

# thirty

By the time daylight arrived, the muffled rumblings had increased and the high-pitched sigh from the mountain had started again. This time, however, the note of the whistle was higher and more of a shriek and somewhere down in the background, as though it were an ugly orchestration from the bowels of the earth, there was a rattling noise like the roll of iron-bound wheels over the cobbles of the Piazza del Mare. The air was full of the smell of sulphur.

When the Porto awoke, the sun was shining but there seemed to be no brightness anywhere. The pantiles of the roofs had changed overnight from the russets and reds and blues to grey – a dull flat grey that reflected no light and, in fact, seemed to absorb light into itself. The window ledges were grey, too, every horizontal plane the same monotonous colour. The whole town had been changed by a thick film of cinder dust in which the blurred footprints of human beings mingled with the neater round ones of dogs, and the small criss-cross marks where pigeons had landed. Wavering down the middle of the streets through the grey-white covering were the tyre marks of bicycles and the wider marks of cars.

'Mamma mia! Mamma mia!' A woman on a balcony was complaining in a high-pitched wail over the clothing she had left out overnight to dry, now covered with a muddy-looking film where the grey dust had stuck to it.

There were people at every window, their hands grimy, the dust sticking to their faces and filling the lines on their foreheads and round their mouths and eyes. The plume of smoke still hung over the mountain, mingling with the obscuring clouds so that they couldn't see the summit properly, bigger than on the previous day and darker, and directed by the wind over the town in heavy rolls of brown and black which seemed to lift hideous stomach sounds from the mountain's inside and spill them down among the alleys and courts of the Porto.

The Piazza Martiri was full of people and dogs and mules as the refugees from San Giorgio began to arrive in the town. Gaunt-faced women, some of them with babies at the breast, were squatting on the pavement, their backs against the withered orange trees with their bright fruit. Behind them their menfolk argued above the noise and gesticulated among themselves, their pathetic belongings piled on to barrows. Some of them were only half-dressed and people from the alleys round the piazza, with a full-hearted generosity, brought shabby clothes and old blankets and bowls of pasta for them. There seemed to be hundreds of human beings in the square, and hundreds of scared-looking children and homeless dogs. A couple of nuns, Don Alessandro and Don Gustavo, his curate, and the priests from the Church of Sant' Antonio on the edge of the town were moving among them muttering prayers that were drowned by the sullen roaring from the mountain that continued to increase as the sun grew weaker and the dust grew worse where it was stirred into clouds by the moving feet.

Patch pushed through the crowd as though in a dream, stupefied with weariness and lack of sleep, his face and hands grimy, his shoes and clothes smeared with the mud that had overwhelmed San Giorgio.

The police who had arrived with a lorry in response to frantic telephone calls had had to leave their vehicle a mile below the village because of the condition of the road, and climb the rest of the way through the wilting foliage. The mud had flowed straight down the main street and had swept into the church where the sacristan had been pulling the bell in a warning. They had been bringing out his body, unrecognisable under the mud, as the police had arrived. About the fields, the women had sat with their children, collecting their few treasures in little groups as the men struggled down the long street to rescue them. It had been impossible to clean anything as the mud had blocked the streams and stopped up the village wells and covered the water taps in the square; and all they could do was stare with a helpless despair at the slimy blankets and bedding, the stained pictures of the saints and the cheap terra cotta statuettes of the Virgin Mary.

Patch had helped to cram them into lorries as the hopelessness of trying to provide accommodation in San Giorgio became obvious, leaving their belongings for the most part scattered over the scrubby grass and draped on the olive trees at the mercy of the weather. They were taken down the hill, through the gap they'd cleared in the road, and down to the Porto to schoolrooms and the Aragonese castle and the churches of Sant' Agata and Sant' Antonio.

Don Dominico had run him up from Fumarola on his return to the town. He had been trying to get hold of Patch all morning, desperate for reassurance.

'Signor Patch,' he had said. 'If anything happens, Fumarola will be swept into the sea. I'm bringing my people round to the Porto.'

The old man's urgent voice was still in his ears as Mamma Meucci grabbed him, her face grey-white with fear, not quite certain what to be afraid of first.

'It's still falling on the slopes, Signor Tom. There's dust all over the sea. It no longer shines.' Her voice held a trace of surprise, as though sunshine on the sea were something to which she had awakened every day of her life, and to find it gone had destroyed the pleasure of coming to consciousness.

'They say it's worse in San Giorgio,' she went on. 'They say a man was killed.'

'Two men,' Patch corrected her. '*And* a woman and a child.'

Mamma Meucci stared up at his haggard face and crossed herself.

'The holy Mother of Jesus have pity on them! It is the will of God.'

Among the hubbub, Hannay stood surrounded by members of his crew, his face and clothes also grimy, the deep lines in the peeling redness of his skin carved in with jetty black.

He had left Patch in San Giorgio and returned to the Porto with Emiliano when the police had arrived, deciding that his duty in the case of an evacuation lay with his ship. He had insisted, however, on taking Cristoforo down with him, too, and in the town, in spite of Devoto's protests, had refused to let the boy out of his sight until he had reported the incident to the police. The harassed sergeant in charge, although promising to keep an eye on Cristoforo, had been swamped immediately afterwards by the flood of refugees from San Giorgio and Hannay was now uneasily aware that nothing had been gained.

He looked up as Patch arrived and he seemed to be bristling all over. The time for talking was past, it appeared, and he was reacting typically to a call for action.

' 'Annay threw open the stores,' he said. 'It's an emergency.' He indicated a couple of Lascar seamen with a steaming tureen. 'That's soup,' he pointed out. 'You can't expect Eyetalians to keep a stiff upper lip on a cup of sergeant major's.'

He was talking at the top of his voice and it was hard to tell whether the note in it was one of despair or triumph at being proved right.

'They're trying to get up a deputation to see Pelli again,' he continued. 'He's in his office. They say he's been there since dawn. What was it like up there?'

'They found young Givanno,' Patch said, unemotional with weariness. 'It had come right over the house and through the windows. He was in there with the dog,'

'Oh, Christ, not *another* Givanno?'

'*And* the sacristan at the church. And a woman and a kid. They must have been bloody near cooked. They're slithering and sliding about up there like pigs on a greasy pole.'

Leonardi appeared with Cecilia through the clouds of dust that put a yellow haze over the sun and enveloped the town in a dim kind of twilight. His thin legs were creaking as he ran, and under his arm, weighing him down, was the ancient portrait camera from his studio, complete with a tripod that trailed on the ground, making three little grooves through the dust.

'Clearly there has been an eruption of lava into the lake in the crater,' he shouted. '*Now* let me face Mayor Pelli. Now who's the old crackpot who's prophesied disaster so often and always been wrong? I am about to take photographs. They will sell to the magazines of the world. I shall be first there. They will laugh on the other side of their faces. You couldn't perhaps lend me a few thousand lire for a taxi?'

Without waiting for a reply, he dashed off, the legs of the tripod clattering over the cobbles.

Cecilia stopped in front of Patch and stared up at him, her eyes wide and horrified.

'Tom,' she said. 'What's going to happen?'

As though in answer to her question, Cristoforo came running across the piazza, his dog at his heels, its muzzle swinging under its jaw, and Hannay scowled as he realised the police had had to let him take his chance in the chaos.

'Signor Hannay,' he shouted. 'Sir Captain!' He pushed fiercely between a bunch of women who were trying to dress children in the old clothes which were being offered to them. 'Signor Hannay, the fishermen have gone to the Town Hall again. The Givanno family are there demanding help from the main land. They *insist* that the Mayor telephone at once.'

'Come on,' Hannay said to Patch. 'Let's go!'

# thirty-one

The crowd outside the Town Hall was already being whipped up from the background by Bruno Bosco, who was standing on his favourite pillar outside the Archivio, gesturing wildly. Beneath him stood his group of stern young men, and this time the police were too occupied to appear in force, so that only two nervous-looking men waited in the doorway of the Town Hall.

'Demand your rights,' Bosco was shouting. 'Demand your rights from the Signori!'

Pelli appeared on the steps. He looked pale and shaken and there was no ready smile on his face this time. Old Leonardi, still with his camera on his shoulder and obviously unable to borrow any money for a taxi, was there shouting abuse and almost decapitating his neighbours with the tripod every time he swung round to gesture at the people behind him. The crowd hooted and someone began to throw vegetables from the basket of a fruit-seller, and a tomato made a red star on the pillar by the doorway. Pelli held up his hands for silence but the crowd was in an ugly mood and refused to be quiet.

'Now who's wrong?' old Leonardi shrieked. 'Now who's an old fool?'

'Answer that one, Pelli,' Giuseppe Givanno shouted. 'Answer that one!'

There was more abuse and Patch thought for a moment the crowd was going to take the Town Hall by storm, but

Pelli managed to stand his ground. He was afraid now, though, and terribly aware of the mess he was in, and was trying hard to bluff his way out of it.

'I'll not talk to you,' he shouted, just managing to make himself heard over the noise of the crowd and the racket of the mountain. 'I'll not talk to you until you've got rid of the opposition elements who're trying to make this into a political meeting. I've done my duty and I'll not have this disaster used for party ends.'

'Nobody's asking you what you want,' he was told. 'You're being told what we want.'

Pelli waved his arms in a desperate appeal for order. 'This is serious,' he shouted, 'and if you want to see me, come by all means, but come without my opponents.'

The crowd began to argue among themselves, shoving and gesturing. Pelli's request seemed reasonable enough, and while they were still shouting, Hannay kept pushing forward until he and Patch were on the steps at the front with old Leonardi.

'Take no notice of him,' Bosco was yelling from his pillar at the back of the crowd. 'He wants to put you off again.'

'That's right,' yelled old Leonardi. 'He'll put you off as he put me off.'

'I'll talk to any of you,' Pelli shouted, and Patch could see the perspiration standing out on his face as he waved his arms 'As many of you as can get into my office. But this dreadful thing can't be solved by election slogans.'

'That's right, be quiet, Bruno.' The crowd started to yell against the opposition element who were trying to push Bosco forward. 'Leave it to us this time.'

'They'll talk you out of it again,' Bosco warned. 'Don't listen to them. Tear the place apart!'

'Shut up,' Meucci shouted at him. 'We want no violence. Tearing the place apart won't help anyone.'

At first Bosco refused to be silent and went on shouting slogans, then someone pushed him off the pillar into the arms of his followers and the whole bunch of them, some of them with torn shirts, were driven out from under the arcade.

As they went, there was another movement from the back of the crowd and it surged forward so that Pelli was bundled unceremoniously backwards into his office. At the front, Patch and Hannay found themselves swept into the room with the fishermen who had been leading the argument. Piero Tornielli was there, pressed against the wall, his handsome face distorted with fear.

There was a great deal of noise during which Pelli tried to make himself heard, then at last Meucci's voice emerged and as he was the oldest and most respected of the fishermen, the others quietened down.

'We can't all talk at once,' Pelli said, mopping his face, aware that events had suddenly got beyond his control, beyond reach of the elaborate plans he had made. 'You must elect a spokesman.'

'Meucci then! Meucci'll speak for us,' someone yelled from the back of the room.

'Not me.' Meucci shook his head. 'I can shout but I'm no talker. Find somebody who's been to school.'

Leonardi pushed forward, tripping people with the tripod and cracking them over the head with the camera.

'I'll speak,' he shouted in his thin voice. 'I'll speak. *Mamma mia*, I've plenty to say!'

'Not you, you old fool!' He was bundled out of sight again immediately, the camera rattling significantly as though something were loose inside it.

'Tomaso!' Meucci pushed his partner forward. 'How about Tomaso?'

'Tomaso's a Communist. Let's have no politics.'

The hubbub started again, the room echoing the shouts like the inside of a drum. Patch saw Piero Tornielli against the wall, cowering from the gestures of an angry Tomaso, while Pelli sat in his chair with all the others towering above him, and Meucci, with one great hand splayed on his blotter as he tried to restore order, fought to make himself heard above the shouting and the frightful roaring from the mountain that seemed to echo and re-echo down the peeling corridors of the Town Hall.

'Ask Signor Patch! He's got no politics!' Tomaso said unexpectedly. 'He's not even got a vote. Let him talk to the Mayor.'

Patch started to back away in alarm, but the crowd behind, having found a representative they could agree on, pushed him forward again so that he half-fell across Pelli's desk. Meucci clapped a huge hand on his shoulder and dragged him upright.

Pelli began to gesture wildly, frankly scared now as he glanced up at Patch's gaunt figure, his face grey with fatigue, his clothes and hands still daubed with mud. 'Signor Patch's not even one of us,' he shouted, his face red. 'It's no concern of his!'

'Don't worry,' Patch said. 'I want no part in it.'

'Then you'd better leave.'

'Signor Patch can speak for us,' Meucci said in his heavy determined way. 'Signor Patch is one of us. He's worked like one of us today. I can vouch for him. He lives in my home.'

'Signor Patch doesn't represent the rest of the island!' Pelli lost his temper and banged the desk furiously so that the dust which had sifted in through the windows rose in little clouds. 'Perhaps he represents *you* but he doesn't represent the other residents – the shopkeepers, the property owners, the people from Colonna del Greco – '

'For Christ's sake, man,' Patch said fiercely in English. 'Stop dodging. Stop worrying about representatives. Listen to the mountain.'

The hollow rumbling seemed to shake the whole building as though it were a cart rolling on crooked wheels. The glass in the windows rattled sharply in the frames and Patch saw Piero Tornielli's eyes swing fearfully towards them.

'I've done my duty,' Pelli said. It seemed to be the only thing he could think of to say.

'Look at the sky,' Patch shouted, pointing to the gloom outside. 'It's getting darker all the time. Telephone the mainland and have done with it. Or they'll tear the place apart. If you don't, I'll tell them that no telephone call left the island the other night when they think it did. For the love of God, ring up before it's too late and while they're all here and can see.'

Pelli looked up at him, his eyes big and frightened, trying to collect his wits in the bedlam of noise. Then he stared round him at the circle of angry fishermen, and reached slowly for the telephone...

# thirty-two

The sky had become quite dark as the crowd moved slowly away from Mayor Pelli's office, straggling in noisy groups across the square, their ears battered by the mechanical clacking noises that came from Amarea.

They had left Pelli slumped in his chair, his face grey and haggard, his mind obsessed with his own guilt and the thought of his downfall. All his plans for the island had disappeared in the darkness that had been thrown over them.

During the day the pall over the mountain grew bigger, a wild-looking column that towered thousands of feet into the sky, billowing and rolling, a hideous mixture of black smoke and white steam. Below it, the mist and dust and ash hung round the crater, hiding the sun and bringing increasing darkness to the island.

As the hours wore on, the rumbling became louder, and more terrifying in the growing gloom. From time to time, they heard explosions from inside the mountain, a kind of ghastly growling like the hollow sound of a jet aircraft streaking across the angry sky.

There seemed to be no breath of air left and the suffocating atmosphere was held close to the earth by the growing cloud of smoke. The election was forgotten and only Bruno Bosco tried to remind them of it with a loudspeaker van led by a motor-cycle outrider that beat its way up the crumbling alleys from the Piazza del Mare.

'People of Anapoli,' he was shouting. 'Now you know what the authorities are made of. Now you know how they play with your safety for the sake of a few votes – '

But no one wanted to listen. The motor-cyclist ran into a cart that was pushed into his path and fell off, and a group of men and youths started pelting the car with vegetables. The loudspeaker stopped abruptly, then started to appeal for calm.

'Go home, Bosco,' the crowd shouted, still throwing. 'This is no time for your lies. We've had enough of politics.'

The limping motor-cyclist picked up his machine hurriedly and began to push it away with a buckled front wheel. The car reversed in an alleyway and disappeared down the hill, its loudspeaker silent.

Then the word got about that rescue ships were beginning to arrive and torches started to flicker in the grey-green smoky streets. There were a few people arguing in the Via Pescatori then suddenly enormous numbers began to appear as the word of rescue got around. Doors crashed open and the crowd huddled together in groups, clotted and tight, from which odd individuals ran backwards and forwards as it edged towards the Piazza del Mare, so that the mass of people swelled and jerked in heaves like a huge snake in the steep little street.

The rumours were wrong, however, and the ships had not arrived, but the frightened crowd in the Piazza del Mare squatted down on the black basalt sea wall in the darkness and cowered in doorways out of the breeze and the drizzle that had started. Every minute more people joined them.

In the afternoon, there was a puff of smoke from the summit like an atomic explosion and several hundred mouths opened in a long-drawn-out 'aaaah'. Women clutched their children more closely to them and men stood up and stared awe-stricken at the mountain.

A few seconds later, with the smoke emerging with the underbelly of the clouds, the colossal gasp from the mountain reached the town, like the sound of a tremendous belch.

Hannay watched it from the bridge of the *Great Watling Street* as he stared over the houses. Behind him in the semi-darkness the Haywards stood, gazing towards the mountain, their eyes frightened, their faces strained and tired. They had arrived ahead of most of the crowd, driving slowly through the streets in their car, which was now standing in the Piazza del Mare, abandoned.

Already jumpy with nerves, they were in a mood to be panicked, and the ordeal of having to pass through the frightened shoving people had been almost as terrifying as the noise of the mountain. They had seen a fist fight between two men who were arguing over the ownership of a dropped blanket, and had had to force their way through a gang of youths from Corti Marina who had tried to drown their fears with wine and were argumentative to the point of truculence.

Even Patch, whom they had bumped into as they had left their car, had seemed indifferent to their plight.

'Tom!' Mrs Hayward was still unconvinced that she had lost all control over him. 'Tom Patch, for God's sake, help us through this damned mob!'

She had shrieked through the struggling crowd, her voice rising in panic as he failed to hear her. 'Tom Patch! Damn you, what's the matter with you?'

She had stared after his stooped heedless back as he trudged on, her expression a mixture of bitterness and fear.

'It's that Italian girl,' she shouted at her husband above the din. 'It's that damned Italian girl he's going back for.'

And she burst into a flood of bad language which, born of hysteria and nerves, told her husband all he had ever wanted to know about the affair he had suspected between her and Patch. For a moment the knowledge of her faithlessness shocked him, then he realised he hadn't the strength of character to treat her as she deserved and would go on suffering from her indifference and faithlessness in all probability until he was too old to care, and he took her arm again and began to lead her down towards the harbour.

The battered old *Great Watling Street*, with its rust-streaked side, had seemed a haven from the chaos ashore and the only thing they required to complete their thankfulness at being on board was to hear her engines throbbing and feel her in motion away from Anapoli.

Anderson, the Mate, was staring over the heads of the Lascar firemen lining the rails. His girl friend huddled in the saloon, frightened as much by the strangeness of her surroundings as by the confusion and noise.

'They say they're coming into the town from Fumarola,' he told Hannay. 'They were coming down the side of the mountain on horses and donkeys when I left. There are still a few coming by cart and car round by Corti Marina.'

'God 'elp 'em,' Hannay said fervently. 'God knows where they'll sleep. The town must be as full as a last bus already.'

'There's not a soul in San Giorgio,' Anderson went on. 'And when I rang Orlesi from Emiliano's about that loading sheet, I couldn't get a reply. The taxi-driver told me they're busy packing up at the Villa Forla.'

Hannay nodded. 'I've seen 'em,' he said. He indicated a car standing on the mole. 'They've been loading all afternoon but they've had to stop now. They can't get off the mole for that lot in the square. They've moved the yacht.'

His hand swept across the harbour to where the *Canzone del Mare* was anchored just off the shore.

'The old boy aboard yet?' Anderson asked.

'I don't think so. I've not seen anything. Maybe they're trying to get him into a boat somewhere else — perhaps at Corti Marina — so they can row him out. If he tried to get along that mole now, they'd tear him to pieces after that business at the Town Hall yesterday. They've heard he's been emptying his house of valuables.'

There was another muffled explosion from inside the mountain and immediately half a hundred strained anxious faces swung round to stare at it. The crowd in the Piazza del Mare had increased by now, those in front trying to hold back from the edge of the sea wall, those behind trying to get nearer to the shore. There must have been two thousand people standing in the square, some of them holding infants, while all the dogs that slithered and wormed their way among the legs of the human beings barked madly, caught by the obsessive sense of panic.

Hannay turned round and spoke to the Haywards.

'Why don't you go down to the saloon and get a cup of tea?' he said. 'The cook's been brewing up.'

Mrs Hayward stared at him in silence and Hayward shook his head without speaking. They appeared to have lost the use of their voices and seemed loath to leave Hannay as though they wanted to be certain that he wouldn't abandon them. Then Hayward suddenly recovered his power of speech. 'When are we leaving?' he asked.

'I dunno,' Hannay said. 'Can't say.' He had been once more to see Devoto – as soon as he'd returned from Pelli's office – and he still hoped the increased bribe he'd offered would produce Cristoforo. It was a slender chance but Hannay had no other option within the law. The thought of Cristoforo still among the quivering old houses scared him in a way the noise and the smoke never could, but there seemed little he could do to remove him.

'Isn't it dangerous to stay?' Mrs Hayward persisted.

'Mebbe,' Hannay said.

'Why can't we go now?' Mrs Hayward burst out. 'Why can't we? You've no right to stay!'

'Lady,' Hannay said stiffly, his mind still on Cristoforo. 'I like to think I'm a humanitarian. If them people think they're in danger, then I'm ready and willing to take 'em off. 'Annay stays 'ere till the Navy arrives.'

Mrs Hayward stared at him, frustrated to the point of loathing for people like Hannay and Patch who ignored her appeals for help and seemed blind to the fact that she was a woman and attractive. She glanced at her husband, hating his sagging, unintelligent face suddenly, then she went into the chart room and sat down and burst into tears.

From Emiliano's, Patch watched the crowds streaming through the town to the mole. Emiliano was more concerned with getting his bottles into the cellar and locking up.

'Signor Tom,' he shouted, waving his fingers in Patch's face. 'I'd be glad if you'd drink your whisky. I'm anxious to leave.'

Patch nodded. He was still weary and a little stupefied. There had seemed little else for anyone to do after they had made sure that everyone from San Giorgio was safe, except to go back down the hill to the Porto and, in the anti-climax after the horror, little else to do until the ships came but stand around and talk.

Emiliano waited impatiently, jigging from one foot to the other and beating his forehead with his fist in despair while Patch slowly finished his whisky. Then, driven into the street, Patch tried the mole in the hope of finding Hannay. But there were as many people about as on festa days and there was as much noise, and moving about was difficult. The only things that were missing were the balloon sellers and the laughter and the fireworks, and the clear blue of the hot Italian sky.

On the way from the harbour in the oven-like atmosphere, he bumped into Piero Tornielli standing behind a group of women kneeling by a crude shrine set in the wall where a stub of candle guttered, trying to gain some comfort from their prayers.

Piero had been badly scared all day and had been drinking to help him fight off the confusion of fear and jealousy that atrophied his brain. As Patch passed him, he turned away, the fact that he had been seen paralysed with terror in Pelli's office adding to his humiliation and hatred. Then abruptly he sensed that Patch was too weary and too shocked to respond to anger, and he began to follow him. Catching him up in the Piazza Martiri, he grabbed his arm and swung him round, and saw immediately that he had been right.

He made a wild gesture at the crowds, aware of a freedom to say almost anything he liked without retaliation. 'This is all your fault,' he shouted. 'All this panic! It's your doing!'

'Go away,' Patch said heavily.

Piero grabbed at his arm again. 'But for you there'd have been no panic,' he stormed, trying to wipe from his mind the staining memory of his own fear. 'You and your clever words!'

'Go away,' Patch said once more, brushing Piero's hand from his sleeve.

Piero thrust forward, carried away by his new courage to the point of rashness.

'Liar! Cheat! Trouble-maker! Why don't you leave?' he yelled. 'And take all your countrymen with you! We don't need you here! None of you! Leave Anapoli! Now!'

'Go away,' Patch roared furiously and Tornielli stepped back, shocked into silence by the expression on his face.

He watched Patch push his way through the crowds, his hatred burning into his vitals. With it grew an equally inflamed desire to keep Cecilia away from Patch, a desire that became physical as it gripped him. Glaring after Patch, he turned and set off hurriedly for the Via Pescatori.

In the confusion of noise and movement, Patch couldn't remember where he went after he left Piero. He simply pushed through the people, indifferent to the shouting and the hands that grabbed at him.

Old Leonardi was almost gleeful when they met in the Piazza Martiri, and just a little drunk. He was still carrying

224

the camera, tied to his back now with a piece of frayed string, and was wearing motoring goggles, gauntlets, and a cap jammed back to front over his white hair. He had managed to borrow Piero Tornielli's Lambretta.

He laughed up at Patch from the saddle and hitched up the camera which was proving a little difficult to manage.

'They're abandoning the Villa Forla,' he said. 'They're leaving it to be ruined.' He cackled cheerfully. 'I wonder what Forla thinks of my prophecies now? At the first sign of an outbreak from the crater, I'm going up the mountain. I don't need a taxi now. Piero says he doesn't need his machine because you can't get through the crowds to the mole on it. But I'm going the other way. I'm going to get pictures. Magazines all over the world will buy them. I shall make a great deal of money.'

He looked suddenly depressed. 'There is only one thing, though,' he said. 'Nothing happens. Nothing but darkness, and you can't photograph darkness.'

In the Church of Sant' Agata the lights were blazing as Don Alessandro conducted masses for the dead, the sick and the bereaved, and for the homeless of San Giorgio.

'*Requiem aeternam dona eis Domine –*' His high chant insinuated itself through the clamour in a knife-like note above the roaring; and the high echoing alto of boys' singing could be heard through the glowing doorway that brought the gilt and biscuit-coloured stone and the glittering candelabra into the gloomy street where Don Gustavo was bending over an old woman who had collapsed, exhausted by the noise and the panic, on the steps.

As he turned into the gloomy hall of Mamma Meucci's, Patch heard shouting on the stairs, and Mamma Meucci's screaming. Then he heard Cecilia's voice raised in fear and he went pounding up the dark stone steps two at a time.

The door of the Leonardis' apartment was open, a shaft of light astride the landing, where Piero Tornielli's overcoat was sprawled on the top of the staircase like a dead body. Old Tornielli stood in the darkness on the landing below with Mamma Meucci, who was yelling stridently, her hands pressed into her fat cheeks, as though that were the only thing she could think of to do, and the harshness of the sound echoed round the upper storeys.

His passion for Cecilia roused by his hatred for Patch, Piero had arrived home, dazed and bewildered by the drinks he'd had, suddenly obsessed by the need to prove his manhood by rescuing her.

'There's no time to lose,' he'd shouted, bursting in on her and gesturing wildly at the door. 'If you don't come now it'll be too late. We can get a place on Forla's yacht if we hurry. Pelli promised me.'

Cecilia had risen to her feet and was staring back at him, her eyes blazing. Piero seemed stupid and adolescent in his panic.

'I'm not coming,' she said above the din. 'I'm staying here.'

The blank refusal was like a lash across Piero's face.

'You're waiting for the Englishman,' he said, his voice breaking with disappointment at her reply, and he noticed she didn't deny it.

'Go if you wish to,' Cecilia snapped. 'Coward! Craven! Go with Forla if you wish. Go with all the other toadies. I'm staying here.'

'You can't refuse to come with me. You love me.'

'I don't. I never did. Get out.'

'I've waited months while you ogled Tom Patch. You're the whole of life to me. You've got to come.'

Making a dive for her, Piero staggered back as one of her swinging hands hit him across the nose, then he grabbed her wrists and bore her backwards.

All the frustration of months, when he had watched her watching Patch, all the time aware of the thing Patch was not aware of, all the thwarted longing, all the shuttered passion, blinded him. He forced her back on the settee, her screams harsh in his ears, and fell across her, his mouth seeking hers as she wrenched her head sideways away from him with an expression of revulsion on her face that drove him all the harder.

Then Patch burst through the doorway and grabbed him by the shoulders, and he felt himself swung bodily into the air and flung across the room. Falling against a chair, he sent it crashing into a corner, a leg flying off it to scar the lacquer of a mock Renaissance sideboard by the door.

Patch was standing in the centre of the room, his eyes blazing, his hair over his eyes, his face still grimy with the dirt of San Giorgio. Cecilia had dragged herself up on to the settee, pushing her clothing straight and the hair out of her face, and even then, in his shame, Piero saw a glowing look in her eyes he had never seen directed towards himself.

'Seducer! Adulterer! Fornicator! Cheat!' he shrieked, scrambling to his knees, his handsome face distorted by fury. 'We don't want you now. She's suffered enough at your hands.'

Patch took a giant stride across the room and, grabbing him by his arm, yanked him to his feet so that the battered chair fell to pieces from his shoulders.

'I know she stayed in the same hotel when you went to the mainland,' Piero yelled, his arms flailing as he fought to free himself. 'I know. I made her tell me. I forced her. I know everything that happened. She told me it all. Every bit of it.'

'Get out,' Patch said, swinging him off his feet again with a brutal, almost insane, violence, so that his legs dragged round behind him like the limp limbs of a rag doll.

Half-throttled and gasping for breath, Piero's inflamed jealousy still managed to drive him to defiance. 'She doesn't want you,' he screamed. 'She doesn't want you! She wants one of her own people!'

Patch picked him up again and, holding him in front of him, his toes barely touching the floor, smashed him through the doorway, knocking the wind out of him on the door-post as he went, and flung him sprawling across the landing where his cries echoed round the high roof and came back at them again. Then he grabbed him by the collar and dragged him backwards to the top of the stairs and flung him down them, so that he slid on his back upside down across several steps, tangled up in his own overcoat.

Humiliated, bruised and defeated, Piero stumbled to his feet, reaching for the wall, his fingers spread into a star on the scarred plaster, while Patch stood above him, his chest heaving with the deep breaths he took and the violence of the dislike inside him. The sight of Cecilia's terrified eyes, and her screaming mouth and her hands fighting against the clawing fingers that tore at her clothes seemed to have burst some safety valve.

He made a swift move towards Piero, ready to murder him, but Piero slithered backwards down several more steps, his mouth still babbling defiance.

'You'll regret it,' he shouted, half-crazed with his hatred. 'I'll remember this.'

'Get out!' Patch snapped. 'Get out! I'll tear your dirty little heart out if you come near Cecilia again!'

Piero grabbed for his overcoat and hurried down the stairs, trailing it after him, disappearing without looking back at Patch. His father turned and stared upwards.

'Cecilia,' he began apologetically. 'Signor Tom –'

He stopped, at a loss for words, then he too turned and ran down the stairs after his son. Mamma Meucci was still standing with her hands to her cheeks, still screaming, her eyes rolling first after Tornielli and then up to Patch.

Patch turned into the Leonardis' apartment and slammed the door against the noise outside. Then he went to Cecilia and gently pulled her to her feet, his hands under her elbows, and held her close to him while she shook with her sobbing. The fire had gone out of her and she clung to Patch, hiccuping with great dry paroxysms.

'Tom, he'll not hesitate to harm you!'

Patch snorted, indifferent to the threats of Piero, and, sitting her on the settee, knelt in front of her.

'Cecilia,' he said gently. 'Are you hurt?'

She shook her head and pulled her torn blouse together.

'No. Nothing. You came too quickly.'

'By Christ – ' Patch's face darkened with fury again and he seemed to choke over his words, ' – Cecilia, you're never really going to marry that bloody little worm?'

She shook her head again, desperate that he should understand. 'No, Tom. I never told him I would. I swear I didn't. He took it all for granted, like everyone else.'

Patch took her hand and looked at her tenderly. 'Cecilia, I'd like to think of you happy. That fool would make your life miserable. He acts like something out of a bad film all the time. Find somebody decent.'

She nodded weakly, her fingers tight on his. 'Tom, please be careful. I'm afraid. And it seems so wrong to be afraid just now.'

He listened to the racket outside for a second then he rose to his feet. 'I don't know about that,' he said, and a faint lopsided grin took the tension out of his face. 'I'm afraid too.'

There was a crash at the door and Mamma Meucci put her head in, her face grey with terror.

'Signor Patch,' she babbled. 'Mother of Mercy protect us! Old Tornielli says we may go down into his cellar until the ships come. Piero's gone out now. The Holy Mother of God have pity on us!'

She slammed the door behind her and they heard her on the stairs shooing her flock towards the ground floor.

229

Cecilia had moved to the open window where Patch stood staring out at the angry sky. He was calm again now.

'Let's stay here, Tom,' she said. 'Don't let's go down.'

He turned and looked at her, the little grin persisting so that she knew he had control of himself again.

'OK.' He stood beside her and as he took her hand, she stopped trembling. 'Hannay was right all the time, Cecilia,' he said. 'How right he was! It must be an odd feeling to be proved right when nobody expects you to be – a bit like being God.'

'When will the ships get here, Tom?'

'Soon. They'll take away anyone who wants to go.'

'Will you go, Tom?'

He turned again and smiled crookedly at her, as though he were jeering at himself. 'No,' he said. 'Oddly enough I don't think I will.'

'You always said you would.'

'I know. I never expected to be behaving like a hero but Cecilia,' he said gently. 'I'm glad you're here too. It makes it a bit easier.'

Outside everything was darkened by the grey-green twilight. The street lights had not been turned on and there was only a few glimmers in the windows of the Porto. It was as though the little town were dying.

*t h i r t y - t h r e e*

---

They were all a little startled to discover the following morning that they were still alive. The crowd that had spent the night on the mole and in the Piazza del Mare stirred with the first light to realise that Anapoli was still above water and that they were all still drawing breath.

The first ship to arrive, the Italian gunboat *Procida*, dropped anchor just outside the harbour in the early evening. There was an immediate burst of cheering from the crowd in the Piazza del Mare, a surge of relief and joy at the promised safety that the grey steel shape beyond the gloom brought to them. There was a concerted instinctive move along the mole and out of the piazza towards the beach, but the ship made no attempt to get closer.

Almost immediately afterwards, the *Ladybird*, a British frigate from the direction of Malta, began to signal from beyond Capo Amarea and the Italian ship began to flash back at her. Over the roaring of the mountain, another cheer went up from the people on the mole. The flickering white lights seemed to bring hope to them.

The British ship drew nearer and came to anchor alongside the Italian, then suddenly the bay seemed to be full of boats. The water that had seemed so abysmally empty during the whole of the day was now crowded with whalers, gigs and tenders, scuttling to and from the bigger ships like a lot of noisy beetles on the smooth surface of a millpond. Lights began to appear everywhere round the little harbour to break the funereal darkness of the town and the abandoned houses.

Half an hour after the British ship, the *Francis X. Adnauer,* an American destroyer from the fleet in Naples, let her anchor splash into the water and the rattle of her cable rang across the bay, sending up another cheer from the crowd. Boats began to arrive alongside the *Great Watling Street,* and the wharfside and the darkness echoed to the sound of voices from the Bronx and Minnesota and Nebraska and Carolina. Before midnight, the *Amsterdamster*, a Dutch freighter, was also asking in halting Italian if assistance was required and dropping her anchor too.

The Americans were grievously disappointed to find that no one was in immediate need of their wealth and man-power, but with transatlantic generosity they had started to land stores and men at once.

A conference was held in the saloon of the *Great Watling Street*, the Italian captain, who was the senior officer present, doing Hannay the honour of asking his opinion. Hannay confidently suggested that in spite of the crowds and the noise from the mountain the situation wasn't half as bad as it had been earlier in the day, and pointed out that Mont' Amarea was curiously quieter than it had been at noon; that the people were calm now that help had arrived and that there seemed no immediate need to evacuate any more than those who really wished to go. Daylight, he concluded, might be better than dark to start any serious evacuation and would cause less accidents.

The Italian captain concurred and an announcement was made over the ship's loud-hailer that comforted the people on the mole in their chilly vigil through the night.

As the first faint tinges of grey edged into the purple of the night and it became possible to pick out faces among the mass of people in the piazza, they all stirred their stiff limbs and began to get to their feet to prepare for embarkation.

The boats now stood ready to carry people out to the warships and the crowd began to bunch together in families, collecting their bundles around them.

Then someone pointed towards the summit of Amarea and his frantic, relieved shout split the morning air.

'The mountain! Look! It's stopped!'

Several heads were turned, then people struggled to their feet and stared at the slaty sides of the mountain in amazement.

The pall of mist and cinder dust which had been hanging over the crater for days had disappeared in the breeze which had sprung up, and only a steady column of smoke rose into the sky to mingle with the low cloud. Then they became aware that the noise they had listened to on and off half the night was dying and that now there was only the faint whistling sigh high again in the heavens.

There was a thin cheer from the crowd, which was broken by the whimpering of babies. Then someone stared at the ships in the bay beyond the *Great Watling Street*, and the knowledge that rescue was at hand gave them courage, and courage gave them the ready optimism of mankind.

'It's 1892 all over again! The mountain's fooled us once more!'

There was a lot of laughter, some of it ashamed, some of it relieved, then old Tornielli, who had finally abandoned his cellar in the hope of being taken aboard a ship, claimed that he had not made his way to the shore through fear of the mountain but because he felt that the authorities might need some help if an evacuation were to take place.

'I came to be close to the boat,' Tomaso the fisherman said. 'I can run faster than Meucci.'

'I came because my wife insisted,' someone else replied. 'And because the children were frightened.'

Emiliano, on the fringe of the crowd, where he had been crouching with his family through the night, suddenly realised that among the crowd around him there were many from the topmost outskirts of the town, some of them even from the villages on the slopes above Forla's palace, and that many of them would be seeking coffee and food as soon as they discovered they had come to no harm. Only a small bar at the end of the mole was there to provide it. Danger suddenly didn't seem quite so imminent.

He rose to his feet and tucked up the apron he had still been wearing when he had put up the shutters and joined the crowd heading for the mole the night before. Then he set off hurriedly up the hill again towards the Piazza Martiri, shooing his children before him with gestures. Old Tornielli, seeing him go, realised what was in his mind, and it occurred to him that in the uproar Emiliano might well need some assistance if his custom grew too big for him to cope with – particularly if his waiter were not around. So, seeing the possibility of earning some money, he began to push his way out of the crowd.

Then Tomaso, realising why Emiliano and Tornielli had gone, thought of breakfast and headed after them, followed by Mamma Meucci and her children. As they pushed out of the mass of people, two men started to disagree over the possession of a goat, and in the argument that followed fear was forgotten as everybody took sides.

One by one and in families, the crowd began to break up. With the coming of daylight, new courage had come to them all. All those fears which had hemmed them in with darkness were dispelled now that they could see what was happening and life suddenly became normal again. The men began to laugh – nervously at first and then at their own fears. Mothers began to shriek at their squalling children, and Hannay, watching from the bridge of the *Great Watling Street*, saw the crowd grow thinner, first at the edges, then in the middle where the people had huddled together for warmth during the night. There was still a touch of hysteria in the behaviour of everyone but a tremendous relief that it had been no worse.

A chestnut seller was hunting round the piazza for his baskets which had been upset in the darkness. The owner of the little bar by the Via Maddalena, seeing Emiliano heading up the hill, had realised what was happening and was whipping down his shutters as fast as he could in the hope of being ready first. Next door to him, the fruit shop proprietor, eyeing the wreckage of his stall which had been knocked over and smashed by the surging crowd the night before, set about putting it together again.

A beggar picked up an abandoned umbrella, decided it might be worth a few lire still, and hurriedly slipped away with it under his coat. The rubbish and the wreckage of the crowds in the piazza were gradually picked over and dispersed, while the growing breeze sent the scraps of paper that had contained loaves and sausages fleeing before it to whirl with the last of the dusty ash from the mountain into the corners and up the Via Maddalena where they were finally scattered under the arches of the Musco.

The ships' captains watching from the bridges of the *Procida*, the *Ladybird*, the *Francis X. Adnauer* and the *Amsterdamster*, seeing the crowd thinning out in the Piazza del Mare, immediately cancelled the orders they had given to send away all the ships' boats which had been lowered during the night.

'I'll be god-damned!' the captain of the *Francis X. Adnauer* said in amazement. 'They're going home again.'

Sailors from New York and Nebraska, from London and Sheerness and Chatham, from Anzio and Salerno and Genoa, from the Hague and Rotterdam, watched in astonishment as the islanders, with their ready adaptability, accepted the fact that they were safe and immediately started to behave normally again, disappearing into the narrow streets off the Piazza del Mare, among the alleys and the little shops and the courtyards where the washing still hung out among the rubbish and the pots of geraniums and the broken tiles like so many flags of truce. They felt cheated and annoyed, as though all their work and lack of sleep was for nothing.

'The ungrateful sods,' said a hairy-faced petty officer from the *Ladybird* as he sat in the stern of a whaler under the ship's side, waiting for the final word that would send him into the shore. 'The sods don't sodding well *want* rescuing now.'

They stared up at the mountain but, even in their annoyance, they had to admit there was nothing particularly threatening about it at that moment. A slight breeze had sprung up in the night and had carried away the dust pall from the summit, and the sun was actually shining weakly on the slopes. The column of oily smoke climbed slowly into the clouds in a calm way that indicated no danger at all.

When the orders came to pick up evacuees, the few boats that headed for the steps of the mole and the chosen spots against the Piazza del Mare found they were returning empty. Only a few of the more timid, a few of the oldest, and a few of those people who had come only a few months before from the mainland in the hope of picking up an easy living among the tourists who had recently discovered the island, were anxious to depart. The rest of them, thinking of their meagre savings and the price of rents on the mainland – if there were rooms to be had at all – were only too anxious to get back to their shops and benches, and their fields and stables. Even the tragedy at San Giorgio seemed to have been forgotten in the general feeling of relief.

The frustrated sailors shouted and argued and grumbled from the boats bobbing under the mole and off the beach and occasionally, when they lost their tempers, pretended they hadn't understood and jammed some protesting and angry old man into the boats and took him out to one of the ships only to bring him back again on the next trip. But for the most part they were beginning to realise that their recall from canteens and cinemas in Malta and Naples, their frantic loading of supplies and bandages and food on the mainland the night before, the changes of course and the mad dash across the Tyrrhenian, and their all-night slog over boats and equipment were all suddenly pointless. The mountain had played one of its splendid jokes on them all.

In the Palazzo di Città, where he had spent the night with his family, sitting close to the telephone, blank-eyed with defeat, Mayor Pelli became aware of gaiety outside in the piazza. He hurried to the window and looked out. To his amazement, the people who were crossing the square were moving up the hill, not down. And they were laughing, their dusty features creased with happiness and relief. A glimmering of hope in his face, he hurried from his office to the back of the building and, staring at the mountain, he saw that the smoke pall had cleared and that the column of jetty vapours that rose from the crater had subsided a little.

The explosions and the unspeakable roaring of the night before had given way again to the familiar high-pitched whistling sound.

'We're safe,' he shouted as he ran to his wife, his voice echoing through the corridors. 'The mountain's quiet again! It's all over!'

He embraced his wife and each of his children, relieved that nothing worse had happened; then, as he realised that the mountain's traditional behaviour meant reprieve for him if he were quick, he seized the telephone and rang up the coastguard's office where he got a first-hand account of how things were progressing in the Piazza del Mare.

He put the instrument down again, his eyes beginning to show relief. 'Piero, Piero,' he shouted, and Piero Tornielli, his face haggard with sleeplessness, appeared in the doorway, rubbing his aching behind which was suffering from a night in one of the office chairs.

'Piero,' Pelli said, his voice growing firmer all the time as his politician's resilience brought strength back to his decision. 'There'll be no evacuation now. Everybody's going home. It's all over. It's 1892 all over again.' He thumped the table confidently, not noticing Tornielli's agonised face and sluggish movements.

'Piero, we've got the answer now to Bosco. *We* were right all the time. We were right to wait. Get in touch with the coastguards again and get them to pass a message to the captains of the ships in the bay. Ask them to come to my office for wine. We must formally offer our thanks and our apologies for the trouble we've caused.'

His face split into a smile to which the miserable Piero failed to respond. 'This is going to prove expensive,' he said gaily. 'Somebody's going to present us with a nice bill for last night. There was a lot of damage done, too. It's heaven-sent to lay at Bosco's door.'

He stopped dead, his expression changing to one of amazement as, through the open window, he heard the sound of a loudspeaker blaring from in front of the Archivio at the other side of the square. Bosco, also seeing the opportunities in the night's events for Pelli, was endeavouring to undermine his arguments by getting in his own blow first.

'People of Anapoli,' he was saying, 'you've seen how the authorities waver, how they have to be told what to do by the workers – '

Pelli whirled round.

'Piero,' he shouted. 'Quickly! Ring up Giovanni and tell him to get the loudspeaker car moving. Get hold of a bill-poster. Get some pamphlets out. Make sure everyone knows our meetings are still on.'

He thought suddenly of Patch and his angry gestures the day before.

'And, Piero,' he said, his voice dropping, 'get the police headquarters. There are things I wish to do.'

## thirty-four

By mid-day it was all over. The crowds had left the Piazza del Mare and the mole and the grey-sand beach where the whalers with their angry crews bobbed. Only the homeless from San Giorgio still hung around, still shocked-looking, still dazed, still bewildered, still unable to appreciate the relief of everyone else, waiting for the assistance that Pelli's workers were organising for them. They had little else to be thankful for.

Don Dominico was the first to make a move to find out what damage had been done outside the Porto. Perched behind a motor-cycle volunteer, his skirts tucked up around him, he roared round the island road to Fumarola. But all there was to see were the evidences of the previous night's panic. The stray dogs and cats were still in the streets, the pigeons were on the roofs, the goats were still on the mountainside – even, he was delighted to note, in Amadeo Baldicera's field where they had found the dead birds.

He immediately hurried to his untidy study followed by his dogs and telephoned the news to the café in the Piazza del Mare.

When they got his message, the people of Fumarola set off for home, and those from Colonna del Greco and Corti Marina sent motor-cyclists to *their* villages. As soon as they heard their homes were untouched also, they set off again with their motor-scooters and their Fiats and their motorcycles, with their mule-carts and donkey carriages, and their bicycles, and on foot, queuing for buses or trailing their families and their dogs behind them out of the Piazza del Mare after the people of the Porto, who were hurrying home to make sure no one had slipped into their houses while they had been away.

Even the Haywards, startled to an awareness of being alive again by the sunshine that was beginning to warm the slopes of Amarea, noticed the sudden absence of people in the Piazza del Mare and, to their surprise, their car, still standing unharmed where they had left it the night before. It took them some time to make up their minds, but the fact that none of the other English people on the island had turned up on Hannay's ship during the night gave them increased courage, and they thanked him stiffly, trying to pretend they'd never been afraid, and climbed down the swaying gangplank to the mole.

By the time the afternoon sun had crept round, instead of the terrified, half-clothed people who had occupied the Piazza del Mare the night before, the panicky mules and donkeys and the noisy dogs, there were now English, Dutch. American and Italian sailors, sitting round the smoky little bar near the Via Maddalena and exchanging with each other in stumbling three-word sentences their disgust at the fiasco of the evacuation. Whatever their nationality, they were at one in their lower-deck fury at what they considered the brass-hats' bungling. A few of them even wandered into the Piazza Martiri to jam the delighted Emiliano's bar with their noisy demand for 'vino', and even as far as the Town Hall where Pelli was marshalling his arguments for an assault on the politics of Bosco.

It was the very normality of the place that made all the more puzzling the appearance of the policeman at Mamma Meucci's in the afternoon with a request for Patch to call at the Town Hall.

Pelli was sitting in his office when Patch arrived. His carpet was marked with the dust from the shoes of his numerous visitors. Behind him stood Carpucci, the sergeant-major of police, and the captain of the *Procida*, and to one side, a little out of his depth, the captain of the *Ladybird*. The hall outside seemed full of naval officers of all nationalities.

'Good afternoon, Signor Patch,' Pelli said in English, and immediately, from the stiff tone of his voice, Patch realised something was wrong. 'Please sit down.'

'Thanks,' Patch said warily. 'I'll stand.'

Pelli introduced the naval men. 'This is Commander Havanter, of your own country's ship, *Ladybird*,' he concluded and the British officer nodded. 'We thought it might be a good idea to have him hear what we have to say. We shouldn't like a garbled report to go out of the island – even over a trivial affair like this. He agreed to be present.'

The words had an ominous note in them.

'What trivial affair are we talking about?' Patch asked. Pelli ignored him and spoke in whispers with Carpucci before he turned to him again.

'This is a most unfortunate thing, Signor Patch,' he said, looking up. Patch stared back at him, conscious of the disapproving features of the immaculate Commander Havanter and, for the first time, of his own untidy, paint-daubed clothes. 'What is?' he asked. 'Tell me what's wrong?'

Pelli put his finger-tips together. 'I'm obliged to ask you for your residence permit,' he said. Patch gazed unbelievingly at him for a moment. There was an atmosphere of artificiality about the whole scene – the policemen, the two naval officers, Pelli, a little shame-faced as he waited, and Piero Tornielli in the background with a smooth expression of triumph on his face.

'Why?' he asked, his expression becoming hostile. 'It's quite in order.'

241

'That's not the point, Signor Patch. We're asking you to return it.'

'Why?' Patch was leaning forward over the desk now, his brows down in a dogged, driven look.

'You can hardly expect to be allowed to remain here after the trouble you've caused.'

Patch smiled bitterly as he began to realise what Pelli was up to.

'I see it now, Mr Mayor,' he said. 'You want me out of the way.'

Pelli shrugged. 'The town has been very badly frightened, Signor Patch. We can't take chances on the possibility of disorder. The police feel it would be best for you to leave.'

In the silence as Pelli sat back, Commander Havanter blew his nose in a loud trumpeting noise that made everyone stare at him.

'We've no option, Signor Patch,' Pelli said. 'If you'd behaved with as much dignity as the other foreigners on the island in the recent upset we should have had no complaint to make. But you've been concerning yourself with affairs that should be of no interest to you and, with the excited state of the population, the police are afraid of what might happen if it started again. They have cause even to suspect the reason for your activities.'

He sat back, wringing his hands with the gesture that meant so clearly that he had already washed his hands of the affair.

'What the authorities on the mainland will do, I don't know,' he went on. 'There is nothing to stop you making an application for a residence permit elsewhere. I'm only asking you to leave Anapoli.'

Patch was silent for a while, still unable to accept that he was being driven out.

'There's no appeal against this?' he asked.

'The police have made up their minds. You could approach your consul, but I'm afraid he'll naturally contact us for our report. Would you like us to make arrangements for your passage to the mainland?'

Patch drew a deep breath. 'I'll make my own arrangements,' he said. 'Doubtless the captain of the ship at the mole will take me when he leaves.'

'That's very helpful of you, Signor Patch. When is this ship due to leave?'

Patch's hot temper flared up and he answered sharply: 'I don't know. Tomorrow or the day afterwards. Why should you worry? It's before the election.'

Pelli kept his eyes on his blotter as he replied: 'Thank you, Signor Patch. We should have liked to be generous but with the population as deeply stirred as it has been and with the election so close we can't take any chances with the police at our disposal. Will that be enough time?'

Oh, God, Patch thought, why didn't they throw him out by the scruff of the neck and have done with it?

'It's enough,' he said heavily.

'Very well. I won't detain you any more. You must have a great many affairs to attend to. Perhaps you'd produce your permit some time for the police.'

Pelli picked up his pen, vaguely ashamed of himself and anxious to be finished with the affair. The policeman who had brought Patch in laid a hand on his arm. Carpucci and the captain of the *Procida* began to talk earnestly together, obviously trying to look as though it were no business of theirs. Piero Tornielli had turned away to hide the pleasure on his face.

Patch stared round the room, his temper boiling up again, then he shook off the policeman's hand and stalked out. The captain of the *Ladybird* followed him, his cap under his arm.

243

Patch rounded on him in the sunshine at the top of the Town Hall steps. 'Well?' he said furiously. 'Can't you do something about it?'

Havanter stopped dead. He had obviously expected to leave unmolested and Patch's vehemence startled him. 'What do you want me to do?' he asked coldly. 'They only brought me along to see fair play. That's what I did.' His features were clearly disapproving.

'But all that damn' nonsense in there,' Patch said. 'Pelli's lying.'

'I'm not in a position to judge. I can only go on what I'm told. For the record, it might interest you to know that even your own fellow-countrymen here couldn't find much to say on your behalf.'

'Fellow-countrymen? Who?'

'Woman by the name of Hayworth or Harwood or something.'

'Mrs Hayward, by God!' Patch's face was dark with anger.

'That might be the name,' Havanter said. 'I met her on my way up here. I lent her a party of men to help with her belongings. She seemed distressed. Naturally, I asked her if she knew you. Apparently she knew you well.'

Patch laughed bitterly and Havanter went on.

'Pity you didn't keep your nose out of the affairs of these people,' he said. 'Our reputation's low enough in the Med. at the moment without it sinking any further. They told me in there you were a Communist. Are you?'

'Oh, God,' Patch said in desperation, as Havanter's words built up a case against him blacker than it should have been, a case founded on hearsay and half-truths. 'Can't a man grow up?'

Havanter waited until he was calm before he spoke again. 'Did you interfere in their affairs?'

'No, I didn't.'

'They told me you led a deputation to the Mayor yesterday. What do you call that?'

'They asked me to speak for them.'

'Who did?'

'The fishermen. I didn't want to.'

'Are they Communists?'

'God knows. Ask 'em yourself. I didn't bother.'

'You've been to see the Mayor before, haven't you? You took everything he told you straight to the Communists. They got some good copy out of it. Posters all round the town.'

'What is this – an inquisition?'

'I'm only making my position clear. You've been having a fine time one way and another – you and this Leonardi, who it seems is well known as a – trouble-maker.'

' "Crackpot" would be nearer the mark.'

'You even tried to drag the Yanks into it.'

'Raphael's an old friend of mine. He still is.'

'He's a Yank.'

'He said he'd do what he could.'

'He didn't do much, did he?' Havanter said contemptuously. 'He didn't want to get mixed up with politics. He said so.'

'Look –' Patch made a desperate attempt to explain before it was too late, and it seemed already too late, ' – it wasn't like that. It wasn't like that at all.' He waved a hand at the people crossing the piazza, relieved people, still a little excited and hysterical at their reprieve. 'Ask all those people out there. They'll tell you.'

Havanter turned his cold intelligent face towards the sunshine. 'I don't think I'll bother,' he said.

Patch flared into a rage. 'No, you god-damned pale edition of a better generation of sea-dogs, you won't! You've made up your mind already, haven't you?'

'Cut that out!'

245

Patch made a supreme effort to control himself. 'Where did you get this information?' he asked slowly.

'Pelli's assistant. He got it from some woman friend of yours.'

Patch gave a harsh shout of laughter. 'My God, stabbed in the back!'

'I beg your pardon.'

'Nothing. I suppose you made frantic signals to check up on it all, eh?'

'Some of it. I like to be in possession of the facts.'

'So that your own lily-white hands would be clean at the end of it, I suppose?'

'I did my best for you,' Havanter said calmly. 'It might interest you to know that this is not my concern. I'd no need to be here at all. I thought I might be able to help you. Now I'm not sure that you need help. I don't know what you're complaining about. *You* did all the agitating. Not me.'

He put his hat on and pulled the peak over his eye. Then, without another word, he stalked across the dusty piazza where the breeze was already blowing the sifting dust into the corners and into great grey-green swathes under the arcade of the Archivio.

## thirty-five

Patch sat on the bed in his room beneath the ugly picture of the Virgin Mary Mamma Meucci had given him. He had been smoking one cigarette after another, his expression angry.

The rain had started again unexpectedly, just when they had all looked forward to a good day, and was lancing down across the window-panes out of a leaden sky which had boiled up from nowhere before a growing wind that had blown the dust clear and then brought the rain to wash away the last traces of the previous night's panic.

He had been storming round the room for a couple of hours now, picking up half-finished canvases to pack them and then, in an explosion of fury, flinging them down again in a heap.

'That god-damned officer,' he said. He seemed to have forgotten Pelli in his dislike of Havanter.

They all stopped what they were doing and looked up at him – Hannay, from the streaming window where he was sucking his pipe; Mamma Meucci, who was trying with tears in her eyes to tie a bundle of small canvases together with a lot of old string, sighing and groaning and wiping her eyes as she worked; Cecilia, trying to push his clothes into a battered old green suitcase; her grandfather, sitting in a corner, his head in his hands, his white hair disarrayed, staring at the floor.

'Damn his smug self-righteousness,' Patch said. 'Behaving as though he were sitting in judgement on me. God, Cecilia, when he talked about you as some "woman friend" of mine, – as though I'd picked you up off the streets – I could have knocked the words down his throat.'

Cecilia looked up again, gratefully, then she folded a shirt and put it in the case. 'You should buy yourself some new clothes, Tom,' she said gently.

'I don't need new clothes,' Patch said fiercely. 'I don't need new clothes to paint with or to punch naval officers on their snotty noses with. My God –' he seemed to choke ' – that bloody Piero!'

He flung away again, wanting to smash something in his rage, then he found himself in front of Leonardi who looked up and sighed. 'Again,' the old man said. 'Again! They're laughing at me again all round the town.'

Patch turned away, deflated, his anger suddenly gone. Old Leonardi had no sympathy to spare for anyone but himself. His only concern was that the mountain had played its infamous jest on him just when he appeared to have been right. His indifference seemed like a symbol. In a month they'd all have forgotten Patch. Any anger they might feel now would have gone cold and he'd be just a name – just one of the many painters who'd once lived there.

'Never mind those little canvases,' he said wearily to Mamma Meucci. 'You can have 'em. They're not worth taking away. They belong to my pre-Hannay period when I was happily drinking myself silly and not worrying about anything.'

'Look –' Hannay turned round, feeling he ought to say something, ' – there isn't all that much of a hurry. I can hold the ship till the weekend.' He caught Patch's eye and glanced pointedly at Cecilia. 'So long as you're on board they won't worry.'

Patch looked quickly at Cecilia, too, then he shook his head. 'No! For God's sake, let's make it tomorrow at the latest! The noose's round my neck. Don't let's delay the drop.'

'It's all my fault,' Hannay said in a heavy self-accusing growl, strangely humble for once. 'I pushed you into it.'

'Don't lose any sleep over it,' Patch said with another smile. 'I'll get over it. I was getting stale here, anyway.'

Hannay sucked his pipe for a second and stared out at the bulk of Amarea. Over Mamma Meucci's loud sighs and sympathetic wheezes, they could hear the high whistling sound through the rain still and from somewhere deep in the mountain's throat, a faint grumble, a mere shadow of the previous night's roaring.

'Pelli's team of experts came after all,' Hannay went on. 'But not when he said they did. They were on the *Procida*. And they came off their own bat. They're supposed to be starting work tomorrow. They'll say I'm daft.'

'That was always *my* opinion.'

'A lot of fuss about nothing.' Hannay sucked his pipe again unhappily. 'The ships have laid off in the bay now even. There's only the Eyetie handy. They're only sticking around because they don't want to go home and they're spinning it out as long as they can. Did you know the Haywards was packing up?'

'There's no need to make conversation,' Patch said, and the heaviness had gone out of his voice. 'I can bear to think of leaving without that.'

Hannay flushed. 'Have you contacted the British Consul?' he asked.

Patch nodded. 'He said he'd look into it, but he didn't think he could do anything about it. That means he won't.'

'Havanter won't help you by the sound of him.'

Patch grinned unexpectedly. 'If *he'd* said the things I said, I wouldn't help *him*.'

249

As he finished speaking, they heard a motor-cycle outrider shatter the silence of the Via Pescatori and almost on top of the racket the sound of Pelli's loudspeaker car.

'– you've seen the irresponsibility of the Communists. You've seen the trouble they've caused. Destruction, not construction, is what they stand for –'

'Don't take 'em long to get the rat race going again,' Hannay growled in his throat. 'Did you know Orlesi came to see me? In person. Took them crates back ashore. Everyone. I coulda strangled him with his own necktie. The work and the radio messages it entailed! They've been unloading that flipping yacht again too!'

He knocked out his pipe on the window-frame and walked slowly towards the door.

'Cristoforo came to see me. He says to say good-bye to you and thanks for all the cigarettes. He couldn't come himself. His uncle's watching him – especially now the ship's due away.'

Patch nodded.

'Emiliano looked as though he was going to cry.'

'I'm not surprised. He's losing his best customer. He'll be able to put that plaque up now I shan't be here to stop him. "*On this spot Tom Patch defied the combined forces of Mayor Pelli and the British Navy. Inghilterra ed Italia. Loved by one and all.*" Looks patriotic. They might even look on me as a sort of Lord Byron in years to come.'

Mamma Meucci indicated the canvas attached to the easel – the *Primavera* on which Patch had worked spasmodically throughout all the upheavals.

'Throw it through the window,' Patch said with sweeping cheerfulness. 'It makes me feel ill. In the light of present events, it's plain silly. My next will be a symbolic design presenting the dictatorship of the masses by politicians, petty Caesars and potty little jacks-in-office. All dwarfs and gnomes wearing girdles of forms and slogans, garlanded with dogmatism and reclining on bowers of red tape and indifference. Throw it away.'

'Nay – ' Hannay moved forward, ' – I've taken quite a fancy to them pansies of yours.'

'Help yourself,' Patch said. 'Old Tornielli'll get it down to the mole for a couple of hundred lire.'

Hannay moved to the door again then he turned and glanced through the window. 'Not thinking of going anywhere, was you, because there's a cop across the road watching this place. That Pelli's not going to let you do any dodging, Mister.'

The door slammed behind him in that thunderous way he had of making his exit – as though he were a tank backing out of a barracks – and they heard his feet on the stairs.

Mamma Meucci finished tying up the canvases. 'That's all, Signor Tom,' she said. 'I'll get you something to eat.'

'I don't want anything, Mamma,' Patch said. 'I'll be all right.'

Mamma Meucci sighed, nodded and rolled out. Old Leonardi heaved himself to his feet and followed her, his head hanging between his shoulders.

Lights were coming on in the houses outside one by one as the daylight lessened. The column of smoke from Amarea moved lazily upwards, cutting the full moon in half with its jetty pall as it emerged briefly from the clouds.

Patch stared at the roof tops caught by the silver light, knowing he'd looked at them dozens of times before without feeling, and tried to sort out his mixed emotions. With one breath he wanted to say 'To Hell with the place!' and with the next he knew he would never quite be able to shake its dust from his shoes. He had become too involved with its people.

'For the first time,' he said aloud to himself, marvelling at the power of the emotions in him, 'I'm afraid to leave this damn' place. I want to stay here even if it sinks under my feet.' He turned and grinned at Cecilia. 'It's a matter of principle chiefly, I think,' he said. 'I'd do it all again if I had to.'

Cecilia looked up at him, her face showing her loneliness and her helpless rebellion against a world which had become too big to be controllable. 'Is there no way out, Tom?'

He shrugged. 'Doesn't look like it. They'll see me safely off and that will be that. I'm a political risk to Pelli as long as I try and to a politician there's no bogey so frightening as a political risk.' He smiled. 'Poor little Pelli. I can't say I blame him. Bosco's a crafty devil and he's got a lot to think about.'

'Tom, you don't agree with Pelli, do you?'

'No.' He smiled again. 'But I feel a bit forgiving all of a sudden. I don't know why. I think Anapoli means a lot to the poor little soul. He just took a chance for it that didn't quite come off.' He turned away hurriedly and rubbed his chin. 'My God, if I go on like this I'll be apologising to him.'

Cecilia was watching him as he moved about. 'Tom, where will you go?' she asked.

'I don't know. Some scruffy little dive in Streatham or Chelsea.' He laughed. 'A nice concrete road a couple of kilometres long. Full of trim little trees in trim little gardens, all looking as though they've been kicked to pieces by the kids or worried by the cats.' His smile disappeared suddenly. 'My God, what a prospect!'

'Must you go home?'

'It depends on Pelli. It depends on whether I can get a permit to stay somewhere else.'

He pushed a pile of pictures straight, aimlessly, obsessed with a sudden feeling of uselessness, as though all he had done up to now had been pointless and aimed nowhere and at nothing. There seemed to be no direction to his life. It had been nothing but a series of events, none of them apparently linked, occurring in first one country then another, a series of different lives lived in a succession of shabby houses where the size of the studio and the shape of the window had been more important than the comfort.

There seemed no point in it suddenly, without roots in the ground somewhere to make it all worth while, and he felt for a moment as though he had been wandering with one-night stops throughout the whole of his existence.

He went to the window where Hannay had been standing and stared out at the rain. In the doorway of the apartment block opposite, a man stood smoking, and as he glanced upwards, Patch recognised him as a policeman who lived in the Via Garibaldi.

'The bloodhound's still there,' he said. He laughed shortly.

'Odd, isn't it?' he said. 'When for the first time in my life I show some signs of responsibility, everybody who represents responsibility comes down on me like a ton of bricks and tells me I'm being *irresponsible*. Everybody's come safely out of it but me.'

He turned away and Cecilia felt tears stinging her eyes as she realised her own share in the events which were driving him away. She sat on the bed, her legs weak, and he crossed to her and blew in her ear from behind.

'Tom, what are you going to do?'

'Blow in your ear.'

'Tom, be serious.' He swung away again, smiling, but restless. 'If I were serious, I'd probably cut that damned officer's liver out.'

'You can't let them drive you out.'

'Cecilia, my little love, I'm out already.' He shrugged. 'It's probably a good thing. It'll stir me up. That damn' *Primavera* was beginning to look as if it had been painted by a three-year-old with a box of birthday colours.'

He came up behind her again and kissed her gently on the cheek. His eyes were tender and as she searched his face she prayed he wouldn't spoil the moment with something angry or sarcastic. She'd thought many times in the last few days of a time like this; lying in her bed hearing him moving upstairs, her body crying out with this incredible new longing for his hands in her hair and his lips on her throat.

Please God, she prayed, don't let him go without me. Let him understand.

But he seemed not to notice her and shattered the moment with the commonplace sarcasm she'd feared.

'Time you were off now,' he said. 'Or you'll be a lost woman.'

He indicated the old lady watching with interest at the window of the room across the street. 'Besides, I'm an international spy now – allied to Bosco and in the pay of the Kremlin.'

He gave her the wry grin she loved so much and without another word, went out, slamming the door behind him.

# thirty-six

There was a full moon when Patch left the dark chasm of the Via Pescatori. The colour-washed walls of the houses alongside him rose in the pale blue light to the balconies above that ended in black oblique slashes where the spikes of a big cactus in a pot threw stark shadows across the stone-work like great clawing fingers.

The rain had stopped again and the air was fresh with the dampness of it. In the gutters, the puddles picked up the moonlight in bright glints. Below him, towards the sea and the lights of the *Great Watling Street*, the russet tiles of the roofs were dusted with silver, and the houses looked like cubes of black and white on a checkerboard. Through the leaning walls, he could see the harbour and the sleek shapes of the battleships out in the bay marked with the yellow lines of their portholes, and against the mole the tubby shape of the *Great Watling Street*.

Hannay was waiting for him by the gangway when he arrived. He carried his old green suitcase and a bundle of small canvases, and behind him Meucci wheeled a handcart with his easel and another bundle of canvases. As he reached the ship, he noticed that the policeman who had followed him from the end of the Via Pescatori had stopped in the Piazza del Mare and was surreptitiously lighting a cigarette in a corner.

'Thank you for the escort, Pasotti,' Patch shouted. 'You can go home now.'

The policeman's head came up for a moment, then he was engrossed again with his cigarette.

Hannay greeted him without a smile.

'Ready?' he asked.

Patch nodded.

'Said good-bye to Cecilia?'

'Yes.'

Hannay glanced curiously at him. He had seen the tears in Cecilia's eyes when Patch had gone to see Pelli, had seen the doubt and the anguish as she waited for him to return. 'Dead keen on you, that kid, Tom,' he said and Patch looked up at the unexpected use of his Christian name.

'Yes, I know she is,' he said.

'Meeting her again?'

'No.'

'Never? Aren't you – er – sort of fond of her, too? I always thought you was a bit.'

'Of course I am, you bloody fool!'

'But – '

'Let's cut out the "Love's Old Sweet Song",' Patch said quickly. 'She's better off without me. She's only a kid and I'm approaching forty.'

'She doesn't seem to think it's a drawback.'

'Maybe not. But I'm a bad-tempered bastard, too, with a tongue like barbed wire. I've quarrelled with every established and decent society in London and New York and now I've done it here. Enemies stick to me like flies to a jam-pot. She deserves something better than that.'

Hannay seemed about to say something in protest. He stared at Patch, baffled, his realistic, honest soul which had been caught up in a fragment of romantic hope, bitterly disappointed, then he shrugged and took the suitcase.

'Let's have you aboard,' he said.

They spoke to each other without warmth but there was an odd sort of affection between them.

'You'd better have Anderson's cabin,' Hannay went on. 'He's up in town with his woman. He'll not leave her till we're due to sail, so you might as well. He'll be on duty then, anyway, and I'll leave a message for him with the watchman.'

As a tearful Meucci passed Patch's few belongings aboard, Hannay stared up at Amarea and the column of smoke that was moving slowly across the moon.

'Is it my imagination,' he said, 'or is there more smoke?'

'I expect it's your imagination. You've got a good imagination.'

Hannay accepted the rebuke without speaking. Patch seemed to have lost all interest in anything but getting away from Anapoli, and he followed Hannay through the ship without another word.

Anderson's cabin was a locker-like compartment hung with its owner's clothes. Tucked into the sides of the spotted mirror were one or two yellowing photographs of Anderson's girl friends whose backgrounds seemed to vary between the palm trees of the far east and the plain brick walls of a Manchester backyard, and one of the boat-hooks was girdled with the dusty pink frill of a woman's garter.

'It's a bit small but I reckon it'll do you for a bit,' Hannay commented.

He stepped towards the bunk and, yanking the ginger cat from the covers, threw it through the door.

'That damned cat,' he complained. 'It'll be pupping in his pocket one of these days and serve him right.'

When Hannay had left, Patch took off his jacket and threw himself down on the hard bunk.

A dog howled among the houses round the Piazza del Mare, and Patch, suffocating in the stifling heat of the little cabin, heaved over on the bunk, lit a cigarette, puffed once on it, and forgot it. Of all that he had left behind on Anapoli only Cecilia remained vividly in his mind at that moment and he wondered if she would ever get away from the island now.

He began to think that perhaps he'd been a damn' fool to leave her but for the life of him he couldn't imagine her living out her days with him – or even wanting to. He knew he loved her – he must have done for ages – but he couldn't see her giving up security and dignity in her own country and all that someone like Piero could offer her for the knock-down-drag-out kind of life he'd been used to, living in hired rooms, with the smell of turpentine getting into the food, and the paint spotting the furniture, the noisy, quarrelsome, crowded places like Mamma Meucci's. She'd never seemed to fit into that scarred and faded block in the Via Pescatori and somehow now, in Anderson's cabin with its stale souvenirs of his shabby love affairs, she seemed even more decent and desirable.

The cigarette burned his fingers and he threw it out of the porthole. The dog howled again and Patch noticed the sighing sound from the mountain had increased, like a rising wind.

By the time he turned out the light and lay in the dark, still unable to push Cecilia from his mind, more dogs had started howling, and now and then he heard a fishermans donkey bray, raucous and abrupt in the stillness, from its stables behind the Via Maddalena.

He woke up panting. The air seemed charged with heat to the point of explosion and the place was full of the smell of smoke.

Then he became conscious of a whistling roar that filled the air, and the sighing sound now grown as harsh and grating as escaping steam. Even as he swung his legs from the bunk the din increased and he heard the sound of footsteps on the deck. He leapt for the door, almost crashing into Hannay who had come to fetch him.

'Brother,' Hannay said, in his flat voice. ' 'Old your 'at on. The perisher's started again. Half an hour ago, and it's increasing fast.'

They turned on their heels and ran for the deck. Just as they reached the bridge, they saw an immense flower of flame shoot from the top of the mountain and go roaring up into the sky in a majestic column of smoke. As they ducked back, unharmed but instinctively cowering, there was a sound like a million batteries of artillery firing a barrage, followed by another puff of flame that illuminated the ship and threw up the crooked houses of the Porto into yellow squares dotted with the blind eyes of their windows. Then the glow died in some sort of mysterious ebb and flow, like the breathing of some gigantic monster, and the houses disappeared again into the darkness.

For a while, still crouching and unable to believe that they could be safe, they stared at Amarea, the breath caught in their throats at the magnificence and the evil of it, the words stuck to their tongues. Then a fountain of sparks exploded from the crater and fell in long slow arcs to the sides of the mountain. It was as though the town were on fire, for the glare lit up the whole island and the sea.

There was a sudden chatter of excitement from the Lascar seamen lining the rails and a distinct human wail from dozens of throats that came from the town and was drowned immediately by the roar that accompanied a new cascade of flames and sparks.

'Some of that lot's coming down near Fumarola,' Hannay said and they both thought immediately of Don Dominico and his big black boots and his dusty soutane and the tired eyes that had lit up so at the news that they would help him.

The fires in the crater died away again – but only for a second, then there was another explosion and another salvo of sparks shot thousands of feet into the air among the rolling smoke. In spite of all that had happened in the past three weeks, they were still surprised and shocked by the sight.

'Sudden activity on the *Canzone del Mare*,' Hannay said laconically, apparently unmoved by the din as he indicated Forla's yacht with his thumb. All its lights were blazing and as they stared they saw a small rowing boat move out from the shadows near the shore and cross a strip of brightly illuminated water that shone like burnished copper. It disappeared again into the blackness alongside the yacht and several people were helped on board. Immediately they heard the low thrum of the yacht's engines starting up, and the *Canzone del Mare* began to move slowly towards the sea.

'What do you bet that's Forla?' Hannay said. 'Running like a mad rat off a sinking ship.'

Patch had said nothing during the explosions from the mountain and now he turned away from the rail abruptly.

'I'm going ashore,' he said.

Hannay swung round on him. 'That cop's still there at the end of the mole,' he said. 'You'll never get past him.'

'Just watch me.'

'Where're you going?'

'Cecilia. She's on her own.'

'She's got the old man.'

'He's more a hindrance than a help. Let go of my bloody arm.'

Hannay swung Patch round again to face him with a surprising strength. 'OK, Tom,' he said gently. 'OK, I'm going to. But give us an ear for a sec.'

Patch disengaged his arm and stared impatiently at Hannay who held out a rubber-covered torch. 'First of all,' he said. 'Get your 'ooks on this. It might be useful. And, Tom, bring her down here. The old man as well, if you like. But bring Cecilia with you especially. Don't take no for an answer. Don't let her refuse. If you don't bring her, lad,' he said earnestly, 'you'll regret it for the rest of your life.'

The noise from the mountain was increasing all the time and they found they were having to shout as what sounded like a fault in some gigantic boiler muffled their words. It was followed by another series of violent detonations like a prolonged bellowing that shook the whole of the mole.

People began to run about in the Piazza del Mare, black figures against the glow that was reflected from the sky, as the whole crazy joke started all over again.

Hannay gave Patch a push.

'Hurry up now, lad,' he said. 'And, lad – '

'Spit it out, for Christ's sake.'

'If you see Cristoforo, send him down here. Dead smart.' Hannay's face seemed suddenly twisted with worry. 'I can't leave me ship to look for him. Not now. I might have to take her to sea in a hurry.'

Patch nodded and as he leapt for the gangway, he heard Hannay's voice trailing after him, shoving its hostile way through a halt in the din.

'And if you see that bloody Anderson,' he was shouting, 'give him a kick up the arse for me.'

Patch clattered across the swaying gangway and headed up the mole. As he reached the Customs House, the policeman, who was standing there staring at the mountain, spotted him and jumped out, throwing his cigarette away hurriedly.

'Signor Patch. I'm sorry. You can't go up there.'

'Good God, Pasotti,' Patch said scornfully. 'With the whole world falling apart round your ears, you're not going to worry about me.'

'I'm sorry, Signor Patch.'

The policeman reached out a hand to lay it on Patch's arm but it halted in mid-air as the mole seemed to heave underneath their feet as the mountain rocked in its agony. They staggered together at the dim violent movement beneath them, holding on to each other for balance.

Amarea gave another thunderous roar and there was a flash of blinding yellow that seemed to leap straight across the sky, as though the whole crater were edged with fire that lit up the underbelly of the clouds and the billowing smoke that rolled upwards into the night sky. Then, as the roar subsided into a series of indistinct explosions, the glare reddened and died away again.

The policeman had turned and was staring back at Amarea with frightened eyes.

'What about your wife and children, Pasotti?' Patch shouted at him. 'Anybody looking after them while you're keeping an eye on me?'

The policeman looked agitated, then he shook his head again. 'I'm sorry,' he said. 'You can't leave. I have my orders.'

'Do your orders say you've got to let your family chance it just to see that I don't get away?'

Another outburst of rage from the mountain lit their faces. In the Piazza del Mare, groups of people from the houses around who had been staring towards the crater were now moving agitatedly, like a lot of disturbed ants. The noise for a few moments was unspeakable and the groups split up and started for the mole.

The policeman was gazing at the sky as the racket grew worse, and while his attention was diverted, Patch gave him a shove and, bolting past him, started to run.

'Signor Patch!'

Pasotti shouted and started after him, then as Patch doubled backwards and forwards among the frightened people in the Piazza del Mare, he stopped dead, thought of his wife and children, and headed for the Via Garibaldi.

# thirty-seven

In the Via Maddalena, the noise of the volcano had brought the people into the street in large numbers. Lights had appeared at windows and the crowds began to gather outside the doorways of the blocks of apartments. Nobody seemed able to make up their minds what to do and stood about in the dust-filled air of the streets, shouting at each other.

'We were told there was no danger,' someone said indignantly, as though he'd been cheated.

'No danger!' A man laughed harshly. 'Take a look at Amarea.'

Another great fountain of flame had burst upwards from the summit, shooting skywards in a hideous column, flame-red at its base and darkening to a deep purple that twisted and writhed in agony as it joined the rolling mass of black cloud and smoke, starred and split with lurid flashes like summer lightning. The noise was unbelievable as the stones and scoriae whistled thousands of feet into the sky, and everyone in the street became silent, listening and waiting.

Then a woman on the fringe of the crowd that was spilling out of the Piazza Martiri began to shout 'Castigo di Dio, the Punishment of God,' in a harsh bestial way that tore at the ears, her frozen agonised face devoid of tears, her throat stringy with shrieking; and the crowd began to heave like a monstrous caterpillar again, making it harder for Patch to push through them on his way to the Via Pescatori, so that lie had to use his fists and the rubber-covered torch to force a way.

The falling dust seemed to be growing worse and the windows of the houses glowed dimly as though through a fog. Coughing, gasping, weeping people were beginning to take shelter as it tore at their lungs. The lights were all on in the Church of Sant' Agata and through the gritty glow of the open doorway Patch could see women huddling with their children. Above the hubbub came the faint high sound of singing as Don Alessandro knelt in prayer before the altar where the lights smudged the old stone of the pillars with gold.

A policeman, looking badly in need of a shave, his jacket unbuttoned, was standing in the middle of the mob, his pistol out of its holster, trying to calm the panic. He had been literally rolled out of bed by the shaking of the floor, so he had dressed quickly and hurried on duty.

The ground shook again and there was a crash as a piece of masonry fell from a building. The crater had glared up again and they saw bursts of vivid red projectiles dropping back from the column of smoke to the sides of the mountain. The throaty clacking noise beat at their ears, half-submerging the whistle of steam that came like the bronchitic gasping of a colossal animal in pain. Then there was a flurried rattling of descending stones and everyone began to push harder as the buildings shook with the noise. The furniture, the floors and the doors buzzed under the vibration while the little pots of geraniums that adorned the balconies jiggled together in a hideous serenade.

The wind had died suddenly, shrivelled to nothingness by the stuffy air, and as the fall of stones stopped again, more groups of agitated people began to spill from the doorways and join the crowd, grey-faced in the terrifying gloom, chattering nervously, cowering at every hideous explosion that set the dogs barking and sent the pigeons fluttering noisily, among the roof tops. Every corner of the little town, every alley, every courtyard, seemed to hold the sickly smell of sulphuretted hydrogen and the acrid taste of cinders.

Patch, thrusting towards the Via Pescatori, saw Mamma Meucci standing in the street with her family, clutching the two smallest children to her skirts and trying to prevent them being knocked over.

'Mamma Meucci, where's Cecilia?'

'In her rooms, I suppose. Meucci's gone to the boat. Signor Tom, for the sake of the Lord Jesus Christ – !'

'Get to the beach, Mamma! Go by the back streets! Hurry, before the crowd starts! I've got to go now!'

As he turned away, Patch bumped into Emiliano who had stopped to help Don Gustavo with a crippled woman.

'Father, will it be all right?' he was asking.

'It will be all right, Emiliano. Pray to the Holy Mother that no harm will come. The Church's a strong building.'

'It's my bar I'm thinking of, Father. I've already built it twice.'

'Then have you any reason to fear that the Holy Mother won't be as merciful as ever?'

A flurry of shouting people blocked the street again, sweeping Emiliano away, and Patch had to wait for them to pass. Then someone remembered the *Great Watling Street* and started shouting to the crowd to head for the mole.

'The ship,' he yelled. 'Make for the ship! We'll be safe there!' Through the swarming people, Patch saw the Haywards pushing towards him.

'Patch.' Hayward's face was drawn with fatigue and his wife, her normally immaculate hair over her face, her makeup and jewellery missing for once, hung over his arm. 'Patch, old boy, the car ran off the road.'

'Get to the mole,' Patch shouted above the din. 'Get going. Now. Before the crowd, or you'll never make it.'

Hayward nodded, not questioning why Patch was heading the other way, and set off for the ship, dragging his wife.

As they thrust down the street, the press of the crowd swept round Patch again. The panic had spread like wildfire and everyone was heading uncertainly towards the mole now. A man went past dragging a goat which squatted on its haunches against the pull of the rope.

'*Andiamo*' he was shrieking. 'Get going!'

A Fiat was nosing among the crowd, hooting furiously, followed by two or three couples on motor-scooters who had obviously come into town from higher up the slopes of the mountain. There were farm carts, too, lumbering and awkward, probably belonging to people who had left San Giorgio after the rush of mud from Amarea had destroyed their farms.

Patch pressed back into an alleyway out of the way and stumbled over a box. Then, above the din, he heard a boy's voice, crooning in the darkness.

' 'Niello. ' 'Niello.'

It was Cristoforo, kneeling on the cobbles alongside his dog, which was stretched out in the shadows. Patch could only just see it in the reflected glow from the crater.

'Cristoforo,' he shouted in the boy's car. 'What the hell are you doing here?'

'Masaniello, Signor Tom!' Cristoforo swung round and faced Patch. 'I followed him. He'd run from the noise. I escaped from my uncle.'

'What's happened to him?' Patch knelt alongside the dog.

'A cart, Signor Tom. It broke his back. The policeman had to shoot him.'

The alleyway was illuminated by a fresh outburst from Amarea and Patch straightened up.

'Cristoforo,' he yelled. 'Captain Hannay wants you. He wants you aboard his ship. You must get down there. The whole town's going to the beach and the mole. Get to his ship. Don't wait any longer.'

Cristoforo lifted his face again, the tears on his cheeks glinting in the glare. 'What about Masaniello?' he asked.

He gently pulled the dog's muzzle from behind its ear and lifted it over the bloodied jaws. Then he looked quickly up at Patch.

'Signor Tom, I shall have to bury him.'

Another explosion lit up the alley as though all the lights in the houses around had been switched on and all the shutters thrown back at once. The din made the glass shudder in the window-frames, drumming it noisily with an increasing viciousness so that Patch and Cristoforo instinctively huddled together as the alleyway seemed to expand and contract, and the very stones of the buildings seemed to rattle against each other.

Then, as the din subsided again, Patch straightened up and, grabbing the boy by the arm, swung him out of the alley, spinning him round into the middle of the street.

'For God's sake, get going, Cristoforo! Before it's too late.'

Cristoforo hesitated for a moment, staring at Patch, then he saw the expression on his face and turned and started walking.

'Hurry,' Patch shouted after him. 'Go by the back streets!'

Cristoforo glanced back and set off running as hard as he could.

When Patch came out of the alley, the street had emptied and he was alone in a nightmare of noise and lurid light. From somewhere among the houses the crackle of flames came thinly through the roaring of the explosions, where a lamp had been upset in the rush and set fire to curtains, and he ducked again as he heard another flurried rattle of stones on the roofs and saw a shower of glowing cinders bounce into the roadway.

The street was deserted. The pigeons had disappeared in one vast flapping of wings at the first terrifying snore and the dogs had vanished after their owners. The cats had melted into the dark corners and down the alleys. From inside the houses, lights still flickered. The windows of the Church of Sant' Agata still glowed but the chanting was indistinct now beneath the noise of the shouting.

Symbolic of the abandonment of the town, a rat ran unheeded out of the shadows, paused at a box dropped by someone on the cobbles in their fright, and disappeared again in a slithering jerky movement. Patch watched it go, his face lit by the glow from Amarea, feeling like the only living soul in a town of the dead.

Then he swung on his heel and ran up the Via Pescatori.

## thirty-eight

The first indication of the mass of people bearing down on the *Great Watling Street* was the appearance on board the ship of Anderson, the missing Mate. His face like his figure was at that moment loose and disjointed with mingled surprise and excitement.

'Skipper,' he panted. 'They're all coming down the main street. Talk about panic. They say the cable to the mainland's broken. The houses are on fire and the water supply's dried up. It's burning the whole east end of the town.'

He paused for a word of praise which he thought in a moment of self-gratification might be forthcoming but the grim-faced Hannay disappointed with his reaction.

'Shut your mouth, Mister,' he said. 'You look like a spent whippet!'

Anderson's jaw clicked shut and Hannay scowled at the mountain. 'Ever read anything in *Instructions to Masters* about what to do in an eruption, Mister?' he said. 'Thank God, we've got steam up. Turn everyone out if they're not out already. Let's have the Chief Engineer up here. We'll post a couple of men at the top of the gangway. We might as well be ready for 'em. If they're coming on board, they've got to come in an orderly fashion and not like the tap-room at opening-time.'

He had switched on the deck lights, covering the ship with a bright white glare that showed up the booms and stanchions with an etched sharpness against their own shadows. The crew lining the rail were staring along the mole, waiting, their eyes strained towards the town.

Then a boy came running out of the shadows, stumbling with exhaustion.

'Cristoforo!' Hannay almost fell down the bridge ladder to the deck and, pushing aside the men clustered round the gangway, he caught the boy as he fell into his arms.

'Thank God, Chris boy! You made it. Mabel'll be glad to see you.'

'Sir Captain, Signor Tom told me to come. I came over the walls and through the gardens. The crowd's just behind me.'

'Where's your uncle?'

'I don't know. I escaped.'

'Glory be to God!'

Hannay's troublesome conscience deserted him as he swung the boy triumphantly into the arms of a brawny sea-man.

'Put him in the saloon,' he said. 'Cover him up. Tell the steward to keep an eye on him. Then come back to the gangway. They're on their way.'

They had just reached the deck again when the crowd burst out of the darkness.

The first person to appear was a woman, then came a group of youths, and a man carrying two children under his arms, their heads bobbing as he ran. Both of them had their mouths open and they were screaming with fright. Then the whole crowd behind them flooded into the light and Hannay found himself staring from the wing bridge at a dense mass of people swirling about on the mole.

Half of them held children. One or two of them had snatched up parcels of belongings, blankets and even chicken coops.

'Signor Capitano,' he heard one man shout. 'Let us aboard!'

The women were beating their breasts and snatching at their hair in their anxiety, bobbing their heads and muttering Ave Marias, their faces puffed and ugly with weeping and fear as they tried to quieten their children.

Hannay's face was troubled. There were a great many people by the ship now, all wailing and shouting at him, and he was afraid of a panic which might destroy his command. Then he saw the lights of the *Procida*, swinging as she turned to head in towards the shore, and he made up his mind quickly.

'Single up the moorings,' he told Anderson. 'We might need to get away from here dead quick. Station your men at the top of the gangway. If there's any sign of a rush, push 'em back.

'Now,' he shouted in his appalling Italian down to the mole. 'You can start coming aboard. Women and children first. Keep calm.'

The women pushed the children forward, shouting their thanks up to Hannay. '*Grazie, Signor Capitano! Mille grazie!*'

The crowd began to open up to let the children approach the gangway and scared figures began to shuffle forward, pushed from behind by the men.

They could see the *Procida* closing the shore now, and they heard her cable rattle as the anchor went down. Then her searchlight flared out, sharp and white in the night, and through its beam they saw a squadron of small boats heading for the shore, forcing their way among the fishing boats which were already heading out to her from the Piazza del Mare, where the crowd was lining the sea wall and the narrow strip of dark sand. Behind the *Procida*, the *Ladybird* and the *Francis X. Adnauer* had appeared and Hannay could see the lights of another ship he assumed were those of the *Amsterdamster* closing up. A few small yachts were alongside the wall already, their crews cramming the frightened people below on to the chintzy cushions while they tried to single up and get clear without losing anyone in the water.

The children and women were still hurrying across the gangway to the *Great Watling Street* when Hannay saw a commotion among the surging crowd as a big hatless figure in a torn shirt began to push through to the front.

'Thief! Murderer! Child-stealer!' His face tautened as he heard the furious voice of Angelo Devoto carrying above the wailing of the crowd. 'Give me back my Cristoforo!'

Using his fists and feet, he was thrusting people aside in an effort to reach the gangway, watched all the time by Hannay from the wing bridge.

'Robber! Assassin! Savage! If he goes, I go too!'

'Hold up, you ape – ' a fisherman with long hair grabbed him by the arm and swung him back, ' – you wait your turn!'

Devoto wheeled and, in the glare from the deck lights, Hannay saw his mean handsome face twisted into rage as he drove his fist into the fisherman's face and began again to thrust forward.

The fisherman recovered quickly and, wiping his bleeding mouth with the back of his hand, made a grab and Devoto disappeared in a tangle of flying fists.

Then the mountain roared up again and Hannay forgot him as the high-pitched whistle became agony to his ears.

One of the crew pointed.

'Look!'

Hannay stared upwards. Three great fiery streaks were spilling through the broken cone of the crater and down the mountainside, like immense crimson serpents, glowing golden at their source and dying away to a dull red at their probing tips. They moved down the slopes with incredible speed at first, then disappeared for a while behind a fold of rock, reappearing again a little lower down. A thick incandescent column of spurting lava that fell back into the crater hovered permanently over the throat of the mountain while all the time flying projectiles were flung out in a fantastic fountain like the crucible of some vast furnace that could be seen right round the island.

At the first uproar, the people of Fumarola had run out into the streets, gathering in the flat little piazza alongside the sea. The glow from the mountain top reflected in dancing points of light on the water around them clear across the bay to Anapoli Porto.

The lights had gone on in the church immediately as Don Dominico gathered around him in the vestry the elders of the village. It didn't take them long to ascertain that the coast road was already too dangerous to use and an attempt to telephone to the Porto confirmed the rumours that the tremors had damaged the line, so that they could only prepare for a slow evacuation across the bay to the Porto with what they had at their disposal.

At once, they started dragging the heavy fishing boats to the water's edge and the women and children began to gather in an orderly fashion at the back of the church, kneeling in the smouldering scent of incense in front of the life-size figure of the Virgin, praying while the moving shadows behind the statue seemed to bring it to life. The newcomers at the back, still tying the scarves on their heads in their hurry, genuflected towards the cross on the high altar as they passed between the doors.

There was no thought of blame for anyone in Don Dominico's gentle mind as he grouped the people together, the oldest and the youngest first, so that as soon as he received the message from the beach that they were ready, they could march down and take to the sheltering sea.

'Light all the candles!' His voice was quite steady as he spoke to the sacristan. 'Turn on all the lights! It will be more cheerful.'

The lights blazed up, shining on the shabby brass haloes of the saints he had himself helped to polish only that day from the top of a pair of rickety steps. He was pleased in his simple fashion that everything was spick and span.

Another explosion from the mountain set the shabby chandelier tinkling madly and he heard a huge piece of plaster fall with a crash outside. The candles round the walls shuddered and their flames lengthened abruptly as though a great draught of air was sucking them up, then they dropped back again to an unsteady flicker. There was a momentary pause in the rising and falling of the prayers around him, then they went on again as though in defiance of the mountain.

The sacristan came up alongside him, his face pasty, his mouth opening and shutting several times before he could get the words out.

'Father,' he said, 'lava's begun to flow.'

'Is the village in danger?'

'Not at the moment, Father. It's heading towards San Giorgio. But Baldicera's here. He's in the vestry. He's seen steam coming from under rocks in his fields. His cattle are mad with fear. He's brought his family down. What shall we do?'

Don Dominico listened patiently as the prayers echoed softly round the high ceiling that seemed to soar away into the shadows but he couldn't think of anything they hadn't done already. Every precaution had been taken that could be taken and they were as ready as they could ever be. All they wanted was the word that the fishing boats were in the water.

'There's nothing,' he said. 'Nothing at this moment that we can do but pray.'

He moved forward to the centre of the church and his thin voice rose above the muttering and echoed round the high eaves.

'*Siccome Voi, o Gran Dio, siete giusto e santo in tutte le opere Vostre –* '

The voices in the church seemed to come together under his guidance and the bent humble old priest, his tired eyes watching the doors for the man who would bring the signal, felt a surge of pride in himself and his church and his people, as the chanting grew stronger and the men and women and children gathered confidence from his words.

'*O, sommo Bene, noi fermamente proponiamo di no offender Vi mai piu –* '

Above the sound of his own voice he heard a violent roaring outside and underneath his feet the floor of the church seemed to rise and fall like waves. He seemed to be borne upwards and then carried downwards again, then the roaring burst – above the church it seemed – like a clap of thunder, and a frightful screaming like the agonised release of a tremendous pressure of steam beat on his ears.

Up on the dark hillside, the fissure hidden under the rocky surface of Baldicera's field had burst open and a monstrous flood of hot water gushed out and began to pour down towards the village.

'*– E come umilmente Vi preghiamo –* ' Don Dominico was saying, his voice never wavering.

'*– E come umilmente –* ' replied his flock, their fears held in check by his calmness.

'*– Vi preghiamo de accettare queste nostre pene –* '

They were still proclaiming their humility and their faith, with the old priest standing in the centre of the church, when a man from the beach ran to tell them that all was ready. He was panting his way up the little hill when he saw the great gush of water flooding down the street, splashing and roaring as it carried away houses and swept carts before it in a vast cloud of steam. Then it struck the church and he heard a wail of horror go up and the shrieks of women as it rushed inside and swept from one end to the other in a tremendous tidal wave.

He paused a second longer, wondering what to do as he saw the lights disappear, then realising he was too late to do anything at all, he turned tail and ran, just before the wall of water swept down on him too and carried him with it across the square and the beach, bearing all the little boats and their crews with it into the greater depths of the sea.

# thirty-nine

The lava that burst out of the mountainside after the hot water swept through Fumarola, shouldering aside walls and trees as it headed for the bay. There was no one to see its downward surge except for the few who had taken refuge on the slopes, for the village was already silent, and it poured onwards over the end of the piazza and fell into the sea which immediately exploded into a tortured roaring as the water dissolved into vast screaming clouds of steam. Gigantic waves leapt up as the sea sprang back from the touch of the white-hot moving rock and receded from the little beach, before recoiling on itself to sweep back again and carry away all the houses nearest to the waterfront. Beneath the shrieking of the steam, the waves then hurtled in whirlpools across the bay towards the Porto where the lights indicated the people being embarked on the ships.

Urged on by the crew of the *Great Watling Street*, the women and children of the Porto were spilling across the deck, hurrying along under the pushes of the officers, until the whole afterpart of the ship was jammed with yelling people.

The men on the shore were still struggling round the end of the gangway, trying to be in an advantageous position for the moment when Hannay gave the order for them to join their families, shouting advice to their relations across the strip of turbulent black water that separated them.

'Hurry up,' Hannay was shouting. '*Avanti!* Come on, let's have the men aboard now!'

Two or three men and a youth pushed forward, then the commotion broke out again in the crowd, and Hannay saw Devoto emerge from the turmoil and struggle to the front, his shirt torn from his back, his eyes wild, his mouth bleeding.

'Now stop me,' he screamed up to the bridge. 'Now stop me, you robber! If he goes, I go! If I can't go, then he stays and suffers too and the Holy Mother of God have pity on us both!'

The crowd broke apart beneath his blows as he wrenched aside one of the men on the gangway and plunged towards the deck of the *Great Watling Street.*

Then, from nowhere, violent waves, stirred by the tremendous upheaval at Fumarola, began to smack against the side of the ship – rolling into the entrance of the harbour from the south, great lifting swells that shone with a weird green glow as the searchlight from the *Procida* cut across their tips. The *Great Watling Street* begin to heave so that the crowd on the after deck staggered together and a woman fell down the companionway and started to scream as though she had broken a limb; then they heard the ship groaning, and the monstrous thumps and clangs as she ground against the mole. The gangway started to swing and, jamming against a bollard ashore, buckled like a pulled bow.

Another violent wave smacked against her and everybody grabbed for a hold as a flood of water shot up over the seaward side, drenching the wailing women and children. The three on the gangway, Devoto, the youth and the other man, jumped for the ship, but the gangway shot violently upwards again, and Hannay saw Devoto and the boy, who were in the middle, lose their balance, spin round as they were flung against the slack ropes, and disappear, their arms and legs whirling like catherine wheels.

Suddenly the crowded gangway was empty, its planks still swaying, its ropes swinging as the ship slammed against the wall. A woman, who appeared to be the mother of the youth, began to shriek in a harsh animal fashion and, fighting her way to the side of the ship, hung over the rail, moaning, her hair over her face, all her neighbours supporting her as she stretched her arms helplessly downwards. The crowd on the mole moved cautiously to the edge and peered down and, for a moment, the shouting welled up round the woman's grief.

Hannay swallowed quickly and turned to Anderson.

'A torch 'ere,' he shouted and Anderson directed a light downwards between the ship and the wall. But in the pit between the steel and the stone, the black water that lashed and swung ferociously was already empty.

'They never had a chance,' Anderson said.

Hannay drew a deep breath. 'God 'ave mercy on their immortal souls,' he added quietly.

Before he could let his thoughts dwell any further on Devoto's death, the Chief Engineer appeared beside him.

'You'll need to get away from here,' he shouted, 'or you'll be aground. The tide's gone mad. We touched bottom just now.'

'We'll stay,' Hannay said.

'You'll lose the ship.'

'We'll stay,' Hannay repeated, and he began to shout down his megaphone again to the people on shore to hurry.

A couple of men, plucking up their courage at the sight of their families wailing on the swaying deck, made a dash across the buckling gangway as the ship settled, and flung themselves on board as she rose again to hammer herself against the sea wall on the vast rollers that smashed across the harbour and overturned the small boats and yachts on to the beach, beating them back in splintered wreckage and scattered spars.

The masts of the *Great Watling Street* were swinging majestically across the ugly sky and the lights of the *Procida* and the other ships beyond the wall rose and fell in crazy angles, crushing the mat of whalers and gigs that lay under their sides.

'For Christ's sake,' Anderson yelled in alarm as he stared at the sea.

'Shut your rattle, Mister,' Hannay said, unmoved, 'and get these people aboard.'

He swung an arm in the direction of the beach where the *Procida's* searchlight picked out the stumbling figures splashing in the surf among the wrecked boats.

'Take a look at that lot. We're the only means now of getting these poor bastards off.'

He could see the flames now in the harbour area as the fires there began to catch hold. In the glare, he saw the crowd huddled in the Piazza del Mare begin to split up as they realised the boats on the beach could not possibly remove them all now, and begin to run towards the mole and the *Great Watling Street,* at first in ones and twos, then in groups, then in a great flood that left the piazza bare and swelled the shouting mass round the ship's gangplank.

The gusts of wind that had started to spring up again were whipping showers of sparks into the blood-red curtain of smoke that coiled upwards to join that belching from Amarea. Then, while the people were still scrambling aboard the rolling ship, the light from the mountain died and the noise suddenly stopped and they were enveloped in a stillness over which they could hear voices calling on the beach, and the barking of dogs in the Piazza del Mare. The red streaks of lava glowed bright again at the crater and, as a new outflow spilled over the old, a swifter stream flowed down the mountain.

High above their heads, the whistling sigh seemed to fill the whole of the heavens. The scene was still tinted red like a view of hell but the glow was dying and the moon was blotted out by the smoke pall that hung over the island. The golden streaks of lava died and the glare faded out of the flames. Then the town went dark and there was no sign of anything beyond the lights of the ship and a few scattered fires.

Hannay sniffed, hanging on to the wing bridge to keep his balance as the ship rolled.

'Sulphur,' he said.

Almost as he spoke, there was a cry from the edge of the crowd and he felt something on his face, brushing it like cobwebs.

'Ash!'

He could see it now, falling through the curtain of light round the ship, a drifting grey pall in which the dust motes gleamed and danced; then bigger particles began to fall, some of them as large as plums and still red hot, bouncing and clattering across the mole and the decks and falling into the sea as they hit the booms of the ship. The crowd ashore began to yell again.

'Mister Anderson,' Hannay shouted, 'send someone round the ship. Close all the ports and all the ventilators. Come on, jump about a bit! Push planks across to the mole. They've got to take their chance. Get these people aboard faster and get 'em under cover. Get 'em below. Pack 'em in anywhere. Then stand by the mooring lines. We'll be leaving soon.'

The crowd farther down towards the Piazza del Mare had started to wail again in a high hopeless note, then they began to break away and run back along the mole, at first in ones and twos and finally in whole groups, breaking off the mass of people like the crumbling away of a landslide, holding handkerchiefs over their mouths as they scuttled along the basalt blocks to hammer at the doors of houses in the square until they were let inside, crowding into the entrances of the tumble down tenement buildings, cramming the little shops and cafés and the hovels of the fishermen which lined the beach. Their faces were already grey, the ash caking on the perspiration, and the air was thick with dust. There was a film over everything, and small pellets of hot cinder fell from Hannay's shoulders and down his clothes every time he moved.

Then an unrecognisable figure supporting a woman appeared in front of him, their feet squeaking on the cinders that littered the decks.

'Captain Hannay! Thank God!'

Only the voice told him it was Hayward. The lines on his face were etched in by grey dust and caked with sweat.

Hannay bawled at a scared apprentice: 'Saloon. Take 'em to the saloon.'

'Thank you. Thank you, Captain.'

'You're welcome, I'm sure.'

The air was hot enough now to catch at the throat and the few people who still remained on the mole were lifting their arms to guard their faces, while the women were shrouding the children with their shawls and their coats, even stripping off their frocks to wrap around them, as the ash left grey-white layers as it fell.

The whole world seemed to be on the move and above the cries of the people ashore Hannay could hear an ugly hissing sound from the cinders that fell into the sea.

The last few people were dragged aboard. A man who couldn't make up his mind turned and ran for the piazza, and Hannay stared after him for a few moments longer, standing on the bridge, his eyes on the empty mole waiting for stragglers, hoping against hope that Patch would appear, then he turned and shouted to Anderson who was fighting his way through the crowd to the forecastle head.

'All right,' he said. 'Stand by to let go.'

## *forty*

---

The Via Pescatori was deserted when Patch arrived and as he stumbled out of the darkness, the great block of apartments where he had lived rang hollowly to the clatter of his shoes in the hall. The shouts of Mamma Meucci's children and the cries of babies, the noise of footsteps and the slamming doors had gone. Old Tornielli's breathy trombone was silent and there was no sound of argument, no brassy blare from the inevitable wireless set. The whole building seemed forsaken.

Then he saw Piero Tornielli huddled at the bottom of the stone stairs, his shape enormous against the chipped plaster in the light that was reflected through the doorway and off the tiles of the hall.

He looked up briefly as Patch appeared alongside him, then his head slumped again.

'Tornielli! Where is everybody?' Patch felt no emotion for the boy at that moment, no dislike, no enmity, in spite of his lies, only a great thankfulness at finding someone alive.

Tornielli shook his head wearily and made no attempt to reply.

'Where is everybody?' Patch repeated.

There was a burst of muffled drumming from the mountain that made the banisters buzz, and Tornielli jumped.

'Tornielli!'

The boy looked up but his expression was dazed and he seemed stupefied by the noise and his own fear. As he crouched down again on the stairs, Patch jumped forward and snatched him up by the padded shoulders of his smart city suit.

'You pathetic imitation of a politician,' he said, losing his temper and shaking Piero so that his head rolled round on his shoulders, limp and uncontrollable. 'Where is everybody? Answer me!'

'They've gone. They've all gone to the mole and the beach. There's no one left.'

As Patch brushed past him and set off up the stairs, Tornielli raised his head, his face grey with fatigue. 'She's not there,' he said heavily. 'She's gone.'

Patch bounded down the stairs again and, grabbing the boy, hoisted him to his feet once more.

'Where's she gone?' he demanded.

'Up the mountain. Towards the Villa Forla. After the old man. He's gone to the crater. He took his camera.'

Patch stared out into the dark street. Through the open doorway, the brutish roaring of the mountain came to him like an enraged animal.

'Up the mountain? My God, how?'

'He took my Lambretta – '

'Never mind the old man. What about Cecilia?'

'She went on foot.'

Patch threw Tornielli aside and he sank down on the stairs again.

In the street, Patch stared round him, then he saw Meucci's bicycle standing in the hall. He dragged it through the doorway with a rattle of loose mudguards and jumped into the saddle, heading out of the Via Pescatori for the slope of the hill towards Forla's palace.

The road out of the town was dark and narrow and several times Patch almost fell off the ancient bicycle as he ran into ruts. The air between the clustered buildings was stifling and his clothes were clinging to his body. There was no lamp on the machine but he managed to find his way by the rising and falling glare from the mountain and from the flames where a portion of the eastern end of the town was blazing. Several times he ran into bundles which had been dropped in the rush for the beach and the mole, scattered across the street and in the doorways that stood agape, empty and desolate, just as they had been flung open in the first frantic dash for the ships.

Near the Church of Sant' Antonio on the edge of the town, he came across a cart with a broken wheel, a tasselled mule still attached to it by one twisted leather harness strap.

It looked up at him in mute appeal as he approached, so he stopped and released it. As it stumbled away, it put its foot on the front wheel of the bicycle where he had dropped it in the road, and halted again, patient, stupid and dumb, the wheel round its hoof like a broken wreath.

For a while, Patch tried frantically to disengage it but the mule refused to lift its foot and he was almost reduced to tears of frustration and impatience.

'Oh, Christ,' he muttered to himself in desperation as he struggled. 'Oh, God Jesus Christ!'

Then he realised he was beginning to panic and that the din from the mountain had been acting like a spur and was making him drive himself harder and harder until he was almost exhausted. He forced himself to pause and lit a cigarette to calm himself down. Blowing out smoke, he patted the mule's sweaty flank.

'OK, chum,' he said. 'You keep it. It's all yours. You won it in fair fight.'

A roar from the mountain made him look up and he caught his breath as he saw the lava stretching down the slopes like golden veins. It was the first time he had realised the crater had overflowed at last after all its threats, and he stood motionless, staggered by the majesty of it.

Tearing himself away as he remembered Cecilia, he set off at a stumbling run up the road and, as though in return for his efforts to behave rationally, just beyond the last of the houses he saw a little green Fiat, which he recognised by the number as the Haywards', slewed broadside on, its rear wheels hanging over the ditch, jammed against one of the Agipgas signs that studded the roadside all the way round the island.

'My God,' he breathed. 'If only I can!'

With torn and bleeding fingers, he dragged down the wall behind it and tossed the stones under the overhanging wheels until he had almost filled the ditch. Panting, he climbed inside the car and released the brake so that the weight of the vehicle pushed over the sign and flattened it to the stones he had thrown there. Climbing out again and leaving the door swinging, he jammed more stones behind the rear wheels.

He was gasping in the hot noisy air as he dropped behind the wheel again. With a shaking hand, he put the car into gear and revved the engine until it was screaming. Then he slammed off the brake and let the clutch pedal out.

The Fiat leapt forward, flinging the stones backwards, rocked dangerously so that he thought it was going over on its side as he wrenched its nose round, and leapt out of the ditch with a jerk. Swerving madly across the road, its headlights sweeping the fields as he fought with the steering-wheel, it finally rocked back on to an even keel in the centre of the road, with Patch huddled gasping over the dashboard.

'Thank God,' he breathed. 'Thank God, thank God, thank God!'

For a second, he sat motionless in the driver's seat, alone, like an oasis of life in the deserted road, blinded with sweat and weak with exhaustion. Then he wiped his face with his hands and put the car in motion, climbing slowly up the hill, holding the wheel with trembling fingers, knowing that without the great luck he had had in stumbling across it, his attempt to find Cecilia was almost hopeless.

The road was getting steeper as he drove, winding in and out of the high-banked fields. He had left the town behind now and was heading upwards between the tall hedges of oleander and fuchsia that bordered the neat little villas strung along the mountainside. They all seemed empty, their owners left for the mole and the beach, and their doors stood open, black mouths in the glare that stretched the sooty shadows of trees across the road.

Then, as he rounded a bend, he saw Cecilia in the headlights, waving madly, a ghostly figure in the glow.

'Stop, stop!' she was shouting. As he halted the car and started forward towards her, she recognised his lean shape in the light of the headlamps and began to stumble towards him, her heels clicking on the macadamed surface of the road. He caught her as she fell into his arms.

'Cecilia, you must have been mad! You should be going the *other* way!'

There was another explosion from above them and she huddled terrified in the circle of his arms, her face buried in his chest, so that he could feel her body shaking through the thin dress she wore.

The cascades of spark were obscured from them by trees which were flung into stark silhouette, every leaf and twig distinct with the glow of the lava flows behind it. Then, as the glare died, the roaring stopped and the whistling sigh that seemed to prelude each new evil started out of the sudden silence and they caught the smell of sulphur, and felt first dusty cinders brushing against their faces on the wind.

'Cecilia – ' Patch stared round him, ' – we've got to get under cover. It's ash!'

He pointed to the beam of the headlights where they could see it sifting down, dropping gently and silently to the road in a slow but deadly cloud, the bigger cinders bouncing on the surface and into the ditch.

'Tom, my grandfather! We must find him. We can't leave him outside.'

He began to move back to the car, pulling her after him. 'Take it easy,' he said, and already he could feel the dust grinding between his teeth. 'He probably knows more about the mountain than we do. He knows how dangerous this ash is. He'll find somewhere to shelter. Come on, Cecelia. We can't stay here.'

'Tom!' Cecilia's voice was broken with weariness. 'I can't go any further.'

As she drooped against him, he swung her up into his arms and stood with his legs braced, wondering what to do. Then he bundled her roughly into the car and, dropping into the driver's seat, put the vehicle into gear and began to cruise onward.

Eventually, through the thickening cloud of cinders that bounced off the bonnet and obscured the windscreen, he saw what he was looking for, a group of little villas – their doors gaping wide and empty. Stopping the car outside the first of them, he dragged Cecilia from the seat and swung her into his arms again.

There was a thud and a puff of dust and something fell alongside him as he stumbled up the flower-decked stone steps from the road, half-blinded by the flying grit that got into his hair and eyes and ears and mouth, his feet crunching on the growing layer of ash. Kicking open the front door, he stumbled inside and stood panting, his mouth dry with a chlorine-tasting thirst that scraped his throat like emery paper, but conscious immediately of the relief, the incredible, blessed relief, at being out of that ghastly choking cloud.

'All right now, Cecilia,' he croaked, his voice hoarse with exhaustion. 'I know this place.'

Groping in the darkness, he saw a slit of light alongside him which he realised was a partly opened door with the glare of Amarea behind it. Kicking it open, he saw the mountain framed in a window opposite him and, from the direction of the golden streaks spilling down the slopes, he knew they were safe.

By the far wall, there was a wide divan bed and he laid Cecilia gently on it and turned back to the hall. He managed to find a switch by the entrance and, as he flooded the place with light, he saw through the open outer door the cinders falling on to the step outside, catching the light as they drifted down, a few of the bigger ones bouncing into the hall.

As he reached out to shut the door, he felt the grit on his face and even inside the air was thick with the smell of ash and sulphur. The sound of the door slamming echoed through the empty house, and he could hear the cinders brushing against the panes as he hurried from room to room shutting the windows. His jacket was spotted and scarred by tiny scorch marks, and he took it off and dropped it on the floor as he ran.

He was sweating when he returned to the room where he had left Cecilia and he brought with him a couple of glasses and a bottle in a straw sheath which he had found in the pantry. Back in the bedroom, he glanced at the photograph by the bed, the wedding group of a man and woman in neat white drill, the ground underneath them striped with the tattered shadows of palm leaves. He stared briefly at the image of Mrs Hayward, thinking cynically of the irony of his presence there with Cecilia.

She was lying with her head sideways on the pillow, her dark hair tumbled against the roundness of her cheek, the winged eyebrows making curves above the smoky eyelashes.

He stood for a long time, looking down at her, with the drifting grey-curtain of ash outside, and for a moment in some way he couldn't explain, Cecilia seemed set apart from him by her very youth and he felt desperately alone.

The thought brought a lump to his throat. Envy for her youth that swept over him, for the very freshness which lay over her like a cloak as she slept, envy too for the simplicity and credulity he knew to be part of her and which seemed to have slipped past him years ago, totally unseen, lost in egoism and cynicism and jeers. For a while he thought how much he'd like to be as young as she was once more, to believe in truth again, and honesty and courage, as she believed in them; then he thought of what lay ahead of her, of the failures and disappointments, and of how much she had already been wounded by the treachery of human beings, and he realised he was the luckier of the two with his hard shell of disbelief and his period of discontent behind him.

He sat on the bed beside her with his glass and lit a cigarette, his hands trembling. Overcome by tiredness, he sagged back beside her, the wine spilling in a dark pool to the floor as the glass tilted in his hand. The cigarette burning his fingers awakened him long enough only for him to grind it out in the ashtray beside the bed, then his eyelids began to droop again.

There seemed to be some slackening in the noise from Amarea when Cecilia opened her eyes. She had slept with the exhaustion of weariness and fear and as she came to her senses, not knowing where she was, she experienced a cold feeling of terror as she remembered only the desolation of the empty road, the abandoned houses, and the glare from the mountain and the din that racketed through her head.

She sat up abruptly and in the faint glow of the bedside light she became aware for the first time of the figure alongside her. Startled, she stared at it for a while, then with relief she recognised the paint-spotted shirt that was scorched here and there by falling cinders.

She bent over Patch and saw his face, all the deep lines smoothed out by sleep, the strength strangely gone from him so that he looked young and hopeless, and she suddenly wanted to cry.

Silently she slipped down again beside him, taking care not to wake him. But he stirred and his eyes opened. He smiled faintly and winked, and the crooked grin she loved so much spread across his mouth so that his whole face became strong and virile and confident again immediately. He reached out to her and, putting his arm about her, drew her close to him and, as her cheek touched his, she knew he was whispering what was echoed in her own heart.

'Thank God, Cecilia!' he was saying. 'Thank God I found you!'

# forty-one

When Patch finally awoke, the first light of the day was pushing through the windows of the room.

He lay on his back for a while, staring at the ceiling, aware of Cecilia beside him, her head against the hollow of his neck, her hand still in his. He could feel her body warm against him and her hair soft against his cheek. As he turned his head, he saw the ash had stopped and the tremendous relief he felt was because of a selfish thankfulness that he had survived and Cecilia had survived. In spite of the disaster, they still had their lives before them, and his own was suddenly full of meaning.

He lifted himself slowly and kissed her gently on the cheek. All the frustration, all the anger that had been in him the previous night had gone in this new and tender experience which had left him cleansed of unhappiness and with only a great faith in himself and Cecilia, and a desire to get on with living. None of his previous cheerful promiscuity had given him much to remember, but this thing which had swept away the old laughing, angry Tom Patch had had a simplicity, a lack of self-consciousness and a beauty which had left him filled with an extraordinary sense of exhilarating elation.

He swung his legs to the floor, feeling the room was smaller and shabbier than he had ever noticed before, and he had a sudden feeling of pity for Mrs Hayward in her ambitious groping for glamour. Outside the door, a cupboard was open that he hadn't noticed the previous night, and Hayward's clothes spilled out of it across the oak-blocked floor, dull, English and honest-to-God, and he felt another wave of pity for his unhappy, frustrated wife to whom all of these things meant nothing.

He crossed to the window and stared out. As far as he could see, the mountainside was a waste of smoke and grey ash, all the colour gone from everything, a sombre volcanic world of grey, dark blue and brown, fading to black. It gave him an odd dead feeling to see the roads and the fields, the sparkle of flowers, the mud-plastered houses, all dulled to a uniform grey beneath the rolling, bubbling column of hydrangea-coloured smoke that poured out of the mountain like a hideous cauliflower and rose five miles into the sky, varying constantly at its source to rich reds, viridians and gaudy greens as though someone were up there unloading chemicals on to the flames.

Then he saw that the vapours clinging to the mountainside came from a hundred-yard-wide stream of grey-black lava creeping slowly downwards as though from a suppurating sore, following the valleys and the clefts of rock, scorching trees and withering plants as it went, but curiously not so terrifying with its glow turned to the colour of cinders by the daylight.

Across the little valley that separated him, he could see the ruins of San Giorgio. The lava appeared to have followed the road and, like the mud before it, had passed clean through the middle of the village. The houses, the untidy farms and the church, everything had been swept aside. The church tower was still visible, the campanile sticking sturdily out of the grey sea which moved without any apparent sign of movement, but as he watched, a wide fissure appeared up its side and lengthened until the whole structure began to disintegrate. A piece of masonry fell off and the great cracked bell he had heard on the night of Marco Givanno's death beneath the mud pealed madly for a few seconds as the tower rocked, then the whole lot crashed down in a shower of dust and sparks and smoke.

Unaware that Cecilia had awakened too and had crossed towards him, he watched as men on the lower side of the village hastily slashed down apple trees, oaks and chestnut in the fields. Others were trying to dig up a few of the precious vines from the fertile soil that the catastrophic river was about to cover up for ever. Even the children tore at the nearby grass until the heat of the moving grey wall drove them back, trying to save some scraps of hay for the donkeys and the cattle.

On the slopes to the east and west of them, people whose property had already been engulfed stood silently, watching with dulled eyes as the monster from the mountain swallowed the years of work, the few bare stalks of corn that withered where they stood like doomed armies, the dying trees and the fading bushes.

'Tom!' Cecilia's voice close behind him made Patch turn, and he swung an arm round her and pulled her to him in an instinctive movement. 'We must find my grandfather.'

She indicated the window at the other side of the room and through it he could see the castellated towers of the Villa Forla, surrounded by the groves of cypresses that marched up the slopes with the precision of squadrons of soldiers.

He nodded without speaking and they ran down the garden path, their feet crunching in the grey desert of ash and clinker, small puffs of dust flying as they sank ankle-deep in the stuff. The car was covered in a grey swathe, and they moved round it, knocking it from the pitted windscreen.

Behind them down the hill there was an overturned cart, its bunchs of tomatoes and garlic spilled into the ditch, and even from these the ash had taken away the shape, rounding the angles, flattening the curves and dulling the colour. A candle still guttered in the lamp that was jammed into a bracket on the empty shafts.

They climbed into the car and set off with a jerk, the wheels spinning in the ash, and slithered forward, throwing the cinders aside in two unbroken tracks as they headed upwards.

Beyond San Giorgio, among the drying mud, the lava was piling up near to the road, the vegetation crackling and smoking already, a few trees in the distance blazing like torches. Groups of people were limping past towards the Porto, one or two of them with burned hands, one or two with faces wrapped in scraps of linen, trudging unspeakingly downwards with what they could carry, here and there passing a house with its occupants up on the roof shovelling off the heaped cinders before the beams collapsed under the weight.

Patch parked the car well below the Villa Forla and at the top of the hill so they could get away quickly if necessary, and they ran through the gates hand-in-hand. Two or three people in the courtyard piling up linen and other things they were obviously looting from the abandoned palace stared curiously at them, and as they halted, doubtful as to their directions, they heard a sound like someone rattling the clinker in a firegrate. Beyond the low wall that surrounded the house, a group of trees started to move agitatedly, the foliage withering before their eyes. On the branches were shreds of what looked like dried grey dough where lava bombs had fallen and cooled immediately to rocky hardness.

The gardens and the cypress grove the Forla family had planted round their home through three or four generations came to a dead stop in a hideous pile of moving slag as high as a three-storey house. The heat was intense and from the hot grumbling wall small onrushes of pebbles and stone rolled towards them with a noise like breaking crockery. The fine rain that dripped from the trees vaporised as it came into contact with it and the atmosphere was as humid and as full of steam as a Turkish bath.

'We've got to hurry, Cecilia,' Patch said. 'He must be here somewhere. Perhaps he's upstairs with his camera. He couldn't be higher up the mountain.'

Even as he turned away, he saw a great spar of rock thrust upwards from the lava pile, rising with a fascinating slowness that held them in their tracks, until it stood on end, a dark menacing outline against the purple sky behind it. Slowly it began to tilt over, its gloomy base sapped away here and there by the trickling of red-hot sand. Then there was a flash and a narrow fissure ran from top to bottom of it and the whole mass split apart and collapsed in a blinding avalanche that sent red-hot boulders rolling across the ground, leaving scorch marks on the grass even as they cooled and turned to black. Almost at once, a new spar of rock began to be forced upwards.

The Villa Forla was silent inside and they stopped dead in the vast hall, awed by the magnificence of it. All that was beautiful in Italy and on Anapoli had been gathered in this vast soundless museum now covered with a film of ash that had sifted through the windows. The walls were white, with doors of black wrought-iron, and the furniture was of heavy old oak, so that the whole room was splendid with colour and grandeur from the thick silent carpets that centred the floors to the marble statues that had been dug out at Colonna del Greco, and the crystal chandeliers that graced the frescoed ceilings. Four generations of Forlas had built this magnificent palace, and now it was ended.

At first they were unable to take their eyes off the splendour, then they ran forward, shouting old Leonardi's name along the echoing corridors, their teeth gritting on the dust in the air. The atmosphere seemed more stifling now and through the windows they saw the bank of lava piling higher against the walls of the house, the edges crumbling and clattering like dumped heaps of coke into the garden.

Then one of the men from the courtyard appeared behind them. 'Signore,' he shouted. 'Hurry! the north wall is cracking!'

Outside again, they heard a crash of falling masonry behind them and saw the dust spurt like an explosion through the windows, and knew that the lava was now trudging through the house and over the carpets, pushing the oak furniture before it into heaps, charring the tables and chairs until it finally swallowed them up in a blazing pyre.

More people had arrived in the courtyard by this time and were running about like a lot of ants, laden with looted clothing and linen. One of them, a carpet under his arm, halted in front of Patch, as though he guessed what he was seeking.

'On the mountain,' he said. 'I saw him out there. But don't waste time, signore, or you'll be cut off! It's reached the road already!'

They ran through the courtyard, across the panic litter of clothes, their throats parched with the heat and the acrid fumes. As they reached the gate, they heard casks of wine exploding in the cellar and saw the surrounding wall crash down. The flowing, slow tide began to eat it up, bricks, mortar, everything, then the garage alongside began to crack as the lava flowed round it and a split like a vein ran up the brickwork.

As the lava reached the petrol tank, there was a tremendous explosion that bulged the walls and lifted the roof in flying tiles that arced across the sky in twisting fragments.

While the pieces were still clattering down around them, someone shouted from the roadway and they saw mules looming out of the smoke and steam, coming on at a trot, men pulling at their bridles and encouraging them with shouts.

The last of them came unsteadily, no one leading it, and they saw at once its rider was old Leonardi, his white hair hanging about his grimy face as he clutched to the torn alpaca jacket he wore the tripod of a broken camera.

They ran forward to meet him and, thrusting through the steaming mules, Patch reached the old man's side just as he swayed in the saddle. As he rolled into Patch's arms, the tripod cracked him at the side of the head and fell over his shoulder to the ground.

'He was caught in a pocket of gas,' one of the mule-riders said, swinging off alongside Patch. 'He was taking photographs and he wouldn't come away. We pushed him on to the mule but I think we were already too late.'

The heat that came to them from the blazing garage was appalling now and Patch could feel it scorching his face as he laid the old man down on the wet grass. Cecilia was beside him, dirty, her eyes full of tears, and beyond her a woman with her hands full of looted clothing was muttering a De Profundis. One of the muleteers crossed himself as Cecilia began to cry quietly.

Old Leonardi opened his eyes. '*Eccole!*' He lifted his hands weakly and showed them the ruined camera he held in his bleeding fingers. 'The pictures here that have never been taken before.

'Fancy,' he said in surprise as his voice grew weak. 'I was right all the time. After all those years.'

# forty-two

The ships were close inshore again now, the American and the British and the Italian and the Dutch. Already stores and food had been landed and even vehicles. A relief centre had been set up in the Town Hall for the people who had lost everything, and a crowd of shabbily dressed peasants sat on the steps and under the arches of the Archivio, lost and bewildered, watching the crates and boxes that were piling high round the headquarters of the first-aid parties, and demolition, electrical and mechanical squads from the ships.

No one was concerned with the election now. The papers which had been put ready for the voting, the symbols of Pelli's futile will, lay forgotten in the Town Hall and in the various voting booths about the town. In the charred corners of the eastern streets where the lava was still steadily pushing its way to the sea, they were scattered about the pavements, trodden into the ash and sticking to the rain-wet walls.

Up there, where the houses were still crumbling before the inexorable thrusting of the grey stream, lorries were lining up to carry away the contents of the doomed houses. Englishmen, Americans and Dutchmen were carrying out chests and battered dressing-tables and kitchen furniture for aged Italian ladies, and cramming them into the lorries with the plaster saints and the faded photographs and the treasured wedding dresses. Some of the old people were even trying to cling to their homes, and the naval and civic officials had given orders for their forcible removal. There

299

was blasting to turn aside the new streams of lava that were approaching and even talk of aerial bombing.

Stumbling groups of people in need of food and shelter were still heading into the town, shuffling through the ash and the dust and the sand the mountain had thrown out, halting at the information centre that had been set up in the Archivio for news of relatives, and then continuing in a straggling line towards the beach for evacuation.

A little procession went by, led by Don Gustavo, Don Alessandro's curate. Following them came a group of men carrying a terra-cotta figure of the Virgin Mary dressed in dusty clothing and crowned with a wreath of fading laurel. Behind it trailed boys carrying incense and crowds of people from the Porto, beads and crucifixes clasped to their breasts, gathering numbers as they went.

As they entered the Piazza Martiri, the little carts from Fumarola began to pass them, pushed by red-eyed men and women with grimy faces, or drawn by jaded horses, carrying bundles or coffins as crude as packing cases. The priests from the Church of Sant' Antonio were busy in the little graveyard above the town where the lava of 1762 still lay banked against the thick wall, waiting among the lopsided gravestones and the tombs which had been thrown open by the immense stresses of the earth as the mountain had heaved. The bell of the little chapel among the cypresses rang slowly and with a nerve-racking monotony over the rising and falling sound of grief.

All of Hannay's inborn love of human beings, all that incredible desire to be at one with everyone around him that had driven him to plague Patch, flowed out to the pathetic little groups. He turned to Patch, who stood alongside him near the mole, his peeled red face glowing with a confident belief in mankind, not looking back on the destruction but, true to his nature, hopefully forward to the future.

'I'm off now,' he said. 'I got 'em all on board. Hayward and his wife and all their pals. I'll look you up when I'm next on this run.' He paused, his face worried. 'Ain't seen Cristoforo, have you?' he asked. 'He's disappeared again. I expect he got whipped away with that lot going to the mainland and I don't suppose he'll come back now. Not if he's got any sense.'

His voice crumbled suddenly in a way that didn't go with his normal brash confidence. 'I'd sorta like to have said good-bye,' he concluded weakly. 'That's all.'

He shook hands with Patch then he turned on his heel and marched down the mole, a short, square figure dressed in flannels, brown shoes, a captain's square rig jacket and felt hat.

A few minutes later the old ship swung out and moved stern-first into the centre of the little harbour, neatly missing the group of fishing boats which bobbed at the far side. Then the siren boomed and the propellor thrashed the water to a yeasty foam as the ship began to head round the mole towards the sea.

Hannay stared over the stern from the bridge as the black basalt wall grew smaller, linked to the ship now only by the wake and the cries of the gulls. The island was basking in an unexpected sunshine. The smoke from the mountain still poured upwards into the sky towards the west and from the slopes where the lava lay in streams, but curiously he knew the danger was over. The worst that could happen now was the maddeningly slow destruction of a few more houses and a few more fields and gardens.

He suddenly felt lonely and began to think of what he and Mabel could have done for Cristoforo. The kid had possibilities. Distinct possibilities that he and Mabel might have done something with. He could have stayed on the *Great Watling Street* directly under Hannay's eye and it would have been dead good to see him fill out on ship's food and Mabel's suet puddings. A bit more flesh would have improved him, a decent suit of clothes, some food in his belly, and none of those damn' cigarettes he'd been smoking. All these things and a couple of years on his back and there'd have been a proper change in Cristoforo. Now it would all slip back into the routine of lack of hope, the easiest way, the little vices that gave comfort in hopelessness, until his spirit was sapped and he began to look like so many others on Anapoli, even as Devoto had looked.

Hannay walked gloomily along the deck towards the poop where he took his daily walk among the engine-room ventilators and the motor that worked the ship's refrigerator. As he passed the starboard lifeboat he noticed that the tarpaulin was loose and at first he thought of passing on the information to the bosun, then he decided to make it fast himself.

He reached up for the cover to yank it straight, but as he lifted it he found himself staring first at the ginger cat sitting on the canvas of a folded sail, and then at two large dark eyes which peered out at him from beneath a fringe of black curls.

'Cristoforo!' He jammed the canvas down quickly and stood for a second with his hands on the edge of the lifeboat, resting on the tarpaulin, listening to the frantic shuffling that was going on beneath it. He stared at the hump made by a small body that moved farther under the tarpaulin towards the bow of the lifeboat, and the smile that started on his red face spread into an expression of amazement and pure delight as his troublesome conscience reminded him with joy that he had had no hand in this.

He glanced backwards briefly. Anapoli lay five miles behind him already, only a dwindling hump on the sea. Ten miles more and nobody in the world could make him turn the *Great Watling Street* back. Another hour or two and nobody could dispute his actions, even if they could find it in them to question him taking an orphan under his wing.

He patted the gunwale of the lifeboat with his two hands in a satisfied gesture.

'Food,' he said out loud. 'That's what this damned cat wants. No cat that's nesting for kittens can go without food. I'll bring you some up 'ere.' He leaned closer, his face stiff and expressionless.

'Stay 'ere, kitty,' he said out loud. 'Stay 'ere, and I'll bring you some dinner.'

The *Città di Salerno*, lying among the other island boats that were helping with the evacuation, was already crowded with homeless people when Patch and Cecilia went on board. They were pushing into the saloon, demanding food, and spilling across the decks, blocking all the alleyways with their belongings. Most of them would never return to Anapoli.

The grey dust-laden water overside was stirred to a scummy froth by a jet of water from the engine-room, and nearby a group of bedraggled gulls fought among the floating pumice for a few scraps of food which had been flung overboard from the galley. Patch pushed through the crowd until they found a corner up against the entrance to the saloon, and he wedged Cecilia in there and stood alongside her. Neither of them possessed much more than what they stood up in. At the end of the Via Pescatori the six-foot-high bank of clinker was still spilling along the narrow street, flowing into doorways and burning the woodwork and the rubbish in the courtyards. The police had cordoned the place off while they were still at the Villa Forla.

Up the hill the Porto lay in ruins, the Church of Sant' Agata only a gaunt square of roofless walls now, the remains of its dome rearing starkly to the sky, its treasures buried beneath the debris of the collapsed roof. The schoolroom lay broken under the fire-scorched houses, its contents scattered under the bricks and rubble and shattered furniture.

In the two days since the eruption so much had happened Patch no longer felt he was completely whole again. Individual fragments of him seemed to be scattered about the island. Anapoli had become a part of him, its experiences his, its sufferings scarred on his flesh. Too many of his emotions had been left behind in those shabby little streets where private lives had been thrown open to the passer-by.

But, with true Italian resilience, everyone was already accepting their loss and he drew courage from the sight of Mamma Meucci seeking out a new home, her arguments with the old woman from across the Via Pescatori going on uninterrupted every time they bumped into each other; and from Emiliano painting new phrases among the daubed pillars and frescoes on the tower of his bar in the Piazza Martiri, which had miraculously escaped damage.

'O, *Gioia*,' he had painted. 'O, *Fede*,' and he was now at work on the final words, 'O, *Speranza*.'

'Oh, Joy,' Patch had read. 'Oh, Faith, Oh, Hope.'

Beneath all this he had hung a wreath for the Virgin he was convinced had saved his property and, dissatisfied with its size, had improved it with painted flowers on the wall behind. It seemed a symbol for the future.

Forla was gone and with his palace destroyed, his vineyards laid waste, his sulphur buried, would not be back. Pelli was gone. Bosco had left the island, his part in the disaster as well known as Pelli's. It was said he had been offered a political appointment on the mainland but it would never amount to much now. Don Alessandro would never be a bishop. They'd all disappeared into the limbo of ordinary and over-ambitious politicians who had guessed wrong, and the parties had declared a truce.

Tomorrow or the day afterwards, someone would say something which would bring a hot reply and probably a loudspeaker car from the courtyards from behind the party offices. Then they would all be at each other's throats again, forgetting the tragedy about them in their passionate gift for living, for the dead didn't stay dead long in Italy. The people were as fertile as the soil and all those who had disappeared would be replaced, their spirit and their vitality untouched, for they had the kind of courage that stemmed from faith as deep as the roots their own writhing vines pushed down. They would rebuild what was left of their life, brick by brick, and stone by stone, enduring, because they'd endured before, as their fathers had, and their grandfathers.

Patch glanced at Cecilia. Her face was calm, her eyes steady as she smiled back at him. She'd had no qualms about putting the old life aside, and the fact that they were starting with nothing in no way dismayed her. She had Patch. In that sad world about her only two people existed just then.

They had not even tried to save their belongings. By mutual consent, they had made no attempt to conceal what had had happened between them, moving into the little hotel in the Piazza Martiri, not excusing themselves, satisfied to be together. For the first time in his life, Patch wanted a home. He wanted to shake off the old life completely and put on the new.

He felt selfishly happy. There was still the whole of Italy before him. The world still had meaning and stability and he had got Cecilia out of the catastrophe. He had got more than he deserved, he thought, and a man was entitled to be selfish once in a while.

A blast from the ship's siren made them jump and, as the engine-room bell clanged, the ferry began to head out into the harbour, its mooring ropes splashing into the water. A few minutes later, the ship cleared the end of the mole and headed north-east towards Naples.

By the evening, they'd be picking up the lights on the twin bastions of Ischia and Capri that stood astride Naples bay and an hour or two later disembarking hard by Santa Luci. By midnight they would have been swallowed up in the teeming mass of people who made up the city, from the Vomero to the Via Roma.

Patch took a deep breath, thinking of all the places he could sit and draw, thinking of all the people around him jamming the ship he could draw too if only he had the paper and the pencil – but even those simple necessities were missing at that moment, and he turned and took Cecilia's hand.

She smiled and put her arm through his, so that he could feel her warm flesh against his own, and he was oddly content.

Together they went into the saloon and out of the cool wind that was blowing over the tip of Amarea, bringing with it the last scent of cinders before they caught the damp smell of the sea.

# John Harris

## China Seas

In this action-packed adventure, Willie Sarth becomes a survivor. Forced to fight pirates on the East China Seas, wrestle for his life on the South China Seas and cross the Sea of Japan ravaged by typhus, Sarth is determined to come out alive. Dealing with human tragedy, war and revolution, Harris presents a novel which packs an awesome punch.

## A Funny Place to Hold a War

Ginger Donnelly is on the trail of Nazi saboteurs in Sierra Leone. Whilst taking a midnight paddle in a canoe cajoled from a local fisherman along with a willing woman, Donnelly sees an enormous seaplane thunder across the sky only to crash in a ball of brilliant flame. It seems like an accident... at least until a second plane explodes in a blistering shower along the same flight path.

# John Harris

## Live Free or Die!

Charles Walter Scully, cut off from his unit and running on empty, is trapped. It's 1944 and though the Allied invasion of France has finally begun, for Scully the war isn't going well. That is, until he meets a French boy trying to get home to Paris and so what begins is an incredible hair raising journey into the heart of the French liberation and one of the most monumental events of the war. Harris portrays wartime France in a vividly overwhelming panorama of scenes intended to enthral and entertain the reader.

## The Old Trade of Killing

Set against the backdrop of the Western Desert and scene of the Eighth Army battles, Harris presents an exciting adventure where the men who fought together in the Second World War return twenty years later in search of treasure. But twenty years may change a man. Young ideals have been replaced by greed. Comradeship has vanished along with innocence. And treachery and murder make for a breathtaking read.

# John Harris

## The Sea Shall Not Have Them

This is John Harris' classic war novel of espionage in the most extreme of situations. An essential flight from France leaves the crew of RAF *Hudson* missing, and somewhere in the North Sea four men cling to a dinghy, praying for rescue before exposure kills them or the enemy finds them. One man is critically injured; another (a rocket expert) is carrying a briefcase stuffed with vital secrets. As time begins to run out each man yearns to evade capture. This story charts the daring and courage of these men, and the men who rescued them in a breathtaking mission with the most awesome of consequences.

## Take or Destroy!

Lieutenant-Colonel George Hockold must destroy Rommel's vast fuel reserves stored at the port of Qaba if the Eighth Army is to succeed in the Alamein offensive. Time is desperately running out, resources are scant and the commando unit Hockold must lead is a rag tag band of misfits scraped from the dregs of the British Army. They must attack Qaba. The orders...take or destroy.

'One of the finest war novels of the year'
– *Evening News*

## TITLES BY JOHN HARRIS AVAILABLE DIRECT
## FROM HOUSE OF STRATUS

| Quantity | | £ | $(US) | $(CAN) | € |
|---|---|---|---|---|---|
| | ARMY OF SHADOWS | 6.99 | 11.50 | 15.99 | 11.50 |
| | CHINA SEAS | 6.99 | 11.50 | 15.99 | 11.50 |
| | THE CLAWS OF MERCY | 6.99 | 11.50 | 15.99 | 11.50 |
| | CORPORAL COTTON'S | | | | |
| | LITTLE WAR | 6.99 | 11.50 | 15.99 | 11.50 |
| | THE CROSS OF LAZZARO | 6.99 | 11.50 | 15.99 | 11.50 |
| | FLAWED BANNER | 6.99 | 11.50 | 15.99 | 11.50 |
| | THE FOX FROM HIS LAIR | 6.99 | 11.50 | 15.99 | 11.50 |
| | A FUNNY PLACE TO HOLD | | | | |
| | A WAR | 6.99 | 11.50 | 15.99 | 11.50 |
| | GETAWAY | 6.99 | 11.50 | 15.99 | 11.50 |
| | HARKAWAY'S SIXTH COLUMN | 6.99 | 11.50 | 15.99 | 11.50 |
| | LIVE FREE OR DIE! | 6.99 | 11.50 | 15.99 | 11.50 |
| | THE LONELY VOYAGE | 6.99 | 11.50 | 15.99 | 11.50 |
| | THE MERCENARIES | 6.99 | 11.50 | 15.99 | 11.50 |
| | NORTH STRIKE | 6.99 | 11.50 | 15.99 | 11.50 |
| | THE OLD TRADE OF KILLING | 6.99 | 11.50 | 15.99 | 11.50 |

ALL HOUSE OF STRATUS BOOKS ARE AVAILABLE FROM GOOD BOOKSHOPS
OR DIRECT FROM THE PUBLISHER:

Internet: **www.houseofstratus.com** including author interviews, reviews, features.

Email: **sales@houseofstratus.com** please quote author, title and credit card details.

## TITLES BY JOHN HARRIS AVAILABLE DIRECT
## FROM HOUSE OF STRATUS

| Quantity | | £ | $(US) | $(CAN) | € |
|---|---|---|---|---|---|
| | PICTURE OF DEFEAT | 6.99 | 11.50 | 15.99 | 11.50 |
| | QUICK BOAT MEN | 6.99 | 11.50 | 15.99 | 11.50 |
| | RIDE OUT THE STORM | 6.99 | 11.50 | 15.99 | 11.50 |
| | RIGHT OF REPLY | 6.99 | 11.50 | 15.99 | 11.50 |
| | THE ROAD TO THE COAST | 6.99 | 11.50 | 15.99 | 11.50 |
| | THE SEA SHALL NOT HAVE THEM | 6.99 | 11.50 | 15.99 | 11.50 |
| | SO FAR FROM GOD | 6.99 | 11.50 | 15.99 | 11.50 |
| | THE SPRING OF MALICE | 6.99 | 11.50 | 15.99 | 11.50 |
| | SUNSET AT SHEBA | 6.99 | 11.50 | 15.99 | 11.50 |
| | SWORDPOINT | 6.99 | 11.50 | 15.99 | 11.50 |
| | TAKE OR DESTROY! | 6.99 | 11.50 | 15.99 | 11.50 |
| | THE THIRTY DAYS' WAR | 6.99 | 11.50 | 15.99 | 11.50 |
| | THE UNFORGIVING WIND | 6.99 | 11.50 | 15.99 | 11.50 |
| | UP FOR GRABS | 6.99 | 11.50 | 15.99 | 11.50 |
| | VARDY | 6.99 | 11.50 | 15.99 | 11.50 |
| | SMILING WILLIE AND THE TIGER | 6.99 | 11.50 | 15.99 | 11.50 |

ALL HOUSE OF STRATUS BOOKS ARE AVAILABLE FROM GOOD BOOKSHOPS
OR DIRECT FROM THE PUBLISHER:

**Hotline:** UK ONLY: **0800 169 1780**, please quote author, title and credit card
details.
INTERNATIONAL: **+44 (0) 20 7494 6400**, please quote author, title,
and credit card details.

**Send to:** **House of Stratus Sales Department**
**24c Old Burlington Street**
**London**
**W1X 1RL**
**UK**

Please allow for postage costs charged per order plus an amount per book as set out in the tables below:

| | £(Sterling) | $(US) | $(CAN) | €(Euros) |
|---|---|---|---|---|
| **Cost per order** | | | | |
| UK | 2.00 | 3.00 | 4.50 | 3.30 |
| Europe | 3.00 | 4.50 | 6.75 | 5.00 |
| North America | 3.00 | 4.50 | 6.75 | 5.00 |
| Rest of World | 3.00 | 4.50 | 6.75 | 5.00 |
| **Additional cost per book** | | | | |
| UK | 0.50 | 0.75 | 1.15 | 0.85 |
| Europe | 1.00 | 1.50 | 2.30 | 1.70 |
| North America | 2.00 | 3.00 | 4.60 | 3.40 |
| Rest of World | 2.50 | 3.75 | 5.75 | 4.25 |

PLEASE SEND CHEQUE, POSTAL ORDER (STERLING ONLY), EUROCHEQUE, OR INTERNATIONAL MONEY ORDER (PLEASE CIRCLE METHOD OF PAYMENT YOU WISH TO USE)
MAKE PAYABLE TO: STRATUS HOLDINGS plc

**Cost of book(s):** —————————— Example: 3 x books at £6.99 each: £20.97

**Cost of order:** —————————— Example: £2.00 (Delivery to UK address)

**Additional cost per book:** —————— Example: 3 x £0.50: £1.50

**Order total including postage:** ———— Example: £24.47

Please tick currency you wish to use and add total amount of order:

☐ £ (Sterling)    ☐ $ (US)    ☐ $ (CAN)    ☐ € (EUROS)

VISA, MASTERCARD, SWITCH, AMEX, SOLO, JCB:

☐ ☐ ☐ ☐ ☐ ☐ ☐ ☐ ☐ ☐ ☐ ☐ ☐ ☐ ☐ ☐ ☐ ☐ ☐ ☐

**Issue number (Switch only):**

☐ ☐ ☐

**Start Date:**               **Expiry Date:**

☐ ☐ / ☐ ☐               ☐ ☐ / ☐ ☐

**Signature:** ————————————————

**NAME:** ————————————————————————

**ADDRESS:** ——————————————————————

——————————————————————

**POSTCODE:** ———————————

Please allow 28 days for delivery.

Prices subject to change without notice.
Please tick box if you do not wish to receive any additional information. ☐

House of Stratus publishes many other titles in this genre; please check our website (**www.houseofstratus.com**) for more details.